The Saxon Marriage

Anna Chant

Anna Chant asserts the moral right to be identified as the author of this work. No part of this publication may be reproduced, distributed, or transmitted in any form or by any means, including photocopying, recording, or other electronic or mechanical methods, without the prior written permission of the author, except in the case of brief quotations embodied in critical reviews and certain other non-commercial uses permitted by copyright law.

Standard Copyright Notice
All rights reserved
Copyright © Anna Chant
2017

Cover image by Gali Estrange/ shutterstock.com

Prologue: The Year of our Lord 919

Eadgyth stared at her parents, trying to make sense of the angry words between them. Around them her brothers and sisters waited silently, their faces similarly bewildered. Her younger sister, Elfgifu, slipped a hand into hers. At the age of nine Eadgyth was four years older, but she was too busy trying to keep her own tears under control to be of any comfort.

"So, I am to be cast aside as if I were nothing. Edward, you cannot do this to me," Eadgyth's mother, Aelflaed cried.

Edward, the King of the Anglo-Saxons, was a powerfully built man with grey streaked hair. "Do not be foolish. You will never be treated as nothing."

"But I am to be cast aside," Aelflaed bit back.

"It is for the best," Edward said. "I am thinking of your health, my dear. You nearly died bearing Ethelhild. You should not have to bear more."

Eadgyth glanced at her youngest sister, mercifully asleep in her cradle, remembering those frightening days when everyone had spoken of her mother in fearful voices as they awaited her death. She looked hopefully at her father, thinking perhaps matters were not as bad as she feared.

"I could bear you more," Aelflaed said, looking beseechingly at her husband. "Although I would be glad not to in the next year or two. But you have many children. Why do you need more?"

"Mostly girls." Edward gave a dismissive glance at the group clustered behind their mother. Eadgyth bit her lip, a painful lump coming to her throat. Her father had always claimed to be so proud of his pretty daughters. Never before had she realised how bitterly she had disappointed him.

Aelflaed pulled her two sons, Aelfweard and Edwin forward. Both avoided looking at their father. "You have two sons." She gestured impatiently at the young man stood with Edward. "Three if you include your bastard."

The man shook his head, but he did not comment as Eadgyth's misery was swiftly replaced by anger. After her father, her half-brother Athelstan was the man she most adored. He was always ready with a jest or some promised treat and she hated seeing him belittled. Her lip trembled, terrified by how quickly everything was changing. Squeezing her eyes shut, she longed to wake from the nightmare and find herself back at the heart of the lively, but happy court.

"Do not refer to Athelstan as a bastard," Edward snapped. "He is my son."

"Yet you have never acknowledged his mother." Aelflaed gave a bitter laugh. "I see. That is to be my fate is it not? Never to be publically acknowledged, my children treated with contempt."

"Athelstan was not treated with contempt by any other than you," Edward said. "My father held him in high regard and my dear sister loved him as her own. Our sons remain Athelings and will be respected by all."

"But you will marry again and beget more sons. You cannot promise me our sons will not suffer."

Eadgyth could not restrain a gasp, unable to believe her father would marry again while her mother still lived. Her eyes met Athelstan's, but with the pity in his gaze obvious, his smile was anything but reassuring.

"Yes, I will marry again," Edward said.

Aelflaed sank her head into her arms and uncertainly her eldest daughter, Eadgifu put her arms around her. Edward scowled as he took in the shocked faces of his daughters. He put his hand on Aelfweard's shoulder. Both he and Edwin looked as shaken as their sisters. "Aelfweard is a man now. I do not see how any further sons can rival him. Aelfweard is to be my heir. Nothing will change that."

Aelflaed looked up, relief flickering across her face at the knowledge her son was safe. "What of our daughters? What is to become of them?"

Edward gave another dismissive glance. "They can stay with you. They are mostly too young to be of any use to me."

Eadgyth's eyes filled with tears as she realised her father did not want her. Her earliest memory was of him returning to the Palace of Winchester and swinging her high in the air, proclaiming her to be the fairest of daughters. Her entire life had been spent at his court, moving around the realm with him and he always claimed he hated them to be parted. But now she, like her mother, was to be sent away. In spite of her best efforts, tears trickled down her cheeks.

Aelflaed gestured at Eadgifu. "What of our firstborn? Is she to rot with me at Wilton?"

Edward grinned triumphantly. "Not at all, my dear. She has a glorious future." He smiled at Eadgifu. "My child, I have arranged a fine marriage for you with King Charles of West Francia. You will be one of the highest ranking women in Christendom." He turned back to Aelflaed. "She goes to West Francia soon. Ensure she is prepared with whatever she needs."

The fight had gone from Aelflaed and she simply bowed her head in acquiescence. Eadgifu looked stunned, but not displeased. In the silence which followed, Eadgyth darted forward.

"Don't go away, Father," she cried. "Please don't leave us."

"Do not be foolish, Eadgyth," Edward said, looking down at his daughter in disdain.

Eadgyth cried out from the pain of his obvious disgust, flinging her arms around his leg. "Take us with you."

Edward tried in vain to extricate himself from Eadgyth's grasp. He looked helplessly at Aelflaed. "Control your daughter, my lady," he snapped at her.

Pressing her lips tightly together, Aelflaed stepped towards them. Eadgyth dug her fingers into her father's leg more desperately than ever, unable to believe how cruelly he was treating her. But before Aelflaed could reach them, gentle hands pulled her away.

"Come, little Eadgyth. This won't do," Athelstan said, lifting her into his arms.

Eadgyth burst into tears, putting her arms around Athelstan's neck. "Why do we have to go away? I don't want to leave Father. I don't want to leave you."

"I know, Little Sister," he said, stroking her hair. "But he is your father and your king. You must trust him to do what is best."

Edward straightened his tunic and scowled at Aelflaed. "I trust you will teach that one to behave as befits a princess of Wessex." He looked again at Eadgyth, still cradled in Athelstan's arms. A ripple of guilt crossed his face, as he patted her awkwardly on the head. "I do not want to hear of such outbursts again, my child or no man of rank will ever want to wed you." He turned on his heel and strode from the chamber with no further words for any of them, the door slamming hard behind him. Eadgyth raised her head from Athelstan's shoulder to stare wide-eyed at the thick oak door, the thump as it closed reverberating in her heart.

Athelstan handed Eadgyth back to Aelflaed. "Do not be too harsh on her, my lady. I have always considered this one a fine little maid."

Aelflaed drew herself up to her full height to glare at her stepson. "I will thank you, Athelstan, not to instruct me in how to raise my children. You heard your father. It is my son who is to be his heir, not you."

Athelstan shrugged and kissed Eadgyth on the forehead. "Farewell, Little Sister. You will be in my prayers."

The pain in Eadgyth's chest increased as Athelstan left the room closely followed by Aelfweard. Edwin's eyes darted between his mother and the door, before hurrying after his brothers. As the door shut behind him the pain burst from Eadgyth. Her sisters stared helplessly at the huge tears rolling down her cheeks.

"Eadgyth, Eadgyth," her mother cried, shaking her by the shoulders. "Stop this."

The harsh thud of the door rang on in Eadgyth's ears drowning out her mother's words. She could not stop crying. Sobs tore from her throat, causing spasms to hurtle through her body. She tried to hold them back, but choked, her face growing scarlet as she gasped for breath. The room spun around her in sweeping circles, ever faster until she fell senseless to the ground.

She was barely aware of being transported to Wilton later that day. There the nuns tried in vain to soothe her tears and tempt her appetite. It took years before the tears stopped flowing every night, silently into her pillow and she took to merely picking at her food. Nightmares plagued her sleep so severely she spent many a dark hour staring into the blackness, terrified to close her eyes. The happy little maiden who had charmed Edward's court seemed vanished forever into the thin, solemn eyed girl.

Part One: The Year of our Lord 929-30

Chapter one

"Well, well, little Eadgyth. You have changed since last we met," Athelstan said, looking at his sister from twinkling eyes.

Eadgyth blushed, remembering the broken hearted child he had last seen. She was now nineteen, with fair hair framing a serious face. The years of ill health no longer plagued her, but had left their mark in her slight frame. Elfgifu, who stood next to her, was only fifteen but already she was taller.

"I do not think you remember me, Elfgifu," Athelstan continued. "But I am most glad to see you again."

Elfgifu murmured her greeting, overawed by the presence of her older brother, now titled King of the English.

Aelflaed had accompanied her daughters to this meeting in the grand hall at Canterbury and she tapped her foot impatiently, waiting to hear why they had been summoned. Her contempt for her stepson had never completely gone away, although she had learnt to conceal it. When Edward had died a few years before, Aelflaed had high hopes Aelfweard, who had been proclaimed King of Wessex, would release them from their obscurity. But her hopes had been dashed in the cruellest fashion, when Aelfweard died a mere month after his father. With Edwin too young to rule, Athelstan had taken the throne of not just Mercia, but also Wessex. Aelflaed had remarked bitterly to her daughters that they might as well all take religious vows, for they would now undoubtedly be forgotten.

But Athelstan had not forgotten them. Three years before

he had summoned her sister, Eadhild, to be married to Hugh, Duke of the Franks. Aelflaed had not been appeased, particularly when she heard what Athelstan had gained in return. Eadgyth had tried in vain to stop her mother interrogating the messenger, who reluctantly gave details of spices, jewels, horses and relics said to have once been the possession of the great Emperor Charles. Aelflaed had become more outraged as the list went on.

Athelstan smiled at the three women and bade them be seated. "Since the noble marriages your sisters made in West Francia, it seems East Francia, or Germany as I believe many call it, does not wish to be left out of an alliance with the House of Wessex."

"My daughters are to be married to East Franks?" Aelflaed inquired.

"One of your daughters, my lady," Athelstan said. "But it is not a Frankish man who seeks a bride. The Kingdom of Germany is now ruled by one of our own kind – a Saxon."

"The Saxons have conquered East Francia?" Eadgyth asked in surprise. Shut away at Wilton she had heard little of the situation in the nearby realms. The possible marriage held very little interest to her, but news of such a Saxon victory was intriguing.

"Not conquered exactly," Athelstan replied. "Ten years ago the Dukes of East Francia asked Henry, Duke of Saxony to take the throne on the death of King Conrad. I believe it caused considerable surprise, as it is the first time anyone other than a Frank has ruled that region."

Eadgyth looked down. The last thing she wanted to think about was the events of ten years before.

"Is it this King Henry who wishes to wed one of my daughters?" Aelflaed asked, bringing Athelstan back to the purpose of the summons.

"No, my lady. He has been long wed. He seeks a West Saxon bride for his son, Prince Otto. A fine young man, from what I have heard."

"Is Prince Otto the King's oldest son?" Eadgyth asked.

A flicker of a frown crossed Athelstan's face. "His oldest legitimate son. It is assumed Otto will be his heir, at least for the Duchy of Saxony. However I suspect he is seeking a bride from the royal house of Wessex to confer such prestige on his son as to make it likely he will succeed his father as king."

"Which of my daughters is he to wed?"

Athelstan hesitated, looking from Eadgyth to Elfgifu. "I do not know. It seems Prince Otto is to be allowed a choice, so King Henry has requested I send two of my sisters."

Aelflaed frowned. "What of the one he does not choose?"

"King Henry assures me he will arrange an advantageous match for the other."

"And you trust him?" Aelflaed looked at Athelstan as if he were losing his mind.

"I would not let my sisters out of Wessex if I did not. Besides, Cenwald, the new Bishop of Worcester, will accompany them. I trust him."

"What do you gain from this, my lord?" Aelflaed barely kept the sarcasm out of her voice.

"I gain a valuable ally," Athelstan replied. "Naturally there is some exchange of treasures. King Henry has sent some fine books."

"I don't think I want to go," Elfgifu whispered, as Aelflaed visibly ground her teeth at Athelstan's reply.

Athelstan took hold of her hand. "My sister, you must trust me to know what is best. It is a custom for our family to wed into the Frankish realms. Have you not heard how our aunt married the Margrave of Flanders? And our great-grandfather, the noble King Athelwulf, took a princess of West Francia as his own second wife. Such alliances always bring us great prestige. You must do your duty, Elfgifu."

"Of course you will pursue this alliance," Aelflaed said firmly.

"At least we will go together," Eadgyth said. She was not displeased to hear of this news. At nearly twenty years of age she had begun to think there would never be a match made for her. This Otto or another German nobleman would suit her well. "All will be well, Elfgifu."

"Yes, of course. Forgive me, my lord." Elfgifu sounded more flustered than ever.

"Perhaps you will excuse us, my lord," Aelflaed put in. "My daughters are tired after their ride."

Athelstan got to his feet. "Of course, my ladies, although if Eadgyth is not tired, perhaps she will stay and talk with me awhile."

Eadgyth nodded and sat back down. Athelstan did not return to his throne, but took a chair next to hers.

"I was with our father when he died. He spoke lovingly of you and your sisters."

Eadgyth shrugged. "Those words mean little. He rarely saw us, even when he was near Wilton. It was obvious he did not regard us with affection."

Athelstan raised his eyebrows. "I wonder what King Henry and his son will make of such frank words. You might do better to curb this, Eadgyth."

"It sounds to me that these Germans need our noble blood far more than we need them."

"You may be right, but even if he marries you, Otto does not have to care for you. Is that truly the marriage you seek?"

Eadgyth shook her head. "I have no expectation my husband should care for me, any more than our father did."

"Our father did love you. I truly believe that."

"You always did see the best in everyone, Brother."

"You seem bitter, Eadgyth. I hope whoever you marry brings you happiness. The little maid I remember was always laughing."

Eadgyth shrugged again, uncomfortable with the conversation. "What do you know of Prince Otto?"

"He is a fine warrior. He acquitted himself well when fighting the Slavs for his father."

"What else has he done?"

"You are impatient. He is young yet. I do not suppose he

has acquired much experience in administration or other such matters."

"How old is he?" Eadgyth demanded.

"He will soon turn seventeen, I believe."

Eadgyth stared at her brother. "Not yet seventeen? I am nearly twenty. I do not think he will choose me, when Elfgifu is younger and so pretty. She is stronger than I too."

Athelstan gave her a long look. "You do not do yourself justice. The few years' difference in age between you will soon mean little. Oh, Eadgyth perhaps you do not realise how pretty you are and your appearance would be finer still if you would only smile. I have kept myself informed so I know your health is much improved. You have a grace Elfgifu lacks. Otto would be fortunate indeed to gain you as his wife."

"Would I be fortunate to gain him as a husband? I would prefer to wed a man, not a boy."

Athelstan took hold of her hands. "But the boy will soon be a man. And if what I have heard is true, he will be a fine man indeed."

∞∞∞

Over the next weeks Eadgyth settled into Athelstan's court, glad to spend time again with her brother. As a child she had adored him, but had been unaware of his powerful intelligence. The household reflected this, with many learned scholars making the evenings in the grand hall stimulating occasions. As she listened intently to the discourse she often caught Athelstan's eyes on her in approval.

The sombre garments Eadgyth and Elfgifu had worn at Wilton were deemed to be unsuitable for their new life in Germany. Aelflaed's spirits rose as she savoured the experience of preparing two of her daughters for marriage and even Elfgifu brightened at the fine cloths and silken threads. But Eadgyth was indifferent, showing no pleasure in the elaborate raiment and jewels which were bestowed upon her. Even the embroidered blue kirtle she would wear for her wedding caused no delight, although the soft cloth made it the finest she had ever possessed. A serving woman combed her fair hair, leaving it loose to flow over her shoulders. Athelstan nodded approvingly and there were murmurs of appreciation from all who stood around. One held up a mirror for Eadgyth to see. The reflection showed a face of enchanting delicacy, with clear blue eyes almost the same colour as the cloth staring steadily back. She did not smile.

"I would try to enjoy these riches, my child," Aelflaed said tartly, observing her daughter's disinterest. "There will be little else for you to enjoy."

"Mother," Eadgyth protested.

"No, Eadgyth, it is important you are prepared for married life. Look at me. Nearly twenty years your father and I were wed. I bore child after child, but it was not enough. I was cast away as if those years were nothing. He cast off Athelstan's mother and he cast off me. He would undoubtedly have cast off his last wife if he had lived longer and found a suitable replacement. That is the reality you could face."

Elfgifu began to cry and Eadgyth quickly put an arm around her, shaking her head at her mother.

"This is not always the case, Sister," Athelstan said quickly. "Our grandfather was wed just the once for many years until death took him. And the first marriage of his father lasted thirty years. I heard she was much mourned when she died."

"What do you know of marriage, Athelstan?" Aelflaed asked. "Why have you not wed if you consider it such a desirable state?"

"Marriage is not for me," Athelstan replied. "For which I thought you would be glad, since it means Edwin remains my heir. But Eadgyth and Elfgifu go with my protection. The German king and his son want my friendship. They will not gain that by treating my sisters ill."

Chapter two

Although the winter was advancing, Eadgyth and Elfgifu made their way to Dover as soon as their belongings were ready. The German envoys had reported that King Henry was eager for the marriage to be solemnized at all speed. To Eadgyth the extreme haste of the German king to see his barely seventeen year old son so quickly wed, merely confirmed her suspicions that Otto was not the prize everyone was proclaiming him to be.

With the weather so mild, there were no delays at Dover. Elfgifu wept to leave her native land, but Eadgyth was mostly calm. Guiltily she felt relieved to be leaving her mother's bitter complaints behind, feeling only a surge of pity as she gave her a last embrace. But as she turned to Athelstan, a lump rose in her throat. It was cruel to be parted just as they were getting to know one another again.

"Farewell, little Eadgyth. Send word to me if you can, so I know you are well." He put his arm around her and kissed her on each cheek.

"Will we meet again?" Eadgyth asked, her voice trembling.

Athelstan gave a gentle smile. "I would like to see you again, but I cannot wish for it. My hope is that you find such contentment in your new land, you never need to return."

Eadgyth wiped away a solitary tear as Athelstan hugged Elfgifu, before resolutely taking her sister's hand to board the boat. Bishop Cenwald and the other envoys on board surrounded their charges solicitously, obscuring their last view of Kent and their family. Eadgyth reflected this was just as well, as from the look of her trembling lip and watery eyes, Elfgifu seemed likely to completely break down at the slightest encouragement. The sounds of oarsmen shouting instructions filled the air as the boat glided towards the harbour mouth. Eadgyth sat up straight, not showing any emotion. There had been little for her in Wessex. Germany, whatever it was like, would at least be different.

"Why aren't you afraid, Eadgyth?" Elfgifu asked, pulling a cloak tightly around herself against the brisk sea breeze.

Eadgyth wrapped a blanket around their knees. "What is there to be afraid of?"

Elfgifu stared at her sister. "We are going to people we know nothing of. All we know of this Otto is what a fine warrior he is, nothing more. One of us will wed a man we know even less of. They might be cruel."

"Athelstan would not send us to one such as that."

"What does Athelstan truly know of these people? All he knows is what the envoys have told him and of course they have sung Prince Otto's praises."

Eadgyth looked at Elfgifu, thinking, not for the first time, she had a common sense which few realised she possessed.

"Even if the envoys are reporting the truth," Elfgifu continued. "They cannot truly know what Prince Otto would be like once he is alone with his wife. You must know this, Eadgyth. So why are you not afraid?"

Eadgyth put her arms around her sister. She stared out to sea, seeing not the grey waves but a sturdy oak door slamming, as once it had slammed behind her father. That door had haunted her nightmares often over the years and each time she woke, she felt afresh the searing pain of her father's desertion. She was sure no pain could ever be as severe. Even if her husband beat her on her wedding night, she did not think it would be as bad.

Adopting her usual calm manner she squeezed Elfgifu tightly. "We have to pray our husbands are kind, god fearing men and we must strive to ensure we never give them cause for complaint."

∞∞∞

Upon arrival in West Francia, they found the marriages of their kinswomen ensured a warm welcome wherever they went. In Calais messengers from their sister, Eadhild, brought costly gifts, and they were greeted with ceremony in Bruges by their cousin, Arnulf, the Margrave of Flanders. Their aunt, Aelfryth, had died earlier that year, but Arnulf clasped their hands warmly, exclaiming on how much they both resembled the mother he still deeply missed.

Messengers from Germany told them King Henry and his family were at Harzburg in Saxony and he was eager for the princesses to proceed there at all speed.

"It is still some way, but the ride should not be hard unless there is too much snow on the ground," Arnulf told them.

Elfgifu, who was in no hurry to reach her destination, shuddered, but Eadgyth agreed with Bishop Cenwald that they should swiftly continue their journey. Arnulf bestowed further gifts on them and accompanied them to the edge of his realm.

"Have you ever met Prince Otto?" Elfgifu asked Arnulf as they prepared to say their farewells.

"Once, several years ago when he was still a boy," Arnulf replied. Eadgyth nodded her head at this comment, thinking privately that Otto was still just a boy. "But his father, King Henry, is a fine man," Arnulf continued. "All were surprised when he was proclaimed King of East Francia. The previous king had been his enemy, yet even he recognised King Henry's nobility. He asked on his deathbed for Henry, then Duke of Saxony, to be named king. The Duke was so far from expecting the crown, he had gone hawking in the mountains and it took some time to find him. Young Otto is well known for his valour in fighting the Slavs."

Eadgyth smiled, hiding her irritation that yet again all she was hearing was how great a warrior Otto was. As if that would make any difference to whichever of them was to be his wife.

Arnulf bowed to them both. "I wish you all prosperity in your new roles, my dear cousins. God speed."

Several long days of riding followed, with the weather growing steadily colder. There was a dusting of snow on the ground as they made their way further east, but the skies remained clear. They were given a curious but warm welcome everywhere they passed through and at nights rested in abbey guest chambers. The land appeared to be a fair one as it rose up into the hills where one of their entourage informed them they were not far from their destination.

A messenger was sent on ahead to inform the King of their imminent arrival, but shortly after setting off he skidded on an icy patch, falling from his horse. They only discovered he had not yet reached his destination when their own arrival two days later in Harzburg took everyone by surprise.

"Welcome, my ladies," cried the confused looking serving man who was the only occupant of the hall. "Please, sit and refresh yourselves."

The bishop muttered to the envoys, shocked at the lack of welcome as Eadgyth and Elfgifu took nervous sips of hot ale, their honeyed cakes remaining untouched. They were still sitting in silence when there was a sound of running footsteps.

A woman swept into the hall, finely dressed in an embroidered red dress over a white tunic. She was not a young woman, but her face was a beautiful one, with strands of dark blonde hair escaping from her mantle.

"Greetings to you both and welcome to Harzburg. Allow me to present myself. I am Mathilda, Duchess of Saxony and Queen of Germany." She indicated another woman, who looked to be a few years younger than Eadgyth. "This is my daughter, Lady Hedwig. I have another daughter but Gerberga is not often at court since she was wed to the Duke of Lotharingia."

Eadgyth swiftly dropped into a curtsey. "Thank you for your welcome, my lady. I am Eadgyth, Princess of Wessex, sister of the most noble King Athelstan." She gestured to Elfgifu, who seemed unable to speak. "This is my sister, Lady Elfgifu. We are most happy to meet you both."

"Well, you have made such swift progress here, I fear you find us most unprepared. None of the menfolk are here this day." Mathilda gave them a kind smile. "But perhaps that is not such a bad thing. You will have time to rest and refresh yourselves after your journey and can be presented to King Henry and Prince Otto this night."

Eadgyth gave no sign of the relief flooding through her at this welcome as she smiled calmly back, taking an immediate liking to the queen. Elfgifu too murmured her thanks.

"I am honoured to meet you," Hedwig said. She was dark haired and attractive with a warm smile very like her mother's. "Please continue with your food. I know you must need the refreshment after so long a journey."

Eadgyth was about to sit back down when she noticed a child peeping out from behind Mathilda's skirts.

Mathilda followed her glance and laughed, pulling a dark haired boy of around four years forward. "Come young man, this is not the way to greet two fair ladies who have travelled so far. Lady Eadgyth, Lady Elfgifu, I can at least present one of my sons to you. This is my youngest, Lord Bruno."

The boy favoured them with a wide grin as he bowed to them. Eadgyth nodded at him and stretched out her hands, bending her knees into a slight curtsey. "I am honoured to meet you, Lord Bruno."

As she sat down she noticed the look of approval on the Queen's face. Mathilda and Hedwig continued to talk as they ate, telling them of the family and life in Germany.

"The King is out with the falcons this day with two of his sons. He does love hawking," Mathilda said. "He has often said his one regret in accepting the crown of Germany is that it gives him less time with his beloved birds."

Elfgifu gave a few murmured responses, but mostly it was left to Eadgyth to carry the conversation as she answered Mathilda's gentle questions. She longed to ask more of Otto, confident that from his mother and sister she might hear of more than just his prowess as a warrior.

"Does Prince Otto also enjoy hawking, my lady?" she ventured.

"Not as much as my Father does," Hedwig replied.

Mathilda shrugged. "I believe Otto has ridden out with some companions this day. Perhaps they are hunting, although who knows what that boy gets up to when I and his father are not present."

Eadgyth did not let her face display the surprise she felt at hearing of Otto in less than flattering terms, perhaps hinting at some deeds his mother disapproved of, but Mathilda said no more of her eldest son. "You must both be tired." She summoned a serving woman. "Conduct the princesses to their chamber. There will be a feast in your honour this night, my ladies, but take your time to rest for now."

"Do I look fitting?" Elfgifu asked, as they prepared for the feast.

Eadgyth gave a slight smile at her sister, looking very pretty in a pink kirtle, with white embroidery. "You look lovely, Sister. I think I know who Otto will choose." A hint of regret stirred in her heart. Mathilda had seemed a kind and intelligent woman. It would be good to spend more time with her.

Elfgifu shook her head. "I would not be so sure of that. You look pretty too and you always know what to say, while I must appear stupid by comparison."

"You are far from stupid. Do not be afraid to speak the words in your heart." Eadgyth smoothed her own kirtle, in a darker shade of pink. "Come, we are Princesses of Wessex. We shall not allow Otto or any of these Saxons to intimidate us."

Hand in hand with their heads held high, Eadgyth and Elfgifu followed Father Cenwald to the hall.

Chapter three

The hall was ablaze with torches and filled with people whose conversations quickly stilled as Eadgyth and Elfgifu entered. Eadgyth tried to smile graciously at the curious faces, relieved to see many welcoming smiles as heads bent in obeisance. The walls were lined with elaborate tapestries, alternated with banners and weaponry, but she had no time to admire them as they made their way towards the end. In front of a fresco depicting a battle scene, a group of richly dressed people were gathered around finely carved chairs.

Mathilda seemed to guess how daunting this was for them, for she rose from her chair to take them by the hand. "How charming you both look. I trust you have rested yourselves this afternoon."

"Thank you, my lady, we have," Eadgyth replied.

"Is your chamber comfortable enough for you? Please tell me if there is anything further you need."

Eadgyth's heart warmed towards this kind lady. "It is most comfortable, my lady. I cannot think we have lacked for anything."

"No, my lady, thank you," Elfgifu murmured.

Mathilda smiled as she led them onwards to where a man had just risen from the other chair. He appeared considerably older than Mathilda, his dark hair and beard streaked with grey. It was obvious from his fine raiment and the gold circlet on his head that this was King Henry and Eadgyth dropped into a curtsey before Mathilda had finished presenting them.

"No need for that, my dear ladies." Henry bowed over their hands. "I bid you both most welcome and can only apologise for our poor preparations."

"Not at all, my lord. We have been most warmly welcomed and this looks fine indeed." Eadgyth gestured at the laden table.

Henry looked pleased and stroked his beard, his eyes moving speculatively from her to Elfgifu. Eadgyth guessed he was trying to decide which of them he preferred. She held her head high, while Elfgifu blushed. Refusing to be daunted, Eadgyth looked at the others who stood near Henry, receiving a warm smile from Hedwig. The one standing closest to the King was a dark haired man, whose face was marred by a faint scowl. As he met her eyes his lips curled into a tight smile, but Eadgyth looked steadily back without flinching. She had given little thought to how she expected Otto to appear, but this was certainly not the fine young man of Athelstan's description. Apart from the scorn on his face, he was not ill-looking, although he looked much older than seventeen years.

"Please meet my oldest son, Lord Thankmar," Henry said indicating the dark haired man.

Firmly Eadgyth quashed her surprise. She remembered now Athelstan saying Otto was Henry's oldest legitimate son. She nodded her head to Thankmar with a sense of relief and the man bowed back. Like his father he too looked from her to Elfgifu, a look of wry amusement spreading over his face.

Eadgyth did her best not to shudder and looked at the other stood with the King, but being a boy of no more than ten or eleven years he was too young to be Otto.

The King laid his hand on the boy's shoulder. "And this is my son and namesake, Lord Henry."

Mathilda smiled proudly as young Henry gave a low bow. "I am honoured to meet you, my ladies."

He was a good looking boy with a strong resemblance to his father, although his hair was as fair as Mathilda's. Eadgyth returned the greeting, trying not to show her impatience as she waited to be presented to Otto.

"I believe you have already met this young rascal," Henry continued, gesturing at Bruno.

"Yes, indeed," Eadgyth smiled. "We have had that privilege."

Henry and Mathilda exchanged irritated glances. "I do, of course, have another son, but unfortunately he is not currently here."

"Where is Prince Otto?" Mathilda asked a serving lad.

"I believe Prince Otto has not yet returned, my lady," the serving lad replied.

"That boy," Mathilda muttered.

Henry shook his head. "I must ask you to forgive my son for his absence, my ladies."

"Yes, my Lord King," Elfgifu stammered.

"Prince Otto cannot know we are here, my lord," Eadgyth said. "No forgiveness is necessary."

"I trust this is not one of those occasions where he stays all night at the hunting lodge." Mathilda looked at the table, obviously wondering whether to bid everyone to be seated.

At that moment the sound of raised voices and laughter came from the doorway and a group of young men entered.

Mathilda raised her eyes to the ceiling. "Otto!" she called.

One of the young men separated from the group and bounded up the hall. He was tall, with dark hair and vivid blue eyes. He caught Mathilda up in a hug, sweeping her off her feet despite her protests. Releasing her, he looked quizzically at her clothes.

"You look very fine, Mother. Is there some occasion I have forgotten?" Otto was dressed in costly, but plain garments. He glanced in surprise at Thankmar, who had cracked a loud laugh.

Mathilda shot an irritated glance at Thankmar, and looked with no more pleasure at Otto. "Yes, my son. The Wessex princesses have arrived."

Eadgyth's lips twitched at the look of dismay spreading over the young man's face. "Already?" he asked.

Mathilda sighed. "Lady Eadgyth, please meet my eldest son, Prince Otto."

Eadgyth curtseyed politely, as Otto stared at her. Suddenly recollecting himself, he bowed deeply before her. "Please forgive me, my lady. I did not know you would be arriving today." He still looked dismayed. "Although I am very glad to meet you," he added hurriedly. "And of course am pleased you have arrived safely."

Young Henry snorted with laughter, leaving Eadgyth unable to keep her face expressionless. Otto's cheeks flushed a crimson red, making him appear more uncomfortable than ever. Feeling sorry for him, she stretched out her hand. "Truly it is of no matter, my lord. We were fortunate with the weather on our journey and arrived far quicker than I expected."

Otto took her hand, still looking anxious. Hesitantly he raised it to his lips. "Thank you for your understanding, my lady." Eadgyth was shocked by the pleading expression in his eyes and could do nothing more than nod.

Otto turned to greet Elfgifu and Eadgyth took the chance to study the man… boy. It was hard to decide which word fitted him the best. His muscular body had the look of a toughened warrior, yet his tousled hair and the anxious expression gave him a boyish look. Eadgyth found the contrast unsettling. As he smiled at Elfgifu, she tried to work out if his expression had been as warm towards her. Catching Mathilda's eye, she flushed to be caught staring and hoped her flicker of jealousy had not been apparent.

"This is a fine hall, my Lady Queen. Are any of these tapestries your work?"

"Some of them, Lady Eadgyth. How does this compare to the palaces of Wessex and Mercia?"

Eadgyth hesitated. "I am not sure, my lady. Until I was summoned to Canterbury by my brother, King Athelstan, I had been for many years at the Abbey of Wilton. From my memory, the Palace of Winchester is very fine, but I have not been there since I was a child."

"I too was raised in an abbey," Mathilda said. "I intended to make my vows, but dear Henry had other plans."

The King patted her hand. "Far too pretty to remain in an abbey, my dear. So are you and your sister, Lady Eadgyth. Don't you agree, Otto?"

Otto went scarlet. "Yes, Father, of course."

"Well, I am sure the princesses are ready to dine now you are here, Otto. Shall we be seated?" Mathilda asked.

Otto nodded silently, making it clear this was not the meal he had planned for the end of a day's hunting, but he took Eadgyth by the hand and led her to a seat, before seating Elfgifu on his other side and they all bowed their heads in prayer.

"Did you have a successful day's hunt, my lord?" Eadgyth asked as the meal was served, understanding it would be up to her to start the conversation.

"Yes, my lady. Some deer and a boar. It was a good day."

"You are a skilled huntsman, my lord."

"Thank you, my lady."

The conversation continued in a similarly stilted fashion and Elfgifu was of no assistance, no matter how Eadgyth tried to draw her in. When Mathilda turned to them, she and Eadgyth spoke easily, while Otto lapsed into silence, occasionally murmuring his agreement. Throughout the meal she was aware of the surreptitious looks the King was giving her as well as the less discrete glances from his other sons. The evening seemed to pass slowly and she was relieved when it came to an end.

Otto rose to his feet to bid them good night, no doubt looking forward to relaxing over a drink once they had gone. He bowed over Elfgifu's hand, smiling warmly. Eadgyth drew herself up to her full height as he turned to her, aware he was looking anxious once again.

He took a deep breath. "I'll bid you good night, my lady. I fear I have been poor company, but I look forward to talking again with you in the next days."

As he pressed his lips against her hand, Eadgyth felt the need to reassure him. "This night has been most pleasant, my lord. I shall be glad to renew our acquaintance in the morn."

Otto's face brightened into a more genuine smile than any she had yet seen. "So shall I."

Eadgyth's eyes widened, unprepared for how that smile transformed his face. Unable to say more she nodded back and took her sister by the hand. Feeling as if a weight had been lifted from her, she left the hall, but could not resist a quick glance back to Otto, now sat talking with his father. She wished she knew what he was saying.

Chapter four

In their chamber Elfgifu fell on her bed in relief. "Oh Sister, what a night. I am glad it is over."

Eadgyth sat down next to her. "The King and Queen seem kind."

"Yes, but what of Lord Thankmar? He did not stop scowling at me the entire night. Who is he? The King called him his eldest son."

"I assume he is illegitimate, but still of high rank," Eadgyth replied.

"Like Athelstan?"

"I suppose so," Eadgyth said. "Although we do not know if Athelstan is illegitimate, just that his mother was never spoken of. Apparently our grandfather treated him as a possible heir. But Lord Thankmar… I thought at first he was Prince Otto. I am glad he is not. I would not care to be wed to him or see you wed to him either."

"What did you think of Prince Otto?" Elfgifu asked.

"An overgrown puppy dog," Eadgyth said promptly.

Elfgifu laughed, but Eadgyth immediately regretted the words. Otto had been so obviously unprepared for their arrival, yet he had spent the evening trying to say the right words to welcome them. Inwardly Eadgyth admitted to herself that she was being churlish because when he had smiled at her, she had been struck by how handsome he was. To indulge in any emotion would be foolish indeed.

Suddenly impatient with the bed chamber, Eadgyth got to

her feet. "I do not think I can sleep yet. I am going to the church. Do you want to come?"

Elfgifu shook her head. "No, I shall stay here. Otto seems acceptable enough, I suppose. If I must marry, he would not be so bad. But I wish I could remain unwed."

Eadgyth hugged her. "It doesn't matter what we want. We must both do our duty, whatever that is."

∞∞∞

The church was deserted, but candles flickered in finely wrought candlesticks as Eadgyth knelt down at the altar, her eyes fixed on the jewelled cross.

"Heavenly Father, Blessed Saint Oswald, please grant me strength for these next days. Guide me to fulfil my duties to the noble alliance Athelstan has arranged and help keep my heart free from inappropriate emotions."

It took some lengthy prayers before she felt sufficiently at peace to think she would sleep. She made her way to the doorway, but paused as she heard voices outside.

"I know you have not been keen on the idea of marriage, my son, but it is time." It was the King. Eadgyth froze, knowing it must be Otto he was speaking to.

"Yes, Father. I know."

"Do either take your fancy yet? The younger looks to be stronger," the King said.

"But Lady Eadgyth has more assurance, although I suppose Lady Elfgifu may acquire more grace as she grows older," Mathilda put in.

"Both are pretty girls. You cannot deny that, Otto," Henry said. "Either would please me as a daughter. You must not take too long over your choice. The King of the English is eager to hear the alliance is sealed."

"I know, Father. I think I know which one I will choose, but I will sleep on it and make my final decision in the morn. I'll bid you both good night now."

"Good night, Otto," Mathilda replied.

Eadgyth was terrified the King and Queen would enter the church and she would be caught listening, although it had not been her fault. She was unsure what to do, as they continued their conversation.

"Do you truly think Lady Elfgifu is the better choice?" Mathilda asked.

"My dear, I do not mind which of them he chooses, but you have made your preference obvious. I want him to know he has a choice."

"The choice is obvious. Really, Henry, have you ever seen such grace and charm as Lady Eadgyth displayed? She would be the perfect wife for him."

"I suppose so." Henry did not sound convinced. "But what of the times when Otto is alone with his wife? Will she still behave with perfect grace and charm or will there be some genuine warmth towards him? I sensed some reserve in her."

"This is nonsense, Henry. Of course she will be a dutiful wife. What more can you want?"

"That is not what I meant. This alliance with the English is useful and will remain useful long after I am gone. But Otto will not tread the easiest path in life. I want the boy to be happy."

"She appears truly devout. I have spoken on this to the bishop who accompanied them and he praised her deep piety. Think how good that will be for him. Why should such noble character not make Otto happy?"

"Perhaps she will, but we do not know. I have no objections to Lady Eadgyth. Quite the opposite, but I promised Otto a choice." Henry's voice faded and Eadgyth gave a sigh of relief as she realised they were moving away. "Please do not try to influence Otto. You know how he longs to win your approval."

Feeling ashamed of herself, Eadgyth strained to hear Mathilda's reply, but they were too far away. She stared back at the altar, knowing sleep would be impossible.

Elfgifu was already sleeping when Eadgyth finally returned to their chamber. She slid into bed and lay as quietly as she could to avoid disturbing her.

∞∞∞

"Lady Eadgyth," Otto said, dazzling her with a joyous smile. "I wish to inform you that I am to wed your sister." He strode away from her, slamming the door on his way out…

Eadgyth sat up in bed, her heart thudding. That door dream again, but this time Otto had taken the place of her father. She lay back down, staring into the darkness, remonstrating with herself. It was ridiculous. Otto's choice made very little difference to her. She would either wed him or another, as yet unknown, man. No doubt either would treat her with the same carelessness as her father had treated her mother. But as dawn broke Eadgyth was still wide awake, feeling sick as she reflected on a day which would seal her fate.

∞∞∞

Eadgyth dressed neatly for the day in a dark green kirtle, which her mother had told her flattered her fair hair. Wordlessly she and Elfgifu made their way to the church to join the court in the first prayers of the day. Mathilda greeted them both warmly. Eadgyth was not sure if this meant Otto had not yet confided in her, or if this was her natural courtesy towards guests, but she returned the greeting calmly.

Otto strode in shortly after with his brother Henry on one side and Thankmar on the other. All three bowed to them. Eadgyth looked surreptitiously into Otto's face in the hope of gaining some clue, but it was expressionless.

"Good day to you, my ladies," Otto said. "I trust you both passed a peaceful night."

"Yes, thank you, my lord," Eadgyth replied, wondering if telling such falsehoods to a man who might soon be her husband was appropriate.

"That is good." Otto looked at them both, obviously trying to think of what to say next.

Thankmar gave a muffled snort of laughter as he and Henry moved on.

"What a fool," Henry said with a backwards glance.

Eadgyth looked again at Otto. His face had gone red, as he glanced swiftly from her to Elfgifu. Eadgyth had been struggling to keep her face composed, but at the miserable look in his eyes, she felt ashamed of her mirth. However before she could think of anything to say, Otto gave another slight bow and moved away from them to take his place beside his father.

Still torn between amusement and fear, Eadgyth knelt with the rest of the court as the mass began and did her best to calm her racing heart. The whole journey she had been supremely indifferent to the marriage, yet now she was there, she no longer knew how she was feeling. She bent her head lower, trying to focus on the words of the mass.

At the end Otto did not approach them as he left with his father and Thankmar. Henry was talking intently to them both, but from the few words she caught it did not seem to be anything to do with her. Still in awe of the German nobility, Elfgifu muttered something about returning to their chamber and swiftly left the church. As others from the court filed out, Eadgyth moved forward to kneel again before the altar.

Whispering the familiar prayers, she felt herself calming at last. The church had become silent and she remained a long time on her knees, glad of the peace. Unsure what she should do next, she got up, grimacing slightly at her cramped knees. She turned and gasped. Otto was standing by a pillar, his arms hanging awkwardly at his side. He was staring at her and all Eadgyth could do was stare back. She looked longingly at the door beyond him, wanting to run from him until she had prepared herself.

He bowed. "Forgive me, my lady, I did not mean to startle you," he said, running his hand through his hair.

Firmly Eadgyth straightened her back, smiling graciously. "No, forgive me, my lord. I did not hear you enter. I did not mean to disregard you."

"You seemed so intent on your devotions, I did not want to disturb you."

Eadgyth tried to think of something to say, cross with herself for becoming distracted by how his blue tunic matched his eyes. Belatedly she realised she should have curtseyed to him. It seemed too late to do this now and Otto did not appear displeased, although he looked as anxious as he had done the previous night.

Finally some words came to her. "I like to say some prayers to Saint Oswald in the mornings. I do not think he is a saint your people entreat very often."

Otto shook his head. "I fear we do not, my lady. He was your forefather was he not?"

Eadgyth nodded, feeling pleased Otto had known this although she knew it was foolish. Her ancient lineage was the main reason King Henry had wanted her there.

Otto swallowed nervously. "Lady Eadgyth, if you can spare a little of your time, will you come with me somewhere we can talk?"

Eadgyth's heart thumped. Otto looked so solemn, she still had no idea what he was thinking. Hoping her own expression was calm, she nodded. "Of course, my lord."

He gave a tight smile and started to stride from the church forcing Eadgyth to quicken her own pace to keep up with him. Otto suddenly recollected himself and his face reddened. He slowed down, gesturing courteously to allow Eadgyth to leave the church first. Bowing her head to hide her smile she went out into the windy winter's day where he became even more flustered. "Forgive me. I had not realised how cold it is."

Eadgyth pulled her cloak around herself, shivering as Otto looked frantically around. Just inside the main doorway to the palace was a small chamber.

"Shall we step in here a moment, my lady?"

The relief of being out of the wind was immense, although Eadgyth continued to tremble almost imperceptibly. Otto did not seem to notice as he resolutely straightened his shoulders and took a deep breath.

Chapter five

"Lady Eadgyth, I would like you to do me the honour of becoming my wife," Otto said, his voice unsteady.

Eadgyth's first thought was one of unexpected pleasure, but the habit of keeping her feelings to herself was deeply ingrained and her face remained expressionless. "Of course, my lord. If that is what you wish, naturally I will oblige."

"Yes, yes, of course." Otto looked crestfallen. "I feel we would deal well together."

The phrase overgrown puppy dog floated again into Eadgyth's mind, but this time without any malice. The anxious expression in Otto's eyes as he looked at her was remarkably similar to the look of a puppy who is unsure whether he has pleased his master. Eadgyth was left with the uncomfortable feeling that if he had been a puppy, she had just kicked him. "I am sure we will," she said in an effort to make amends.

"I will try to make you happy," Otto continued desperately.

Eadgyth couldn't help but feel touched by the sight of this seasoned warrior, trying so hard to win her favour. She clenched her fists, trying to think of something to reassure him she was content with the arrangement.

"Otto," she said, slipping without thinking into using his name. "You know I have no choice in marrying you, but truly it is an arrangement which pleases me."

Eadgyth wondered if she was being too outspoken, but Otto's face broke into a dazzling smile. "Truly?" he said, eagerly taking her hands.

The smile was impossible to resist and Eadgyth's steadfast expression melted into one of her own. "Truly," she replied, breathless as his fingers entwined with hers.

Otto pulled her hands to his lips and kissed them. "I must inform my father. We should be betrothed this day."

"I would like that," Eadgyth replied. "But first may I speak to my sister?"

Otto's face fell. "Of course. I do not mean to offend her. She is charming and the man she weds will be fortunate indeed. I could not marry you both... not that I want to... I mean..." Otto stuttered to a halt.

Eadgyth shook her head, still smiling. She imagined Otto on the battlefield or in the hunt, completely in control. Yet here he seemed lost. "Do not worry. Elfgifu is not eager for marriage. She will not be upset."

"I see. I had a feeling I was not the great matrimonial prize everyone was telling me I was," Otto replied in mournful tones.

The laughter Eadgyth had been restraining since she met Otto burst from her, surprising her by how good it was to truly laugh. Otto's dismayed look changed into one of appreciation. "Oh, Eadgyth, I was struck by your appearance the moment I laid eyes on you. But when you smile like this, your beauty is beyond anything I have seen."

She blushed and looked down, feeling shy at the look in his eyes. He pulled her closer to him. "Eadgyth," he whispered. "I know we are not formally betrothed yet, but can I kiss you?"

Eadgyth was certain such a thing was not at all proper, but the pleading look in his eyes was hard to resist. Unable to speak, she nodded, lifting up her face. Very gently Otto slid an arm around her as he brought his lips down to meet hers. All thoughts vanished from her mind at the touch of his lips. Never had she expected to enjoy such an experience. Tentatively she raised her hand to his cheek. He was clean shaven and the skin felt smooth. Dark locks of hair fell forwards to cover her fingers. When he pulled his head back, all Eadgyth could do was stare at him, shocked by the warmth of her feelings.

They smiled at each other, their fingers still entwined. "I shall wait for you by the hall, while you talk to Lady Elfgifu," Otto said. "But hurry. I can scarce wait for the moment we are formally promised to each other."

Eadgyth nodded, reluctantly letting her hands slip away from him. "I shall be there soon," she said.

∞∞∞

Elfgifu looked up when Eadgyth came into their chamber and laughed. "I can see Prince Otto has chosen you," she said.

"But, how?" Eadgyth stammered.

"Oh, Sister, your face. I have never seen you look so happy. I do not need to ask if this is what you want."

"Well, of course this is a great honour," Eadgyth said sharply.

"I think to you it is more than that." Elfgifu gave her sister a wistful look.

Eadgyth bit back her reply and took her sister's hand. "Elfgifu, are you sure you do not mind?"

Elfgifu shook her head. "I would have been flattered if Prince Otto had chosen me, but terrified. Everyone here is so learned. The Queen is kind, but very clever. I would always feel a fool and I think I would struggle to find my place in such a family. You will not."

Eadgyth hugged her. "You are not a fool. You should not say such things."

Elfgifu laughed again. "Never mind about me. Are you formally betrothed?"

"No. Otto and I are to go to his father now."

"Then why are you here? Go!"

∞∞∞

Otto was waiting where he had promised, talking to Thankmar. His face lit up when he saw her and she smiled shyly back.

Thankmar arched an eyebrow. "I thought you were going to choose the other one. Did she refuse you?"

Eadgyth stopped, looking questioningly at Otto. He scowled at his brother. "I confided nothing about my choice to you."

"But you were full of praise for her beauty last night." Thankmar grinned as he looked insolently at his younger brother.

"I did not… that is, I praised them both. Damn it, Brother. I do not need to justify my choice to you."

"Not at all," Thankmar agreed. "Indeed it is clear from your face that of all the ladies you have ever seen, you consider none to be as fair as Lady Eadgyth. Would that be correct, my dear brother?"

Otto's eyes narrowed. "Please excuse us, Thankmar. Lady Eadgyth and I must see my father."

With a malicious grin Thankmar bowed to Eadgyth, who was staring open-mouthed at them. "I am sure I wish you both every happiness."

Otto released his breath as Thankmar moved away. "Are you ready?" he asked, kissing her hands.

Eadgyth nodded, still bewildered by the exchange between the brothers. She straightened herself to face the court for the first time as Otto's intended bride. Knowing how much curiosity there had been she longed to impress everyone. Resting her hand lightly on his arm, they entered the hall where King Henry had just finished receiving petitioners. Groups of people smiled on them as they made their way. Henry was standing at the far end of the hall, talking to Mathilda, but at the sight of Otto and Eadgyth coming towards them he sat back down on his throne.

Eadgyth was warmed by the smiles of the people, feeling herself taken to their hearts. Thankmar's unpleasant attitude faded from her mind when she saw Mathilda's delighted smile, as she took her seat next to her husband and waited for Otto's words.

"Greetings, Otto," Henry called. "Is there something you wish to say to me?"

"Yes, Father," Otto replied, giving Eadgyth a quick smile. He went down on one knee before his father. "I intend to take Lady Eadgyth, daughter of the late Edward, King of the Anglo-Saxons, as my wife. I ask most humbly for your blessing."

Henry nodded, laying his hand on his son's head. "I willingly give you my blessing, my son. Lady Eadgyth, please come forward."

Keeping her head high, Eadgyth took the few steps towards the throne and sank into a curtsey. Henry quickly raised her up and kissed her on both cheeks. "My dear lady, I regard it as a great honour to call you my daughter."

Henry's words struck Eadgyth like a needle to her heart, as she remembered the rejection of her own father. She murmured her thanks to the affable man, struggling to keep her tears back. Henry had kept her hand in his and he extended his other hand to Otto. Putting their hands together enclosed in his own, Henry nodded his head. "You two have my blessing and my wholehearted approval." He raised his voice to address the court. "My people, we will soon have a wedding to celebrate."

The room erupted into cheers and in the mayhem, Mathilda beckoned Bishop Bernard of Halberstadt forward. Henry held up his hand for silence.

"Prince Otto, please speak the words to pledge yourself to this woman," the Bishop said.

Otto did his best to keep his features solemn as he turned to Eadgyth. "I, Otto, son of Henry, Duke of Saxony and King of Germany, pledge myself to wed you, Eadgyth, daughter of

Edward, King of the Anglo-Saxons."

"Lady Eadgyth, please repeat the words to pledge yourself to this man."

"I, Eadgyth, daughter of King Edward of the Anglo-Saxons, pledge myself to wed you, Otto, son of Henry, King of Germany and Duke of Saxony, with the permission of my noble brother, Athelstan, King of the English."

"Present the rings as a symbol of your sacred promises."

Eadgyth was glad to lower her head under the pretext of looking in her pouch for the betrothal ring, Athelstan had said should be presented to her intended husband. She hated referring to herself as Edward's daughter. By the time she looked up at Otto, her face was calm once again. Otto took her hand to slip a band of gold set with three gems over her finger. Eadgyth's hand trembled at this momentous step as she pushed her own ring onto Otto's finger.

"Prince Otto, Lady Eadgyth, you are now bound by sacred promises to wed."

There were more cheers in the hall and Otto grinned with pride, pressing his lips against hers. Eadgyth was glad they had already kissed, so the stirring in her heart was not such a shock. But still the unfamiliar surge of happiness almost frightened her as she looked into the handsome young face of the man she would soon call her husband.

Chapter six

Elfgifu had to be coaxed out of their chamber to celebrate the betrothal at a feast even more magnificent than the previous one. Although pleased to see her sister's happiness, she hated being viewed as the rejected one. In the hall Eadgyth was quickly swept up in conversation with Mathilda and the other ladies of the court, so Elfgifu was standing alone when Otto entered. He paused, looking awkward but as Elfgifu appeared even more uncomfortable he straightened his shoulders and went directly to her.

"My dearest sister," he said, kissing her hand. "I am pleased to see you here this night. I look forward to getting to know you better." Eadgyth was certain he had rehearsed this greeting, but still she was grateful to Otto for trying to put her sister at ease.

By the time Eadgyth reached Elfgifu, Otto was the centre of a crowd of courtiers, eager to offer him their best wishes. She was unable to help smiling as he accepted their words with a proud grin.

"I think you are falling in love with him," Elfgifu commented softy.

Eadgyth frowned. "Nonsense."

"Are you sure? I think he loves you," she said, observing how Otto's face had lit up as he glanced in their direction.

There was a rustle of amusement as he strode across the hall towards them and many laughed as he swept Eadgyth into his arms, spinning her around. For a moment Eadgyth laughed too, enjoying the exuberant affection. But suddenly she found herself transported back to Winchester, where another pair of strong arms had spun her off her feet, back in the days when her father had appeared to love her. The smile faded from her face and as Otto set her down, she stepped abruptly away from him.

"Try to behave with a little more decorum, Otto," Mathilda muttered as she made her way to the dais at the head of the table.

Otto looked confused. "I am sorry. I did not mean to offend you."

Eadgyth bit her lip, unnerved by the hurt on his face. "I am not offended. You just surprised me."

A forced smile told her Otto had not been convinced, as he bowed to her and Elfgifu and moved away. Eadgyth flushed as she caught Henry's eye, aware of the reproachful look he was giving her.

"That was foolish," Elfgifu murmured.

"I do not know what you mean," Eadgyth said crossly.

Elfgifu shook her head. "If the man they find for me, regards me with half such devotion as Otto just showed you, I would consider myself fortunate indeed."

"Such devotion from a man is meaningless," Eadgyth replied. "Our father once seemed devoted to us, but that did not stop him sending us away."

"Why do you think Otto will be like our father?"

Eadgyth glanced swiftly around, but none were listening to them. "What of his father? I have heard how he cast off Lord Thankmar's mother."

"I heard it too and it seems their marriage truly was illegal. She had taken holy vows. I am not certain King Henry wanted to cast her off."

"I know not, but he married the queen very soon after, while Lord Thankmar's mother was abandoned in a convent as our own mother was."

"Otto cannot deny the legitimacy of your marriage. I think

you may regret being so cold towards him."

The call for everyone to be seated saved Eadgyth from replying to this. In her heart she did regret it, but at the mere thought of giving into her feelings, she found her breath catching in her throat. Silently she took her place at the table between Hedwig and Otto. Hedwig murmured a pleasant greeting, but Otto's face was solemn. Thankmar brushed passed them. "I think you are losing your touch, Brother," he muttered.

The regret in Eadgyth's heart deepened, as Otto simply gave his brother a furious look before staring again at the table. She was unable to catch his eye before the King seated himself, smiling benevolently at them all.

"I intend to move the court to Quedlinburg in the next few days," Henry announced. "I want Otto's wedding to take place there." He nodded at his son. "It seems Otto is now most impatient for marriage and has been pestering me all day for the ceremony to take place as soon as possible." Otto shook his head as the people around them laughed. Henry looked pointedly at Eadgyth. "I trust that does not displease you, my daughter."

Eadgyth smiled at the king. "Not at all, my lord. I will be honoured to become his wife."

Otto's face had gone a dull red and Eadgyth cursed herself for using the word honoured. She tried to catch his eye, but he was looking down. The King's eyes were still gravely on her, no doubt condemning her distant manner. Hesitantly, worried everyone would wonder at such boldness, Eadgyth placed her hand next to Otto's on the table, allowing her fingers to brush against his. He glanced sharply at her and she smiled, hoping to return the smile to his face.

"I do want the marriage to take place soon," he said. "But I understand how strange everything must seem. If this haste appears unseemly to you…"

Eadgyth edged her hand even closer. "No bride was ever as warmly welcomed as I. Truly I shall be glad for the wedding to take place as soon as it can be arranged."

Her smile faltered, fearing her words had not been enough as Otto took her hand and raised it to his lips. He was smiling, but it was far from the dazzling smile he had previously shown and although he kept her hand in his, he did not repeat the exuberant affection she had earlier rejected.

A slight frown marked Henry's face, but he nodded at them both. "Then it is settled," he said. "Let us head to Quedlinburg as soon as can be arranged."

∞∞∞

The courtyard outside the palace resonated with the noise of horses' hooves and men shouting, while Eadgyth and Elfgifu waited in the hall with Mathilda and Hedwig to be summoned. It had taken only a few days to make the arrangements, but in those days she had seen little of Otto and when she did his manner towards her was friendly, but proper. It was the attitude she had hoped for in her husband, yet it was not pleasing her.

"I am sorry. You have scarce had time to settle here and already we are moving you on," Mathilda said to them. "Quedlinburg is Henry's favourite palace. It is where he was proclaimed King of Germany, so it is natural that he wishes the wedding of his son to take place there."

"It is of no matter, my lady. I have heard much of Quedlinburg and am eager to see it for myself."

Mathilda laid her hand on Eadgyth's shoulder. "My dear, you are soon to be my son's bride. I do not think there is need for any formality between us. Please use my name and I trust I may use yours."

"I would like that," she said, pleased by Mathilda's affectionate manner. She knew how fortunate she was to receive such a welcome from Otto's family.

"The horses are ready for you, my ladies." Thankmar's voice

came from the doorway, reminding her of the one exception to the welcome.

"At last," Mathilda muttered, making her way outside.

"There is your horse, my lady," Thankmar said, completely ignoring Elfgifu.

"Thank you, my lord." Eadgyth tried to sound warmer, but something about this man made her uncomfortable.

"And soon we will be at Quedlinburg, where you will be wed to perfect little Otto."

The sneer in Thankmar's voice shocked Eadgyth and she strove for a light hearted reply. "I would not call Otto, little." She gestured to where Otto was engaged in a playful scuffle with young Henry, towering over his younger brother.

Thankmar grinned, but it was not a friendly smile. "I wouldn't call him perfect either."

Eadgyth stared after him, her brow creasing. It relaxed as Otto ran over to her, young Henry scampering behind him. He took her hand, but unnerved by Thankmar, she shrank closer to him. After a shocked moment he tentatively put an arm around her. It felt reassuring and she smiled gratefully.

"Is anything amiss?" he asked, observing her expression.

"Not really. Lord Thankmar made a strange comment. He said you were not perfect."

Otto's face froze, but then he smiled. "I have never claimed to be perfect. Are you perfect?"

Eadgyth laughed. "No, of course not."

A teasing gleam lit up his eyes. "Are you sure? I think you are." Otto stared at her a moment longer before brushing a swift kiss against her lips. It was the first time he had kissed her since the betrothal and Eadgyth slid her own arms around his waist, forgetting how everyone was watching. His eyes widened at her response and he kissed her again, his lips lingering against hers.

"Otto, it would be nice if we could arrive at Quedlinburg before nightfall," the King called.

Otto released Eadgyth and she saw Henry already mounted

on his horse, Mathilda at his side. Eadgyth blushed, not used to such public embraces. But Henry was smiling and it was obvious the affection between his son and his intended bride was pleasing him.

Not remotely embarrassed, Otto grinned at his father and helped Eadgyth onto her horse. "Wait a moment, my sweet. I would ride alongside you."

As Henry and Mathilda moved off, Eadgyth watched as Otto stopped to talk to Thankmar, elbowing him sharply in the ribs. She was puzzled. It seemed very different to the affectionate scuffle he had shared with his younger brother.

∞∞∞

Quedlinburg was every bit as impressive as Eadgyth had heard. Set among steeply wooded hills, a fine palace rose before her. She slid down from her horse to stare in wonder at the majestic looking hall, surrounded by a vast complex of outbuildings.

"It is very fine, is it not?" Otto said, putting his arm around her shoulders. He had ridden beside her the whole journey, not once joining in the races with his brothers. Along the way he had told her amusing tales of sights they had passed and the last awkwardness between them seemed to have faded.

"It is. I understand this is where your father accepted the crown of Germany."

Otto nodded. "But soon it will take on even more importance. It will be where the most beautiful young woman in the land weds the luckiest of men."

Eadgyth rested her head against his shoulder and laughed, feeling she had laughed more on that day than in the whole of the previous decade. "You exaggerate." But she was flattered by his comments, delighted to find she was beautiful in Otto's eyes.

The King came over to them, his smile towards Eadgyth

looking genuinely affectionate. "Welcome to Quedlinburg, my daughter. Come inside. The afternoon grows cold and we cannot have you catching a chill."

If it had been possible, Eadgyth would have said the inside of the palace was even more magnificent than the exterior. The hall was far larger than the one at Harzburg and the tapestries adorning the walls were more elaborate, gleaming with golden threads.

In the comfortable bed chamber she would share with Elfgifu until her marriage, Eadgyth took out the kirtle Athelstan had said should be worn for her wedding and frowned at the creases. She forgot the indifference she had felt the first time she had tried it on, suddenly longing to appear beautiful for Otto. The blue dress, edged in bands of embroidered silk and adorned with jewels around the neck, was finer than anything else she possessed, but she wondered if it would be suitable for the splendour of Quedlinburg. However Mathilda quickly put her mind at rest.

"It is beautiful. The style appears a little unusual in my eyes, but it is fitting you should appear as a princess of Wessex for your nuptial. You will look lovely."

"I hope so," Eadgyth murmured.

"I will be glad to see Otto wed. I know you will keep that boy in order."

"Does Otto need keeping in order?" Eadgyth asked, puzzled by Mathilda's tone. Surely Otto, the handsome young battle hero, was the pride of his parents' hearts.

Mathilda shot Eadgyth a sideways glance, but smiled. "All boys need keeping in order. You will discover that when you have a son of your own."

Eadgyth smiled too, imagining her son, perhaps with Otto's blue eyes, never giving her a moment's peace as he rode off on mad escapades, but always able to charm her from her scolds with a smile as infectious as his father's.

"You are coming to care very much for Otto, are you not?"

Eadgyth blushed, but nodded. "I did not expect to. On the

journey here I only prayed I would not find my husband repellent. But, Otto…" Eadgyth's voice trailed off, unwilling to explore how strong her feelings were becoming.

Mathilda squeezed her shoulder. "Otto is a fortunate boy. I hope he realises it."

∞∞∞

Any last fears Eadgyth had about the suitability of her wedding attire were put to rest when, on the morning of her wedding, the King arrived to escort her to the church. He looked her up and down, a proud smile lighting up his face.

"It is an honour to be performing this service, my dear daughter. By rights, it should be your father doing this. He would be a proud man indeed if he could see you this day."

Eadgyth's nervous smile faded, as memories of the disdain on his face the day he had cast off her mother resurfaced. Determined not to allow thoughts of her father to intrude, she laid her hand on the King's arm. They followed Bishop Cenwald along the pathway to the church which was lined with courtiers, all eager to get a first glimpse of the bride. Eadgyth's good looks and assured manner had already won her many supporters at court.

Surrounded by a crowd of well-wishers, including his mother and siblings, Otto stood in the doorway of the church before the Bishop of Halberstadt. He was dressed in a blue tunic a similar shade to her raiment, with his hair uncharacteristically neat. Eadgyth was glad to see young Henry and Bruno were both stood nearer to Otto than Thankmar, guessing the comments his older brother might make if he had the chance. He looked nervous enough as it was. But as Eadgyth drew near he smiled and stretched out his hand.

Chapter seven

A hush descended on everyone as Eadgyth took Otto's hand. Otto looked at her and wet his lips nervously.

"I, Otto, take you Eadgyth as my wife from this day until death parts us, with the permission of your noble brother, King Athelstan of the English and the blessing of my father, Henry, Duke of Saxony and King of Germany."

Otto released his breath as he finished and smiled at Eadgyth. Until that moment she'd had no fears at these vows, but suddenly the words caught in her throat. She gazed into his eyes, gaining reassurance from the expression in them. His face, so open and honest, drove away any fears he might one day forget those vows. A faint rustle as the watchers stirred brought Eadgyth out of her thoughts and with a smile she made her own vows.

"I, Eadgyth, with the permission of my noble brother, Athelstan, King of the English, take you Otto, son of King Henry of Germany, Duke of Saxony as my lord and husband from this day until death parts us."

Otto beamed as he slipped the ring onto her finger and Bishop Bernard of Halberstadt nodded his approval. "Otto and Eadgyth, in the name of God, the father, son and holy spirit and with the blessings of Saint Oswald, I declare you wed."

Eadgyth had to blink back a few tears, touched that Otto had instructed the bishop to remember Saint Oswald in his words, but Otto had clearly had enough of the formality. He scooped his bride up in his arms, spinning her off her feet and kissing her. For once not caring about the people watching, Eadgyth put her arms around him, delighted she was now his wife. Everyone laughed and although a few heads shook at the lack of solemnity, no one truly disapproved of the joy their prince was taking in his new wife.

Bishop Bernard cleared his throat. "Prince Otto, I bid you and your fair wife to enter the church so we may celebrate mass."

Still grinning ear to ear, Otto took Eadgyth by the hand to enter the church as husband and wife.

∞∞∞

The rest of the day was given over to feasting and musicians struck up merry tunes, drawing many into dances and songs. The stream of gifts bestowed upon her seemed never ending. It was the custom, but even so Eadgyth was overwhelmed by the generosity of the court. She was presented to so many of the nobles of the realm she soon forgot most of their names and could only hope she would not offend them by asking them again. She was pleased to meet Duke Gilbert of Lotharingia, Otto's brother-in-law, although his sister Gerberga was recovering from the birth of her first child and was not able to be present. She also met two of the other most powerful dukes of the realm, Arnulf of Bavaria and Hermann of Swabia, both apparently good friends of King Henry.

The day passed in a blur of laughter, until the time came when Eadgyth was escorted to the chamber she would now share with Otto. The women fussed around her, wrapping a robe around her shoulders and some pushing charms to aid fertility under the pillows. It was a relief when they finally left her alone. She looked around, noting the elegant wall hangings and the finely carved chests and coffers which already held her possessions and jewels.

She did not have long to wait before Otto joined her. He sat down beside her on the bed and put his arms around her, giving her a long kiss.

"Alone at last," he said. "I thought the feasting would never end."

Rather self-consciously he removed his robe as Eadgyth watched him curiously. Unclothed his body appeared more muscular than ever, his chest covered in dark hair although marked by a few faint scars. He slid under the covers with her and held her tightly for a moment. Slowly he pushed away her own robe.

Eadgyth rarely gave her appearance any thought, but at that moment she was very aware of how slender and delicate looking her body was. She was struck by a pang of regret that she was not more voluptuous. However Otto drew in a sharp breath at the sight of her and his eyes widened.

"You are so beautiful," he breathed, running his hand almost reverently down her body.

At the touch of his hand on her bare skin, Eadgyth's heart began to thud. She moved closer to him, delighting in the warmth of his strong arm encircling her, as he brushed his lips against hers.

"You are not afraid?" he asked.

Eadgyth shook her head, smiling. "Do I need to be?"

Otto shrugged. "It is the first time you will lie with a man. It would be understandable if you were a little afraid."

"I do not think I need to be afraid of you, Otto."

Otto kissed her again. "There may be a little pain at first. I hope it won't be bad. I would hate to hurt you, but…"

Eadgyth stroked his face, trying to smooth away the anxious look. "I know what to expect. Do not worry about me."

Otto smiled, gently stroking her cheek. With a look of wonder on his face, he ran his fingers through her fair hair, raising a few strands to his lips.

"Is this the first time you will lie with a woman?" Eadgyth asked, confident she already knew the answer. Otto was young still and in spite of his high spirited ways, he was truly devout. He looked too, to be considerably more nervous than she was that night.

"No," Otto replied.

Eadgyth stared at him. "Oh…"

"There have not been many," Otto added quickly. "And nothing of any importance, except…"

Eadgyth's arms fell away from him. "Except?"

Otto began to look very wary. "Eadgyth, I do not want there to be any secrets between us."

She folded her arms and raised her eyebrows.

More than ever Otto looked like a boy who was about to be beaten. "I have a son."

Eadgyth's mouth dropped open. Her first thought was that she now knew what was behind Thankmar's sly insinuations and Mathilda's faint disapproval. She wondered too if it was the knowledge his son was fathering bastards which had caused Henry's determination to get Otto quickly married. "Where is he?"

"He is still an infant, just half a year old. He is with his mother."

"Where is she?" Eadgyth asked through gritted teeth. "Who is she?"

"She is a Slavic woman. After one of my father's victories we took some hostages, including a Slavic prince and his widowed sister. She is his mother. I did not force myself on her," Otto swiftly added, correctly understanding the question in Eadgyth's outraged eyes. "It was a very enjoyable liaison. For her, I mean. And, well, obviously I…" Otto looked down, miserably aware of the mess he was making of his explanation.

Eadgyth unfolded her arms and did her best to reclaim her dignity. "This is none of my concern. It is inappropriate for me to question you in this way."

Otto looked up, shamefacedly meeting Eadgyth's eyes. "I am sorry to have disappointed you. I never wanted that. Perhaps I have given you a disgust of me."

Reluctantly Eadgyth smiled, unable to resist the worry in his eyes. "No. I am not some naïve young girl. I know these matters happen. I was just surprised." Surprised was an understatement. She was shocked at the jealousy surging through her at the thought of Otto with other women. She wondered what had happened to her determination to make a marriage of comfortable indifference. "This is truly none of my concern, but may I ask you one question?"

"Of course. I meant what I said. There should be no secrets between us."

Eadgyth clenched her fists, bracing herself against the pain she would feel. "Do you love her?"

Otto shook his head. "I thought I did at the time, but no. There is nothing between us now. The boy is very fine and I shall ensure he and his mother are always well provided for, but she no longer has any place in my heart."

Eadgyth relaxed and smiled at Otto, taking hold of his hands. "Is there anyone else now in your heart?"

"Yes," Otto replied.

She stared at him again, but there was no time to feel the pain which struck her, before recognising the tender look in his eyes. He smiled and put his arms around her. "Can I tell you of her? She is a noble lady from far away. Very, very beautiful." Eadgyth blushed, leaning her head against his chest. Otto ran his hand through her hair. "She has hair brighter than any gold."

She began to laugh. "Stop it."

"And eyes the blue of the sea,"

Eadgyth looked up at him, filled with merriment. "Otto, have you ever seen the sea? I have crossed it and I can assure you, it is not blue. I do not know why the story tellers say it is. It is dull and grey."

But Otto was not to be dissuaded. "The sky, then. Yes, eyes the colour of the summer sky."

Very tenderly Eadgyth stroked his face. "Oh, Otto. You are a fool."

A smile ruined Otto's outraged look at that comment. "A fool? I have sung your praises and you call me a fool! If you cannot say any kind words to me, my lady wife, I may have to stop you talking altogether."

Eadgyth raised her eyebrows in mock fury and wound her arms around his neck "How do you plan to do that?"

"Like this," Otto replied, bringing his lips against hers with more eagerness than ever. His strong body pressed against her, pushing her against the pillows. Responding just as eagerly, Eadgyth tried to pull him even closer. As his lips moved to gently kiss her neck, she stroked the dark hair which was falling across her.

"You are the most handsome man," she murmured, overwhelmed with the sensation of his hands stroking her body.

Otto raised his head, a hint of mischief appearing in his face. "That is better. If you are going to say kind things about me, I might sit up and listen."

Eadgyth tightened her arms around him. "No, you will not."

The playful look faded and the desire returned. His hands moved again gently over her. "You are right," he whispered into her hair. "I most certainly will not."

Chapter eight

It was not yet light when Eadgyth woke with a feeling of having been awake more than asleep. She had lain awake for a long time after Otto had slept, trying to make sense of everything she was feeling. One thing was certain. There was no chance now of the passionless, dignified marriage of her expectation. She blushed as she remembered her contemptuous words to Athelstan about preferring to wed a man, rather than a boy. But how could she have known then, that Otto, just on the brink of manhood, would prove to be everything she could want? She had to smile too at her calm assertion to Otto that she knew what to expect from her wedding night. Nothing had prepared her for the feeling his hands had aroused nor could she have anticipated how caring Otto would be, tempering his eagerness with continual assurances for her well-being. Not that there was any need for it. The one brief moment of pain, had quickly been overwhelmed in myriad of other sensations.

Even after she had fallen asleep, the unaccustomed presence of a man in her bed meant she had woken frequently. It seemed that every time he stirred, Otto had reached out to her again, drawing her closer into his arms. He was lying now with one arm flung across her body, his hand resting lightly on her shoulder. Eadgyth smiled as she shifted herself into a more comfortable position, nestling against him and drifted off again into a pleasant dream.

The next time she woke it was full daylight. Otto's arm was

no longer around her, but he was lying next to her propped up on his elbow, gazing down at her. He grinned as her eyes focused on him and leant over for a kiss.

Sleepily Eadgyth smiled back, unsure of what to say to him. But words were unnecessary as Otto pulled her into his arms, so her head rested on his chest. Very gently he stroked her hair. "Are you happy, my sweet?"

"Very. More than I knew was possible."

"I am glad. I want you always to be happy." Clumsily he presented her with a cloth wrapped package which had been lying on a nearby coffer. "Your morning gift."

Eadgyth unwrapped the cloth and could only stare at an intricate necklace set with pearls and sapphires.

"Of course this is not all you will get," Otto said hastily. "We are to present you with the City of Magdeburg at a ceremony later this day. It is very fine, but I wanted to give you something which was solely from me."

Eadgyth was still beyond words. She knew how much more valuable the gift of a city was, but somehow it could not compare with this gift which was from Otto alone.

Otto swallowed. "If you do not like it, I shall present you with something else."

She found her voice at last and looked up at Otto, her eyes shining. "Oh, Otto, I love it." She slipped her arms around him. "Thank you."

"Are you sure?"

Eadgyth smiled at him, running her fingers over the fine workmanship of the necklace. "I shall treasure it always. I know the City of Magdeburg will be a very fine gift, but I do not think I can wear it close to my heart as I can this."

Otto grinned. "That is true."

Eadgyth snuggled back against his chest. "Can I assume we are not going to attend the first prayers of the day?"

Otto stroked her hair, his hand drifting lower with each stroke. "Yes and I don't think we are going to make the second prayers either." His other hand tilted her head up to meet his lips. "I really don't think anyone will be expecting us."

∞∞∞

It was hunger which eventually drove them from their chamber. They entered the hall to find everyone already partaking of the midday meal. For the first time Eadgyth wore the mantle of a married woman in a blue which matched her eyes and with Otto's gift clasped around her neck, she made her entry into the hall with a dignity, which soon collapsed at the cheerful, but lewd comments many called. Otto grinned, but made no reply as he swiftly brought his wife to their places.

At the head of the table, Henry set down his cup of ale as Otto favoured him with a bland smile. "Good day to you, Otto. How nice that you and your wife have decided to join us."

Otto, filling up cups for himself and Eadgyth, almost spilled the ale as he tried to stifle his mirth and Eadgyth had to bite her lip to stop her own laughter escaping. With a shake of his head, Henry laughed delightedly and returned to his meal, while Elfgifu looked curiously at her sister's joyful, blushing face and clearly could not wait to get her alone. Under the table Eadgyth squeezed her hand and prayed that her sister would find the same happiness in her own marriage.

∞∞∞

The court remained in a festive mood as everyone gathered yet again so Eadgyth could be formally presented with the charters granting her the rights of the City of Magdeburg.

"It is a charming place," Hedwig told her as she waited for the summons. "It is around a day's ride from here on the River Elbe. The castle there is a splendid one."

"It is not far from the Slavic border, which Otto will no doubt find handy," Thankmar commented with a malicious smile.

Hedwig glared daggers at him, but Eadgyth remained calm, feeling superior now she knew what his comments referred to. "Of course, I understand how useful it will be for King Henry to have Otto, one of his finest military commanders, based so near the border."

Gilbert exchanged a look with Thankmar and snorted with laughter. "Very useful," he replied.

Eadgyth did not show her distress, but the attitude of Thankmar and Gilbert bothered her. This had seemed such a contented family and she could not understand why Otto's brother and brother-in-law were trying to stir trouble just a day after her wedding.

"Perhaps you two should take your places," Hedwig suggested.

"The King is not yet in place," Gilbert said, lounging back against the doorpost. "I am enjoying this talk with my new sister very much."

"As am I," Thankmar added. "Tell me, my dear Eadgyth, is marriage with a fool of a boy pleasing you? You do realise if matters had been different it would undoubtedly have been me you wed. Perhaps you would have preferred to have had a man in your bed." He leered at Elfgifu. "Although of course there is no guarantee I would have chosen you."

Elfgifu gasped and shrank against Eadgyth, who had gone red in mortification.

"Thankmar, do not talk to Eadgyth in that way," Hedwig snapped. "If Otto could hear you…"

Eadgyth lifted her head. "I consider myself wed to a very fine man indeed. I am most grateful to have been given to the finest of husbands." She narrowed her eyes. "I am sorry if that disappoints you, my lord."

She felt some satisfaction as it was Thankmar's turn to redden in anger. But before anyone could say anything more, the King entered accompanied by Duke Hermann of Swabia.

"Come everyone, take your places," the King said. "There will be plenty of time for you to get to know dear Eadgyth better."

Eadgyth was relieved as everyone left her and felt even better as Henry embraced her before continuing into the hall. His manner had become so affectionate, she truly felt she was gaining a new father in him. The Duke bowed to her. He was a man of compact build, who looked to be a little more than thirty years of age. As he straightened himself, Eadgyth noticed the shrewd look in his eyes and wondered how much he had understood of the scene he had walked into.

"Greetings, my lady," he said. "I know you were presented to so many yesterday, so permit me to introduce myself again. I am Duke Hermann of Swabia."

Eadgyth took an immediate liking to the Duke. "Of course I remember you, my lord. I am delighted to further my acquaintance." She meant the words. After the sly comments of Gilbert and Thankmar, there was something calming about this man.

As Hermann bowed again and followed the King, Eadgyth took some deep breaths to calm herself until Bishop Bernard of Halberstadt delivered the formal summons.

"Lady Eadgyth, wife of the noble Prince Otto, King Henry of Germany summons you to present yourself."

Eadgyth walked slowly into the hall, a gracious smile on her lips. From the corner of her eye she could see the smiles on the faces of the people, but she kept her own gaze directly ahead to where Otto was sitting next to his parents, his smile widening as she drew closer. At the dais Eadgyth sank into a deep curtsey.

"Please rise, Lady Eadgyth," Henry said. "Just one day passed you were united in marriage with my noble son, Prince Otto of Saxony. As that union has now been honoured by your body, it is our privilege to present you with a morning gift of the City of Magdeburg, including all incomes from the city and the surrounding district." Henry passed Otto a scroll. "Prince Otto, present the morning gift to your wife."

Otto's face was solemn, but his eyes shone with pride as he handed the charter to Eadgyth. "Lady Eadgyth, you have honoured me indeed with your marriage vows. From this day I grant you the right to title yourself Lady of Magdeburg."

Chapter nine

Even before their wedding, the news there was an unwed and very pretty West-Saxon princess at the court of King Henry had begun to filter across Germany and beyond. Envoys and noblemen alike gathered, eager to state their intentions towards Elfgifu.

Henry considered the offers of each one and began to compile a list of those offers he considered most advantageous to him, so he might make some recommendations to Athelstan.

Elfgifu hated the scrutiny. She became more tongue tied as each guest arrived and eventually confessed tearfully to her sister that she wished she could retire to a convent.

"You know you cannot," Eadgyth said. "Athelstan is depending on us to bring him allies."

"You have done that and so have our sisters. I do not see why it is a very great matter if I adopt a religious life."

"If Athelstan wanted you to adopt a religious life, he would have allowed you to do so in Wessex. You must marry."

"I do not think I can bear it. I do not want to preside over a grand household as you will. And the thought of sharing my body with a man makes me shudder."

Eadgyth could not help smiling. Somehow the blissful start to her own marriage had become even more joyous with each night that passed. "The marriage bed is not what you expect. Truly it is not bad."

"Perhaps that depends on the man. None who have come

here have looked at me as Otto looks at you."

Eadgyth could offer no reassurance to that. All those men were strangers and she had no idea if they would show the same consideration as Otto.

"Few of these men even look at me at all. Please, Eadgyth. Will you speak to Otto? Ask if I may enter a convent."

Eadgyth sighed. "I will try, but it is not Otto's decision. It is down to Henry and Athelstan."

But Otto refused to even consider the idea. She had approached him as he was preparing himself for bed that night in an antechamber.

"No, Eadgyth," he said tossing his cloak onto a coffer. "Elfgifu must fulfil her duties to the alliance as we all must."

"She is so unhappy and frightened. Can you not understand that?"

"Of course I can. But she must overcome it and obey her brother's commands. Perhaps if she tried greeting some of these men, instead of looking at the ground the whole time, she might feel more comfortable."

Eadgyth frowned, displeased to hear Otto criticising her sister. "She finds it hard. She is young and afraid."

"I know you are older than her, but not by much. Yet you had to make that same journey away from your native land for a new life among strangers. She must follow your example. You never appeared afraid."

"I was never afraid because I did not care," Eadgyth snapped. "Elfgifu does."

Otto stared open mouthed at her. "You did not care?"

"No. I did not care whether I was left in the abbey in Wessex or sent away to be married." Eadgyth did not notice the dumbfounded expression on Otto's face, as the anger built in her. "I did not care whether I stayed in my native land or left it. I did not care whether I married a man who regarded me with affection or indifference. The whole journey here, I did not care if you chose Elfgifu or me."

"You made your indifference fairly obvious the first time we

THE SAXON MARRIAGE

met." Otto's eyes narrowed. "I can see that now. You showed no pleasure when I asked you to be my wife and barely concealed your contempt at my attentions. If I had not been so blinded by your beauty I might have realised it earlier. Perhaps I should repudiate you now and wed another. Even then I don't suppose you would care."

Eadgyth froze. "No, Otto, no." She ran into her bedchamber, crying out as the door slammed behind her and collapsed weeping on the bed.

After a shocked moment Otto followed and stood, staring at her, unsure what to do as he took in the sight of his wife sobbing into her pillow. Tentatively he sat down on the bed and laid his hand on her shoulder, snatching it back when she flinched at his touch.

"Eadgyth, whatever I have said to upset you, I am sorry. Please don't cry."

"Go away, Otto." Eadgyth did not even raise her head from the pillow.

Uncertainly Otto stood up, then sat down again. "No, I will not go away. Tell me what I have done to upset you. That is an order. Damn it, in Wessex do wives not obey their husbands?"

Eadgyth reluctantly raised her head. Otto's voice had been stern, but his eyes were looking pleadingly at her. "My father repudiated my mother."

Otto looked puzzled. "I know, but… I am sorry, I never realised how that would upset you."

"No, you wouldn't," Eadgyth said bitterly. "The husband can continue his life, while the wife must go meekly to the convent and pretend she doesn't care. It destroyed my mother. She was never the same again and nor was I." She shuddered at the memories she had no wish to relive. "I was happy as a young girl. I thought my father loved me. At feasts he would often take me onto his lap and feed me the finest of food or lift me up high so I could see the story tellers perform. But when he repudiated my mother, he made it clear I was worthless to him."

"Oh, Eadgyth." Otto hesitantly put an arm around her.

Eadgyth stiffened, but did not push him away. Ineffectually she wiped at the tears which trickled relentlessly from her eyes. "After that nothing mattered. For years I have not cared what happened to me. When Athelstan told me of this marriage, I was indifferent. The whole journey here I did not care who I married. When we arrived in Saxony, even though I could see this life was a fine one, I still did not care if you chose me. Then we went down to the hall that night and you came in."

"And made a fool of myself," Otto commented wryly.

Eadgyth couldn't help laughing at that. "I had not cared whether you were there or not. But then I looked into your eyes as you smiled at me and I started to care. You asked me to be your wife and I cared even more. I know I did not show it, but truly I was so happy in that moment. And on our wedding night you showed me such affection as I had never dreamed of and I knew I was coming to care for you more than I had believed possible."

Otto gave an uncomfortable smile. "This whole time I have felt I was not quite good enough for you. I thought you had hoped for someone better, someone a little older and a lot finer. Someone who did not behave as foolishly as I."

Eadgyth flung her arms tightly around him. "Never think that. There is no one finer."

Otto held her at arm's length. "Really? I felt I always appeared foolish in your presence. I was sure you held me in contempt. Often I saw how you laughed at me."

"Oh, Otto, I am sorry I made you feel that. I never held you in contempt."

"What about our betrothal feast? You made it plain I was not the sensible man you hoped for."

Eadgyth bit her lip in guilt. "No, Otto," she said softly. "I was cold towards you because I was afraid of my feelings. I was the foolish one, not you."

"I know you laughed at me. Do not say you did not."

He looked so hurt, Eadgyth wished she could deny his words. Very gently she pushed back his hair to gaze into his eyes. "Perhaps I was a little, but it was no bad thing. All those years at Wilton I so rarely laughed. Athelstan told me I was too solemn. I think it is in part because you always make me smile that I have come to care for you so much. If I had wed that fine, older man you spoke of, I would have taken my place with him as solemnly and graciously as I attended mass at the convent. I would never have cared for him, as I care for you. I could never have loved him."

Otto's eyes widened. "Do you mean..."

She nodded, tears brimming in her eyes again. "Oh, my dearest, did you not know how I love you? I thought the pain when my father walked away from me, was the worst I could ever feel. But I was wrong. That would be nothing compared to the pain if you repudiated me. I do not think I would want to live. I tried to be cold towards you, for I was so afraid of loving you. I am still afraid, but you made it impossible for me not to love you."

Otto shook his head, almost laughing. "You do not need to be afraid. I would never repudiate you. You are my wife. You have made me the happiest man alive, particularly now I know how you care for me. How could I ever want to give that up?"

"We cannot know what will happen. What if I am unable to bear you children?"

"I will never repudiate you," Otto repeated, looking earnestly into her eyes. "If you are unable to give me children..." He shrugged. "Perhaps then I will forgive my parents for saddling me with two little brats of brothers."

Eadgyth laughed again. "They are not so bad," she said sternly. Suddenly she remembered how the conversation had started. "But what of my sister?"

"I am not unsympathetic to her," Otto said. "But she must do her duty as bravely as she can. I am sure she can find the courage, after all is she not the sister of the bravest person?"

"Athelstan?"

"No. You."

Chapter ten

Elfgifu accepted her fate with resignation. Otto did his best to help her, trying to draw her into conversation with the guests at the court, but she remained downcast.

One day Eadgyth was sitting with her in one of the galleries. They were alone and were spending more time talking than stitching. It was unusual for her to see Otto during the day, so she was delighted when the door opened and he came in, accompanied by a slightly older man.

Both men bowed to her. "I would like to present an old companion, Lord Ludwig of Burgundy. He and I fought together once on the Slavic front. Ludwig, my wife, Lady Eadgyth. And this is her fair sister, Lady Elfgifu."

"It is an honour to meet you, my lady," Ludwig said bestowing the usual kiss on her hand.

Eadgyth was unsurprised to see him give Elfgifu a long look, as she guessed why he was there. As was her custom, Elfgifu stammered a greeting and looked down. But to Eadgyth's astonishment she looked up again, a shy smile on her face.

Ludwig elbowed Otto in the ribs. "Well, you are a lucky man, getting to choose between these two beauties."

"I most certainly am," Otto replied. "While I am confident I made the right choice, I would not condemn a man who disagrees."

Eadgyth frowned, knowing such outspoken conversation was undoubtedly sending her sister into a panic. Ludwig's brown eyes looked speculatively from Eadgyth to Elfgifu. "My friend, I would not wish to offend either of these fair ladies by voicing any opinion." He winked at Elfgifu, who went scarlet, but smiled more than ever.

Eadgyth stared at her in amazement. "My lord, if you have ridden far I am sure you would be glad of some refreshment. Otto, can you assist me with that?"

Otto had been about to sit down, but followed his wife's unusual instruction with no more than a raised eyebrow.

"Who is he?" Eadgyth hissed, as soon as she had Otto a distance away.

"He is the brother of the King of Burgundy," Otto replied. "His lands are not extensive, but they include a pass over the Alps, so are of great importance. I do not know him well, but he was a valuable addition indeed to our forces last year."

Otto picked up a jug of wine but before he could head back to his guest, Eadgyth grabbed hold of his arm, irritated that once again all she was learning of a man was how fine a fighter he was. "Does he want a wife?"

Otto looked back at him, still talking to Elfgifu. "I think perhaps he does." He smiled innocently at Eadgyth and returned to Ludwig, who appeared to be recounting an outrageous story to Elfgifu. "I trust this tale is fit for the ears of my sister," he said sternly.

Elfgifu giggled and Ludwig winked at her once again. "My dear friend, how can you even think otherwise?"

∞∞∞

Henry was pleased to add Ludwig to the number of suitable candidates for Elfgifu's hand, but with several other powerful names to be considered, Eadgyth was concerned that Athelstan would have no reason to choose him. The night before the messenger departed for England, Otto came to their chamber to find Eadgyth had just finished dictating her own message to a scribe. He took the scroll from her and read it aloud.

"My most beloved and noble Brother, I send you greetings from Quedlinburg and wish to assure you that I am well and have found great contentment in my marriage." A smug smile spread over Otto's face, but he made no comment. "I know you have received many offers for Elfgifu's hand, but I would urge you to favour the suit of Lord Ludwig of Burgundy. Although his realm is not as extensive as some, it occupies a position near the mountains which would be most beneficial for any of our people who wish to make a pilgrimage to the Holy City. In regards to the Lord's character, I can assure you he is a fine and god-fearing man." Otto lowered the script and stared at Eadgyth. "Fine, yes, but god-fearing?"

Eadgyth laughed. "I know, but Athelstan will likely never meet him."

Otto grinned as he finished the message. "I conclude, dear Brother, by saying he would be a good husband for Elfgifu and worthy to ally himself with our family. I pray this message finds you well and beg that you pass my greetings to my mother and sisters. Your loving sister, Eadgyth."

"Do you think he will listen?"

Otto looked from the script to his wife. "My sweet, I do not think he will dare disobey you."

∞∞∞

Whether Athelstan had been moved by Eadgyth's words, she never knew, but Bishop Cenwald was instructed to negotiate a settlement with Ludwig.

"Try to act god-fearing," Otto muttered to his friend as the negotiations started.

All proceeded well and the spring saw Elfgifu as a nervous, but happy bride. Soon after the festivities she and Ludwig prepared to depart for his realm in the south.

Eadgyth had been delighted for her sister, but as the day of her departure came closer a weight seemed to descend on her at the thought of saying farewell. While their horses were assembled, Eadgyth clung to her, tears swimming in her eyes and a lump in her throat almost choking her. It was with difficulty that Elfgifu pulled away.

"Eadgyth, this is not like you. It is usually I who am the foolish one."

"I know," Eadgyth said, the tears not stopping. She did not know why this was affecting her so much, when she had barely shed a tear at bidding farewell to her mother and Athelstan. "I am going to miss you so much. I wish you weren't going."

"I shall miss you too, but we are not so far away. I know the King has residences in the South, so I am sure we will see each other again before too long."

Again Eadgyth flung her arms around her, the tears coming faster than ever. Otto pulled her away looking helpless at her misery. Through blurry eyes she could see a frown on Henry's face and he muttered something to Mathilda. She too looked at Eadgyth, her disapproval obvious. Eadgyth did not blame them. She was disgusted with herself. The last time she had made such a scene in public was when her father had left them. Such a thought made her cry all the more and she had to raise her hand to her mouth to stop the sound from escaping.

"Control yourself, Eadgyth," Otto muttered. He embraced Ludwig and kissed Elfgifu on the cheek. "Farewell to you both. We are brothers now, Ludwig. We shall certainly meet again soon."

"Farewell," Elfgifu replied. "I thank you all for your kindness and hospitality." She looked uncertainly at Eadgyth who had turned away, trying desperately to compose herself.

Otto shook his head, looking even more irritated than Henry. "Do not worry, Sister. I shall look after her."

As Ludwig helped her onto her horse, Elfgifu called out a last farewell to her sister. This was the final straw for Eadgyth and she abandoned her position, running for the privacy of her chamber. The gathered crowd parted, their faces shocked. There was a murmur of curiosity and a few called out to her in concern.

"Eadgyth, come back," Otto called, but she ignored him and did not stop running until she had reached their chamber. There she collapsed on the bed, giving way to her emotion until her sobs almost made her sick.

Chapter eleven

"Has Otto taken to beating you, my dear sister?" Thankmar asked a few mornings later when Eadgyth had again arrived in the hall, her face white with dark circles under her eyes.

"Leave her alone," Otto snapped back, putting his arm protectively around her. But as Thankmar wandered away, looking delighted to have angered his brother, Otto frowned at Eadgyth. "He's not the only one wondering why you seemed so happy with me one day and so miserable the next."

"I am sorry, Otto," Eadgyth replied wearily. "I am not unhappy with you."

"Then try to appear happier, in public at least." Otto scowled and strode away without kissing her.

Eadgyth had little heart for the day ahead as she joined Mathilda and the other ladies in their work. Mathilda had been working for some time on a wall hanging to replace the faded one which adorned one side of the hall. It was vast, but like all of Mathilda's work, exquisite in its details. She permitted only the most skilled of needlewomen to assist her and Eadgyth had been flattered when she had been asked to join them.

That day Eadgyth did not join in the light hearted conversation between the ladies, although both Mathilda and Hedwig tried to draw her in. Often she did not even hear the questions as she remained distracted by her own thoughts. Sometimes her mind went to Elfgifu as she wondered how she was settling in to her new home, but such thoughts made her eyes swim with tears and she quickly pushed them away.

She was glad when Mathilda announced they had worked enough for one day and stood up, stretching her cramped limbs. Mathilda looked pleased at the progress made, as she strolled around the table.

Suddenly she exclaimed in annoyance. "Who was stitching the robe of Saint Anna? That is the wrong thread."

She held up the cloth, the two different shades of blue obvious and jarring. There was silence among the women and Eadgyth went scarlet.

"Forgive me," she whispered. "I do not know how I came to do that."

"That will all have to be cut away. What a waste." Hedwig frowned. No expense had been spared in the hanging and the blue threads were of a costly silk.

Eadgyth bit her lip, not understanding how she had come to make such a mistake. Mathilda looked at her, then glanced meaningfully at Hedwig. Hedwig nodded slightly and ushered the other women from the room.

"Eadgyth, the behaviour you have displayed these last days is not what we expect," Mathilda said as soon as they were alone. "Of course I understand you have left behind your home and your family, but we have tried to make you feel welcome."

Eadgyth could not look at her mother-in-law. "I know. I am grateful."

"Are you? You have barely spoken a single word to Hedwig and myself this day. I did not expect such rudeness from you. And you have made it clear to everyone how unhappy you are in your marriage. Of course you cannot be forced to enjoy marriage to Otto, but it is most inappropriate to make your feelings so obvious."

"I am not unhappy," Eadgyth protested. "I did not mean to be rude. I shall beg Hedwig's pardon as I do yours."

"My dear, I urged Otto strongly to choose you. I thought you would be the better wife. You need to strive harder to be worthy of him."

Eadgyth nodded dumbly. "I will try," she whispered, trying to keep the tears back.

It was an effort to get through the remainder of the day. She apologised to Hedwig, who accepted it graciously, but she suspected it would be futile to hope for a closer friendship with her sister-in-law. As the evening came she sat at Otto's side, nibbling on a little food, trying to converse politely with all around, but she knew her manner was a long way from what was expected of her.

When Otto came to their chamber that night, he took her in his arms as he always did. Feeling overwrought, Eadgyth burst into tears.

"What is wrong? Why are you so unhappy?" Otto stroked her hair helplessly.

"I don't know," she sobbed into his chest. "I miss Elfgifu and my mother so much. I wish they were here now."

"I am here. Why is that not enough for you? Have I done something wrong?"

"No, nothing."

"I am trying to make you happy. It's obvious I am not succeeding." Otto sounded hurt and Eadgyth cried more than ever. He looked down at her, the anxiety obvious on his face. "I don't know what to do. I would do anything to make you happy, but I can't if you won't tell me what is wrong." His arms fell away from her leaving her suddenly chilled. "When you are ready to tell me, just let me know."

He lay down, turning his back on her as Eadgyth wept into her pillow feeling bitterly lonely. More than anything she wanted his arms around her, but Otto pulled the covers over his ears and ignored her.

When she woke the next morning, Otto had already risen. She was glad not to have to face him that day, finding the hurt in his eyes hard to bear. Hoping it would make her feel better she splashed water over her face. Her eyes still felt swollen, but the mirror simply showed her as looking pale.

Mathilda had not forbidden her from working on the

wall hanging and Eadgyth was determined to make amends. She knew Otto held his mother in high regard and her recommendation had probably been one reason why he had chosen her. If Mathilda urged him to repudiate her, perhaps he would listen. A sudden wave of dizziness at that thought made her clutch onto the doorpost to steady herself. Wishing she could return to bed, she muttered a quick prayer to Saint Oswald that she would get through the day without any problems and left her chamber.

Mathilda made no comment on her mistake the day before, welcoming her pleasantly. Hedwig too nodded at her, but neither woman displayed any affection. Resolutely Eadgyth settled down to work, taking extra care with her stitches and trying to reply courteously to any comments directed at her. The chatter of the women flowed around her and the brightly burning fire made the room warm. Eadgyth's eyes grew heavy.

Cries of shock jolted her awake again and she stared in horror at a crimson wine stain spreading across the beautiful wall-hanging. Her cup lay on its side, where she had evidently knocked it. Mathilda rose up, her face frozen.

"Do not stand there gaping, you fools," she snapped. "Take the cloth and clean it as best you can."

As several of the women gathered up the cloth, Eadgyth slumped her head into her hands, unable to stop the sobs. It no longer mattered. She did not see how she could ever win Mathilda's affection now.

"Mother, it is ruined. It will be impossible to get the stain out." Hedwig looked in fury at Eadgyth. "How could she be so careless?"

"We shall have to do what we can to salvage it," Mathilda sighed, looking thoughtfully at Eadgyth who continued to weep. "Hedwig, go make sure they are doing everything they can to clean it. Everyone go. I wish to speak to Lady Eadgyth alone."

Being alone with Mathilda was the last thing she wanted, but there was no avoiding it. Eadgyth wiped her eyes and waited for her inevitable anger.

"My dear child, what is wrong with you?" Mathilda asked, pulling up a chair next to her.

Mathilda's soft tone brought a painful lump to her throat. She looked down, desperate to keep her voice steady. "I don't know. I am so sorry. Your beautiful hanging... I do not know how you can forgive me."

"Never mind about the cloth, my dear. I am concerned for you." Mathilda refilled Eadgyth's cup. "Drink this and try to calm yourself."

Obediently Eadgyth sipped, although the wine tasted bitter. A wave of nausea sent her hand flying to cover her mouth. With difficulty she held it back. "I can drink no more," she said, setting the cup down on the table.

"Are you ill?"

Eadgyth shook her head. "No, I don't think so. The smell of the food makes me feel a little unwell sometimes. I think because it is different here, although it is very fine," she added quickly, not wanting Mathilda to think she was complaining.

"The smell of the food did not seem to concern you when you first arrived here," Mathilda commented.

Eadgyth summoned up the courage to look her mother-in-law in the face. The kindness on it made her eyes well with tears again. "I know. In truth I have little appetite at the moment."

To Eadgyth's surprise a smile spread over Mathilda's face. She placed her hands over Eadgyth's. "My dear, have you bled since your marriage?"

"Bled?" Eadgyth was puzzled, thinking of that crimson wine stain, spreading like blood across the cloth.

"Yes, the bleeding which comes every month. Has it come since your marriage?"

Eadgyth stared open-mouthed at Mathilda. "Yes," she breathed. "But just once." They had been wed now for nearly four months. Eadgyth's hand flew to her stomach. "Do you think...?"

"Yes, I do. No bleeding, you are feeling sick, you are tired. You are absent minded." Mathilda looked faintly amused and Eadgyth blushed. "You are displaying emotions without knowing why."

"Is that a sign?" Eadgyth asked.

"Oh yes, my dear. When I was carrying Otto, poor Henry scarcely dared come near me, I was so quick to anger."

Eadgyth laughed. "I truly cannot imagine that." She looked down again at her stomach, her face growing radiant as the joy flooded through her. "A child. I can scarce believe it."

Mathilda put her arms around her. "It is the most wonderful news."

"But your beautiful hanging…"

"They will clean it and we shall sew over the stain. Oh, Eadgyth, you foolish girl, as if a hanging can compare with such news as this. But, my dear, you must look after yourself. If you are tired or unwell, there is no shame in needing to rest."

Eadgyth nodded. "Should I announce the news yet?"

Mathilda hesitated. "Perhaps wait a little as it is early days. Although I expect many will guess."

"I must tell Otto. I do not think I could keep such a thing from him. We have promised not to have secrets from each other."

Mathilda's smile froze. "Of course, my dear. Well, I know he has been worried about you, so you can put his mind at ease."

Eadgyth hid her smile as she understood the look on Mathilda's face, but she had no intention of discussing the illegitimate son with her. "I can scarce wait to tell him. He will be so pleased and I know he will be a fine father."

"I hope he will," Mathilda muttered, but her expression softened at the happiness on Eadgyth's face. "He has won your heart, so perhaps the boy has a little more sense than I give him credit for."

Chapter twelve

The day had passed excruciatingly slowly, but at last night had come. Eadgyth sat next to Otto at the table, bubbling with excitement. When she rose up at the end, she laid her hand on Otto's shoulder.

"You will not be too long, will you, my love?" she asked.

Otto caught hold of her hand and kissed it. He was obviously pleased to see her in better spirits. "I shall retire soon."

Mathilda gave her a secret smile, as Eadgyth drifted happily to her chamber. Unclothed she looked down at her body. Her stomach was flat and she pressed her hand against it, still finding it hard to believe there could be a child in there.

Otto joined her quickly as he had promised. "I am so pleased you are happy again, my sweet," he said, folding her gently in his arms.

"I know I have been difficult these last days." Eadgyth put her arms around his neck and looked into his eyes, savouring the perfection of this moment. "But I know now the reason." She smiled. "My dearest, I am with child."

Otto sucked in his breath, his eyes widening. Just as Eadgyth had earlier, his hand drifted down to her stomach. He ran his hand over it, a proud smile spreading across his face. "Well, that did not take long, did it?" he said. He leant forward, kissing her as if she were made from glass. "Oh Eadgyth, this is the most wonderful news. When will the child come?"

"Late in the autumn, I think. Before Christmas tide."

Otto pulled her into his arms once again. "We must take good care of you. You are so precious to me," he whispered into her hair. "But now you are doubly so."

∞∞∞

Mathilda smiled at them as they arrived hand in hand at prayers the next morning, afterwards embracing Otto. Eadgyth smiled, realising she rarely saw Mathilda initiate affection towards her eldest son, although she was lavish with her attentions towards young Henry.

The three of them walked out together to stand a while in the spring sunshine. Flowers were springing up and Eadgyth had a sudden sense of being completely at home. Otto hesitated, unwilling to leave her.

"I know childbearing can be dangerous, but all will be well with Eadgyth, will it not?" he asked, looking pleadingly at his mother.

Eadgyth felt a flutter of fear. She had been imagining cradling her child in her arms and was determined not to think of the birth.

"There can be no guarantees, my son," Mathilda said. "But we will take good care of Eadgyth and pray everything goes well for her and the child."

"I know it will be hard," Eadgyth replied, thinking back to her years of ill health. She was not certain her body was built for childbearing.

"It will, but I will be with you, my child." Mathilda squeezed Eadgyth's hand. It was obvious that by conceiving so quickly, she had gone up considerably in Mathilda's estimation.

"Will you?" Eadgyth was surprised. "But I thought Henry wanted Otto to deal with some matters in the West and I was to accompany him?"

"Well, Henry will have to change his plans. Such a journey would not be good for you. And yes, Otto, I know you will not want to be away from Eadgyth too much at such a time."

Otto grinned sheepishly. "That is true, but if I do need to be away, I shall be glad to know Eadgyth is safe here with you."

"Or you could move to Magdeburg if you would prefer a household of your own. It would be understandable if you did, my dear."

Not for the first time, Eadgyth was touched by Mathilda's thoughtfulness. "One day I would like my own household, but at such a time I would prefer to be near you."

Mathilda looked pleased, but gave Otto an exasperated look. He was still watching Eadgyth anxiously. "Your father will be waiting. Go! No harm will come to Eadgyth this day."

Otto kissed Eadgyth and left with obvious reluctance.

"Did you not say that telling Otto would ease his mind? I think it has had the opposite effect," Eadgyth said with a laugh.

"I fear he is going to be hard work these next months," Mathilda replied, taking her arm. "But it is because he cares so much for you."

∞∞∞

It did not take long for news of Eadgyth's pregnancy to spread. Otto's new protectiveness of his wife was immediately commented upon and Eadgyth was aware of the whispers surrounding her. After several days of this Henry arrived one evening in the hall before Mathilda. As the highest ranking woman present, Eadgyth picked up the wine jug to fill her father-in-law's cup.

"Let me do that, Eadgyth," Otto said, quickly taking the heavy jug from her.

Eadgyth shook her head in exasperated amusement.

Henry looked at them, his eyes twinkling. "Thank you, Otto. Is there perhaps some news you would care to share with me?"

Otto gave Eadgyth an apologetic look, but the pride was bursting from him. "Yes, Father. Eadgyth is with child."

Henry embraced his son delightedly and kissed Eadgyth on

the cheek. "Well, my dear, it is a fine day indeed when a man learns he is to have a grandchild."

"It is still early days yet," Eadgyth replied. "But I pray I shall present Otto with a son before the year is out."

Henry patted her hand. "We shall all pray for your good health, my dear and a happy outcome."

"What wonderful news," Thankmar put in with a broad smile. "I am sure you are delighted, Brother and must feel as if Eadgyth is the only woman ever to bear a child."

Eadgyth's smile faded, upset Thankmar was using her happy news to needle his brother. Otto took a step towards Thankmar, but Henry put a hand on his arm.

"What a foolish thing to say, Thankmar. How would I have had my fine children if Eadgyth were the only woman to bear a child? But I trust you will also pray for the good health of both Eadgyth and her child."

With Henry's eyes boring into him, Thankmar could do nothing more than mutter his assurances. Otto was still frowning until young Henry provided a welcome distraction. "How delightful. Another little brat like Bruno."

"Henry!" his beleaguered father exclaimed. "My dear Eadgyth, I must apologise for the poor manners of my son."

Otto cuffed his younger brother lightly about the head. "I can assure you, Henry, my child will not be as much of a brat as you."

"Well, I think this is indeed happy news." Hedwig embraced Eadgyth. "If there is any help I can give you, please ask."

"Thank you, Sister," Otto replied. "I am glad you will help look after Eadgyth. Make sure she does not over exert herself."

Hedwig assured Otto she would indeed do everything she could to help, but burst out laughing at the infuriated look on Eadgyth's face. Eadgyth joined in the laughter, finally believing her sister-in-law had become truly her friend.

∞∞∞

Eadgyth's pregnancy went smoothly. The sickness and tiredness gradually eased and although she still found herself easily moved to tears, no one now condemned her. Her status at Quedlinburg soared, as Henry treated her with special favour and Mathilda cossetted her as if Eadgyth were her own child. Most of all she was grateful to Otto, who no longer considered her tears a reproach to him, but instead was always ready to enfold her in his arms until the weeping stopped, often whispering comments to make her smile once again.

However as the months passed Eadgyth began to find Otto's over protectiveness irritating and was almost relieved when Henry ordered him to attend to some matters in the West.

"I can't leave Eadgyth at such a time," Otto said.

"Of course you can, my love. I feel very well now," Eadgyth replied, smoothing her hand over a stomach which was starting to swell.

"Sometimes infants come too soon… I should be here." Eadgyth's heart melted at the anxiety in Otto's face. Guilt struck her that she had ever found him irritating when she knew how lucky she was to have a husband caring so devotedly for her.

"Eadgyth is now past the point when women most commonly lose their babies," Mathilda put in. "Of course we cannot be certain, but I am hopeful all will be well. If we even suspect something is amiss, I will send a message and you can return."

"As a King's son, you must fulfil your duties, Otto," Henry added. "After that I shall need you to meet me in Mainz. I want the nobles to start accepting you as my heir."

"Is that necessary already, Henry?" Mathilda asked.

"Well, I hope I will not die just yet," Henry said. "But this is, after all, what I have long planned." He smiled at Eadgyth. "He has a wife of ancient royal lineage and his prowess as a warrior is much admired. With a child already on the way, I think this is the time to raise the matter."

∞∞∞

Eadgyth missed Otto intensely while he was away. Mathilda too was subdued as Bruno also departed with his father. It had been decided that he should enter the church and was being placed in the care of Bishop Balderic of Utrecht.

"I know he will receive a fine education and the bishop is a most kindly man, but I do miss him," Mathilda confessed to Eadgyth.

Thankmar too had left the court, so it was left to young Henry to preside over everyone in the King's place. Eadgyth found it amusing to see him strutting grandly into the hall every evening, but she longed for Otto to return.

She wept for joy as she felt the first signs of life stir in her and wished he could be there to share the moment. Beginning to feel hopeful the pregnancy would have a happy outcome, she started work on soft shawls and blankets, happily daydreaming of the moment she would hold the baby in her arms

It was early autumn when Otto returned. Eadgyth had grown great with child and was working with Mathilda, stitching tiny infant robes when Otto strode into the hall. She struggled to her feet.

"Otto! I am so glad you are back, but I am a sight. I wish you did not have to see me like this."

"You are more beautiful than ever," he replied.

Mathilda laughed and for once did not object when Otto swept her into a hug. "Welcome back, Otto. We have heard much of your progress." She kissed his cheek. "I shall leave you two to your reunion."

Otto took Eadgyth very gently in his arms. "I meant what I said. You really are so beautiful. But more importantly, are you well?"

Eadgyth nodded. "Apart from a few aches, yes, I have never

felt so well." She kissed him. "I have so missed you."

"I have thought of you every day," Otto replied.

"Did all progress as your father hoped at the synod in Mainz?" she asked, wondering why Mathilda had not asked Otto about this.

Otto nodded. "Nothing is settled yet and the nobles are surprised Father does not wish to divide the realm in the Frankish custom, but he is confident we have made a good start."

Eadgyth sat back down. Taking Otto's hand she drew it to her stomach. "Feel this."

As if sensing the presence of its father, the baby kicked against it. Tears came to Eadgyth's eyes at the look on Otto's face and Otto's own eyes glistened. "Oh Eadgyth, that is truly amazing." He knelt on the floor, putting his arms around her and pressing his face against her stomach. "Our child."

Chapter thirteen

Eadgyth clawed against a door, her fingers bleeding with the struggle. Splinters sliced open her fingers and she screamed in agony, knowing her child was dying, but no once came to her aid and the door remained shut…

She opened her eyes with a start, unsurprised to find herself in bed. It was not the first time she had suffered such a dream. Next to her Otto stirred. He had insisted they continue to share a bed, in spite of the usual customs. Often he said she should wake him if she needed him, but knowing he had many fears of his own, she tried to keep her terrors from him.

Her trembling body was clammy from sweat, but a sharp kick from inside her brought a smile back to her face, as she tried to settle herself as comfortably as she could. She soothed herself with thoughts of holding the baby in her arms, until she was able to sleep again.

After so many restless nights it was almost a relief when the first pains came in the darkest time of a late autumn night, several hours before dawn. Eadgyth shifted herself on the bed, trying to ignore them. But when the third one came she knew it was useless to keep trying to sleep. She sat up.

"Eadgyth?" Otto swiftly sat up next to her. "Is all well?"

Eadgyth clutched on to his hand. "I… I think I will present you with your child this day." With an effort she kept the tremor out of her voice.

Otto lit a candle, illuminating the fear on his face. "Shall I fetch my mother?"

Eadgyth shook her head. "No, little is happening yet. It will likely be a long day. She should rest as long as she can."

"Do you think you can sleep again?"

"I do not think so."

Otto pulled her against him, so her head was cradled against his chest. His strong arms encircled her, bringing a sense of security even at such a time. "At least rest."

"I'll try," she said, but in spite of the warmth of his arms her fears surfaced once again. "Otto, I am so afraid."

Gently Otto stroked her hair. "I know, my sweet. Oh, you hide it well, but of course you are afraid."

"Is it foolish of me?"

"No, of course not. Do you think I am not afraid when I prepare myself for battle?"

"Are you?" Eadgyth was surprised. "All I have ever heard is how brave you are."

"Well, I hope I am, but I am not a fool. When I prepare for battle, I know it could be the day I face a slow and painful death. My dearest, I do know how you are feeling at this moment. And one day, if I need to fight again, you will know how I am feeling."

Eadgyth tightened her arms around him. "We have been so happy together. If this is my last day, please always be glad we had this happy year and remember how much I love you."

"I'll try." Otto pressed his face against her hair in an effort, Eadgyth suspected, to stop tears from overflowing.

They said no more and snug in his arms, Eadgyth did manage to doze a little between the pains. But as the first grey rays of light filtered into their chamber, she could sleep no more. The pains were closer together and more intense. She pulled on a loose robe and paced around their chamber.

"If we have a son, what shall we name him?" she asked Otto as the latest pain ebbed away. "Otto? Henry?"

"Could we call him Liudolf? Liudolf was a forefather of mine. My grandfather's father and first in my family to be Duke of Saxony. As a boy I loved hearing tales of him. I would be proud to name my son for him, if that has your agreement."

"Liudolf. Yes, I like the name." Eadgyth smiled at Otto.

"What if we have a daughter?" Otto asked.

But Eadgyth did not answer. The sharpest pain yet was building up and she could not withhold a cry. There was a gush of liquid. She doubled over, the wet robe cloying to her legs.

Otto sucked in his breath and ran for the door, shouting loudly for a serving lad. "Fetch the Queen. Tell her the Lady Eadgyth's pains have started."

Turning back, Otto put his arms around her. Gratefully she clung to him as the pain subsided once again. "They are coming even quicker now," she whispered.

He kissed the top of her head. "I know. Be strong, my sweet. Get through this."

It did not take long for Mathilda to arrive. She swept in, accompanied by a group of people including Hedwig, a midwife and a priest. The room felt crowded and Eadgyth clung tighter to Otto in a sudden panic. Mathilda shook her head. "Go the hall now, Otto. We shall look after Eadgyth."

"She needs me. I can't leave her."

"Don't be foolish, Otto. What use can you be here? I would waste all my time comforting you."

"But…" Otto looked in a bewildered fashion from his wife to his mother.

"I shall look after her as if she were my own daughter," Mathilda said softly.

Eadgyth took a deep breath. "Otto, I will be fine."

Otto gave a tortured smile and took Eadgyth into his arms one last time. "Do not pretend for me. The anxiety I must bear this day is nothing compared to what you will have to endure. I love you so much, Eadgyth. I shall be praying for you." He kissed her and reluctantly let her out of his arms.

As he went slowly to the door, Mathilda gave him a swift kiss on the cheek. "I will send word as soon as there is any news, but it will likely be a long time yet."

"She felt the first pains some time ago now. Perhaps it will soon be over?" Otto looked pleadingly at his mother.

"Oh, Otto." Mathilda shook her head. "First borns can take a long time to come, but every birth is different. We do not know how long it will take for Eadgyth."

Eadgyth watched as Otto left the room, turning as he went for what he intended to be an encouraging smile. Hedwig pushed the door shut and the soft thud seemed to echo throughout the room sending another flood of panic into her as she wondered if she would ever see him again. "Otto," she whispered, wishing she could call him back.

Mathilda knelt at her side, putting her arms around her. "There, child. Try to stay calm."

Around her the women were busy covering the windows with dark cloths causing strange shadows to fill the room. Eadgyth cried out, fearing these cloths had summoned the very evil spirits they were supposed to prevent.

Mathilda stroked her hair comfortingly as the priest chanted some soft prayers for the safe delivery, although the monotonous tone of his voice made Eadgyth feel like screaming. She was relieved when he finally made the sign of the cross in blessing and departed. The midwife filled a cup with a herbal infusion sweetened with honey. "Try to drink this, my lady."

It was a long day and it seemed to Eadgyth there would be no end as pain after pain struck her. The women helped her to walk around until she sank, exhausted to the floor.

"I do not think I am built for childbearing," she whispered to Mathilda. "As a child I was so sickly. I fear it damaged me."

"Hush, child. Everything is going as it should so far. Stay strong, Eadgyth. I think it may not be too much longer."

Mathilda was right. The pains soon changed into an overwhelming urge to push. The women became excited and for Eadgyth it was easier now she had a focus, although the contractions tearing through her were more severe than ever. The midwife ordered the women to rub her body with oils, their heavy scent making her dizzy.

Eadgyth was never certain how she got through that day. The birth went on for a long time after she was sure she was at the end of her strength. Often she felt she would not have done it at all, except for the thought of Otto's anxious face and Mathilda's whispered words of encouragement as she sponged down her face.

The pain reached an intensity she was not sure she could bear. "How much longer?" she screamed.

Mathilda put her arms around her. "Not very long now. Another few pushes and the head will be out."

Eadgyth clung on to her mother-in-law's hands as she pushed with all her strength. There was a cry of delight from the women.

"The head is out, my child," Mathilda cried. "One more push."

Almost sobbing with relief, Eadgyth did as she was instructed. There was a curious sensation and then a tense silence. Eadgyth stared at the bundle in Mathilda's arms, clutching fearfully onto Hedwig's hand. She was unable even to whisper any prayers as the midwife rubbed the baby's back, frowning in intense concentration. Mathilda's face was growing grave when there was a faint choke followed by a squawky cry. The women let out a long sigh of relief and Mathilda's eyes lit up. The midwife nodded her head, letting her place the child into Eadgyth's arms. She blinked back tears as the warm little body curled against her. Out of a crumpled, slightly bloodstained face, two shining eyes looked up at her, the mouth forming a perfect ring.

"You have done so well, my child," Mathilda said, putting her arm around Eadgyth's shoulders and looking admiringly at the baby, who was already rooting for Eadgyth's breast. "A fine, strong little boy."

Eadgyth could barely speak. "Welcome, little Liudolf," she whispered.

"Liudolf? Otto always liked to hear tales of him." Mathilda smiled, looking close to tears herself.

Eadgyth laughed with joy. "I think the name suits him."

"Yes, it does."

∞∞∞

"Well, we must summon Otto, before the boy goes out of his mind with worry," Mathilda said as soon as Eadgyth had been cleaned. "And no doubt Henry will want to bother you as soon as you feel up to it, but we shall let Otto have some time alone with you first."

"I shall be glad to present Henry with his grandson, once Otto has seen him," Eadgyth said. The memory of the pain was already fading. She felt tired, but ecstatically happy. "Please do not give him any news yet. I want to see his face when he learns he has a son."

It did not take Otto long to arrive. "What has happened, Mother? Is all well with Eadgyth?" he cried as he arrived breathless in the doorway.

Mathilda got up and took her son by the hands. She had already dismissed the other women. "Yes, my son. If we take good care of her, I am hopeful she will quickly recover."

"God be praised," Otto whispered.

Mathilda pushed him towards Eadgyth. "You are a father, Otto," she said as she left them together.

He knelt down at Eadgyth's side, gazing at the child. "Meet Liudolf," she said, looking up at him. "Oh, Otto, we have a son."

The look on Otto's face was everything Eadgyth had hoped for. "Eadgyth, my beautiful Eadgyth and my beautiful son." He laid his head against Eadgyth's and they both smiled down at the bright eyed baby. "I am the happiest man alive."

Part Two: The Year of our Lord 932-36

Chapter one

"You have a fair daughter, Otto," Mathilda announced when once again Otto arrived in the birth chamber. It was barely a year since Liudolf's birth.

Mathilda had not been impressed when Eadgyth had conceived again so quickly, saying it would have been better for her health if they had waited a little longer. Eadgyth had laughed. She had recovered so quickly from Liudolf's birth it seemed to be of no concern that she was yet again with child.

But now she wished they had waited. The birth had been gruelling, taking far longer than Liudolf's. She felt listless as she watched Otto take their daughter in his arms, hoping he was not too disappointed not to have another son. The memory of how she had disappointed her own father struck her so hard she almost cried aloud, feeling wretched that her daughter might experience the same.

"She is beautiful," Otto said, looking delighted. "She might even be as beautiful as you one day, Eadgyth. I wish to call her Liutgarde, if you agree, my sweet."

Eadgyth had little strength to do anything other than nod. Otto looked at her in alarm and thrust the baby back into Mathilda's arms. He knelt at her side. "Eadgyth, is all well?"

Eadgyth raised a limp hand to touch Otto on the cheek. "The birth was difficult."

"I thought second births were usually easier." Otto glanced up in concern at Mathilda.

"If Eadgyth had more time to recover from the first, it probably would have been easier." Mathilda too looked exhausted. She had been at Eadgyth's side for every moment of the nearly three day labour. "You can have some time alone now, but not too long. Eadgyth needs to rest. Do not rush her into bearing you the next one too soon. You should put your wife's health before your desires."

Otto's mouth dropped open in horror and Eadgyth tried to find the strength to protest that it had not been his fault, but Mathilda had already left the chamber.

"I am sorry," Otto whispered.

Eadgyth shook her head, a futile attempt at a smile struggling across her face. "This was not your fault. I wanted you as much as you wanted me, remember?"

Otto did not look cheered. "I should have been stronger." He kissed her gently. "But at least it is over now."

However it proved to be very far from over. Over the next days the women became concerned by how heavily Eadgyth was bleeding until one morning Otto came to find her face flushed and her breath rapid. He took her hand, almost dropping it in shock at the scorching heat of her skin. His eyes flew to Mathilda, who was watching him gravely.

"It is the fever," she said.

"What does that mean?" Otto asked, looking terrified.

"It means she is seriously ill," Mathilda replied.

Eadgyth had no strength left to do anything, as she took in Otto's stricken look. Her skin may have been burning hot, but inside she was frozen. Even in her years of sickness as a child she had never felt so ill. Throughout that day everyone fussed around her, sponging her down with cool water or trying to feed her with sips of mead. All she wanted was to be left alone.

The efforts of the women were in vain and their faces grew increasingly anxious, with much shaking of heads. Finally they called Otto back. He came so quickly it was obvious he had been sitting just outside the chamber in increasing agitation. With her lip trembling, Mathilda sat next to Otto and gently took hold of his hand.

"My son, we need to summon a priest."

Otto's hand flew to his mouth. "No. She will recover."

The tears in Mathilda's eyes spilled over. "Otto, I love Eadgyth like a daughter. I do not want to face this, but if you love her as I think you do, you will not refuse her Last Rites."

To Eadgyth those words seemed very far away and she felt detached from it all, but the pain on Otto's face pierced her to her heart. She tried to sit up, but could find no strength to do so. Otto was staring at her. "No, no," he mouthed. "Please, God, no. This is my fault, Mother. Mine."

Mathilda put her arm tightly around him. "No, my son. This is the sacrifice many women have to make." Her tears flowed faster than ever. "It is God's will. I know that is hard, but we must accept it."

Otto laid his head in his hands. "I love her so much. How can God take her from me?"

"Otto, the priest. Please, my son. For the sake of Eadgyth's soul."

"Yes, summon a priest, Mother." The words came out reluctantly. His chest heaved with suppressed anguish as he looked piteously at his mother. "Please, can I have a few moments alone with her?"

Mathilda nodded, squeezing his shoulder. Otto flung himself on his knees next to the bed, taking Eadgyth gently into his arms. "I am sorry, my sweet. So sorry. This is not how it should be. This is not fair." Tears ran from his eyes. "This is all my fault. I love you so much, but I have killed you."

Eadgyth wanted to tell Otto not to grieve, that none of this was his fault. But the room was spinning and she could get no words out. It seemed to her there was a door floating above her, swinging backwards and forth, ready to slam, shutting her away from everyone she loved.

The priest entered the room, holding up a cross. He marked a cross on Eadgyth's forehead as solemnly he began the sacred words of Last Rites.

"Credo in spiritum sanctum," he intoned, his voice sounding distant.

Otto laid her back on the bed, clasping a hand over his mouth to stop his sobs escaping. Eadgyth kept her eyes on him, as the chamber began to fade to a merciful blackness.

∞∞∞

When Eadgyth opened her eyes again early morning sunshine was illuminating the room and all was quiet. She no longer felt cold, but snug under the covers. She lifted her arms to push back her hair from her face. The movement took an effort, but at least her hand was doing what she wanted. Turning her head, she smiled to see Otto asleep in a chair as the memories flooded back. Somehow she was still alive. Her mouth felt parched and she looked longingly at a jug on a table beyond him. Gingerly she sat up.

Otto jerked awake. "Eadgyth? Don't move. You must rest."

"Can I have a drink?" she gestured languidly at the jug."

Otto nodded, putting some pillows behind her. He held a cup to her lips, letting the cool liquid trickle into her mouth. She leaned back against the pillows. "Where is the priest?"

"The priest? My love, that was two nights back."

Eadgyth looked at him in surprise. "Two nights? What happened?"

"He had to administer Last Rites," Otto said, looking agonised at the memory. "We did not think you would last the night, but somehow you kept breathing. Then last night the fever broke. How are you feeling?"

"Terrible," she admitted.

Otto took her hand. "You need some food. You've hardly eaten since the birth."

Eadgyth stared at him in sudden panic, realising it had been days since she had held her newborn daughter. "The baby? Where is she?"

"She's fine, my sweet. She's being well looked after. Please, let me have some food brought for you and then you can see her."

"And Liudolf," Eadgyth said.

Mathilda's tired face lit up when she came, bringing the food herself. "Oh, Eadgyth. It is good to see you awake."

"Stay with her, Mother. She wants to see the children."

As Eadgyth obediently ate some bread dipped in the thick broth Mathilda had brought, the door opened and Otto returned, with Liudolf on one arm and the baby in the other. Eadgyth smiled, but Liudolf took one look at his mother and burst into tears, burying his head in his father's shoulder.

Eadgyth stared at him, shocked by his reaction. To her horror she realised Liudolf was frightened of her. She picked up a mirror and felt like bursting into tears herself. Her hair hung limply around a haggard face so white even her lips were pale. It was almost the face of an old woman. She laid the mirror face down, looking at Otto, so young and handsome with his children in his arms. He would be ashamed to have her at his side.

Otto sat on the bed, still holding Liudolf, but put the baby into her arms. "You have never looked as beautiful to me as you do at this moment," he said softly. "Liudolf is being foolish. Come, my son, give your mother an embrace."

Liudolf looked solemnly at her and then snuggled into her arms. Otto put his arms around all three of them. "Get well, Eadgyth. Nothing else matters."

Chapter two

The spring flowers were already in full bloom before Eadgyth felt well enough to re-join the court, although it was almost the autumn before Otto stopped looking anxiously at her and decided she was well enough to travel. He suggested they move to Magdeburg, Eadgyth's own city, a place she had not yet been able to visit. Eadgyth loved Mathilda all the more for the devoted care she had received while she had been so ill, but she was delighted at the prospect of presiding over a household of her own. Henry had also approved the plan, saying it would be good for Otto to have his own court. On a day when the first nip of autumn was in the air, they made the day's ride to the city.

"Welcome to Magdeburg, my sweet." Otto reined in his horse outside the city walls. "Although in truth you should be welcoming me. This is your city."

After the ceremonial opening of the gates, Bishop Bernard of Halberstadt, surrounded by a crowd of the town's burghers and Saxon nobles came out to greet them, his white robes trailing in the dust. Otto dismounted and took the man's hands with a smile, as he spoke the formal words of entry. "I, Otto of Saxony, husband of Eadgyth, Lady of Magdeburg, demand entry to the city."

The Bishop stood aside with a flourish. "Entry is most gladly granted. Welcome, Lady of Magdeburg and you too Prince Otto."

"On behalf of the people of Magdeburg, I welcome you,

Eadgyth, Lady of Magdeburg and Prince Otto of Saxony," one of the nobles announced. "May I say how much you have grown since last you were here?"

Otto grinned ruefully. The man had known him well as a small boy. "Thank you, Lord Billung." He looked up at Eadgyth. "Lord Hermann Billung's brother, Count Wichmann is wed to my mother's sister."

Eadgyth smiled down from her horse. "Thank you for your welcome, Father, Lord Billung. I am most happy to be here."

"Shall we enter?" Otto asked.

"Wait. Can the children ride with us to their new home?"

Otto nodded and a serving lad scurried to take the message to where the children had been riding in one of the carts.

"Father! Father! Father!" an excited voice cried.

Otto turned, holding out his arms to the fair haired little boy running towards him, sweeping him high in the air. Eadgyth smiled. Liudolf was a tiny version of Otto, apart from his blonde hair and light blue eyes. Eadgyth had once expressed regret that he had not inherited Otto's deeper eyes, but Otto had simply replied that the more his son looked like his beautiful mother, the more pleased he was. The eyes she loved so much, had been passed down to little Liutgarde. At less than a year old, she was already considered a beauty. Both children had infectious smiles, although Eadgyth and Otto never could agree on who they had inherited them from.

"Are you going to ride on Father's horse?" Otto asked.

The boy shrieked with delight as he was lifted onto the saddle. Liutgarde was strapped onto Eadgyth's front and together the family entered Magdeburg.

Eadgyth fell in love with the town at first sight, admiring the clusters of buildings by the river and as welcoming cries rang out on all sides, it seemed Magdeburg returned the affection. They made such an attractive group, it was hardly surprising. Otto, now almost aged twenty, had become more muscular with broad shoulders filling out his fine red tunic and his dark hair contrasting with the fair strands which had escaped from Eadgyth's mantle. As her health had improved over the year, so too had her appearance even in her own critical eyes. Pink cheeked from the ride in the cool air, she accepted with a warm smile the compliments many in the crowd called. However most attention was claimed by the children. Liudolf, waving his chubby fist and smiling at everything he saw and Liutgarde, her head nodding sleepily against her mother, melted the hearts of all who saw them.

The palace was very fine, set in a commanding position overlooking the river. As Eadgyth dismounted, she shifted Liutgarde into a more comfortable position on her hip and looked up at the grand edifice, said to have been built by the great Emperor Charles, who had ruled the whole of Francia more than a hundred years before. The complex was not as big as Quedlinburg, but it was finely built in the Frankish style, with a stately hall and a church nearby.

Otto put one arm around her shoulders, his other hand holding on tightly to Liudolf. "What do you think, Eadgyth?"

"It is magnificent," she said. "I am eager to see inside."

"It is reckoned to be a fair palace," Otto said as they reached the steps to the door. "But I fear it is not as fine as Quedlinburg."

Eadgyth smiled at him. "Perhaps not yet."

∞ ∞ ∞

The remainder of the autumn was a happy time. Eadgyth further endeared herself to her city as she regularly rode out, bringing food and warm garments to the poor. She was busy too improving the palace, replacing faded hangings with fine new tapestries.

But one evening a few months after their arrival Otto came to her, a somewhat disgruntled look on his face. "I have had a message from my father. He wants me to go to Erfurt. The nobility are gathering."

"That is not unusual is it?"

"I think this may be different. Listen to his message. 'My dearest Otto, I send greetings from Quedlinburg and trust it finds you, your fair wife and children in good health. I command you to come to Erfurt at all speed. The tribute to the Magyars is due again and I am resolved that we take action. Your loving father, Henry, Duke of Saxony, King of Germany.'"

"What is the tribute to the Magyars?"

"About eight years ago the Magyars defeated my father. In the negotiations for surrender it was agreed we would pay a tribute every year in return for a truce. It infuriates my father. Every year the payment puts him in the most terrible of moods."

Eadgyth smiled. "I am not surprised."

"My father has not been idle these last years. He has had new defences constructed, manned by many of our finest warriors. I suspect this means he considers the truce to be at an end."

"War?" Eadgyth clutched onto Otto's hand. "Will you have to fight?"

"Of course."

Eadgyth bit her lip, knowing it had been a foolish question. The happy few months they had just spent suddenly seemed very distant.

"Will you come with me to Erfurt? I can leave Hermann Billung in charge while we are away. I am sorry. I know you have just settled here, but I would like you at my side."

Eadgyth felt a brief pang of regret at leaving the city she loved already and her children, but she did not hesitate. "Of course I will, although I am not sure what use I shall be on such an occasion."

Otto put his arms around her. "Of great use, my sweet. You know I am the intended heir for both the Duchy of Saxony and for the throne of Germany?"

"Of course, but how does my presence help you?"

Otto laughed. "You really have no idea of what an asset you are to me, do you? If I am to be King of Germany, I will need the support of the nobles, many older and wiser than I. It will enhance my prestige beyond all others when I appear with a fair English princess at my side, particularly one as wise and devout as you." Eadgyth blushed and Otto grinned, kissing the top of her head. "Besides, if this does result in a war, we must make the most of the time we have together."

Chapter three

The nobility of Germany were already gathering in Erfurt when Eadgyth and Otto arrived. Henry and Mathilda received them with pleasure, passing on greetings from Hedwig. Otto turned with a grin to young Henry, cuffing his younger brother about the head and expertly dodging Henry's swift retort. The scuffle ended as it usually did in an exuberant embrace, before the boy greeted Eadgyth more properly. However the friendly mood cooled as Thankmar also came forward.

"It is good to see you, Brother," Thankmar said, giving Otto a tight smile. He bowed and bestowed a perfunctory kiss on Eadgyth's hand. "And you too, Eadgyth."

Eadgyth did her best to smile warmly back. She had tried to like this man. No one knew better than her what it was like to have your mother repudiated, although at least her legitimacy had never been called into question. At times she had found it hard to reconcile the strong affection she had for Henry with the knowledge of how he had treated Thankmar's mother and she guessed it must have been harder still for Thankmar as he found himself supplanted by a popular younger brother.

"What decisions have you made on the Magyar tribute, Father?" Otto asked.

"I hope to convince the nobles and the bishops that the tribute must stop."

"That will likely mean war," Otto commented.

"Have you turned into a coward, Little Brother? Once you

appeared to find war most... pleasurable." Thankmar gave a sly glance at Eadgyth, reminding her of why she didn't like him. "But perhaps now there are greater attractions away from the borders."

Young Henry swiftly covered his mouth to conceal his laughter, while keeping his eyes gleefully on his brothers.

Only a slight clenching of Otto's fists betrayed how Thankmar had riled him. "You should know me better than that. I have fought the enemies of Germany since I was no more than fifteen. I am merely ensuring everyone understands the consequences."

Henry folded his arms and looked sternly at Thankmar. "Don't be a fool, Thankmar. You know Otto is no coward. Otto, I can assure you I have considered the consequences. It may not be easy to convince the church and the nobles. I hope I have your support."

"Of course you have my support. And more than that, I fully agree with you," Otto replied. "It is not right that Germany continues to pay the heathens to stay away."

Eadgyth watched her husband in fascination. Although Otto had grown considerably in assurance over the previous couple of years, she had never seen this side to him, as a confident military commander. She exchanged glances with Mathilda who smiled faintly back. They each knew how the other was feeling. Their husbands would likely soon be riding off to battle and all they could do was pray for them.

∞ ∞ ∞

While Henry, flanked by Otto and Thankmar, spoke to the nobles, Eadgyth took the chance to fill Mathilda in on news of the children. There was much laughter as she recounted Liudolf's latest exploits.

"And is all well with you, my child?" Mathilda asked.

"I think so," Eadgyth replied hesitantly. She met her mother-in-law's anxious eyes. "I had expected to conceive again by now."

"I would have thought you would be glad of the rest. Liutgarde is not quite a year."

"I suppose I am glad, but…"

"Is Otto reproaching you?" Mathilda demanded. "Because if he is, he will have me to deal with. You presented him with two children in barely two years."

"No, no." Eadgyth shook her head, laughing. "Otto has not said a word."

"He is probably glad you have not conceived again so quickly. When you were ill after Liutgarde was born, I thought Otto's own heart would break. I have never seen him so distraught."

"I know I am being foolish to worry. These matters lie in God's hands and I am fortunate indeed that Liudolf and Liutgarde are so strong. I suppose I worry that if Otto is to be king one day, he may become dissatisfied if I do not bear him more sons."

Mathilda raised her eyebrows. "It is by no means certain that Otto will be king, my dear. He is not Henry's only son, you know."

"Of course, but I understood Thankmar is disbarred from the succession."

"Oh yes, Thankmar will not be king. Henry has already declared that. But young Henry is his namesake and he was the first son to be born in the purple. Henry was merely the Duke of Saxony when Otto was born."

"Henry? But he is still a boy. He has seen little more than thirteen years."

"The King is in excellent health," Mathilda replied rather frostily. "I am sure young Henry will be well into manhood before we need consider such matters."

"Of course." Eadgyth swallowed, not wanting a quarrel with her mother-in-law. "Indeed I hope it is many years before such matters need to be considered, but Henry has already made it plain to the nobles that he hopes they will accept Otto as his heir."

"Nothing has been formalised yet, Eadgyth," Mathilda said. "You should not make so many assumptions. Of course I understand that as a king's daughter, you must hope to one day be a king's wife."

Eadgyth bit her lip, hating to be reminded of her father. Being a king's daughter had brought her little happiness and she preferred not to wonder whether being a king's wife would be any better. However she had to say something in support of Otto. "If Otto was to be selected, I know he would fulfil the role excellently."

Mathilda looked uncomfortable. "Perhaps."

Eadgyth frowned, but said no more. She bent her head over her stitching, casting surreptitious glances at Mathilda. Often she had wondered why her manner was sometimes so cold towards her oldest son, especially as she made no secret of her great pride in young Henry. Her piety was famous throughout the realm but even so, it seemed strange to be still holding against him that one youthful indiscretion with the Slavic noblewoman. Eadgyth's heart ached, as she knew how Otto adored his mother.

They were still sitting in silence when the men re-joined them. Henry's face was triumphant and Otto was smiling grimly. Rather to Eadgyth's surprise, young Henry was with them. She had assumed he was too young to be part of such a meeting.

"Everyone has agreed," Henry announced jubilantly. "There is to be no more tribute."

"So we must prepare for a fight," Otto added.

Mathilda forced a bright smile. "I am sure this is for the best. It will be good to have the matter settled." She smiled more naturally at young Henry. "Did you find the synod interesting, my son?"

The boy shrugged. "Some of it."

Henry laughed. "My dear Mathilda, I do not know why you wished such a thing on him. Otto did not attend such synods until much older and even then he found them dull."

Eadgyth felt a faint chill as she wondered at Mathilda's motives. It truly seemed as if she was pushing young Henry forward as the heir to Germany.

"I think it is good for Henry to learn of such matters," Mathilda replied calmly.

"A waste of time. He learnt nothing and Otto learning later did him no harm. Otto was most persuasive this day. I think it is in part thanks to his words that I secured the agreement so quickly." Henry put an arm around Otto and Eadgyth smiled proudly, hoping Mathilda would realise he was no longer the careless boy he had been just a few years before.

Otto grinned. "Some of the bishops were more resistant than I had expected, but we convinced them in the end. If old Arnulf of Bavaria has had similar success in convincing the nobles of his duchy we will muster a fine force."

"Can I join your force, Father?" young Henry asked.

"Not this time, my son. You are not yet grown, although I know you are becoming skilled. Neither Otto nor Thankmar fought alongside me at your age. Another year or two of growth and you will be ready. But for now you must stay with your mother at Quedlinburg."

Young Henry scowled. "I do not wish to stay with the women and babies."

Otto ruffled his head as he passed him to take Eadgyth's hands. "I once thought like that, but now I can assure you, staying with a beautiful woman is infinitely more appealing than going to war." He raised her hands to his lips, squeezing them slightly to show he understood her anxiety.

Henry looked more infuriated than ever by Otto's comment and slumped insolently into a chair.

"Of course you will stay with me, Henry," Mathilda said. "It would not be wise for your father to risk so many of his sons on the same day."

Eadgyth barely repressed a shudder, suddenly afraid Mathilda was hoping Otto would perish to leave the throne free for young Henry. She watched her speaking in soft tones to her second son, the affection she so rarely showed Otto, obvious in every gesture. She knew Mathilda did not think highly of Otto, but never before had she considered how deeply that disfavour ran.

∞∞∞

The Magyar envoys arrived a few days later to collect their tribute. The hall was packed, as everyone speculated how Henry would deal with them. Mathilda sat beside Henry, her beautiful face calm. Otto was standing at his father's other side with one arm around Eadgyth and Thankmar next to her. Again young Henry had been brought into a prominent position, next to his mother. Otto had made no comment, so Eadgyth was unsure whether this was unusual.

She looked around. It had not previously been possible for her to witness such a gathering of the nobles. She could see Hermann of Swabia stood with Gilbert of Lotharingia. They were talking to another man who Otto told her was Duke Eberhard of Franconia, the brother of the previous king. All were engaged in animated discussions as everyone waited for the envoys to be presented. Eadgyth listened as Otto and Thankmar talked over her head, the usual animosity between them non-existent as they tossed around strategies and battle stories. These accounts of injuries and near-deaths did nothing to reassure her, although the two brothers seemed to be enjoying it.

Otto suddenly looked down at her. "If there is war soon, I want you and the children to join my mother at Quedlinburg. It is better defended than Magdeburg and further from the border. We can concentrate the guards there."

"But…" Eadgyth started a protest. She was not certain she wanted to be in the company of Mathilda and seeing the way her mother-in-law was whispering to young Henry did nothing to convince her otherwise.

"Eadgyth, I am insisting." Otto's smile took away the sting of the command. "I know we have only just settled in Magdeburg and we will return as soon as it is safe, I swear it. I need to be concentrating my energies on the fight and not worrying about you and the children."

"Of course, Otto." Eadgyth tried to smile. Otto had not yet noticed anything amiss between her and Mathilda and for his sake, she knew it would be for the best if they could overcome the tension between them.

A flourish of horns heralded the arrival of the envoys and the hall immediately stilled. Henry sat up straight and Otto folded his arms as three men strode in. It was the first time Eadgyth had seen any dressed in the raiment of the Magyars and she had to smile at their curious conical hats. Their tunics were of a lavishly brocaded fabric which she rather admired, although spoilt in her opinion by baggy breeches tucked into boots, which were not nearly as flattering as the tightly fitted breeches Otto and the other German men wore. They swept up to Henry's throne and did not bow.

"Lord King of Germany, we are here on behalf of Grand Prince Zoltan to collect the tribute due to us. Is it is ready?"

Henry stood up, his magnificent robes sweeping to the ground. "Indeed it is." He raised his hand in a signal to a guard at one of the doors.

The door opened and there was a murmur of surprise and disgust. Eadgyth craned her neck to see what was happening, while Otto's lips turned into an amused smile. A pungent smell of rotting meat hit her and she covered her nose with her hand. The envoys looked bewildered, fanning the air to rid themselves of the stench coming ever closer. The faces of the Dukes filled with glee.

"My God, he's really doing it," muttered Thankmar.

"Did you think he wouldn't?" Otto replied in a low voice, his eyes fixed on the shocked faces of the envoys.

Eadgyth glanced at the King. Of everyone she could see,

only his face was impassive. He held up a hand for silence as a soldier came into view bearing the body of a dead dog, its head lolling back over the man's arm. Eadgyth could barely restrain a gasp of surprise at the sight. The soldier's bearing was upright and his face as dignified as the King's with none of the amusement or disgust everyone else seemed to be feeling.

"What is the meaning of this, Lord King?" one of the envoys cried.

"This is your tribute," Henry replied and as he spoke, the soldier threw the dead dog at the feet of the envoys. Eadgyth stared at the pathetic looking body of what had once been a fine hound. Fluids oozed from the carcass and the glassy eyes stared up sightlessly at the three Magyar men. Mocking laughter rang around the hall as the men cried out, jumping back from the lump of rotting flesh.

A ferocious anger replaced the shock of the envoys. With as much dignity as he could manage, one stepped over the body of the dog. "This will mean war, Lord King."

Henry gave the man a chilling smile. "Will it?" he asked. "Then so be it."

Chapter four

After the Synod they had swiftly returned to Magdeburg, but although delighted to be there, Eadgyth was fearful as she wondered what the response of the Magyar prince would be. They celebrated Christmas with feasting and music once the solemn church services had been completed. The night ended informally with the tunes of the pipes and cytharas becoming merrier, luring many a couple into a dance. Otto caught Eadgyth's eye and laughed, stretching out his hand. Joyfully she took it, quickly losing her regal manner as Otto pulled her among the dancers.

Eadgyth could not help thinking back to the previous year when she had been just days away from Liutgarde's birth and very uncomfortable, although blissfully unaware of the ordeal to come. Otto too was thinking of that. As the musicians finished with a flourish, he pulled Eadgyth into his arms and whispered in her ear, "I once thought we would never again celebrate a Christmas together. I praise God every day I was wrong."

She clung to him, praying they would celebrate many a Christmas together, but with rumours of Magyar raids on the borders already reaching them, she feared the worst.

∞∞∞

It was soon after Candlemas when Henry summoned his

men to defend the border and the force which mustered at Quedlinburg was a formidable one. Eadgyth stood quietly with Mathilda as Henry greeted the troops, both Otto and Thankmar at his side. All three were fully armed, but for once Eadgyth's attention was not fixed on Otto. Henry was holding a battered looking lance, its point still keen. Eadgyth crossed herself, her eyes widening at the sight. For this fight Henry had ordered the Holy Lance, the one once used to stab Christ on his cross, to be brought for him to carry into battle. She murmured a prayer, suddenly confident that with such a holy treasure on Henry's side, the heathen barbarians would stand little chance.

Men had come from all over Germany to swell Henry's forces. As the cavalry began to mount, Eadgyth looked unhappily at a group of horses which did not yet have their riders, knowing one would soon bear Otto away from her. Henry entered a conversation with Arnulf of Bavaria and Hermann of Swabia, but after a warm smile to both men, Otto came over to them and embraced his mother.

"Make sure you pray before the battle, my son," Mathilda instructed.

"Of course, Mother."

"And keep an eye on your father. I am not sure he should still be heading into battle at his age. Look after him."

"Yes, Mother."

"And, Otto..."

Otto looked resigned. "Yes, Mother?"

Mathilda's eyes filled with tears as she tried to smile on her son. "Look after yourself. Do not do anything reckless. I want you to come back to me on that horse, not..." Eadgyth's heart melted as she watched them, wondering how she could ever have suspected Mathilda of secretly hoping for Otto's death.

Otto swept his mother into another hug. "Do not worry, Mother. I have every intention of returning."

A tug on his cloak made Otto look down to where Liudolf was grinning cheekily up at him. Otto laughed as he picked up his son. "You take good care of your mother and grandmother, young man. I hope that is clear."

In reply Liudolf gleefully grabbed hold of a handful of his father's hair. Otto kissed him before setting him down on the ground again and stroking the hair of Liutgarde who was in her nurse's arms. He stared intently at his children a moment or two longer before turning to Eadgyth.

Eadgyth tried very hard to smile. Otto in his mail shirt, his dark hair shifting in the breeze looked more handsome than ever. Otto smiled back. "I think you understand now what I said to you on the day of Liudolf's birth."

"Yes, I do."

"Such a pity you did not realise it then and showed a little more sympathy for my anxieties," Otto said in a martyred tone.

Eadgyth couldn't help laughing at that and Otto's smile widened. "That is better. That is the beautiful smile I wanted to see before I left."

"Oh, Otto. Just be careful. Please," Eadgyth begged, putting her arms tightly around him.

Otto gave her a long kiss, which he broke off only when a horn sounded. The army was ready to depart. "Farewell, my sweet," he murmured. "I will see you soon, I am sure of it."

"May God send you victory, my dearest love," Eadgyth replied, somehow keeping back the tears.

With no more words Otto strode away, swinging himself up into his saddle. With a last wave he urged his horse to his father's side. Eadgyth picked up Liudolf and held him close as she watched them trot briskly away. The tears she was unable to prevent springing to her eyes blurred her last sight of Otto. Impatiently she wiped them away, but he was gone. The thud of the horses' hooves was almost drowned by the thud of her heart. Almost she cried aloud at the terrible fear he was gone from her forever.

∞∞∞

The days passed slowly. Henry sent frequent messengers, but there was no news of importance. Eadgyth recovered her affection for Mathilda, remembering how she had cared for her during her confinements. But her concerns resurfaced when she arrived one day in the hall shortly before noon to find young Henry and Mathilda in an intense discussion with a young priest. There was nothing unusual in that so she was puzzled when the three abruptly broke off their conversation.

"Eadgyth!" Mathilda exclaimed, her usual warm smile absent. "I had expected you to be longer at the church."

Taken aback by her curt manner, Eadgyth looked at the other two. The priest was a stranger to her, although as he smoothed the fringe of dark hair encircling his head, she wondered if she had met him before. Certainly there seemed something familiar about him. As Eadgyth nodded to him in greeting, his thin lips curved into a slight smile. Irrationally she disliked him on sight.

"May I present Father Frederick," Mathilda put in. "He is a very fine chaplain from one of the ducal households."

"I am honoured to meet you, my lady," Father Frederick said. "Indeed it is truly an honour to meet a descendent of so illustrious a saint as Saint Oswald."

The words sounded sincere, but none the less Eadgyth felt sure he was mocking her. "Greetings, Father," she replied properly.

"Shall we dine now, Mother," Henry said, as others also entered the hall.

Mathilda nodded and Henry made his way towards the great table. In the absence of the other men, it would be Henry who would sit at the centre of the dais. He paused as he got there, staring at the elaborately carved chair where his father usually sat.

"Is all well, Henry?" Eadgyth asked, surprised by the way he was running his hands reverently over the arms of the chair.

He gave her a startled look. "Of course, Sister. Why would it not be?"

Eadgyth looked back to where Mathilda and Father Frederick were still talking. Always she had been amused by the grand way Henry presided over everyone in his father's absence, but this day she could find nothing to make her smile. She shivered as Henry sat down on the royal throne, fearing she was seeing a portent of the future.

The entrance of Liudolf saved her from having to reply, her face lighting up into a smile as the little boy hurled himself exuberantly into her arms.

"Make your bow to your grandmother and Aunt Hedwig," Eadgyth instructed.

Beaming with pride Liudolf did exactly that, but flung his arms around Henry's leg, grinning up at his uncle. Eadgyth smiled, waiting for Henry to swing him into the air in his usual manner.

"Should he not also bow to me while I sit in this chair?" Henry enquired in a polite tone.

Eadgyth flushed. He was right in a fashion, but given the King was far more likely to encourage Liudolf to climb all over him than bow, she found Henry's words presumptuous.

"Henry, he's just a baby," Hedwig said, pulling her nephew onto her knee. "You cannot expect him to know the proper protocols."

"Then he should learn them," Henry replied.

∞∞∞

Quedlinburg seemed a strange, silent place with so many of the men gone. Eadgyth did not speak of her fears to Mathilda, but by the shadows under her eyes, she guessed her mother-in-law had many of her own. As days went by even Hedwig's determined cheerfulness faded.

It was some weeks after the army departed, soon after noon, when Henry's latest messenger brought the news they were dreading. He bowed before them. "My ladies, I bear a message from King Henry. He states 'My dearest Mathilda, I send greetings from Riade, where we are camped this night. We have had word that the Magyar forces are besieging a town a short distance away. We will launch our attack in the morn. I know you will lend your prayers for our victory and God willing, I will soon report our triumph. Your loving husband, Henry, Duke of Saxony, King of Germany.'"

Hedwig cried out, clamping one hand over her mouth, while putting her other arm around Mathilda.

"When did you leave the king?" Eadgyth asked hoarsely.

"Last night, my lady."

Eadgyth and Mathilda stared at each other. "The battle may be taking place this very moment," Mathilda said.

"Otto will be fighting or he may be injured, lying somewhere I cannot care for him." Eadgyth stared into space, imagining spears and arrows swooping through the air, as Otto moved forward, his shield raised in an attempt to protect himself. "He may be…" Unable to finish, she ran from the room and flung herself on her knees before the altar in the church.

As news spread, many joined her and the monks chanted soft prayers. Eadgyth did not move as she mouthed frantic prayer after prayer to Saint Oswald and to Saint Maurice, the soldier saint Otto had a particular devotion to. Desperately she tried not to think the worst.

A gentle arm around her shoulders made her start and she looked into Matilda's drawn face. Fear clutched Eadgyth afresh. "Has there been any news?"

"No, my child. I think we cannot expect any news before the morning at the earliest. But you have knelt here for hours. Come."

Eadgyth felt so stiff she could barely move as she struggled to her feet.

"And you are frozen. You need some food. Otto will not be happy to find you have made yourself ill while he has been away."

But Eadgyth was not fooled by Mathilda's brisk tone. At the church door she was surprised to find night was falling. She looked down, realising she was standing on the very spot she and Otto had been joined as husband and wife. Pain built up in her chest as she feared they might this day have been brutally torn apart.

"The battle will be over now, at least for this night," Eadgyth said, staring up at the moon. "Whether they are victorious or defeated, it is over. Otto may already be dead and I know nothing of it." Eadgyth sank her head into her hands. "If Otto is slain, I do not know how I will bear it."

Eadgyth waited for Mathilda's inevitable speech on how it would be her duty to bear it as God's will, but Mathilda slipped an arm around her shoulders. "I do not know how I will bear it either," she replied. She shook her head. "Oh, we are being foolish. The troops are the finest in the land. Otto and Henry will be well defended."

Eadgyth half smiled. "That may be true, but you know neither Henry nor Otto are the type of men to hide behind their troops."

"I know." Mathilda pulled her closer. "All we can do is wait and pray that the news will be good."

"I do not think I will sleep this night," Eadgyth muttered.

"Nor I," Mathilda replied. "But we must try. We may need all our strength these next days, although hopefully just for preparing the most magnificent of victory celebrations."

∞∞∞

As she had suspected, she slept little. Quedlinburg was full of so many memories. In her bedchamber, she reminisced of passionate nights in Otto's arms, wondering if she would ever know such joy again. It was torture to lie there alone, not knowing what state he was in. He could be lying grievously wounded, or he might be kneeling beside his father or a close companion, grief struck as he watched them struggle for breath. She hardly dared hope he was sat by a fire, a drink in his hands, raucously celebrating a victory.

When she encountered Mathilda in the hall the next day it was obvious her mother-in-law too had not slept.

"I suppose there is no news yet?" Eadgyth asked breathlessly.

"No. I left orders that if a messenger came I was to be notified, no matter what the hour."

"Henry and Otto will know how anxious we are. I am sure a message will reach us today," Eadgyth said, concerned by Mathilda's pallor.

"I hope so," Mathilda replied. Both of them were struck by the same thoughts that Henry and Otto might be in no state to send messages, but neither spoke them out loud.

The day passed as slowly as the night. Mathilda, Eadgyth and Hedwig sat silently together in the hall, some stitching on their laps that none payed any attention to. Every time someone entered, they looked up sharply.

At midday Mathilda wearily called for some food to be brought to the table. As young Henry took his place as the highest ranking man, Eadgyth had no idea how she was meant to eat, terrified the boy might soon permanently occupy the most prominent position.

Father Frederick began the prayers, beginning with some words for the King's victory. Putting her dislike of the man to one side, Eadgyth repeated his words in her mind, feeling as if she had never prayed so earnestly. The Priest had not quite finished when they heard a clatter of boots running up the steps. Eadgyth froze and reached for the hands of Mathilda and Hedwig, all three holding their breath. Even before the man entered, they knew it would be a messenger.

The man was covered in dust from the ride, but came quickly towards them and bowed. "My ladies, be of good cheer, this is a great day for Germany. The Magyars have retreated."

Chapter five

"The King? My son? How did you leave them?" Mathilda asked.

"Both in excellent spirits, my lady."

"Uninjured?" Eadgyth asked faintly.

"No more than a bruise or two, nothing to cause any concern, my lady. Indeed there have been few deaths. The Magyar forces were besieging one of our towns. King Henry ordered in some foot soldiers and just a few horsemen. The heathens assumed that was our entire force and expected an easy fight. But then King Henry himself led the charge of the main army. It did not last long."

"And Prince Otto?" Eadgyth asked.

"He led one flank of the army, my lady. The fighting was brief, but it was fierce. Prince Otto was in the thick of it and has won much praise."

"What of my brother, Lord Thankmar?" Hedwig asked, leaving Eadgyth ashamed she had scarcely given him a moment's thought while the men had been away.

"He was part of the first attack. He too has won much praise."

"I suppose the men celebrated well last night," Eadgyth commented, remembering her sleepless night now with a smile.

"Preparations were well under way when I left, my lady."

"And there will be another celebration when they return," Mathilda said, the drawn look vanished from her face. She put her arms around her daughter and Eadgyth, smiling in delight. Eadgyth looked around the hall seeing in her mind the lavish celebrations, hardly able to wait for Otto to return. But her joyful expression faded as she caught the eye of young Henry, shocked to see his face looking blank. Otto was always affectionate with his younger brother and although Eadgyth considered him somewhat overindulged, she too was fond of the boy. She wondered what ambitions had been encouraged to cause him to display so little joy in the victory of his father and older brothers.

∞ ∞ ∞

There was no immediate reunion. Henry was determined to leave the border secure and spent some weeks patrolling the defences, ensuring there were enough men stationed to repel any further attacks. Eventually he was satisfied and sent word he would soon be returning.

Eadgyth was certain the hall had never looked so festive as they prepared to welcome them back. Fresh banners hung from the ceilings, while the finest foods were heaped onto the table. Serving men at the palace had spent days preparing roasted meats flavoured with spices, grilled fish, cakes and pastries a plenty, all stuffed with nuts, fruits and honey. Young Henry was sitting back in his accustomed place, the seat at the centre of the dais and the one next to it remaining empty as they awaited the return of their rightful occupants. Bruno had been summoned back to Quedlinburg for the celebrations to the delight of his mother, who was overjoyed at having so many of her children with her again. Hedwig poured out cups of the costliest wine, smiling as Eadgyth entered, leading Liudolf and Liutgarde by the hand.

"You look prettier than ever, my dear," Mathilda commented.

Eadgyth had dressed in a fine blue kirtle, embroidered in a silver thread over a pale tunic. Although her head was covered, in the excitement strands of fair hair had escaped to frame a face lit by a radiant smile. Her cheeks flushed pink with the compliment, but she made no reply as the horns rang out and Henry, holding the holy lance, entered the room with Otto just a step behind him.

Joy surged in her and she barely waited for Henry to reach Mathilda before darting forward and throwing herself into Otto's arms. He swung her off her feet, to much laughter and cheers from the men.

"Oh, Otto, we have heard how well you have done. I am so proud of you," Eadgyth whispered, as she clung to him.

"We showed them, did we not, my boy?" Henry exclaimed, a cup already in his hand. "The Magyar cowards could not face us for long before they turned and ran."

"Yes, Father. It was a splendid victory indeed."

"At the end the men hailed me as emperor," Henry said proudly.

"Emperor?" Mathilda arched her eyebrows. "Henry, I trust you are not thinking of campaigning towards Rome."

Henry laughed. "No, my dear. Germany more than satisfies me. Although, it would not surprise me if one of my line is one day proclaimed Emperor of the Romans."

Mathilda shook her head. "Only Franks, especially those of the line of Charles the Great, are likely to be emperor."

"Well, perhaps, my dear. But no one should underestimate us Saxons. The Magyars did, but they regret it now."

"I wish I had been with you," young Henry put in.

"Another year or two, my son, if you keep applying yourself to your training," Henry replied, putting his arms around his namesake. He embraced Bruno, before pretending to stop and stare at the other boy present. "Who can this young man be? He has a look of my grandson, but I had not thought he was so big."

Liudolf launched himself forward. "Grandfather! Father!"

Otto laughed and swept his son high in the air to the amusement of everyone around him. He kept him in his arms, pulling Eadgyth and Liutgarde to him as well. Eadgyth held him tightly, overjoyed they were all together again.

∞∞∞

The celebrations went on for several days, but eventually the nobility drifted away to their own lands. Eadgyth was in the courtyard with Henry and Mathilda to bid farewell to Arnulf of Bavaria. Gilbert of Lotharingia was also nearby with members of his entourage, waiting to make their departure.

"I thank you most heartily for your hospitality, my lady," Arnulf said, bowing before Mathilda. "I trust we will meet again before long."

"I hope so, Arnulf," Henry replied.

Eadgyth watched them in fascination. Otto had told her of the bitter quarrel which had once raged between Henry and Arnulf, with Arnulf proclaiming himself king even after the Saxons and Franks had chosen Henry. Yet the friendship now between them seemed genuine.

Arnulf stared for a moment at Otto. He was stood with Duke Hermann of Swabia, talking amicably with a group of Swabian men who were hanging off Otto's every word. "That boy of yours is very fine. He has a way with the men I have rarely seen in one so young."

"I agree," Henry replied. "Otto has always been a fine warrior, but what was the mere promise of leadership in our Slavic campaign has blossomed during this one."

"I hear he is to be your heir for Germany as well as Saxony."

"That is certainly my intention, but of course the nobility must agree."

Arnulf smiled. "I cannot imagine any contesting it after the leadership all have witnessed."

Henry gave him a sideways glance. "Would you support him?"

"Indeed I would, although I do not know why you think I would outlive you."

"Who can tell in such matters? But your support is valued indeed, by both myself and my son. Farewell, my friend. A safe journey to you."

Arnulf nodded and bowed once again. As he made his way to his horse, he stopped to talk to Otto.

"Henry, Otto is not your only son," Mathilda said. "You should not be too hasty in deciding the succession. You do not yet know what kind of a man young Henry will be."

"I am sure young Henry will be a fine one," the King replied. "But he will find it hard to match Otto for skill and surely impossible for experience."

Gilbert glanced over. "I trust it will not just be the word of Bavaria which decides the succession," he said. "I am not yet convinced. Just because I am wed to your daughter does not mean you should take the support of Lotharingia for granted. It was not so long ago that we favoured West Francia and might again if we are shut out of such important decisions. My dearest brother, Father Frederick, believes we must consider God's will in the matter."

Eadgyth started in surprise, suddenly realising why Father Frederick looked so familiar. Seeing him stood with Gilbert, the resemblance was even more obvious. The Priest was already making her uneasy. Now knowing how well connected he was, she felt more concerned than ever.

"Exactly," Mathilda said eagerly. "Henry was born a king's son. Otto was not. I feel it is God's will that Henry should rule."

The King raised his eyebrows. "I was not born a king's son nor ever became one. Was it not God's will that I should rule?"

Henry did not wait for an answer before moving away to talk quietly with Gilbert. Eadgyth stared accusingly at Mathilda, who flushed uncomfortably. "I do not want to quarrel with you, Eadgyth, but I truly believe young Henry is God's choice." She gestured at the Priest who was still watching them with a slight smile. "It seems many will agree with me."

"I do not want a quarrel either," Eadgyth replied. "Indeed, after all the kindness you have shown me since I arrived in this land, it would be poor of me to do so. But I cannot agree with you on this. I hope Henry lives for many years yet, but when the time comes to him as must come to all men, there can be no better choice than Otto to succeed him."

∞∞∞

Otto and Eadgyth too departed Quedlinburg not long after the Bavarians. Eadgyth was pleased to be returning to Magdeburg, although she worried it might have been better for Otto to remain at Henry's side. As they entered the gates of Magdeburg she looked at Otto, who had taken Liudolf onto his horse, both of them in great spirits. She hated the thought of shattering that happiness.

At the palace he put his arms around her. "You have been very quiet, my sweet. What ails you? I thought you would be overjoyed to return here."

"I am," Eadgyth replied. "Otto, I would be glad to stretch my legs a while after the ride. Will you walk with me by the river?"

"Of course."

Hand in hand they headed down to the river bank. It was as busy as ever with vessels laden with goods and people. Eadgyth looked out over it, trying to find the words she needed to talk to Otto.

"No secrets, Eadgyth. That is what we agreed upon, remember?"

Eadgyth smiled. "I know. But it is hard to find the words, when I fear I will be speaking ill of your mother."

"My mother? How has she upset you?"

"Oh no, Otto. She has always been kind to me. I love her as my own mother. But… I have to tell you this. She is pushing young Henry forward as your father's successor."

"I know," Otto replied.

Eadgyth stared at him. "You know?"

"Her favour is obvious," Otto said with a wry smile.

"Are you not concerned?"

Otto stared over the river, a slight frown creasing his forehead. "It will not be her decision. The nobles and the churchmen will decide. The assumption among them at the moment is that I will succeed, although nothing formal has been decided. Henry is far too young to be even considered."

"He is now, but your father will likely reign for some years yet. Henry could be a man by then.

"Perhaps. My father is not as strong as once he was, although I hope he will live for some time. If young Henry is a man by then, well I shall just have to be the better man."

Eadgyth smiled proudly. "I have no doubt you will be the better man. But why is your mother so opposed to you? I know she talks of God's will, but I sense it is more than that. Is it because of your illegitimate son?"

Otto glanced down, raising his eyebrows at Eadgyth mentioning the boy they had last spoken of on their wedding night. "Perhaps. She was certainly not impressed." His smile slipped. "She spoke such words on the day she found out, as cannot be unsaid. I know I greatly disappointed her."

Eadgyth put her arms around him, trying to ease the hurt. "My love, as we have no secrets, may I ask you something? Do you ever see the boy?"

"Yes, I see him when I am in the North. He is handsome and intelligent. A boy to be proud of."

"I see."

"Eadgyth, I would do almost anything to make you happy, but I will not forget my son. He could never take Liudolf's place, but he is still my son. I am sorry if this upsets you. My mother's disgust was hard to bear, but it would be far worse to lose your devotion."

Eadgyth shook her head. "You never will and it does not upset me. It would upset me more if you had forgotten him. A father should never forget his children."

"Thank you, my sweet." He tightened his arms around her. "I truly want to be a man worthy of you. I want to be a man worthy of this land."

Eadgyth laughed. "Do not be foolish, Otto. Of course you are more than worthy of me. I am sure soon everyone will know how worthy you are to be king. Even your mother and Gilbert. Even that peculiar priest brother of his."

"Father Frederick?" Otto asked, sounding surprised. "His opinions will not count for much. It is the bishops and archbishops I need to convince, but I am not anticipating many detractors amongst the clergy. Gilbert has always been tricky and of course Eberhard of Franconia has his own claims, but I believe old Arnulf will stand with me."

"What of the Duke of Swabia?" Eadgyth asked.

Otto grinned. "Hermann? I have fought alongside him on many an occasion, but during this campaign I got to know him better. We have become good friends and I am more confident of his support than any other."

Chapter six

Over the next couple of years Henry pushed at the borders in an effort to increase the security of his realm. Eadgyth for the most part remained at Magdeburg, accepting with resignation each time Otto was summoned away. While she never lost her fear when they were apart, the army faced little more than skirmishes and it was not long before they were joyfully reunited.

When Otto was needed to oversee matters in different parts of the realm, Eadgyth often accompanied him. She was even more acutely aware of the need to show the various nobles they met what a worthy king Otto would make. So she dressed finely, greeting the nobles with a gracious smile, never forgetting to extend affectionate greetings to the man's wife and children. They were welcomed everywhere as they moved into the Rhineland to be greeted by Hermann of Swabia.

She watched as Hermann bowed respectfully to Otto, before taking him by the hands. The smile on his face, as he greeted Otto, was warmer than any other man they had encountered.

"Welcome to you too, my lady," he said, bowing even deeper to her. "Swabia is honoured by your presence."

Eadgyth extended her hand for him to kiss. "Thank you, my lord. I am delighted to be here. Swabia appears a fair land indeed." Eadgyth meant those words. The steeply wooded hills they had passed through had struck her with their majestic beauty.

Hermann looked pleased as he gestured to his residence.

"Come rest yourselves after your journey and tell me your news. It seems an age since we were last together after our victory over the Magyars."

Otto nodded. "Too long, my friend."

Eadgyth smiled at the look which passed between the two men. It was one which summed up all the camaraderie of battle companions. Hermann was considerably older than Otto and he seemed unafraid to offer him advice, but his words were sensible. She suspected this friendship would become increasingly important to Otto.

"May I present my wife, Lady Regelind," Hermann said as they stepped into the hall. After the bright sunlight, it took a few moments to become accustomed to the shadowy hall.

Otto bowed over the lady's hand. "I am delighted to meet you again, my lady."

"I am surprised you remember me, my lord," the lady said with a warm smile. "You were still a boy last time we met."

"How could I forget?" Otto replied.

Eadgyth too smiled as Regelind turned to her. She appeared to be several years older than her husband, although still very attractive.

"She was the widow of the previous duke," Otto told Eadgyth, as they changed out of their travel stained clothes for the feast Hermann and Regelind were hosting for them. "Many in Swabia were not happy when my father appointed Hermann as the duke. He married Lady Regelind to appease them." Otto grinned. "She was quite a beauty, so I do not suppose he found it any hardship."

"Do they have children?"

"An infant daughter, I believe." Otto fastened a cloak with a jewelled pin. "Regelind has several children from her first marriage. She is well connected. One of her daughters is married to the King of Burgundy."

"I suppose Hermann too enjoys those connections through her," Eadgyth commented.

"Exactly," Otto replied. "Do not let his unassuming manner

fool you. Hermann is very powerful. He would make a formidable foe."

"But an important friend," Eadgyth replied, as they returned to the hall. "Of course I too have a connection with Burgundy through my sister."

Otto shook his head. "Everyone seems to be better connected than me."

∞∞∞

"With such a wife as you, I do not think I stand any chance of being chosen as King of Germany," Otto commented that night when he returned to their chamber after a lively evening.

Eadgyth looked at him in alarm, praying she had done nothing to offend Hermann. "Why? What have I done wrong?"

"Nothing, my sweet. Hermann has spent the entire night so praising your manner and wisdom that he has all but proclaimed he wants you on the throne!"

Eadgyth shook her head in exasperation. "Do not be foolish, Otto. Now tell me truly, am I helping you?"

Exuberantly Otto scooped her up in his arms. "Helping me? My love, you have the whole of Swabia eating out of your hand. Everyone here adores you. You behave with such grace, but with a true warmth so all present have felt valued. You are truly the greatest of support."

"You exaggerate."

"Nonsense. Why, you even made Lady Regelind's pompous son-in-law, Werner believe he was the most interesting man in the land. How did you do that? I could not have born to speak with him for so long!"

Eadgyth laughed. In truth it had been a long night.

∞∞∞

After some pleasant weeks in Swabia, they returned from that tour by way of Quedlinburg, where they found Henry making plans to invade Denmark. Young Henry was overjoyed, as at last his father had agreed he could join the fight.

"I thought I would place him with your troops, Otto, if that has your agreement," Henry told him.

"Of course, Father."

"I want to fight alongside you, Father," young Henry cried.

"That might be more appropriate," Mathilda said.

But Henry shook his head. "Otto takes more of a lead now. He is still under my command, of course, but increasingly I am allowing Otto to make the decisions. Henry will see more action at his side."

Young Henry scowled and Otto looked at him with amusement. "Are you skilled enough to fight with me, Brother? Shall we see?" He drew his sword.

The boy's eyes lit up and eagerly he seized the sword his father had recently presented to him, following Otto into the courtyard.

Henry looked on with pride as their swords clashed, but Eadgyth bit her lip. "Do not look so concerned, my dear. Otto is very skilled. He will not hurt his brother."

Eadgyth did not say that this was not what was worrying her. She could see Otto was skilled enough to fight without bloodshed, but she was not so sure about young Henry. She suspected his desire to triumph over his older brother would mean he would care little if he hurt him. She almost cried out as the tip of Henry's sword slashed towards Otto's face. But Otto blocked it with a force which pushed the sword from Henry's hand. Swiftly he brought his own sword to his brother's throat.

"My victory this time, Brother." Henry scowled again, but Otto ruffled his head. "You fight well. I am glad you will be on our side."

Later he confided in Eadgyth. "God help me with that young hot head in my troops. If any harm befalls him, my mother will likely never forgive me."

"Perhaps you should let him fight alongside your father."

Otto shrugged. "Perhaps, but managing the young fools in their first fight is part of leading the men. I need to prove I can do it."

∞∞∞

As had become her custom, Eadgyth returned to Magdeburg while Otto was away, but as soon as she heard Henry was returning in victory, she journeyed joyfully to join the court which was in residence at Henry's palace of Memleben.

But from the moment of her arrival, she was unnerved by the undercurrent of tension, despite the celebrations. Young Henry was strutting around as a battle hero, to the great pride of his mother and the amusement of his father and Thankmar. Otto scowled at him, an expression which quickly cleared from his face as he saw Eadgyth had arrived.

"My mother did not fete me as much after my first campaign," Otto commented, once they were finally able to be alone. "Not even before Thankmar told her about the child."

Eadgyth had not realised it was Thankmar who had broken the news, although upon reflection, she was not surprised. She put her arms around him, sensing a considerable hurt in how Mathilda favoured Henry. "How did Henry do?" she asked.

Otto shrugged. "Oh, he managed well enough." He grinned reluctantly, his natural fairness winning through. "No, he did well and I have told him that. Why else do you think he is acting like he won the campaign singlehandedly? He was reckless, of course, but brave and skilled."

Eadgyth said nothing more as she dressed finely for the celebrations. She hated tension in the family and so took the time to add her praise to both young Henry and Thankmar as the festivities got underway.

Already merry on the ale, the King got to his feet to thank the men. "And this campaign was memorable for another reason. My dear son, Henry became truly a man and proved himself a fine warrior. No father could be prouder." The men thumped the table in agreement with loud cheers. Eadgyth was pleased to see Otto joining in the tribute, clapping his young brother on his shoulders. Young Henry's smile spread wider than ever, but his father had not finished. "To one more than any other do we owe this victory. My fine son, Otto. In every battle your ability to lead grows stronger. Soon there will be no man who can call himself your equal."

The hall descended into uproar, with thumps and cheers rattling the platters. Eadgyth's heart swelled with pride at this sign of adoration from the men. She flung her arms around him. "I am so proud of you," she whispered, pressing her lips passionately against his. At this there were more cheers and even a few whistles.

Grinning, Otto also stood. "Father, I thank you for your words. Coming from a king and warrior as fine as you, they are truly the highest of praise. My brothers and I cannot fail to be skilled, when we have had the good fortune to call such a man as you, Father."

With tears in his eyes Henry embraced Otto. Eadgyth smiled mistily, hoping the tension could be put aside.

But her hopes were to be in vain. The next day the family gathered to bid farewell to Thankmar who was returning to the lands he held. Although Eadgyth, Mathilda and the other ladies of the court had retired at the usual time, the men had continued feasting late into the night and all of them appeared somewhat blurry eyed that morning. Mathilda swept in, her sharp gestures and clipped words making it obvious she was not in the best of moods.

"You should not have spoken those words, Henry," she said. "You virtually proclaimed Otto as your heir."

"My dear, must we discuss this now? Otto is the one I intend as my heir."

"You are being too hasty, Henry. There is no need to decide

this now."

Henry shook his head wearily. "There is a need. I have reached an age when God could call me at any time. It is the nobles who will make the final decision."

"You should at least confirm you consider dear Henry worthy to be your heir. Indeed I consider none more worthy than the one who bears your name. I have spoken at great length on this with a fine priest, Gilbert's brother, Frederick. He agrees that Henry, as the oldest son born in the purple, would be the best choice."

Eadgyth looked in concern at Otto, whose face was growing white with anger. "Damn it, Mother, I have served Father loyally for years. I have been ever a dutiful son, yet it is not good enough for you. Why do you consider me to be so unworthy?"

"I will not discuss my reasons, Otto. I love you very much, but your behaviour confirmed to me that you are not suitable to reign over this land and it is God's will for Henry to one day assume the throne." Mathilda's voice was calm and she displayed no distress at Otto's anger.

Thankmar cracked a laugh. "She is referring to your bastard, my dear brother."

There was an instant silence as all eyes went to Eadgyth. She met them defiantly, determined to show no reaction.

"Thankmar!" Henry snapped.

Otto put his arms protectively around Eadgyth. "You can all stop looking at Eadgyth like that. She has long known about the boy. And, Mother, unlike you, she accepted the knowledge without judgement or condemnation."

"I am glad this was not a shock to dear Eadgyth," Henry said. "Thankmar, you had no right to say such a thing. Apologise immediately to Otto and Eadgyth." Thankmar flushed and looked down, muttering something unintelligible. "Mathilda, since the matter has been raised, I must inform you that the existence of such a boy will have no bearing on the decision of the nobles. It is hardly uncommon behaviour for a young man and I do not know why you expect better from young Henry."

Mathilda flushed angrily. "Henry is truly devout. You should not cast aspersions on your own son with no cause."

Otto's face remained unchanged, but Eadgyth saw his eyes flick to Thankmar, apparently forgetting his anger for a moment or two. She was intrigued by the glance which passed between them, and longed to ask exactly what young Henry had got up to during the campaign.

The King's lips also twitched slightly. "I am sure you are right, my dear. My son, forgive me if I have said anything unjust."

Young Henry's blue eyes were clear and innocent looking as he nodded to his father, but there was a distinct smirk to the shape of his mouth.

Otto shook his head, a faint spark of humour remaining in his face. "Father, this tension helps no one. I think the time has come to formalise the succession. If you intend to name me your heir to all or part of the realm, the matter should be settled."

Henry was nodding, but Mathilda glared at her eldest son. "I see, the truth is now out. He is eager to be king. Otto longs for your death."

Chapter seven

The sudden silence descended again and Otto's fingers dug into Eadgyth's shoulder as he tensed. She bit her lip to stop the angry words escaping as she longed to defend him to his family. Young Henry and Thankmar were trying to conceal grins, although Hedwig shook her head at her mother.

"I see," Otto replied calmly. "You regard me as a traitor." He gave his father a slight bow. "Do as you will, Father. Name whoever you choose as your heir. Thankmar is not the only one departing Memleben this day. Eadgyth and I are also leaving. Farewell."

Otto strode from the room, pulling Eadgyth with him. In his agitation he moved quickly and she had to almost run to prevent herself from being pulled over. The courtyard was full of horses waiting for Thankmar and his entourage. Otto came to an abrupt stop, eying the horses speculatively.

"Perhaps we should just steal a couple of those and ride away," he commented.

Eadgyth put her arms around him. "My dearest, I do not think your mother meant those words. How can she? Everyone knows how you support your father."

"Do they or am I just furthering my own interests?"

"Otto." Eadgyth shook her head. "Do not talk this nonsense to me. I know where your loyalties lie."

Otto half smiled. "Thank you, my sweet." He kissed the top of her head. "I do not know what I would do without your support."

"Otto," came Henry's voice. "Do not do anything foolish. You cannot leave this day. Poor Eadgyth has only just arrived. You cannot expect her to ride away again already."

Otto turned to face his father, straightening his shoulders. "Father, I will swear any oath of loyalty you wish me to. I know at times it must have appeared as if I did not appreciate your guidance and strained against the restrictions you placed on me, but I have never once wished for your death."

"Perhaps at times my guidance may have seemed too strict." Henry gave Eadgyth an awkward glance. "I know once I ordered you into a situation you had no wish for."

Otto too glanced at Eadgyth, his face lightening. "Father, you cannot possibly believe I bear any grudge for that."

Henry laughed. "Well, I did think you had become quickly reconciled to that situation."

Otto grinned as he put his arm around Eadgyth. "Very much so! Indeed Father, I bear no grudge for any of your guidance. Young fools never want to listen to their fathers, but I am old enough now to understand your wisdom in everything. Truly, I have never wished for your death."

"Oh, I know that, Otto," Henry replied. "And so does your mother. Her words were foolish ones spoken in the moment. She will apologise. Please do not leave this day."

Otto looked questioningly at Eadgyth. "My dearest, I will support whatever you wish," she said. "But I did just arrive here yesterday. I would be glad not to have so long a ride again just yet."

Otto nodded. "Very well, but Father, what of the succession? The matter needs to be decided."

"I know. I will hold a synod in the spring to formalise the arrangements. I intend for you to inherit the whole realm. My personal lands will be divided among Thankmar, Henry and Bruno, but you are to be Duke of Saxony and, if the nobles agree, King of Germany."

Otto raised his eyebrows. "Definitely no realm at all for

young Henry?"

"No. I truly believe it is for the best if this land stands together under one ruler - you. Dividing it will only weaken it. However I hope you will not forget Henry is a king's son. If he serves you well, I would want you to reward him with a high position."

Otto nodded and embraced his father. "You do me a great honour, Father. I will be proud to one day be King of Germany, but when that day comes, it will be a sorrowful one."

Henry smiled. "Not too sorrowful, my boy. I have lived a long life. My dear Eadgyth, can I apologise again for Thankmar's words. I am glad it was not a shock for you today and hope the shock was not too great when you did learn of the child."

Eadgyth smiled back. "It was a surprise, but I learnt the truth long ago. Otto told me on our wedding night."

"Your wedding night?" Henry gave Otto an incredulous look. "Otto, how have you managed to convince this excellent young woman to regard you with such devotion?"

Otto grinned sheepishly. "I know not, Father. I am well aware of my good fortune."

"You are indeed fortunate. Guard that fortune well. The devoted loyalty of a wife is one of the greatest assets a king can possess."

Thankmar came out of the palace at that moment accompanied by young Henry and Hedwig. The three were deep in a conversation which stopped uncertainly as they saw Otto. The King beckoned them over.

"You all know my plans for the succession, but I will repeat them so there can be no misunderstanding. Otto is the heir to Saxony and with the blessing of the nobles, the entire realm. There are many fine lands for both of you. If you wish for more, serve Otto well once he is king. There is no reason you cannot both rise to considerable influence."

"I know all this, Father," Thankmar replied. He looked at Otto. "Farewell, Brother. Yes, I know you are angry with me."

"Do you blame me?" replied Otto, but he embraced his

brother. "We will not be parted in anger. Godspeed Thankmar, until we meet again."

Thankmar gave a sketchy bow to Eadgyth and she murmured her farewells, but her eyes were fixed on young Henry. In spite of some meaningful looks from Hedwig, he had made no response to his father's commands. Instead he was scowling at the ground. Eadgyth shuddered as she sensed the anger in him, realising the casual affection between him and Otto was now rarely seen. As Hedwig put a hand under his arm to follow the King towards Thankmar's horse, Eadgyth stared thoughtfully after them.

"Otto, we have always agreed no secrets, have we not?"

Otto sighed. "Eadgyth, when my father told me I was to be married, I was not happy. Yes, I begged him to delay a while and to choose a German bride for me. But you know I forgot all that the moment I set eyes on you."

Eadgyth laughed. "Really? I did not know you hoped for a German wife. But that was not what I was going to ask."

"What do you want to know?"

"What did young Henry get up to while he was on campaign?"

Otto grinned. "Such things as are not fit for your ears, my sweet." He looked after his younger brother. "Young fool, but I was no better than that at his age."

Eadgyth flung her arms around him. "Oh Otto, I love you so much."

Otto returned the embrace, but looked surprised. "Any special reason for saying that?"

"Yes, you could have destroyed your mother's pride in young Henry. Yet you chose not to, even as she condemned you. I hope Henry understands how fortunate he is to have such a brother."

Chapter eight

A tentative unity returned to the family. Mathilda took back her words wholeheartedly, assuring Otto they had been foolish ones, spoken in the heat of the moment. Otto accepted her apology and only Eadgyth knew how hurt he remained by her attitude. However the matter was not referred to again.

At Henry's request they returned to Memleben for Christmas with the children. Whatever her attitude towards Otto, Mathilda doted on her grandchildren and the celebrations were merry. All the same they were glad when they could get back to Magdeburg and a household free from any tension.

It was not until after Easter that Henry summoned the nobles to Erfurt to ratify the succession. At the age of five, Otto considered Liudolf old enough to witness the ceremony which would see him proclaimed as his father's heir and so the three of them, accompanied by an impressive entourage made their way to Erfurt and entered the hall in high spirits.

However Eadgyth's laughter caught in her throat at the sight of Henry's pale face, his hair greyer than she remembered. He seemed to have aged years since they last saw him at Christmas just a few months earlier. Although he greeted them delightedly, he did not rise from his chair and as he pulled Liudolf onto his lap, she noticed how his hands were shaking.

"Are you well, Father?" Otto asked after a shocked pause.

"I was ill after Christmas tide," Henry replied matter of factly. "The ride here has tired me."

"You were ill?" Otto asked. "Why was I not told?"

"There was no need to trouble you, my son. I already had your mother and Hedwig fussing over me. I did not need you two as well."

Otto half smiled. "I am sure you were well looked after, but I wish Mother had told me."

"She wanted to tell you, but I forbade it. Otto, I wanted you and Eadgyth to have a last carefree spring. I do not think it will be much longer before your responsibilities increase."

Otto sucked in his breath sharply. "Do not say such things, Father. It is not surprising the ride tired you if you have been unwell, but there is no need to talk like that."

"We are here to settle the succession," Henry commented with a smile.

Otto looked distressed. "I know, but…"

Henry smiled again. "You may be right. But whatever happens, after the synod you will have more responsibilities. Apart from anything else, I do not think I will lead the armies into battle again. That responsibility will be yours."

"Of course, Father."

"Now, no fussing, Otto. I cannot bear it." He kissed Liudolf on the head. "Take this young man to see your mother and I shall enjoy a talk with Eadgyth." As Otto and Liudolf left the room, Henry indicated a space next to himself on the bench. "Come sit with me, my daughter. And I do not use such a term lightly. I have come to regard you with as much affection as if you had indeed been my true daughter."

Eadgyth smiled. "I would say I regard you with as much affection as my own father, but the truth is I so rarely saw my father that you are many times dearer."

Henry looked pleased and patted her hand. "My dear, there is much I need to say and I know Otto will not listen. I do not think you will want to hear this either, but you have a rare good sense, so I think you will listen and remember what I say."

Eadgyth took hold of his hand and squeezed it, feeling a lump come to her throat.

"I am not well and I suspect I will not reign for much longer. Of course I cannot see the future. If in a few months' time I feel much recovered, this may seem a foolish talk. But whenever the time comes for Otto to rule, whether it is this year or any other, I need you to remember my words."

"I shall pray it is not this year or any year soon," Eadgyth said. "But I promise I will remember what you say."

Henry smiled reminiscently. "It is strange. When you and your sister arrived in my realm, I did not think Otto would choose you. Indeed at first I was not even certain I wanted Otto to choose you. I very much admired your charm, but I feared it concealed a cold heart. Of course, I soon realised I could not be more wrong." He gave her an apologetic look, but remembering herself back in those days Eadgyth could not condemn his words. "Your sister was so young and pretty, a little helpless perhaps, but I expected that to appeal to Otto's protective instincts. I thought your grace and assurance, while attractive to a man, would intimidate the boy Otto was then."

"I did not think he would choose me either," Eadgyth replied.

"But now I have seen how you charm everyone, I am not surprised Otto was the first to be won. I know the boy was motivated by his heart, not his mind when he chose you, but all the same his choice has proved to be a wise one. You have won many hearts and are popular with the nobles. Your presence at Otto's side enhances his own popularity."

Eadgyth blushed, flattered by his words but not sure what to say. "I am glad to be of use to Otto."

"I think Otto does not yet fully realise how valuable you are to him. But he will find out when he ascends the throne. My dear, Otto will not have an easy succession. He will struggle to win his brothers' support. I have tried to temper the ambitions of Thankmar and Henry, but I have not succeeded. Mathilda too will not be as supportive as Otto will need."

"Has she not accepted that Otto is your heir?"

"She no longer contests it, but I know it is not what she believes in her heart. She loves Otto and would do nothing to harm him, but she cannot support him wholeheartedly."

"And I can," Eadgyth whispered, suddenly understanding the conversation.

Henry nodded. "You can as no other and he will need that, my dear. On those days when it will feel as if half the nobles in the realm are against him, the loving and unquestioning support of a wife is a blessing like no other. Promise me, Eadgyth, you will always be that for my son."

Eadgyth looked at Henry, touched by the pleading expression in his eye. At twenty-three Otto was not excessively young to take the throne, but he was not old either. She understood why Henry felt concerned for the son, he feared he would soon be unable to protect. "I swear it by the bones of Saint Oswald. While there is breath in my body, Otto will always have my love and support."

Henry put his arms around her in a warm embrace. Eadgyth was shocked by how thin his arms felt and realised the truth in his words. With a burst of emotion she hugged him tightly.

"Thank you, my dear. I shall rest easy knowing Otto has that."

∞∞∞

The synod of the nobles and churchmen proved to be little more than a formality. Otto was popular among the nobles, due to his skill in war and the churchmen too were impressed with how well he had defended the realm from the barbarians, seeing him as a true champion of Christ. Appearing as he did in the church for prayers with his truly devout wife, a descendent of Saint Oswald no less and his sturdy young son, any youthful indiscretions were long since forgotten.

Soon after midday Eadgyth, Mathilda and Liudolf were summoned to the packed hall to witness the declaration. Magnificently dressed, Henry sat on a raised throne.

"I summon my noble son, Otto of Saxony," Henry proclaimed

formally, with no sign of any weakness in his manner. Quite the opposite, his bearing was every inch that of a powerful king.

Eadgyth could not have felt prouder as Otto came forward. He was finely dressed in a dark red tunic, edged in white. He knelt before his father and kissed his hand.

"Rise, my son," Henry said. "This day I name Otto my sole heir of the Duchy of Saxony and ask you to accept him as my successor as King of Germany. Who here will stand to support him?"

The question was a rhetorical one, but even so the deafening cheers made Eadgyth start. Liudolf clutched onto her hand, looking bewildered. She smiled down at him to reassure the child. As the cheers continued she looked around, warmed by the genuine enthusiasm. Arnulf of Bavaria and Hermann of Swabia, two powerful men who might have represented a threat, were both smiling. Eberhard of Franconia was another potential threat and although he did not look happy, his expression was resigned.

Eadgyth relaxed, thinking fear had made Henry paint too bleak a picture, until she saw the faces of those closest to her. Mathilda was smiling, but it did not seem to be a natural one. Neither Thankmar nor young Henry were even pretending to be happy. Although both were standing, their faces were devoid of any expression. Gilbert was not far away, the ever present Father Frederick beside him. Frederick whispered something to Gilbert, who stifled a laugh, as he glanced in their direction. Even Hedwig looked anxious. Of the family only Bruno and little Liudolf, who had now recovered from his shock, looked truly joyful. Both were jumping up and down in the excitement, cheering loudly.

Henry laid his hand on Otto's shoulder and gestured to one of his men. The man came forward bearing a fur lined cloak studded with jewels. Henry clasped the cloak around Otto's shoulders, before sitting down again on the throne. Otto sat beside him, now entitled to call himself king.

"My people, a great honour has been conferred upon me this day. As the one chosen by you and by the grace of God to rule over you, I command all to swear loyalty."

Eadgyth felt Mathilda flinch at Otto claiming God's will. She darted a look of anger towards her but there was no time to respond. With their faces still unsmiling, Thankmar and young Henry went forward to kneel before Otto. He quickly raised them.

"Brothers should not have to kneel, so long as their hearts be true," Otto proclaimed. He smiled benevolently at them, but his eyes were stern. Eadgyth's pride in Otto's regal manner could only increase, as she recognised how he was both honouring and warning his brothers and rivals.

They were followed by Bruno and Liudolf. As they knelt, Otto's face broke into the dazzling smile Eadgyth loved to see. He laid his hand on their heads in blessing before quickly raising them and taking hold of their hands. Eadgyth could not hear the words he spoke, but the affection was obvious and both boys came away grinning.

While not as dazzling, Otto's smile remained genuine as the remaining nobles came forward to kneel. From the murmured comments Eadgyth caught, it seemed Otto's warm yet noble bearing had impressed them all. To her relief everyone knelt willingly. Otto had been accepted.

At the end Henry and Otto rose together and resting on his son's arm, Henry led the way to where a feast had been arranged. Eadgyth smiled as they passed. Henry's face glowed with so much pride, no one noticed how frail he had become.

Chapter nine

"I am returning to Memleben," Henry announced the next day. "You should travel around the country. Ensure your presence is felt throughout Germany."

"I will ride with you to Memleben first," Otto replied. "Perhaps I should stay with you. I do not like to leave you while you are unwell."

"No, Otto. I shall have your mother looking after me. You will be sent for if you are needed." Henry smiled at Otto. "You must do what is right for your realm now, my son."

Otto nodded with some reluctance and beckoned Liudolf over. "I will be away for a while, Liudolf. But I have a most important task for you. You are to stay with your grandfather and I shall send for Liutgarde as well. You must ensure he is well entertained. Can I trust you with that, my boy?"

Liudolf beamed, leaning against Henry. "I love staying with Grandfather."

Henry ruffled his grandson's head, looking as delighted as Liudolf. "Excellent. You will certainly leave me in safe hands, Otto."

Otto looked at Eadgyth. "I know you do not like to leave the children for too long, my sweet, but-"

"Of course I will come with you, Otto," Eadgyth interrupted. She smiled at Henry, letting him know her promise would be kept.

∞∞∞

After leaving Memleben, Eadgyth and Otto made a leisurely way to Bavaria, almost as far as the mountains. The meadows were a riot of spring flowers, enchanting Eadgyth at every turn. From Bavaria they travelled to Swabia, where Hermann and Regelind welcomed them, proudly presenting their young daughter. On each occasion she met him, Eadgyth became more impressed with Hermann and she felt a profound sense of relief that this corner of the realm would ever be true.

Hermann accompanied them as they made the next stage of their journey by boat along the Rhine. It was a pleasant way to travel, as the boat glided through green hills dotted with small settlements. Otto was always at her side, his manner relaxed and light-hearted until they arrived in Lotharingia a few weeks before midsummer.

Gilbert and his wife, Otto's sister, Gerberga welcomed them as they disembarked from the boat. But their greetings were cordial rather than warm.

"I believe you know my dear brother, Father Frederick," Gilbert said.

"Indeed I have met Prince Otto on many an occasion," Frederick said, his thin lips curving into an expression which seemed to Eadgyth to be more sneer than smile.

Eadgyth frowned. Although now entitled to be called King, Otto did not normally use the title out of courtesy to his father. However it was presumptuous indeed for the priest to assume this.

The amused glance Gerberga gave her husband as she stepped forward, led Eadgyth to suspect it was intentional. "Welcome, my dear Brother," Gerberga said, embracing Otto.

Eadgyth studied her before extending her own greeting. Gerberga looked very like Mathilda, yet she was not the beauty Mathilda still was. As Gerberga kissed her perfunctorily on the cheek, Eadgyth suspected this was because she lacked the warmth Mathilda always displayed.

"I shall have my work cut out here," Otto said to Eadgyth that night.

"But they agreed to your accession, did they not?"

"Yes, but half-heartedly. The men of Franconia and Lotharingia have never completely accepted a Saxon on the throne of Germany. Until my father, it had always been a Frank since the days of Charles the Great and perhaps even further back. My grandmother was a Frank, so they accepted my father and will accept me, but it is grudging."

Eadgyth kissed him. "They are fools. We Saxons have proved ourselves ever the equal to the Franks."

Otto smiled back. "We have indeed."

"Did your father not consider a Frankish bride for you as a way of building on the links?"

"He may have done, but he wanted an alliance with a King to boost my position. I suppose he could have looked to West Francia, but of course they were already in alliance with Wessex or England as it had become by then. With your brother becoming so powerful, Father thought an alliance there would bring us more prestige. Of course it emphasises what a noble race we Saxons are!"

"I am glad he did," Eadgyth replied. "But I had thought your own brother-in-law would display more enthusiasm for you."

"So did I," Otto replied. "That is certainly what my father would have hoped for when he arranged that match."

"Gerberga seems an admirable woman. I am sure she could persuade her husband to loyalty."

"Or to disloyalty," Otto commented.

"What do you mean?"

"Gerberga is a trouble maker. She always has been. Be careful of what you say to her, my sweet. She could easily turn it against you."

∞∞∞

Gilbert and Gerberga joined the entourage which accompanied Otto and Eadgyth to Franconia, another region which unsurprisingly regarded Otto as a Saxon upstart. However Otto's demeanour was regarded with approval and Eadgyth too made every effort to be charming towards everyone she met. As they drew close to Frankfurt, Duke Eberhard of Franconia rode out to meet them.

"His brother was King of East Francia before my father was offered the throne and he is related to us as my father's cousin. If he was to challenge me, it would be a serious matter indeed," Otto had told her.

Eadgyth shivered at all these threats to Otto, but Eberhard was welcoming enough and she hoped he was now too old to harbour any ambitions. Hermann, who was also Eberhard's cousin, proved to be a great asset in keeping the mood friendly and she reflected that if Otto did have a trouble free succession, it would undoubtedly be in part thanks to Hermann's quiet wisdom.

They were all still at Frankfurt, when the messenger arrived. It was early evening and Eberhard was hosting a feast to honour Otto. Eadgyth was sat with Gerberga, laughing at some of her stories of Otto as a boy, pleased to find her sister-in-law becoming friendlier.

The messenger was quickly ushered in to the hall where the merriment was taking place. Messengers were common enough and no one took much notice as the man approached Otto.

"My mother?" Otto exclaimed. "My mother sent you?" The room went silent. Swiftly Eadgyth went to Otto's side. A message from Mathilda rather than Henry was unlikely to be good news.

"My lord, your lady mother begged me to inform you that

your father, the noble King Henry, has taken a turn for the worse. She believes you should be at your father's side at such a time and requests you return at all speed to Memleben."

Otto went very pale, but he nodded calmly at the messenger. "I thank you for bringing this message so swiftly. Please, refresh yourself."

Eadgyth rested her hand on his shoulder, as he turned to Duke Eberhard. "My lord, your hospitality has been much appreciated and I regret that I must bring it so swiftly to a close."

"I too regret such sad tidings," Eberhard replied. "If I might make one request, it is that I accompany you to Memleben. The King is a valued kinsman and I would be glad indeed to see him again."

"I too will come," Gilbert said. "I know Gerberga will want to see her father again if possible." He had his arm around his wife and Eadgyth warmed further to her as she saw the tears in her eyes.

The news was not unexpected, but even so everyone was shaken. "I intend to ride at all speed," Otto warned. "Eadgyth, please tell me if you need to ride at a slower pace."

Eadgyth shook her head, tightening her arm around Otto's shoulders. There was no possibility she would leave him alone at such a time. "I will keep pace with you, my love."

Otto kissed her hand. "Thank you." Their eyes met and Eadgyth saw the hint of vulnerability in them, a look he was determined not to show to the others.

∞∞∞

They set off at daybreak the next day and it took five days of hard riding to reach Memleben. During each day Otto focused on the ride, but at night he slid into Eadgyth's arms, saying nothing as he rested his head against her breast. She held him tightly, knowing there was nothing she could say to ease his mind.

"I pray I arrive in time," he whispered to her on the last night of the journey.

"So do I, my dearest," Eadgyth replied, stroking his hair. "But whatever we find at Memleben, remember I am with you."

It was a sombre group of riders who eventually arrived at the Palace of Memleben. Otto gripped Eadgyth's hand almost painfully as they entered the hall, preparing themselves for the worst.

"Father! Mother!" Liudolf cried, running towards them, Liutgarde not far behind.

Otto brightened as he pulled his children into his arms. Eadgyth put her arms around the three of them and for a moment the family clung together. Otto set the children down looking fearfully at Thankmar, Henry and Bruno who had come forward. All three looked subdued.

"Am I too late?" Otto asked.

Thankmar shook his head. "He lives still, but he is in a bad way. I only arrived myself yesterday."

Otto embraced his brothers, for once the four of them in unity. "What happened?"

"He collapsed," Henry replied. "For days he could neither talk nor walk and the priest administered Last Rites. His speech is a little improved now, but his right arm and leg will not move. Mother is with him."

Otto took a mouthful of drink and pushed Liudolf, who was still clinging to his leg, towards Eadgyth. "I must see him."

"Shall I come with you?" she asked.

Otto shook his head. "No. I want some time alone with him, although I know Father will be glad to see you later. Gerberga, you too should see him as soon as you can, but I shall send Mother to you for now. It will raise her spirits to see you." Otto planted a kiss on Eadgyth's head. "You rest yourself after the ride and stay with the children. You have been apart from them long enough for my sake."

∞∞∞

When Eadgyth did see Henry she was horrified. If he had not been lying propped up on pillows in the royal bedchamber she did not think she would have recognised him. His face was white and sagged on one side with one corner of his mouth drooping. His eyes were half shut, but one eyelid flickered open as Eadgyth approached. He reached out to her with his left hand, his right one hanging uselessly as young Henry had said.

"Eadgyth," he whispered.

"Don't try to talk, Henry," Eadgyth replied, kissing him on the cheek. "I know what concerns you, but I think Otto is equal to anything."

"He… has… done… well?"

"Yes, he will be a King you would be proud of." Eadgyth's eyes filled with tears and she remembered how she had not shed any when her own father lay dying.

"And you…"

"I will be beside him. It is both my duty and my heart's desire to support him in everything."

Henry managed a lop-sided smile. "I… know. Proud… of… you… my daughter."

Eadgyth had to squeeze her eyes shut to prevent the tears from escaping and she sank to her knees beside Henry's bed. "Thank you, Henry. Thank you for asking Athelstan to send me here. Thank you for raising such a son and allowing me to be his wife."

∞∞∞

The end when it came was peaceful. Henry had managed to speak again to all his children and laid his hand in blessing on the heads of Liudolf and Liutgarde. The entire family had gathered in his chamber for mass and at its end Henry indicated how tired he was.

Otto kissed his father on the cheek. "I will see you again this evening, Father."

Henry gave a weak smile, as the family went to dine in the hall leaving Mathilda sitting beside him. The meal was a subdued one, but not overly solemn. Bruno and Liudolf chattered to each other, even laughing at a few comments. Eadgyth was smiling at their innocent talk, when she saw Mathilda come slowly into the hall. She drew in a sharp breath, laying her hand on Otto's arm. Otto looked up and the hall stilled as he ran to Mathilda.

"Mother?"

There were tears on her cheek. "He is gone, Otto."

Otto eased his mother into a chair and Eadgyth poured her a cup of wine. "I should have been with him," Otto murmured.

"There was no time, my son. I did not even realise it myself," Mathilda said. "He fell asleep. I watched him a moment and then I took up some stitching. The next time I looked…"

Young Henry rubbed his eyes, giving a slight laugh. "Typical of Father. He was determined not to let us fuss."

Otto managed a faint smile. "That is true. He died quietly with you at his side, Mother. I think it is how he would have wished it."

The brothers embraced each other, all seeming unsure what to do next. Eadgyth put her arms around Mathilda as the widow's tears fell even faster.

At that moment Hermann came forward and knelt. "All hail King Otto!"

There was an instant of surprised silence before everyone in the hall fell to their knees. Even Mathilda slid from her chair to kneel. Eadgyth too knelt, pulling her children with her, and bowing her head before her husband and king.

Part Three : The Year of our Lord 936–37

Chapter one

Otto stared at his kneeling family before swiftly pulling Eadgyth back to her feet. She gazed at him trying to understand the mix of emotions on his face. She could clearly see the grief and pride, but there was something else there she could not read. For the first time in their marriage, she felt as if a barrier had come between them. As Otto raised the rest of his family, a shiver of fear crept icily upon her.

The realisation of what had happened suddenly dawned on Liudolf and he began to cry. Eadgyth bent over him, pulling Liutgarde into her arms as well. She looked around. Mathilda had clutched Bruno to her and was holding the hand of Gerberga, with young Henry's arm around them all, while Thankmar was comforting Hedwig. But Otto had already moved away from the family to take the hands of the assembled nobles, graciously accepting their protestations of loyalty.

Henry's body was moved to the church and the funeral rites were planned for the next day. That night Eadgyth lay alone, as Otto spent the night in vigil with his brothers, even eleven year old Bruno taking his place. There had been no time for any private conversation with Otto. She got occasional glimpses of him looking distracted, needing to attend to many matters at once and it seemed wrong to Eadgyth that she had not yet been able to hold him in her arms to comfort him on the loss of his much loved father.

He was still kneeling with his brothers before the coffin

when Eadgyth led Liudolf and Liutgarde to their grandfather's funeral. The chanting of monks echoed through the space as she took her place next to Mathilda. The widow was dressed all in black, her face pale and her eyes shut as she mouthed prayers while the court solemnly moved into place.

As the highest churchman in the land, Archbishop Hildebert of Mainz proceeded to the altar, swinging his censor to start the requiem mass. Everyone knelt as he spoke the words, an atmosphere of genuine sorrow hanging over them all. Successful in war, affable at court, Henry had been popular with everyone.

∞∞∞

A simple meal followed the rites, but there was no time for rest as the court prepared to move to Quedlinburg.

"Henry loved Memleben." Mathilda wiped her eyes as she spoke to Eadgyth. "It was his birth place and he wanted to spend his last days here. But he requested his body lie at Quedlinburg, so he may rest forever near the spot where he was proclaimed king."

"I think that is fitting for so great a king as Henry." Eadgyth felt guilty she was only giving Mathilda a part of the attention she deserved. Her eyes were on Otto.

Dressed all in black, he was consulting with Thankmar as they prepared to ride on either side of the coffin with Henry and Bruno behind them. It was an awkward conversation. Eadgyth could see Otto was finding it hard to respect Thankmar's position as the eldest son without losing his own authority of the situation, however the words between them were cordial enough. A tug on her sleeve made her look down.

"I want to ride with Father," Liudolf demanded.

"You can't. It would not be fitting on such an occasion."

"I always ride with Father."

"Not on this occasion," Eadgyth sighed. "Liudolf, matters are different now. Your father is the king."

Liudolf kicked his foot against a tethering post. "I wish he wasn't the king. I am not riding in the cart with the babies."

"You must. Please Liudolf, for this occasion."

"I won't."

"Liudolf! You will do as your mother has instructed." Otto strode over to them. He glowered at his son, displaying a fury Eadgyth had rarely seen and never directed towards his children.

Liudolf looked down. "I don't want to."

"Do as you have been instructed," Otto repeated. "If I have to say that again, you will be sorry."

Liudolf gulped, awed by the fury in his father's eyes. He turned away with his lip trembling. Eadgyth's heart ached at his downcast look, shaken by Otto's rage.

But Otto had not yet finished. He seized Liudolf by the shoulders, turning him firmly back to face them. "This is not the behaviour of a king's son. I expect better from you, Liudolf."

Liudolf held back his tears with an effort. "I am sorry, Father. Sorry, Mother."

"That is better, my son." Otto picked Liudolf up and placed him in the cart next to Liutgarde. He kissed him on the head. "You and I will enjoy a ride together as soon as I can find the time."

Eadgyth smiled at Otto, glad to see him soften, but he did not smile back. "That boy needs to behave on such occasions. It will reflect badly on me if men think I cannot control my own son," he said in a low voice. "You need to be firmer with him."

Eadgyth did not let herself display any distress. "Of course, Otto."

He squeezed her hand briefly before returning to his brothers. Wearily Eadgyth mounted her own horse and guided it to where she would ride in the cavalcade beside Mathilda.

∞∞∞

It was not until five days later that they arrived at Quedlinburg. Men and women had gathered along the route of their slow progress through the wooded valleys of Saxony to bid a final farewell to their king. At Quedlinburg he was interred with grief and solemnity, as Archbishop Hildebert again presided over the rites. Monks were instructed to pray for his soul day and night, but as soon as Hildebert had proclaimed, "Requiem Aeternum," and Henry's body was lowered into the ground, all eyes turned to the new king.

Over the next days Otto was endlessly busy. Men flocked to Quedlinburg from all over Saxony and beyond to discuss the future. It seemed to Eadgyth that the only time she saw him was at meal times and even then he barely gave her any attention, but spoke to the various visitors who had gathered.

Remembering her promise to Henry, Eadgyth made no complaint. She smiled graciously at the visiting envoys, engaging them in conversation, never forgetting it was now her role to enhance Otto's popularity. But her face started to ache from maintaining a smile she did not feel.

Even in their chamber she felt the distance between her and Otto grow. Inevitably he came late, looking exhausted, yet he did not turn to her for comfort, but simply bestowed a perfunctory kiss on her cheek and lay down to sleep, with barely a word passing between them. She lay still, tears slipping silently down her cheek, well remembering now Henry's words about wanting her and Otto to enjoy a last carefree spring. She only wished she had appreciated it more at the time.

Four days after the burial a serving boy came to her as she was sitting with Mathilda, Hedwig and Gerberga, showing Liutgarde how to make some stitches. Mathilda was discussing her hopes to found an abbey at Quedlinburg in Henry's memory.

The boy bowed before her. "My lady, the King commands your presence in his council chamber."

Eadgyth thanked the boy and excused herself from her companions with a smile, but inwardly the pain in her heart deepened. Never had Otto summoned her in this way. Normally if he wished to see her, he would burst into whichever chamber she was at, to catch her up in his arms, laughingly pulling her away from the other women. As she approached the council chamber she could hear his voice, although it seemed almost unrecognisable in its solemnity.

"Will the people accept such a change in my wife's status?" Otto was saying.

"I think so." Eadgyth recognised the voice of the Archbishop of Mainz. "It is unusual, but not unheard of. Even in her own family there are examples."

Eadgyth froze at his words, terrified by what she was hearing. There had been too many changes recently and Otto's recent distance from her suddenly took on a sinister meaning.

Holding her head high, she knocked on the door.

"Enter," Otto called.

Eadgyth pushed open the door. Only Otto and the Archbishop of Mainz were present and they both rose to their feet as she came in. Something about the formality of the situation made Eadgyth drop into a curtsey, although she would never normally do this when so few were present. Otto gave a slight bow.

"Eadgyth, come in." He turned to the Archbishop. "Perhaps you will excuse us, Father. I will attend to this matter alone."

"Of course, my son." He turned at the door to nod at Otto. "I certainly think this is a wise course of action. The more I consider it, the more sensible it appears."

"I agree," Otto replied, gesturing to Eadgyth to sit on the bench the archbishop had just vacated. The door closed behind the Archbishop with a soft thud, which should have been barely noticed, but it echoed on in Eadgyth's ears, as she turned her attention to Otto. He sat opposite her on the elaborately carved chair and smiled solemnly. "Eadgyth, I have a matter of grave import to discuss with you. I have been considering your position."

Chapter two

In an instant Eadgyth was transported back seventeen years to the moment her father had come to her mother, bowed and said, "Aelflaed, I have come to a decision of considerable importance. I have been considering your position."

If she had not been sitting down, she was certain she would have collapsed. Feeling completely numb she looked at Otto, trying not to think of the joys of lying in his arms. She could not blame him if he wished to be rid of her. When she had born two children in the first two years of marriage, she had felt secure, hopeful of presenting Otto with a large family. But since Liutgarde's birth she had struggled to conceive and on the two occasions she had managed, it had come to nothing. She knew to have just the one son was not ideal for a king, particularly a king with ambitious brothers. With a sense of tragic inevitability, she remembered how it was her father's succession to the throne which had prompted him to end his union with Athelstan's mother.

"Of course, my lord," she replied, keeping her voice steady with an effort. "I understand much has changed."

Otto looked grim. "Everything is different," he said, a note of regret in his voice. Eadgyth tried to take comfort from it. He did love her, but he would need to do what was best for the realm. "Already I am finding it hard to win all loyalty. Thankmar is furious at how our father left his estates. He believes he should have received more. Henry is continually insolent, whispering behind his hands with that nuisance of a priest, Father Frederick. My mother has never supported me. You have heard of her plans for Quedlinburg?"

Eadgyth nodded, wondering if to preside over the new abbey at Quedlinburg would be her fate.

"I intend to set up my own foundation," Otto continued. "It will need to be grander than the one at Quedlinburg. Oh, I do not begrudge her wish to set up this abbey and it will be a fitting tribute to my father, but I cannot allow her to preside over the greatest institution in the land."

Eadgyth nodded again, realising she would be needed to preside over Otto's foundation. No doubt she would be expected to welcome him and whoever he put in her place to it on occasion. She had made a promise to Henry to support Otto unquestioningly, but she did not know how she would find the strength to do that.

"I thought to set it up at Magdeburg. It is your city, so it would be fitting."

"Yes, it would, my lord," Eadgyth whispered.

Otto scowled. "Stop calling me that, Eadgyth. We have never been on such formal terms when we are alone. Now, your position…"

"I understand my position," Eadgyth said, her eyes filling with tears. "It will be an honour to preside over your foundation at Magdeburg. I will always endeavour to serve you in whatever way I can."

Otto stared at her. "What are you talking about? Eadgyth, you don't think… you can't think…" He slid over to the bench pulling her almost roughly into his arms. Her body was trembling. "My God, you do think it. My love, I swore many years ago that I would never cast you off. How can you think it?"

"You said yourself everything is different."

"Not everything," Otto said, a tortured expression on his face. "Not how I feel about you."

Almost fearfully Eadgyth touched his cheek. "I know you

love me, but I have only given you one son."

"You have given me the finest son and the most beautiful daughter. I have just lost my father. How can you think I would want to lose my wife?"

"You spoke of my change in status and of needing to consider my position. That was what my father said to my mother."

"I did not know that, but you should know I am not like your father."

Eadgyth looked up at him, a smile struggling though her tears. "Have I been a very great fool?"

Otto grinned, suddenly looking like the boy she had married six years before. "Yes, you have, but it makes a nice change for me to be the sensible one of us."

"Oh, Otto," Eadgyth whispered, pressing her lips against his. To her joy he responded eagerly. It had been a while since he had last kissed her in that way.

"But there has been a distance between us these last days. I am sure I have not imagined that," Eadgyth said as Otto relaxed his arms slightly, but kept them around her.

"No, I have felt it too." The strange expression crept over Otto's face once again. "Eadgyth, when I heard my father had died, I did not think about becoming king. All I felt was grief."

"I know," Eadgyth replied.

"When Hermann proclaimed me King, I felt such a sense of triumph. No victory in battle has ever compared to it. But when you all knelt before me…" Otto swallowed, his voice breaking. "I have never felt so lonely in my life."

Eadgyth tightened her arms around him. "I had no idea."

"It felt so strange to see all those closest to me, kneeling. My mother, who used to scold me as a child. My brothers, who have shared the camaraderie of battles. Men like old Arnulf, who I have known my entire life. And you, the one who is usually in my arms, instead kneeling on the ground. Suddenly everything is different between me and those I love most."

"We will not let it be different between us. Of course you are now my king, but when we are alone I will forget that and regard you merely as my husband."

"It is not enough. That is why I have been discussing your positon with the Archbishop. He has agreed to crown you."

Eadgyth gasped. "Crown me? That is not the custom here is it?"

"No, but it is not unheard of. He said it happened on occasions in your land as well."

"It did in Mercia, but rarely in Wessex. My great-grandfather had his second wife crowned, but she was a Frankish princess, so was considered worthy."

"My wife is an English princess, so is most definitely worthy," Otto commented with a smile. "I want this, Eadgyth. As an anointed king my rank will be higher than any in the land. There will inevitably be a distance between myself and all others. I do not want that distance from you. I do not want you to kneel to me, ever." He looked sternly at her. "And I do not want you addressing me as 'my lord'."

Eadgyth smiled at him meekly. "Of course, Otto. It will be as you wish. I shall endeavour never to show you any respect ever again."

"Good," Otto replied, his eyes filled with mischief. "Oh, Eadgyth, this is not the only reason. Truly you are made for such a role. You will be the most noble of queens and are so well loved. Germany needs you. Please, will you accept it?"

Eadgyth nodded. "I shall be honoured to be your queen. Was your mother crowned?"

"No. Indeed even my father was not anointed. He preferred to rule by the will of the people, rather than by the grace of God. I intend to rule by both. It has already been agreed by the dukes and bishops at the synod in Erfurt. The crowning will take place at Aachen."

"Aachen? Why not here in Saxony?"

"Aachen was a favoured spot of many of the Frankish kings, including their great Emperor Charles. His son, the Emperor Louis, was crowned there. It is a fitting place."

Eadgyth's eyes widened. "Otto, you are not thinking of

aiming to be emperor are you?"

Otto laughed. "No, I shall have my hands full with Germany for now at least." Eadgyth raised her eyebrows at that comment, but did not enquire further, as Otto continued, "I need to draw attention to my Frank ancestors. As matters stand I have the firm support of Hermann of Swabia and I believe Arnulf of Bavaria, although he is not in the best of health and I am not so sure of his son. But I fear there could easily be trouble with Gilbert of Lotharingia and Eberhard of Franconia. If I am to rule over them, I need to be accepted as an heir to the Frankish kings as well as the Saxon one."

Eadgyth smiled proudly, thinking how wise Otto had become in the last years. However she felt a pang of regret at the memory of the exuberant boy she had fallen in love with. She vowed that as his wife, she would make it her duty to ensure Otto did not become swamped in his kingly duties, but would still have the chance to be the fun loving husband and father. "Am I to be crowned alongside you in Aachen?"

Otto hesitated. "In Aachen, yes. But I think not alongside me." He grinned. "I am greedy. I want all eyes on me on the day I am crowned, but I know no one will want to look at me if such a beautiful lady as yourself is there."

Eadgyth laughed. "You are the one being a fool now. All eyes will be on you. It will be your day."

Otto pulled Eadgyth close to him once again. "Yes, it will. And then a day or two later you shall have your day."

He kissed her again and secure in his arms, Eadgyth's earlier fears were long forgotten. After a while she pushed him gently away. "You have much to do, my love. More messengers have arrived this day. You should not be taking so long with me."

"I want to take some time with you. I must have been severely neglecting you if you truly thought I would cast you off."

"I was foolish." She stood up, pressing a last kiss against his lips. "Matters will settle down, I know that now. But do not feel lonely, Otto. I am always with you."

Otto put his arm around her shoulders as she walked to the door. "I will find the time for you."

Eadgyth turned, winding her arms around his neck. "Do not worry about me, but if you do have a little time… Liudolf. He misses his grandfather."

"And I was harsh with him," Otto said ruefully. "Oh, Eadgyth, it is so hard suspecting everyone is always judging me, ready to pounce on any weakness. I know he is a good little lad and if he has a will of his own, that is no bad thing. Tell him I will take him riding later." He glanced back into the council chamber. "I shall be glad of the excuse to get out of here for a while."

There was a group of men waiting outside, who all rose to their feet as Eadgyth left the room. Otto smiled at them. "Forgive me for keeping you waiting, my lords."

"Do not worry, my Lord King, I completely understand," Hermann said with a wink.

"That's right, my lord," Arnulf added. "I would not want to talk to this lot if I had such a beautiful woman to talk to either." He gestured laughingly at the others.

Otto laughed, putting his arm genially around Arnulf's shoulders and gesturing to the other three dukes to follow.

Eadgyth smiled as they went into the council chamber, but she caught the look which passed between Eberhard of Franconia and Gilbert of Lotharingia. It lacked the good humour of the other two and Eadgyth shuddered. She had hoped Gilbert, Otto's brother by marriage, at least would be supporting him. Hermann nodded to her in a friendly fashion as he closed the door, but Eadgyth knew he too had seen the look between Eberhard and Gilbert and his eyes were troubled.

Chapter three

Otto's plans for his crowning did not go down well with everyone. When he came to their chamber that night he took Eadgyth in his arms and held her tightly. She could sense the tension in him.

"What did the dukes have to say?" she asked him.

"As I expected. Arnulf and Hermann are happy with the plans, while Eberhard and Gilbert barely concealed their contempt. Hermann thinks I will have trouble with them soon." Otto rolled onto his back and in the flickering candle light, Eadgyth could see the weariness on his face. She wished there was something she could do to help him. He turned his head to look at her. "We could face some difficult times."

She slipped her hand into his. "We will face them together."

She lay awake a long time after Otto had fallen asleep, unable to help worrying about the future and wondering what had annoyed Eberhard and Gilbert. It did not take her long to find out.

She joined the women the next day in time to hear Gerberga say, "This crowning. What is Otto thinking?"

"It is Otto's decision now," Hedwig said.

"I do not know what goes through that boy's head," Mathilda replied, ignoring Hedwig's comment. They all fell silent as they noticed Eadgyth.

"Do not stop on my account," Eadgyth said, sitting down and smoothing out her skirts. She was feeling like an outsider among the womenfolk, but she would do whatever was necessary to ease Otto's path. "Do tell me what your objections are to Otto's crowning. I consider his plans very fine."

"That does not surprise me, my dear," Mathilda said acidly. "Your good sense seems to vanish whenever Otto is concerned."

"So, what are your objections?" Eadgyth smiled with assurance and waited. She felt at a disadvantage as apart from the location of Aachen she knew very little about the coronation. She wished she had asked Otto for more details, but he had looked so drawn the previous night she had not wanted to press him further.

"He expects Gilbert to act as his servant for the coronation feast," Gerberga said. "And not just Gilbert. All the Dukes are to have serving roles."

Eadgyth raised her eyebrows, slightly surprised at this detail. "I believe Otto wishes to honour the Dukes by making them part of the ceremony. I had not heard of any objections from the others." She hoped she was right about this.

"I believe Lord Arnulf and Lord Hermann have no objections," Hedwig said.

"Oh, Arnulf will always indulge Otto," Mathilda said. "He always did, from when Otto was a child. Even when he and Henry were on the frostiest of terms, somehow Arnulf always had a smile for Otto. So if Otto says he shall be marshal, Arnulf will play along."

"Hermann is one of Otto's closest friends," Gerberga put in, making it sound like a fault. "I dare say he does not object to being Otto's cupbearer. But Gilbert should be treated as Otto's brother, not his chamberlain"

"And to expect Eberhard, a brother of a King, to act as seneschal is ridiculous," Mathilda added. "All those years he and Henry were at peace, but Otto just throws that away to boost his own pride."

"If Arnulf and Hermann do not feel insulted, I do not see why Gilbert and Eberhard are. They should be honoured Otto has included them with his most trusted friend and one that I know he regards almost as an uncle. They are being foolish. Otto has chosen them to play an important part in the crowning. While he hopes they will always remain true to the German interests, there is no expectation they will ever act as his personal servants again. It is simply that they must honour Otto on that day."

"As of course we all shall," Hedwig said, clearly hating the conflict as much as Eadgyth did.

Eadgyth smiled gratefully at her, but it was a brief respite.

"No doubt as we shall be expected to honour you," Gerberga said. "Perhaps we should have knelt when you came in."

Eadgyth flushed and Mathilda looked puzzled. "What are you talking about?"

"Have you not heard, Mother? Otto is to have Eadgyth crowned."

Mathilda narrowed her eyes. "I see. I had no idea you held such ambitions, my dear."

"This is not ambition," Eadgyth replied, firmly meeting her mother-in-law's eye. "Otto has requested it and I am supporting him. As a consecrated king, he wishes his wife to be a consecrated queen. The Archbishop of Mainz has agreed it is fitting. I am surprised at you, Mathilda, for questioning the wisdom of this holy man."

It was Mathilda's turn to flush uncomfortably. "Henry ruled perfectly well without all of that. This is a disgrace to his memory."

"Indeed he did," Eadgyth replied. "Otto and I will always honour Henry's memory, but Otto must find his own way to rule and it may be in a different style to his father's. As his wife, it is my honour to support him wholeheartedly. As his mother and sisters, I feel you should do the same."

"Otto is not my only son," Mathilda said icily. "I shall lend my support to the one who appears most worthy."

Eadgyth rose up, aware she was about to utter the cruellest of words to a woman so recently widowed. She understood how Mathilda was feeling at losing her place as the highest ranking woman in the land, but she could not allow such a statement to pass. "The noble King Henry considered Otto to be the one most worthy. I think, my lady, it is you who are not honouring his memory."

∞∞∞

Eadgyth did not tell Otto about this scene, but privately she wept to think she had lost Mathilda's friendship. One of the greatest joys since her arrival in Germany was gaining such a loving family, but Henry's death was tearing it apart. Already mourning Henry who she had come to love as a father, her grief intensified. Every night Eadgyth spent precious moments before Henry's grave, praying matters would improve, but on the eve of the day they were to leave for Aachen, it became obvious such prayers would not be quickly answered.

Otto had ordered the final mass to be said for his father, marking the end of the funeral rites. Eadgyth, who had held him in her arms as he wept the previous night, knew how Otto continued to grieve, but he cast off his dark clothes in favour of a more kingly raiment and she joined him, appearing at the meal in a kirtle of deep pink. Mathilda had remained in mourning as was appropriate for a widow, but the majority of the court followed the example of the new king. Only young Henry remained in grey.

"Henry was devoted to his father," Mathilda said when Arnulf commented on this.

"As were we all, my lady," Arnulf said. "But we must look to the future now. Tomorrow we set out for a crowning."

"I am not certain that is a cause for celebration," Mathilda replied. "Otto rules by the will of the synod. It is presumptuous for him to claim God's blessing. I do not know why you are so sure he is God's choice."

"The oldest legitimate son, my lady," Arnulf replied. "My heir will be my oldest son."

Mathilda said no more, but Henry leant forward to speak in a hushed voice. "What if the people turned against Otto? Whose will then is most important?"

Despite the low tone, Otto overheard and turned away from his own conversation. "God's will triumphs, Brother. The people must obey the will of God."

"I was the first son born after Father's accession," Henry cried. "You know that suggests I am God's choice."

Arnulf shook his head. "Do not be a fool, my boy."

Otto frowned, giving Henry a sharp shove. "I am reaching the end of my patience with you, Henry. I have made enough allowances for you as a boy grieving for his father, but I have done with your disobedience. Get on your knees, Boy and swear an oath of loyalty."

Henry stumbled back, but quickly steadied himself and glared at his brother. Eadgyth caught her breath. At seventeen Henry had become as strong as Otto. "I will not. You should be swearing an oath of loyalty to me."

The hall went deadly silent and all eyes went to Otto. Eadgyth too stared at him, scared for what would happen next. She knew any weakness Otto showed now would be pounced upon. Thankmar was openly grinning at the scene and she could see Eberhard and Gilbert whispering together with Father Frederick. Inwardly she quaked as she wondered what plots might already be hatching.

"You need not ride with us tomorrow, Brother," Otto said. "There is no place for you at my crowning."

The greatest in the land had been summoned to the crowning and the celebrations were expected to be lavish, but Henry did not look put out. "I do not know why you think I have any wish to witness it. I shall be glad to remain here at Quedlinburg. It was the heart of my father's power. One day it will be mine."

There was a gasp, but Otto laughed and shook his head. "I think not. I shall find some other spot for you to stay.

Somewhere you can cause no trouble and discover a little sense. You have much to learn, Little Brother."

A ripple of laughter went around the hall and Eadgyth knew Otto's approach of treating Henry as of little account was a good one. The rage appeared to almost boil in Henry, as he tried to find a retort to his brother.

"I find it hard to believe the great King Henry could have such a fool for a son," Hermann commented, standing shoulder to shoulder with Otto.

"Oh, Henry is no fool, my friend," Otto replied. "Just an impertinent little puppy in need of training."

"Do not say such things about your brother, Otto," Mathilda snapped.

Henry flushed scarlet, mortified by his mother's defence. Hermann laughed out loud. "He may be young, my lord, but surely he is too old to be hiding behind his mother's skirts."

"Well, I thought he was," Otto said doubtfully.

"I hate you Otto," Henry snapped. "You will cower before me one day."

"I hardly think so," Otto said, turning away. "I am finding you most tiresome at the moment."

"My lord, perhaps I could make a suggestion," Arnulf put in. "I have a small residence at Erding, quite fine enough to house a younger son of a king, but where he can cause no trouble. It is at your service if you wish it. Send him there in the company of a sensible man, perhaps Margrave Siegfried."

"Thank you, my dear Arnulf, that offer is most appreciated. I shall be glad to be able to enjoy my meal without having to give any further thought to this fool."

"I am not going to Bavaria," Henry said.

Otto put his hands on Henry's shoulders in a manner which looked affectionate. "Yes, you are. If you have any sense, you will go with dignity. If you oppose this, I will have my men bind you and you will be transported there by force. I suggest you spend your time there in reflection until you become the man our father hoped you would be."

Otto turned away, but the trouble was not yet over. Mathilda was white with anger, as she blocked her oldest son's path. "I do not think I will attend the crowning either."

"As you will, Mother," Otto said, stepping calmly around his mother.

Eadgyth shot her a reproachful look as she followed Otto to the head of the table. Silently the people parted to let her through, although nothing could part the tension thickening the atmosphere of the hall.

"Otto, am I coming with you?" Bruno looked bewildered by the arguments.

Otto stopped, his face lighting up into a smile. He was very fond of his youngest brother. "Well, let me see. Where are we going and why?"

"To Aachen, so you will be crowned in the chapel of Charles the Great."

"By whose will am I crowned?"

"By God and the will of the synod." Bruno's face became sadder. "It was Father's will that you succeed him."

"Very good. I have heard you have become a fine rider, Brother. Is that true? Do you think you can keep up with me?" A nervous ripple of laughter lightened the air as Bruno nodded eagerly. "Then you must most certainly accompany me to Aachen. You shall ride at my side."

Bruno flung his arms around his brother and Eadgyth smiled, relieved to feel the tension in the hall ease. Otto ruffled his brother's hair, before continuing to his place. He looked out at the court. "Now, my friends, can we dine? We have a long ride tomorrow. And I had hoped that I might for once retire early with my fair wife this night!"

There was a burst of laughter as Otto put his arm around her and kissed her heartily in what seemed to be a suggestive manner. Only Eadgyth could feel how desperately he clung to her.

Chapter four

The cavalcade which set off from Quedlinburg the next day was a splendid one. There was a loud cheer as Otto and Eadgyth came out, both dressed in green riding tunics. Otto paused for a moment, acknowledging the cheers. He put one arm around Eadgyth, while his other hand was clasped firmly in Liudolf's. Liutgarde clung to Eadgyth, her eyes wide with astonishment. As ever they made an attractive young family.

Otto grinned, looking every inch the confident king with no sign of the anguish he had displayed the night before, when he had arrived in their chambers to collapse in Eadgyth's arms. She knew young Henry had already departed for Bavaria. Otto had not seen him go, however Arnulf reported that the boy had gone sullenly but without protest. As Arnulf and Hermann came forward to consult with Otto, Eadgyth looked around to see Mathilda standing behind her in the doorway, Gerberga and Hedwig hovering protectively around her. Their eyes met.

"You have become as a daughter to me, Eadgyth," she said. "I do not want to quarrel,"

"Nor do I," Eadgyth replied, but there was no smile on her face as she looked steadily at her mother-in-law. However fond she was of Mathilda, Otto's unhappiness was too fresh in her mind. "Will you change your mind about coming to Aachen?"

"How can I, when Otto has sent Henry away?"

"You know no harm will befall him. Why can you not be proud of Otto this day?"

They both looked at Otto, tall and handsome, laughing with the men. Eadgyth could not imagine failing to be proud of such a son.

"I do love him, but I cannot support this," Mathilda said, her face strained.

Eadgyth shook her head. "I have tried to understand you, Mathilda. I can imagine myself, I pray many years from now, a widow and I know I will be in little mood for celebration. But even so, nothing would stop me witnessing my beloved son on such an occasion."

"But you have just the one son, my dear. Perhaps if you had more, you would understand why I cannot play favourites."

Eadgyth flinched. When she had expressed her fears at bearing no more children, Mathilda had always been the one to comfort her. Despite Otto's assurances, she couldn't help but feel her failure to present him with more sons and it hurt that Mathilda was now using her one weakness against her. Out of the corner of her eye, she caught a glimpse of Gerberga's smirk. Drawing on every bit of strength, she narrowed her eyes. "But you do play favourites," she said. "All the time."

With nothing further to say, she swept out to join Otto in the sunshine, taking comfort from his smile and the respectful bows of the men. With everything prepared, Otto lifted Liutgarde, kissing her head, before placing her in the cart. "You sit there, sweetheart and be a good little maid."

Liutgarde smiled enchantingly at Otto. With Otto's dark hair and deep blue eyes, but Eadgyth's delicate features, she was growing into her promise to be a beauty. "Yes, Father."

Otto looked down at Liudolf and smiled. "Are you going to ride with me?"

Liudolf gasped. "Can I, Father?"

Otto nodded. "For now at least. When we arrive in Aachen I must be alone on my horse, so no arguing when I order you then to sit with your sister."

"I swear I won't, Father," Liudolf said eagerly, making Eadgyth smile at his joy.

"I think that is very wise, my lord," Arnulf said, patting Liudolf on the head. "If you had such a fine young man as this on your horse, the people of Aachen would not know which one of you to crown."

Otto laughed at that comment as he strode towards the horse, his son scampering behind him. It was a spirited black stallion and Liudolf could barely contain his excitement when he saw it.

"One moment, my son. I must help your mother first." He turned to where Eadgyth was standing next to her glossy black mare. They smiled at each other and Otto put his hands on her waist. "Ready for this, my sweet?" he asked.

"Completely."

Otto brushed a kiss across her lips before lifting her onto the horse. She gathered the reins and waited as he swung himself up behind Liudolf. Bruno, not even attempting to hide his pride, was on his other side while Thankmar rode next to her. The four dukes urged their horses behind them. Otto looked again at Eadgyth and her heart lifted at the joy in his eyes.

He raised his hand. "To Aachen!"

∞∞∞

It took over two weeks to reach Aachen, but the ride was an enjoyable one. Everyone was in a festive mood and often along the way they encountered groups of people gathering to cheer their new king. Otto would always slow his horse on such occasions to allow the people to see him as he favoured them with his dazzling smile. Eadgyth too smiled warmly as they passed, delighting to hear the praise of the people directed towards her almost as much as to Otto. She might have been born in land far away, but the people had wholeheartedly accepted her as their own.

Away from the stresses of Quedlinburg, Otto's manner became almost carefree. At nights they rested in the royal palaces, private residences and abbeys along the way and Otto would preside over the meal in great humour. In the privacy of their bedchamber Eadgyth was delighted to find his high spirits had not been forced. Although both were weary from the day's ride, they arrived there full of laughter and far too exuberant to sleep.

They crossed the River Rhine at Cologne, where they were welcomed by Archbishop Wigfried. Otto remained there a few days, holding court with the nobles of Swabia and Franconia, who had travelled to be with him. Eadgyth watched Eberhard and Gilbert carefully as they arrived in Frankish territory, but the two dukes continued to display a respectful manner. At each stage of the journey the numbers of men in the cavalcade increased and it was a vast, but joyous crowd who reached journey's end.

It was a hot summer's day when they finally arrived in the city of Charles the Great. Never had Eadgyth seen anywhere so magnificent. They entered the hall of the palace to enjoy a lavish feast, before spending the night in a chamber of unparalleled luxury. The next morning Otto took the time to show Eadgyth the rest of the palace. As she walked through endless galleries, to a library containing more manuscripts than she had ever seen, she wondered why the family had not come here before.

"Saxony is the heart of our power," Otto told her. "Of course we do come here on occasion, but we have always felt we are tolerated here, rather than loved."

As remarkable as the palace was, the bath house adjoining the palace was even more wondrous. Eadgyth gazed at the huge pools of hot and cold water, big enough, it was said, to hold a hundred bathers.

"You should take some time to relax here after the journey," Otto suggested.

"So should you," Eadgyth replied. "These last weeks have not been the easiest ones."

Otto looked at the water, a speculative smile on his face.

He put his arms around her. "Sharing these waters with a beautiful young woman sounds like a pleasant way to relax indeed."

Eadgyth laughed, standing on tiptoes to kiss him. "Make the time if you can, Otto. It would do us both good."

"I will, but come. I want to show you the church. I do not believe you will ever have seen anywhere so splendid. It is what I want for us at Magdeburg."

Otto was right. Eadgyth did not know what to admire first, as her astonished gaze took in the frescos of the domed chapel, with the summer sun shining through the glass, glinting off the jewelled icons and mosaics lining the walls. She looked at the white marble throne of Charles the Great, lined with silken cloths. Otto was also staring at it and she realised with a jolt this was where Otto too would sit. There was a mix of expressions on his face. The pride was obvious, but also the look she now realised was fear and loneliness. She slid her hand into his.

"I think you will be the finest king to have ever sat on that throne," she said softly.

"I hope so, my sweet. I shall try."

∞∞∞

On the day of the crowning Otto was out of bed before it was light, unable to contain his excitement any longer.

"Otto, it will be hours yet," Eadgyth said sleepily. "Why not come back to bed a while. You know the feasting will go on all night."

Otto sat back on the bed, pressing his lips against hers in a long, but gentle kiss. "You tempt me, but no. I want some time alone in the church. My father began preparing me for this day when I was a small boy, not much older than Liudolf. I want to do him proud."

Since leaving Quedlinburg Otto had not mentioned his

mother. "Your father was very proud of you, my love. No father was ever prouder."

She did not see Otto again before the crowning, but waited in one of the galleries with the rest of the family. Everyone greeted her politely, but it was only from Bruno and the children that she found the welcome warm. Even Hedwig's manner had become uneasy and Eadgyth suspected her loyalty was torn between her mother and brother.

"You look charming, Sister," Thankmar said, making the effort to break the awkward silence.

Eadgyth squeezed his hand warmly, guessing this was a difficult day for him. If his mother had not been repudiated, it would likely have been him crowned that day. "I am glad you are here, Thankmar. I know how Otto values your support."

Thankmar gave a slight smile, exchanging looks with Gerberga. The absence of Henry suddenly hung heavily in everyone's mind. Determinedly Eadgyth turned her mind away from him and Mathilda to focus on those who had come. Even if their support was not wholehearted at least they were present. She hoped they could be drawn further into Otto's circle.

The room stilled as Archbishop Wigfried of Cologne and Archbishop Hildebert of Mainz entered.

"My lords, my ladies, it is time."

Chapter five

It was Bruno who took Eadgyth's arm to escort her to the church. Although expecting a crowd, she was surprised by how many could squeeze inside. The day was warm and no doubt some were finding the wait trying, but there was no sign of discomfort from any, as everyone called their greetings.

The rousing flourish of horns told them Otto had arrived, causing a hush to descend on the crowd, but it was broken almost immediately by a surprised murmur. Eadgyth longed to crane her neck to get a glimpse of him, but forced herself to keep her gaze steady.

Her heart thumped as those closest to her sank to their knees and Eadgyth took her first look at her husband. She quickly realised what had caused the people's surprise. Otto had abandoned the finery of a Saxon nobleman in favour of the splendour of a Frankish king. Her first thought was one of admiration. The scarlet of the tunic, edged in golden silks, suited him. It was tighter fitting than the Saxon style, making him look more muscular than ever. But her next was one of faint fear, as she wondered if the Saxons would feel offended by this. Although she knew how important it was for Otto to win the allegiance of the Franks and Lotharingians, it would be worthless if the Saxons turned against him. However everyone continued to kneel and only flattering comments reached her ears.

Eadgyth relaxed and returned to admiring how handsome he looked. He came closer, causing his siblings to sink to their knees. Hedwig and Gerberga were both raised and greeted with pleasure.

"I pledge my allegiance to you, Otto as my King," Thankmar said.

To Eadgyth's surprise it did not sound false. For the first time since she had known him, she gave him a smile of genuine affection as she prayed all would be well between the brothers.

Bruno repeated the words, before Otto moved on to Liutgarde and Liudolf. Otto's eyes shone as he laid his hand on their silky hair and raised them back to their feet.

"I pledge my allegiance to you, Otto, as my king," Liudolf announced, beaming with pride.

Otto smiled down at his son, much the same expression on his face and he bent to give both children a kiss.

As Otto moved on, Eadgyth sank into a low curtsey as she had been forbidden from kneeling to him. He rested his hand briefly on her head, but quickly raised her, kissing her hand. For an instant they looked at each other. "I pledge my allegiance to you, Otto, as my king and my husband," Eadgyth pronounced.

Otto smiled, his eyes conveying his gratitude for her words. She was pleased to see him look so calm, with no sign of any loneliness as he took the most important steps of his life.

Eadgyth had been so focused on Otto, she had not noticed the four dukes walking behind him. All were magnificently dressed in a manner which reflected their region. They progressed solemnly behind, as Otto followed the two archbishops. At the altar he knelt in the web of sunbeams streaming through the glass, as Archbishop Hildebert began the mass.

When the last chants of the monks died away, Otto looked up at the two archbishops.

"Duke Otto of Saxony, you have been proclaimed King of Germany by the will of the synod. Do you, Otto, Duke of Saxony pledge to uphold God's holy law?" Wigfried asked.

"I do," Otto replied solemnly.

"Do you swear to uphold the authority of His Holiness the Pope?"

"I do."

"Do you swear to defend this realm of Germany from its enemies?"

"While there is breath in my body, I will."

The four Dukes were holding a part of the royal insignia. Each one in turn passed these to be blessed by the archbishops. A mantle of deep blue cloth, edged in ermine fur was clasped around his shoulders. Next they fastened an elaborate sword belt around his waist and braces to his arms.

"I bestow God's blessing on you, Otto to grant you the strength to defend your realm," Wigfried pronounced.

Lastly the Archbishop placed the sceptre in his hands. "Receive this rod as a symbol of your right to administer God's holy law and to uphold the authority of His Holiness the Pope in this realm."

"Otto, Duke of Saxony, you have been affirmed King of Germany by the will of the good men of this land. I now anoint you King by the grace of God." Archbishop Hildebert marked a cross on Otto's forehead and his hands. He slipped a ring set with a ruby onto Otto's finger and held aloft a golden circlet, illuminated by the sunbeams. Slowly he lowered it onto Otto's head, where it gleamed brighter than ever against his dark hair.

"Arise, Otto, King of Germany," both bishops pronounced.

Overwhelmed with pride Eadgyth watched as slowly and with impeccable dignity, Otto rose and climbed the steps to the white marble throne. Everyone burst into loud cheers for their king and with a graciousness, barely concealing his glee, Otto smiled at his people.

∞∞∞

As the coronation feast started, the four dukes carried out

their duties with due solemnity. Remembering their contempt when they had been informed of their roles, Eadgyth watched Gilbert and Eberhard closely. She hoped they would respect the sacred rite they had just witnessed, but their gestures seemed perfunctory and lacking the very real respect she could see in Hermann and Arnulf's service.

But as the meal proceeded and drinks were downed, the solemn atmosphere lightened. Arnulf's manner changed from respectful to affectionate, often addressing his king as "my boy" rather than any more formal address. Otto raised an eyebrow, but grinned, as he took another draught of his drink. Hermann's eyes lit up mischievously and he promptly refilled the cup. He took to repeating this action after every mouthful, often not even waiting for Otto to set the cup down, until Otto put his hand over his cup.

Hermann looked speculatively at the jug and Eadgyth half expected him to pour it out anyway, ruining Otto's elaborate tunic. Firmly she took the jug from him, causing both men to laugh out loud. Otto gestured to the chairs nearest him. "My friends, I release you from further duties for this night. I am glad to know I can always rely on your support, but for now sit with me."

The mood became merrier and as the hour drew late, Eadgyth rose from the table.

"You are not retiring already are you?" Otto asked, pulling her onto his lap.

"I do not think you will want me here much longer, my love," Eadgyth replied, brushing her lips against Otto's.

"Nonsense, my dear lady," Arnulf cried. "Your presence enhances any feast."

Eadgyth tried to look as dignified as was possible when sat on Otto's knee, his arms tightly around her. "Very well," she said with mock sternness. "But I trust you will all watch your manners and ensure any songs sung are appropriate."

Otto laughed, kissing her again. "I think perhaps you are tired, my sweet, and need to retire. My friends, forgive me for denying you my wife's company, but we will not object."

Eadgyth's heart warmed at the burst of friendly laughter, as she got to her feet. Even Gilbert looked to be in good spirits. "I will bid you all good night, my lords."

She walked calmly to the door, nodding and smiling at all she passed. At the doorway she looked back. Otto had pushed back his finely carved chair to rest his feet upon the table, as he laughed with Hermann. Eadgyth smiled in relief. The day had gone well and she was glad Otto could relax.

∞∞∞

Three days later they returned to the church for Eadgyth to be crowned. She was dressed in a deep blue dress, edged in golden threads and amber beads. The wide sleeves fell almost to the floor, to reveal a creamy under tunic. Otto had requested that she leave her hair uncovered and loose, so the blonde mass fell over her shoulders.

"You look very fine, Eadgyth," Gerberga said. She and Hedwig were acting as her attendants, which no doubt accounted for the abrasive tone of her voice.

"Oh, you look lovely," Hedwig exclaimed. "Otto will be so proud."

Eadgyth disclaimed, as she smiled affectionately at Hedwig and they made their way to where the Archbishop of Mainz was waiting to greet them at the church door. Inside it was almost as full as it had been for Otto's crowning. Eadgyth was not sure if men had gathered out of curiosity or loyalty, but the smiles of all seemed genuine, as she passed through them to kneel before the altar.

Otto was seated once again on the throne. He was magnificently dressed, but this time in the Saxon style. His face was grave, but Eadgyth could detect the pride in his eyes.

As for Otto's crowning, the service started with a mass and the bishop prayed over her. Gerberga handed Hildebert a cloak of cream wool edged in white fur. Eadgyth's eyes widened at the sight of the jewelled brooch which was used to fasten it. Otto had said he would present her with a gift on the occasion of her crowning, but the fine workmanship of this was beyond anything she normally saw. She raised her eyes to look at him. There was a faint smile on his face, as she tried to convey her gratitude in her gaze.

"Lady Eadgyth, Duchess of Saxony, daughter of the late King Edward of the Anglo-Saxons and wife of King Otto of Germany, I anoint you queen by the grace of God." Eadgyth held her breath as the cross was marked on her forehead and shoulders. "I bestow upon you this ring and this crown as a symbol of your faith in God's sacred laws." The ring was almost identical to Otto's, while the unfamiliar weight of the crown made her bow her head, murmuring a swift prayer. "In the name of God our Father, son and holy spirit please rise, Queen Eadgyth of Germany."

Feeling completely overwhelmed, Eadgyth got to her feet. Otto too rose, stretching out his hand. Slowly Eadgyth made her way to the throne and climbed the steps, finding it strange how these few steps were to elevate her to such a position. Understanding her feelings only too well, Otto squeezed her hand reassuringly. At the top of the steps, she turned to look at the people.

"All hail Queen Eadgyth!" Otto proclaimed.

Joyfully the cry was taken up as she sat with him on the throne. He gestured to the gathered people and led by the four dukes, the nobles approached to kneel and kiss her hand, swearing their own oaths of loyalty.

∞∞∞

The feast which followed was quieter than Otto's had been, but no less joyous. She expected Otto to start the feast with some words of his own, but there was a mysterious smile on his face, as he indicated to a man to come forward. Eadgyth looked at him in surprise. He was in Saxon dress, but it was not in the style of Saxony – it was the style of Wessex.

The man knelt and kissed her hand. "My Lady Queen, I bring a message from your most noble brother, Athelstan, King of the English. With your permission, I will read it."

Eadgyth's eyes filled with tears. "Athelstan? Please read his message."

The envoy got to his feet, unfurling a vellum scroll. "My dearest and most beloved sister, Eadgyth, Duchess of Saxony and Queen of Germany, I have rarely felt such satisfaction as I did this day when I received the communication from your noble husband Otto, Duke of Saxony and King of Germany that you are to be crowned as his queen. In my life I have encountered few who I consider as worthy of the honour as you. I feel certain you will fulfil your role with a grace and good judgement to be admired by all. You will be in my prayers this day as I implore God for a happy and prosperous reign for you at your husband's side and beg you accept this gift as a token of my esteem and everlasting affection. Your devoted brother, Athelstan, King of the English."

The messenger handed her a package, which contained a finely engraved chalice of silver, with a band of gold adorned with precious stones. Eadgyth wiped at the tears which escaped her eyes as she listened to her brother's words and whispered her heartfelt thanks to the man.

Otto ordered for her cup to be filled and got to his feet. "My people, drink to the good health of Queen Eadgyth, the wisest, most pious and certainly the most beautiful queen to ever grace this land!"

As Otto's toast was repeated, Eadgyth blushed and shook her head, but she could see in Otto's wide smile that he had truly meant every word.

Chapter six

"Will you travel with us, Brother?" Otto asked Thankmar, after they had said their farewells to Bruno, who was returning to Utrecht. Hedwig too had already departed, saying she believed she should be with Mathilda.

"I was planning on returning to my own lands, unless you are commanding me otherwise," Thankmar replied.

"I am not commanding," Otto replied. "Please do as you wish, but I hope it will not be too long before we meet again. It has been good to see you."

"Indeed. I am sure I was honoured to be present at your crowning."

Eadgyth smiled uncertainly at him, alarmed by the edge to his voice. The more amiable manner he had shown during the coronation had been something she had strongly welcomed. "I hope you know Otto and I will always regard it as an honour to welcome you to court, Brother," she said.

"Thank you, my lady." Thankmar gave a slight bow.

"Gerberga and I hope it will not be too long before we welcome you to Lotharingia, my dearest brother," Gilbert said, clasping Thankmar's hands. "We will have much to talk about."

Eadgyth did not need the slight frown Otto directed at Hermann to alarm her at those words. Father Frederick too had been watching them.

"Do you object to your sister welcoming your brother to her

home, my lord?" Frederick asked.

"Of course not. Why should I?" Otto stared unblinkingly at Frederick.

Frederick returned the gaze. "No reason, my lord. I simply felt you were displeased."

"I think, Father, you should not make such assumptions."

Hermann filled the awkward silence with a warm smile. "I too would be glad to welcome Lord Thankmar to my home and the fair Duchess of Lotharingia too if she ever cares to make such a journey." He bowed to Otto and Eadgyth. "I understand you are to travel down the Rhine, my Lord King. If that is correct, any residence of mine is quite at your disposal. I will be more honoured than ever to receive you."

The tension in the group eased at this and when Thankmar made his departure a few days later, the farewell between him and Otto was cordial.

Eadgyth and Otto travelled by boat down the River Rhine, lingering some weeks with Hermann and his family before riding across country with Arnulf to Bavaria, where Otto summoned Henry to join them. He did not show any pleasure at seeing them, greeting them only with a curt bow to convey his refusal to kneel to Otto.

As they were alone Otto chose not to press the issue and welcomed his brother with an embrace. "I am glad to see you, Henry. You have missed some fine celebrations, but that is of no matter. There will I am sure be many more."

"How long am I to remain in Bavaria?" Henry asked.

"Only as long as I," Otto replied. "I have every intention of keeping an eye on you myself."

Henry sent Otto a black look, but before he could say anything a mud stained messenger was ushered in. He knelt to Otto as he delivered the unwelcome news of an attack by a Hungarian army, fighting across German lands. Otto scowled, one hand curling into a fist and striking the other.

"No doubt those damned heathens have heard of my father's death and think this a good time to attack," he cursed. "They will learn of their mistake."

"I shall marshal my men for you, my lord," Arnulf said.

"Thank you, my friend," Otto replied. "My own men too are always ready. This will not take long. Do you care to join us, Brother?"

Henry's sullen mood had vanished upon hearing of the invasion. "Certainly I do. Do you think I am a coward?"

Otto clapped his younger brother on the shoulder. "You forget that I was at your side in your first fight. I know very well you are no coward. I shall be glad indeed to have you in my army for this one."

Henry grew visibly taller at his brother's praise, causing Eadgyth a flicker of hope that in fighting alongside each other the two might grow closer.

"I must find somewhere safe for you, my sweet," Otto said, turning to her.

"My lord, may I suggest the Queen goes to my main residence of Regensburg. It is well defended and not far away. I shall instruct my daughter to make her most welcome."

"That sounds like an excellent plan. What do you think, Eadgyth? I need to know you and the children are safe."

Eadgyth tried to hide her worry at Otto riding off yet again for battle. She was certain it was something she would never get used to. "It does sound a good idea," she replied, smiling at Arnulf. "I thank you for your hospitality, my lord. I shall be delighted to meet your daughter."

It was a hurried farewell the next day as Eadgyth and her entourage rode on to Arnulf's residence. Regensburg was a bustling town, on the banks of a wide river with wooded hills rising up beyond the river plain. Arnulf's castle was impressive and as well defended as he had said. As they arrived in the courtyard, a girl came out to greet them. She dropped into a low curtsey.

"Welcome, my Lady Queen," the girl said. "I am Judith, daughter of Duke Arnulf."

Eadgyth swiftly raised her up and studied the girl. She was

very young, probably not yet twelve years with golden brown hair falling to her waist. Her hands were shaking in awe at being the one to receive the queen.

"Thank you for your welcome, Lady Judith," she said.

"Please enter," the girl said, nervously raising eyes of an unusual green to look at her.

Eadgyth was impressed with the child's beauty as she was shown into a hall where a grand welcome had been prepared.

"This looks very fine, Lady Judith," she said, trying to put the girl at ease. She glanced down at Liudolf, whose face had lit up at the sight of the bounty on the table. "I see my son cannot wait to sample it."

Judith gave a shy laugh. "Please be seated Lord Liudolf. I am honoured to have you dine at my table this night."

Eadgyth became even more impressed. It could not be an easy matter for a girl as young as Judith to be hosting the Queen and the royal children, but her nervous manner soon blossomed into a genuine warmth. Over the next days the two spent considerable time together and Eadgyth found herself increasingly drawn to the girl, greatly admiring her skill and intelligence.

After some weeks Eadgyth got the message she was hoping for, that the Hungarians had been successfully driven out of German lands. Arnulf was on his way to escort her to Saalfeld where Otto had based himself.

"I trust my daughter has served you well, my lady," Arnulf said, as he arrived late one afternoon. "My lady, I wonder if we might have a few days before we start our journey to the King."

"Indeed I have been well looked after by Lady Judith. You must be proud to have such a daughter." Eadgyth looked at Arnulf, concerned by the strained look on his face. "I am happy to wait another few days, but my lord, surely it is not necessary for you to have to accompany me. I do not think Otto should have suggested such a thing."

Arnulf looked even wearier. "Well, perhaps I might entrust the matter to my son, Eberhard." He gestured to a young man with the same stunning green eyes as his sister.

"I would be honoured, my lady," the man said.

Arnulf did appear somewhat recovered by the time Eadgyth left a few days later. "I thank you heartily for your hospitality. And you too, Lady Judith. I have been made to feel very welcome." She pressed a golden brooch set with a fine jewel and coloured glass into Judith's hand. "A small token of my thanks."

Judith flushed with pleasure. "Thank you, my lady. It was an honour to receive you."

"I hope we will meet again soon," Eadgyth said.

Arnulf kissed Eadgyth's hand in farewell. "I feel sure you will meet my daughter again very soon, my lady."

∞∞∞

Eadgyth quickly found out what Arnulf meant by that when she re-joined Otto. Their reunion was as joyful as ever. He was buoyed up by the first victory of his kingship and full of stories to tell. Liudolf sat on his knee, his eyes wide as he listened to the tales from his brave father. But the next day he spoke to Eadgyth alone.

"What was your impression of old Arnulf's daughter?"

"Very high," Eadgyth replied. "She is both accomplished and educated."

"Pretty?"

Eadgyth reflected that with any other man such a question would be worrying indeed, but she had no fears Otto would betray her and so answered honestly. "Very. Why do you ask?"

"Would she make an acceptable bride for Henry?"

Eadgyth's first thought was that Judith deserved far better than sulky Henry, but this was not what Otto was asking. "I think any man would be privileged to gain her for a wife, but she is not yet old enough for marriage."

"I have heard she is not far off. Arnulf said she will soon see twelve years."

"I suppose so," Eadgyth said doubtfully.

Otto looked amused. "Come, Eadgyth speak your mind. Something in this proposed marriage does not meet your approval. Are you concerned she will outshine you? I can assure you such a thing is not possible."

"She will be far prettier than I, but that is not what concerns me. You asked me if she would make an acceptable bride for Henry. She would. But I am not certain he will make an acceptable husband for so fine a girl."

Otto was taken aback. "Well, Arnulf is delighted at the possibility of a match between his daughter and my brother. I do not see any reason to object to Henry. He is the son of a king, a fine warrior and a handsome young man."

"I hope she is pleased," Eadgyth murmured, not liking the thought of that gentle girl in Henry's hands.

Otto shrugged impatiently. "Whether she is pleased or not makes no difference. Were you pleased when you were told you were being sent here?"

With an unwilling smile, Eadgyth shook her head. "Not particularly, but I got you, Otto. Henry is very different."

"He is not that different. I was much improved by my marriage to you. Perhaps this girl will do the same for Henry."

Eadgyth was irritated with Otto for not using Judith's name. "Judith is so young. I know she will be marriageable when she reaches the age of twelve, but…"

"We are just talking about a betrothal at present," Otto said. "The marriage may well wait a while."

Henry was far from grateful when Otto discussed the match with him. "Why do you think I want a marriage with anyone, let alone old Arnulf's daughter?"

"Marriage will be good for you, Brother and in my experience it is a happy state indeed. The Bavarians are a powerful race. This match is a prestigious one."

"I suppose so," Henry muttered.

"Eadgyth tells me the girl is both beautiful and accomplished."

"She is a child. I would prefer to wed a woman not a girl," Henry snapped.

"Don't be so foolish, Henry. It is a fine alliance," Otto snapped back.

Eadgyth choked on her laughter, which further enraged Henry. "I am glad you find this amusing, Sister."

Eadgyth wiped her eyes and laid her hand on Henry's arm. "No, Henry. I am laughing for I once said something very similar when, at the grand age of nearly twenty, I was told I was a prospective bride for a mere boy of seventeen."

Otto grinned. "Did you?"

"Henry, I will say to you, what Athelstan said to me. The girl will soon be a woman and from what I can see, she will be a fine woman indeed."

Chapter seven

Arnulf and Judith joined the court at Meresburg for the Christmas celebrations, as Otto intended the betrothal to take place after the festivities. Eadgyth smiled encouragingly at Judith, who had extended a shaky hand to hers. She sank into a low curtsey before Otto.

He quickly raised her up with kind smile. "I am honoured to meet you again, Lady Judith, although I am sure you do not remember me for it is many years since we last met."

"Thank you, my lord," Judith said in a low voice. "I am most happy to be here."

Otto looked impressed as he kept her hand in his. "Lady Judith, may I present my brother, Lord Henry of Saxony."

Henry was still smarting from Eadgyth's hissed instruction to be kind, but there was no sign of this in his manner as he bowed respectfully over Judith's hand. "It is an honour to meet you, my lady."

Judith stuttered a few words, her skin flushing and Henry's formal manner relaxed into a genuine smile. "I know you have ridden far this day, my lady. Come sit yourself a moment and take some refreshment. With your permission of course, Arnulf?"

"Of course, yes my child, go with Lord Henry."

"Thank you, my lord," Judith replied, summoning the courage to meet Henry's eyes. He smiled reassuringly back. Eadgyth, who well remembered Otto's fumbling attempts at conversation at the same age, was impressed with Henry's manner. For the first time he reminded her strongly of his father and if Henry could grow into such a kindly man as that, Eadgyth felt Judith might not be so unfortunate.

"I do not think this marriage is too bad, Eadgyth," Otto said in a low voice, as they all stared after them.

"Did you have some objections to my daughter, my Lady Queen?" Arnulf asked, a hard edge to his voice.

Before she could reply, Otto laughed. "No, she had some objections to my brother."

Arnulf smiled. "Your brother has been a young fool, but he is growing up. I would be happy to call him my son."

"Then I suggest we proceed with the betrothal as soon as the Christmas celebrations are over," Otto said. "How soon after would you want the marriage to take place? Eadgyth is concerned that your daughter, although marriageable, is still very young."

"In truth I am reluctant to let her go just yet," Arnulf said. "But I am getting old, my boy. I do not think I will be here to protect her much longer."

Otto's face was filled with compassion as he rested his hand on Arnulf's shoulder. "The betrothal will be a binding one, but it could be good for them both if they wait a couple of years."

"It would certainly be better for Judith's health if she does not start childbearing just yet," Eadgyth added.

Arnulf nodded. "I will be glad to keep my daughter by my side a little longer. But if I should die before the marriage takes place…"

"The marriage will still take place. You have my word on that," Otto said.

∞∞∞

Henry seemed pleased with the arrangement, complimenting Arnulf on the beauty and manner of his daughter and assuring him he had no objections to waiting a few years for his bride. Mathilda arrived with Hedwig to spend Christmas with her sons and, upon meeting Judith, proclaimed herself delighted her beloved Henry was to receive so fair a wife.

Eadgyth took an opportunity to speak to Judith alone, enquiring what she made of the proposed match.

"I am honoured the King considers me worthy of his brother, my lady," Judith replied properly. She gave Eadgyth a shy smile. "Lord Henry seems very charming."

Eadgyth squeezed her hands, both shocked and delighted at her brother-in-law's kindness. "We shall be sisters, Judith," she said. "And that certainly pleases me."

"I am honoured to gain you as a sister, my lady," Judith murmured.

Arnulf and Judith returned to Bavaria after the betrothal and to Eadgyth's delight, Otto announced they would head for Magdeburg. It was not quite a year since they had left the city for Otto to be affirmed as his father's heir, but it felt far longer.

The defeat of the Hungarians and the harmony in the family meant everyone's spirits were high as they travelled north. Sometimes Otto and Eadgyth would canter ahead of the rest of the group, laughing as they raced each other. At other times they slowed so Liudolf could mount his own horse, grinning with pride as he rode between his parents.

When they reached the River Elbe, they swapped their horses for boats and glided up the river. For Eadgyth it was an emotional moment when the boat docked near Magdeburg. The palace priest and the leading burghers came to meet them, followed by a crowd of cheering townspeople and nearby farmers. In Eadgyth's city the family were more popular than ever.

Everyone knelt on the bank as Otto, magnificently robed as befitted a king, stepped ashore and the Priest read the address of welcome. "To the most noble Otto, King of Germany, Duke of Saxony, to his fair wife, Eadgyth, Queen of Germany, Duchess of Saxony and Lady of Magdeburg, to Lord Liudolf and Lady

Liutgarde of Saxony, to the noble dowager Queen Mathilda, to Lord Henry, son of our late Lord, King Henry and to Lady Hedwig, daughter of our late Lord, King Henry, we bid you welcome to Magdeburg."

Otto extended his hand to Eadgyth to help her from the boat, the children following behind her and waved up the men.

"Thank you, Father, thank you good men of Magdeburg," Eadgyth said. "I am most happy to return."

Horses were brought for them to ride to the palace, but Otto walked with the Priest. "Father, my Queen and I intend to found a holy order in Magdeburg. I shall bring monks from Trier to serve here and it will become the finest foundation in the land."

"Magdeburg is honoured by your interest, my Lord King," the Priest said. He smiled up at Eadgyth on her horse. "It was a fortunate day for Magdeburg when it was presented to you, my lady."

"I can think of no place more fitting," Eadgyth replied.

∞∞∞

Otto announced the abbey would be dedicated to Saint Maurice, the soldier saint he was particularly devoted to. He and Eadgyth spent much time in consultation with master craftsmen as they planned what would be a magnificent building. Mathilda, who had already laid the plans for her own foundation at Quedlinburg, was happy to join in with her suggestions.

And so in the autumn of 937 they were ready to consecrate the land for building to commence. On the eve of the feast of Saint Maurice, Otto had the charters drawn up and brought for his approval. Eadgyth rested her hand on his shoulder, as the documents were read to them. Picking up his seal, Otto glanced questioningly up at her. Touched by how he was deferring to her, she smiled and nodded. Otto smiled back as he dipped his seal in the hot wax and pressed it against the charter. They both stared at it as the wax dried, overjoyed to finally have reached this point.

A crowd, including those who would take part in the construction, gathered at the site. The marshy ground alongside the river was mostly awkward for building, but a rocky outcrop close to the palace had been declared to be perfect. Otto was delighted, claiming it as a sign from God that this was where the abbey should be. Accompanied by several bishops who had travelled across the realm to be there, Eadgyth and Otto arrived, both soberly dressed, followed by the Priest and a procession of Benedictine monks from Trier. As Lady of Magdeburg, Eadgyth walked to where the centre of the abbey church would be. Solemnly Otto followed and went down on one knee before her.

"Lady of Magdeburg, I entreat you most humbly to grant this land for God's holy church to venerate the blessed Saint Maurice."

Eadgyth was awestruck at the step they were taking. This would be an abbey which would serve God until the day of the resurrection. Normally she would have felt a sense of amusement at Otto kneeling so humbly, appearing as a pilgrim supplicant, rather than a king or a husband, but on that day both were completely serious. "Otto, King of Germany, I most willingly grant your request. From this day, I declare this hallowed ground dedicated for all time to the veneration of Saint Maurice." Slowly she knelt down with Otto.

Holding a cross in one hand, the Priest sprinkled holy water on the ground and everyone fell to their knees. Around them a complete silence enveloped them, as even the oarsmen on the river paused their efforts. It was broken by the voices of the monks, drifting up into the blue sky as the Priest began the mass to bless the sacred ground. At the end Otto and Eadgyth rose, their hands joined. Otto turned to the priest. "From this day, Father, you are the Abbot of Saint Maurice Abbey of Magdeburg. To you and your monks and your successors for all time, I entrust the duty of praying for the souls of myself, my fair queen and our children. May God lend you strength in this task."

Part Four: The Year of our Lord 938-40

Chapter one

In his first year as king, Otto strengthened his position in the West by granting protection to the new King of Burgundy. At the urging of both Hermann of Swabia and Eadgyth's brother-in-law, Ludwig of Burgundy, he kept him at court while the situation in his realm was resolved. On the more volatile Eastern Front he appointed two trusted allies, Lord Hermann Billung and Lord Gero to the Marches, telling Eadgyth it was a relief to know those areas would be well defended even when he was not in Saxony. There was a protest from Lord Billung's elder brother, Mathilda's brother-in-law Count Wichmann, which Otto brushed off. However he was unable to avoid the protest to Gero's appointment, when Thankmar arrived unexpectedly at Magdeburg.

Eadgyth rose to greet him, but he ignored her, storming directly up to Otto. "Why have you appointed that commoner to the Meresburg March?" he demanded.

"He has inherited it from his brother, Siegfried and I trust him," Otto replied coolly.

"Siegfried was my cousin and I am your brother. Our father intended you to grant some honours to me. The Meresburg March should have been mine by the right of my mother."

"When you have proved your loyalty to me, I shall grant you both honour and power." Otto looked firmly at his half-brother, who was unable to meet his gaze. "Stay a while at court, Thankmar. Nothing would make me gladder than to have a brother I truly trust. I cannot yet trust Henry and Bruno is still so young."

Thankmar's face set into bitter lines. "You really have no idea how much I hate seeing you strutting around your court, do you? It should have been me. It would have been me if my mother had not been repudiated. You can never understand what that is like."

"I do," Eadgyth said, unwelcome thoughts of her father stealing into her mind.

Thankmar rounded on her. "Really, my lady? I had no idea your legitimacy was in doubt. Did you know your wife was a bastard, Otto?"

"Be silent, Thankmar," Otto snapped. "You will not talk to Eadgyth in that way."

"My legitimacy was not questioned," Eadgyth replied. "You are right. I do not understand that. But I was banished from court with my mother. That never happened to you. You kept your father's love."

The bitter sneer on Thankmar's face deepened. "Love? That is the way a fool of a woman thinks. My father's love has no value to me, when he was able to disperse the lands my mother brought to him as he willed. First that brat Henry inherits lands which should have been mine and now Otto chooses to favour a commoner over his own brother. But yes, Sister, bleat on about love while all men call me bastard. Tell me, Otto, how does that boy of yours like being a bastard?"

"That is enough," Otto shouted. "If you continue to speak to Eadgyth and myself in this fashion, I shall have you thrown from the court."

Thankmar turned away. "I care not. I am leaving anyway."

Otto put his arm around Eadgyth. "Good riddance," he muttered.

"But he is your brother." Eadgyth stared after Thankmar who had already strode from the door, his entourage scurrying behind him. "Otto, he is right. You do not understand how it feels to see your mother cast away."

Eadgyth turned away to hide her distress, but Otto pulled

her back. "You must not dwell on such matters. I know your mother was cruelly treated. Perhaps Thankmar's mother was as well, but, my love, you know such a thing will never happen to you."

She nodded, wiping her eyes. "What of Thankmar? You should not be parted like this."

"He will cool down," Otto said. "I have more important matters to concern me. Archbishop Hildebert of Mainz has died."

"I am sorry to hear that," Eadgyth said, remembering the kindly man who had crowned her.

"So am I." Otto looked grim. "Especially as that brother of Gilbert's is to succeed him."

"Father Frederick?" Eadgyth felt a chill creep down her spine, as a new fear drove away the memories of her mother's worn face. "I have never liked him."

"Nor have I, but until now he was of little importance."

"Can you not stop the appointment?"

"I could try, I suppose, but Gilbert would be furious. I suspect he is already considering switching the allegiance of Lotharingia to West Francia. I would rather not antagonise him."

"Now he is in a position of power, Father Frederick could be very dangerous." Eadgyth shuddered. Frederick had encouraged enough discord in the family as a simple priest. She hated to imagine how he would be now he was one of the most important men in the land.

"I know." Otto gave a helpless shrug. "Whatever I do will create enemies."

However it was another death which brought the peace in the realm to an end. Some six months after they last saw him, Eadgyth and Otto were saddened to hear of the death of Arnulf, Duke of Bavaria. Henry took their condolences to his son Eberhard, the new Duke of Bavaria and assured him the matrimonial alliance would go ahead as soon the Duke considered his sister to be ready. But by the spring of 938

Otto was feeling impatient, convinced the new Duke was over reaching himself.

"Bavaria is too powerful," Otto said, after summoning some of his closest advisors.

"I must say, my lord, I have always been surprised Bavaria has had such rights as are denied to other duchies," Hermann of Swabia commented.

"I agree," Otto said. "It is not the best situation."

"But it has worked well enough, has it not?" Eadgyth asked.

"It worked because my father and Arnulf were both tired of fighting and so were willing to agree some compromises. My father trusted Arnulf not to abuse his powers and so did I, but his son is a very different matter. Eberhard always hoped to gain the crown of the Lombard's, but that is now beyond his grasp. King Hugh has it well in his possession. So I suspect he will use the power of his duchy to try for the German crown."

"What do you plan to do, my lord?" Hermann asked.

Otto leant back in his chair. "Demand he gives up those powers granted to Bavaria, which are denied the other duchies."

"And when he refuses?" Hermann raised his eyebrow in grim amusement.

"Then I shall have to force him. Replace him if necessary. My forces are far superior to the Bavarians. It should not be hard."

"Well, my forces too are at your disposal if you need them," Hermann said, pushing back his chair. "I would be glad to see Bavarian power reduced."

"You are looking troubled," Otto commented, once they were alone.

"I know you must defend your realm," Eadgyth said. "But I shall be grieved to see trouble within the German lands."

"So shall I, but Eberhard must realise that although I support his right to inherit from his father, the powers his father enjoyed cannot automatically remain his."

"What of Lady Judith?" Eadgyth asked.

Otto looked puzzled. "What of her?"

"Does her betrothal still stand?"

"Of course it does," Otto said impatiently. "I gave Arnulf my word. Besides, it will be useful to have my brother represent my interests in the Bavarian ruling family."

"As long as Henry does represent your interests."

Otto laughed. "If he does not, it will be the worse for him."

∞∞∞

The new Duke of Bavaria responded to Otto's demands as expected and rebelled. Otto left Eadgyth at Magdeburg to ride with his troops to put down the rebellion. He managed it easily enough and returned just after Easter, more confident than ever. Eadgyth was delighted to welcome him back, but there was little time for their reunion, as Otto summoned Hedwig to him.

"It is time you were married, my dear sister," he said.

Hedwig raised an eyebrow. "I was starting to think you had forgotten me and had been wondering whether to take religious vows."

"Certainly not," Otto replied. "I have been waiting for the right alliance and now it has come about. The wife of Hugh, Duke of the Franks has died. He is looking for a new wife. An alliance with the most powerful man in West Francia will be most advantageous."

Eadgyth froze. The Duchess of the Franks had been her sister, Eadhild. But Otto made no reference to her, as he talked to Hedwig. Her questions were eager ones and even the knowledge that the Duke was eighteen years her senior did not seem to dampen her enthusiasm.

"We shall have some grand celebrations for this, shall we not, Eadgyth?" Otto was smiling at his sister's excitement and failed to notice the sorrow in Eadgyth's face.

"Of course." Eadgyth forced a smile.

"I know the Duke will be eager for the wedding to take place with all haste. His wife bore him no children. Let us hope you prove more fertile."

Eadgyth flinched. Her older sister had been a loving one. She remembered in the days when she had been so ill, Eadhild smuggling sweet treats to her in an attempt to coax her appetite. But to Otto she was just an inconvenient, childless wife whose death now presented him with a glorious opportunity.

Otto bowed to them both and Eadgyth half listened to Hedwig's animated comments. Her thoughts were with Athelstan as she wondered how he had taken the news of his sister's death. No doubt he would have ordered prayers to be said for her.

Eadgyth struggled through the day, shocked by the intensity of her grief. It had been years since she had seen Eadhild, but now the sorrow hit her as powerfully as if they had just parted that day. As the evening came to an end, she made her way to her chamber in a daze, before collapsing onto her bed and letting the grief out at last.

She was still weeping when Otto came to their chamber, whistling cheerfully. He stopped, shocked by the sight.

"Eadgyth, what is wrong?" he asked, taking her in his arms.

"The Duchess of the Franks was my sister," Eadgyth choked between sobs.

With her head buried against his chest, Eadgyth did not see the stricken expression on Otto's face. He stroked her hair. "I am so sorry. That was not how you should have heard such sad tidings. I had forgotten she was your sister. That is, I did not think-"

Anger suddenly replaced Eadgyth's sorrow. "No, you did not think who she was. She wasn't anyone to you."

"I'm sorry, but I have much on my mind."

"Really? Is that why you cared so little? It seems to me that you have changed since becoming king. Once you would have remembered who she was, but now all you think about is how such people can be useful to you. The childless Duchess of the Franks was scarce a person to you at all. I am starting to understand why your father refused consecration. It might have been better if you had done so."

"You are a consecrated queen," Otto pointed out.

"I know my rank is higher than any in the land, but I do not forget I am also a woman, a wife and mother like so many other wives and mothers in this land. You are the first in this land, but you are not the only. Yet sometimes you act as if you were."

"That is harsh."

"Is it?" Eadgyth shook off his arms. "I fell in love with a man, not a king. He cared for others. Where is that man now?"

Otto frowned. "It is your duty to love me."

"Duty? Duty never came into it and you know that. But if my dutiful love is all you need now, so be it, my lord."

There was a tense silence. "Don't, Eadgyth, please." He took her back into his arms. "I need you. Not as my queen, but as a woman."

"What for?"

Otto gave a rueful smile. "To remind me to be a king who is a man, not a monster."

Eadgyth managed a shaky smile back. "I do try."

Otto smoothed back Eadgyth's fair hair. "Tomorrow we will have prayers said for your sister and her memory will be treated with all honour. Tell me of her. Not the Duchess of the Franks, but of Eadhild the sister of Eadgyth. Was she kind or overbearing? From my experience sisters are often both."

Chapter two

Hedwig's marriage was celebrated lavishly a week before Pentecost with many attending from across the land. In spite of Hedwig's entreaties, Thankmar remained absent but, to Mathilda's joy, Henry and Bruno briefly came to the court for the festivities. Hugh, Duke of the Franks seemed pleased with his new bride, but Eadgyth was touched when in a moment of private conversation with her, he spoke fondly of Eadhild.

Scarcely had Hedwig and her new husband departed when trouble again reared its head with the arrival in Magdeburg of Brunning, one of Otto's loyal men, who held land on the border between Saxony and Franconia.

"My Lord King," Brunning cried. "A most grievous wrong has been done to me by the Duke of Franconia. He attacked and burnt my Castle of Burchard. All inside were slain."

Otto was furious. "How dare he do such a thing? Do not fret, my friend. He will be held accountable. He has overreached himself and I shall be glad of the chance to put the fool in his place."

"What will you do?" Eadgyth asked nervously. Eberhard, the brother of a King, was highly regarded and the Duchy of Franconia was a powerful one.

"I shall summon him here to make recompense."

But when Duke Eberhard of Franconia arrived in Magdeburg, he was unrepentant. "Brunning's lands are in Franconia. He should have sworn loyalty to me."

Otto had remained seated on his throne, his arms folded while forcing Eberhard to stand before him. "He has sworn loyalty to me. I regard an attack on him, as an attack on myself."

"I think you forget who my brother was. I do not need to listen to this nonsense from an upstart Saxon. I have never pushed my own claim, but perhaps it is time I did so."

Otto slammed his fist against the table. "You have sworn loyalty to my rule and I will not let you forget it. Your own brother did not consider you worthy to be king. On his deathbed he begged my father to be appointed. That is how useless you are."

There was muffled sniggering from the gathered men at this comment. Eberhard's fists clenched and his eyes narrowed. He took a step towards Otto and for a moment Eadgyth feared he would strike him. "You will regret those words, Otto," he spat.

The laughter of the men stuttered to a halt, as Otto rose up, shoving Eberhard to the ground. Angrily he stood over the sprawling man. "Do not address me in such a familiar fashion. You were summoned here to account for your actions and you will listen to my judgement. You will pay a generous compensation to Lord Brunning. As for the men who carried out the burning on your orders, I have a fitting punishment for them."

∞∞∞

Otto forced Duke Eberhard to stand next to him to witness the shame of his lieutenants. For them was the most humiliating of punishments – being forced to carry dead dogs on their shoulders through Magdeburg.

There was a look of malicious amusement on Otto's face, as the men walked past. Eadgyth felt her stomach turn at the sight of those pathetic dogs' bodies, some covered in blood and excrement and from the way Mathilda clasped her hand over her mouth, Eadgyth guessed she felt the same way. Even from her vantage point the stench was powerful, so she was not surprised when one of the men doubled over, the body of the dog slipping down, to vomit on the ground. Eadgyth averted her eyes from the sight, but Otto laughed as one of his guards forced the man back to his feet. Crimson with humiliation, the man hoisted the dog back onto his shoulders to march onwards.

But worse even than that sight was the look of rage on Eberhard's face. It was as well that guards stood all around, waiting to move at the slightest hint of trouble, for it was obvious Eberhard would have liked nothing more than to kill Otto. However he had been stripped of all weaponry and Otto gripped tightly onto his arm, so all he could do was watch helplessly as men from their household and the city also came out to witness the spectacle, many jeering and laughing at the hapless men.

As the men passed from their sight, Otto turned again to Eberhard. "Let this stand as a warning to you. I am your king and you will obey me. If you have any further concerns on the border you will discuss them with me like a reasonable man. Acts of war against my vassals will not be tolerated."

Otto walked away without waiting for a response. Eberhard threw Eadgyth a black look before stalking away himself, without bowing.

"Otto is making a mistake," Mathilda said. "Eadgyth, can you not persuade him to adopt a more conciliatory manner with the Duke?"

"No, I cannot. I support Otto completely," Eadgyth replied.

"You always do," Mathilda muttered. "My dear, there are times when even the most loyal of wives must tell her husband he is making a mistake. I think he will listen to you. Otto has offended Eberhard. The Duke of Bavaria is no happier. Thankmar too is furious with him, as is my dear brother-in-law, Wichmann. Otto needs their support."

"No, they need to remember their oath of loyalty. The Dukes

should concentrate on managing matters in their own duchies and Count Wichmann need not feel offended. The power on the Marches remains in his family. As for Thankmar, if he supported Otto more wholeheartedly, he would find his own power increase. As matters stand Otto does not trust him."

"I don't trust him either," Mathilda said. "So why antagonise him as Otto does?"

"Otto cannot show any weakness to him. It would be disastrous. Besides, in this matter today I am proud of Otto for defending his vassal. Can you imagine what would happen if Eberhard had been allowed to get away with his crimes? Half the border castles in the land would be up in smoke."

"Henry would not rule as Otto does."

Eadgyth narrowed her eyes. "Which Henry are you talking about? Your husband or your son?"

"I am not sure I know."

"Do not encourage Henry into any further pretensions. We believe him to be supporting Otto now, is that not right?"

Eadgyth's heart quailed at the hesitation in Mathilda's manner. The last thing Otto needed was to have another rebellious brother to deal with. Henry had been busying himself on his lands and other than for Hedwig's wedding, they had not seen him for some time. Away from Otto's watchful eyes, she realised they had no idea what Henry was feeling. Mathilda suddenly looked old and weary. "I know not. Henry does not confide in me. If he appears loyal, I assume he is. I am sorry, Eadgyth. I did not mean to upset you. Truly I am concerned for Otto."

Eadgyth smiled and took Mathilda's arm. "Otto knows what he is doing. You must trust him."

∞∞∞

Mathilda's fears turned out to be well founded. Shortly before midsummer, as the court were sitting down for their evening meal, Hermann of Swabia arrived, his hair dishevelled and his fine cloak covered in dust.

Otto went to his friend, his hands outstretched. "Hermann, it is good to see you. I had no idea you were joining the court at this time."

Hermann gave a slight bow to Otto and a deeper one to Eadgyth as she added her greetings. "Forgive the interruption, my lady. My lord, I must speak with you on a matter of considerable urgency."

Eadgyth had poured him a cup of wine, but she froze as she passed it to him. As always she was delighted to see Hermann, having gained a deep respect for his good sense and loyalty. But on this occasion there was something alarming in his manner. "What has happened?"

Hermann glanced uncertainly from Eadgyth to Otto. Raising his voice Otto spoke to the court, which was watching them curiously. "Start to dine, my people. I will join you shortly.

He drew Hermann and Eadgyth to one side. "You can speak in front of Eadgyth. Whatever you have to say, she will soon hear."

Hermann nodded. "There is a rebellion, my lord."

Otto cursed. "Is it the Bavarians again?"

"No, it is Eberhard of Franconia. He is mustering a considerable force."

"I suppose I shouldn't be surprised. He was in a terrible temper when he left here but I do not think it will be a serious matter. I am sure the Saxon forces will be more than a match for the Franks and I assume I can count on the support of Swabia?"

Hermann's grim face relaxed into a slight grin. "You do not need to ask that, my lord. But it is not just Eberhard. Your brother, Lord Thankmar is with them as is your uncle, Count Wichmann. They have acquired a valuable hostage."

Eadgyth held her breath, as the enormity of this situation dawned on her. Otto frowned. "A hostage? Who?"

"They have captured your brother, Lord Henry."

"Henry? I thought he was on his lands," Eadgyth exclaimed.

"He was," Hermann replied. "It is said they dragged him from his stronghold."

"What do they want with him?" she asked.

Hermann glanced at Otto. "I know not. Eberhard might wish to put him on the throne under his control. Lord Thankmar probably just wants Henry's lands."

Otto's face darkened and Eadgyth clutched onto his hand. This was what she had feared most – brother against brother. "What will you do, Otto?" she asked fearfully.

"What do you think I will do?" Otto snapped. "They will be dealt with until they beg for my mercy."

"The new Archbishop of Mainz is with them as well," Hermann added.

Otto scowled. "I should have stood firmer over that appointment. I have never liked him. You were right to come to me, Hermann. This matter is serious indeed."

"You have offended many with your new appointments over the last couple of years. Not that I blame you, my lord," he quickly added. "But others do."

Otto shrugged. "I must have men I trust in those positions. I was clearly right not to trust these men."

Eadgyth wondered if that were true. Thankmar's position was a tough one and she couldn't help thinking there might have been an opportunity Otto had missed when he could have won his half-brother to loyalty.

"My friend, you have ridden hard this day and we can do nothing more this night. Go dine. I shall join you presently."

Otto took Eadgyth in his arms and she held him tightly. "This is worse than the Bavarians, is it not?"

"Yes, it is. Eadgyth, if I do not return-"

Eadgyth clung tighter to him. "Do not speak this way."

"I must and you must listen. Liudolf is too young to take the throne. I think it is inevitable that Henry or possibly even Thankmar would be chosen. Of course if either of them offered to be regent for Liudolf, he could be crowned, but I doubt very much if they will."

"I know."

"You can trust Hermann, but he has no authority to act for you. Put yourself and the children under the protection of Bruno. I know he is barely fourteen, but he will need to act as your guardian with Hermann's help."

"Liudolf would always remain a threat to Henry or Thankmar, especially as he grows older."

Otto nodded. "You and Bruno will need to guard him well. If necessary return to your own land and put him under the protection of your brother."

Eadgyth wiped at her eyes, unable to speak.

Otto smiled. "My sweet, this is just the worst possible outcome. It is not the most likely one. I have every intention of returning victorious."

Chapter three

"I said Otto would have trouble soon if he continued as he did." There was a definite note of satisfaction in Mathilda's voice as the army rode away.

Eadgyth rounded on her. "Do not talk this way. Those men have proved Otto was right not to trust them."

"Otto has made nothing but mistakes. He is too arrogant and it is not popular. This is not how his father ruled."

"Perhaps not, but Henry too spent the early years of his reign fighting to establish his authority, did he not? I do not know why you are surprised if Otto has to do the same. He will be victorious and all possible rebels will learn a valuable lesson." Eadgyth swept away with an assurance she did not feel.

The next days and weeks were spent in an agony of anxiety, waiting for Otto's messengers to return and praying for good news. Eadgyth did her best to maintain her normal manner, seeing to the day to day business of running the household, but her nights were often sleepless ones. As news came of skirmishes, her terror only increased.

She was heartened when she received news that some of the rebels, including Count Wichmann had abandoned their cause and joined Otto's forces, but Thankmar, Eberhard and Archbishop Frederick were still at large and Otto expected a full scale battle to not be far off.

His final message was brief and odd. "My dearest Eadgyth, I send my greetings from Eresburg. I will be returning soon. Your devoted husband, Otto, King of Germany, Duke of

THE SAXON MARRIAGE

Saxony."

"Is that all he said?" she asked the messenger.

"Yes, my lady."

"Is he victorious?"

The messenger hesitated. "He was about to enter negotiations with the rebel leaders, my lady."

"What of Lord Henry?" Mathilda asked. "Has he been released?"

"I am not sure, my lady. I have not heard."

"I do not think Otto would return if Henry was not free," Eadgyth said.

"If Thankmar and Eberhard are using him for bargaining, what do you think Otto will do?" Mathilda asked. "Will he make any concessions? You know how Otto guards his power. I think he would let Henry be slain rather than concede."

"I truly believe he will not desert his brother." Eadgyth prayed she was right. "Indeed I think our fears are foolish ones. If Otto is returning, it means he is victorious."

"You don't believe that. Otto would be overjoyed at a victory. His message would be crowing of his triumph." Mathilda shook her head. "In truth it would be no bad thing if he does have to make some concessions. As long as Henry is well, I shall be content."

"I know Otto is victorious," Eadgyth said, although in her heart she believed no such thing. Mathilda was right. There had been so sense of victory in his message. However Otto was still alive. As long as he came back to her, she would bear whatever else needed to be born.

∞∞∞

Otto sent no further word on when he would return, which at least saved Eadgyth from having to decide whether to prepare a victory feast. In the end the announcement the King's banner had been sighted took them all by surprise, leaving her barely enough time to have the welcome drinks ready.

As soon as Otto walked in Eadgyth knew something had gone badly wrong. He came in alone, his shoulders slumped. She ran to him, but he seemed not to notice her as he glanced at his mother. "Henry is at liberty. He is with Gilbert and Gerberga in Lotharingia, but he is free and unharmed."

"God be praised," Mathilda said.

"Yes," Otto replied, sinking into a chair.

Eadgyth placed a drink in front of him. He picked it up and swirled the liquid around, staring blankly at it. She put her arms around his shoulders. "Otto, if you were defeated, I know that is hard, but it is just one defeat. If you have made concessions, no one will think any less of you. Indeed you will be praised for making such concessions to save your brother."

Otto looked up at that, a tortured smile on his lips. "Save my brother? I was not defeated. I was victorious."

"Truly victorious?" Mathilda asked. "You have made no concessions to the rebels?"

"None. Father Frederick and Eberhard have been exiled."

Eadgyth and Mathilda looked at each other, bewildered by Otto's attitude. "But this is good, is it not, my love?"

Otto put his head in his hands, his shoulders shaking. "Otto, tell me what has happened? You are frightening me," Eadgyth cried.

Otto composed himself, but he did not meet her eyes. "Thankmar is dead. He was killed after he submitted, while taking refuge in a church." He sank his head back into his hands, as both Eadgyth and Mathilda sucked in a shocked breath.

"You killed him in a church? That is terrible, Otto," Mathilda cried. "I can scarce look at you. I am ashamed of the king and the man you have become."

Eadgyth turned on her mother-in-law. "Leave the hall, Mathilda. Otto does not need to hear such things now." She addressed everyone else in the hall. "Everyone go. I wish to be alone with the King."

For a long time Otto stared into space while Eadgyth could do nothing but sit beside him, covering his hands in hers and waiting for him to say something.

"Have I become the monster you feared I would?" Otto asked, looking her in the eye at last.

Eadgyth felt her heart would break at how weary Otto looked. The last signs of any youthful exuberance had vanished, she feared forever. "No, Otto. If you were a monster, you would not ask me such a question."

"Is this how I will be remembered? As the man responsible for the death of his own brother in a church."

"We will be remembered for all our deeds. The good as well as the bad."

"What good have I done?" Tears flowed from his eyes. "My mother is right. I am shameful. I am not fit to be king. I do not think I am fit to be your husband."

Eadgyth put her arms around him. "Do not talk like this. You have done much good. My love, do you want to tell me what happened?"

Otto nodded slowly. "I besieged Thankmar at Eresburg. I sent several demands for his surrender. Dear God, why did he not listen?"

Eadgyth held his hands tightly. "Go on."

"Finally we stormed the stronghold, joining forces with Henry's men. I ordered the men to find Thankmar. I said to bring him to me." Otto's voice broke again, but he kept talking. "When they told me he had been cornered in the church and struck by a lance, I hurried there. I hoped it would not be so bad, but I shall never forget what I saw." He rubbed his eyes as if to erase the memory in spite of his words. "Thankmar lay face down before the altar, the lance sticking from his back. There was blood everywhere. He was dead, Eadgyth. My brother was dead."

Eadgyth knew this was not the time to remind Otto that Thankmar had not acted as a brother to him. She put her arms round him, drawing his head against her shoulder. "My love, his death was not your fault. It is one of those terrible deeds which happen in war."

"When I was a boy I idolised Thankmar. I used to follow him everywhere," Otto went on. "How could I have dreamt then that his blood would be on my hands?"

"Oh, Otto. It is not on your hands. It is on the hands of the man who threw the lance. Do not forget the boy Thankmar was. The boy you loved."

"Perhaps it was impossible for us ever to be friends. When he was an infant he was raised to be my father's heir. My birth shattered his hopes. It is no surprise he hated me. Perhaps if it was just the Duchy of Saxony, we might have reconciled, but the kingship… I don't know. I should have handled matters differently."

"It is always easy to think matters could have been different when you look back, but we must look forward. The rebellion is over. We are safe. Liudolf is safe. You said yourself his life could be in danger if you were killed. Grieve for your brother, but do not let his death destroy you."

Otto managed a smile. "Oh, Eadgyth, you are ever the greatest of blessings. Yes, I must find a way to go on. But the court will go into mourning and there will be no victory celebrations."

"Of course. We shall have prayers said for Thankmar's soul."

"Yes, we shall." He kissed Eadgyth. "Do not look so worried. I shall bear this for the rest of my life, but I will go on. And you, my sweet, please keep reminding me to remain a man."

"You are a man, Otto. That is why matters cannot always go as you wish. This will not be the last time events happen which you cannot control. For you the challenge is that you will have to deal with such matters as a king, while feeling them as a man."

Chapter four

Otto remained subdued for the rest of the summer. In public all seemed as normal, but he was plagued by nightmares and many of those dark hours were spent sobbing in Eadgyth's arms. In the autumn came the unwelcome news that the Bavarians were again in revolt. Somewhat to Eadgyth's surprise, Otto perked up considerably at this.

"I was too lenient with him last time. This time he will be sorted once and for all."

"Otto was born to fight," Mathilda said, when Eadgyth commented on Otto's sudden high spirits. "He first fought against the Slavs when he was little more than a boy and even then everyone commented on how skilled he was."

"I remember," Eadgyth replied, thinking of how when her marriage had been arranged all anyone had talked about was his martial prowess.

"I think he is never happier than at the head of an army."

"If the events of this summer have not put him off, I suppose nothing will," Eadgyth said with a touch of sadness.

However Otto dismissed this, when he kissed her farewell the next day. "I am never happier than when I am with you and our children. Do not forget that. But yes, I am happy to sort the Bavarian problem."

Remembering the ease with which Otto had put the Bavarians down on the previous occasion, Eadgyth did not unduly worry. And sure enough Otto returned to announce that the Duke had been stripped of his title and exiled.

"I have appointed Lord Berthold, Arnulf's brother as Duke of Bavaria, conditional, of course, on him relinquishing all unusual powers."

"What of Lady Judith?" Eadgyth asked.

"What of her?" Otto said.

"Will the wedding still go ahead?"

"Of course it will. Why wouldn't it? The girl will be safe enough in the household of her uncle until we proceed with the wedding."

Greatly cheered by solving this matter, Otto chose Christmas to pardon Duke Eberhard of Franconia and Archbishop Frederick of Mainz. Both were summoned to court and asked to do penance. Upon receiving this Otto graciously reinstated them in their positions, informing them the matter of their rebellion was now over.

"Do you really think it is?" Eadgyth asked. "Eberhard did not seem happy."

"I don't expect him to be happy, just to be obedient. He is getting too old to be much trouble now."

∞∞∞

As soon as the spring came Otto and Eadgyth processed across the country, bringing Liudolf and Liutgarde with them. It was a pleasant journey, with Liudolf, now a handsome eight year old, proving popular with all who saw him.

By midsummer they had arrived at the Palace of Worms, where they were joined by Hermann, accompanied by an enormous entourage as well as his daughter Ida, a charming child of seven years.

"What a pretty little maid she has grown into," Eadgyth exclaimed, as the dark haired girl was prompted into a curtsey.

"Thank you, my lady," Hermann replied. He grinned at Otto and the two men embraced. Eadgyth guessed that in the days immediately after Thankmar's death, Hermann had been the one to comfort Otto. Certainly there was now little formality between them. "I cannot tell you how much I envy Otto his fine son, but in truth I could not wish my little Ida to be anything other than who she is."

"I think you are rightly proud," Eadgyth replied. "Leave her with me, if you will, while you and Otto talk."

Eadgyth found out later what Otto and Hermann had been discussing, when Otto joined her again. They watched from a distance as Liudolf swaggered around in front of Ida, evidently finding her a much more appreciative audience than his younger sister.

"What would you say to a match there?" Otto asked, gesturing to the two children.

Eadgyth stared at him. "You are planning a match for Liudolf already? When Liudolf is older he may wish to be consulted on such a matter."

"In my experience a father's judgement is superior. Who do you think I would be wed to now if my father had consulted me before making arrangements with Athelstan?"

Eadgyth laughed. "That is true. Of course it is a great honour for Hermann."

"Exactly. He has been the most loyal of supporters. I am glad to reward him and strengthen the ties between us. Do you object?"

"I have no objections to Ida. How could I? But why the urgency?"

"Hermann has no son and Lady Regelind is of an age where she is unlikely to bear more children. Married to Ida, Liudolf would inherit the Duchy of Swabia. Think what an advantage that could be to him one day. When he is older, I intend to name him my heir for Saxony and ask for the dukes to support his succession to the throne of Germany. These duchies are very powerful, but if Liudolf was heir to both Saxony and Swabia, I do not believe any could stand in his way."

"That is true," Eadgyth said.

"Hopefully the need to decide the succession is a long way off, but I have a more pressing reason. We spoke last year of what you should do if I was slain, but it was far from an ideal plan. I do not trust Henry. Bruno is not yet old enough or powerful enough to protect Liudolf and raising my son in Wessex should always be a last resort. Betrothed to Ida, Liudolf gains a new father and a powerful one."

"You are right. Of course I would always have trusted Hermann to support Liudolf, but this will legitimise his right to act as Liudolf's guardian. Very well, I agree completely with your plan."

With the Bishop of Worms looking impassively on, the two children were brought before them the next day to solemnize the betrothal.

"My son, I observed that you were on excellent terms yesterday with Lady Ida. Well, I have some good news for you. One day she will be your wife and I am sure she will be one who is as fair and wise as you could hope for."

Liudolf nodded, seeming somewhat uninterested. "Very well, Father."

Otto laughed and ruffled his head. "Yes, such matters do not interest you yet, but one day you will be glad. A charming and loving wife is one of the greatest blessings any man can have. Treat her always with respect and you will gain a devotion which can sustain you through the darkest of days."

Eadgyth couldn't help laughing at the blank look on Liudolf's face. "Be friends for now, Liudolf. When the time comes for you to wed, the affection will grow naturally."

Otto turned to Ida, who was clutching onto her father's hand looking similarly bewildered. He laid his hand on her smooth, dark hair. "I am honoured to be able to call you daughter from this day, Lady Ida," he said.

The little girl smiled uncertainly back as Otto handed Liudolf a ring. "Give this to your betrothed, Liudolf as a promise to one day wed her."

Liudolf did as he was instructed, receiving a bright smile in return as Ida admired the pretty ring.

"Ida, give this to Lord Liudolf," Hermann said, handing a ring of his own to Ida.

The rings were far too big to fit on the children's fingers, so Otto presented them each with a chain so they could be worn around the neck. Both children looked glad when they were dismissed, but Eadgyth felt a sense of relief that it was done. As she looked at Otto and Hermann, two strong, powerful men, she felt certain Liudolf would be well protected throughout his childhood.

∞∞∞

A few days later Otto's actions turned out to be almost prescient as a messenger was ushered in. He did not kneel.

"Lord Otto, Duke of Saxony, I bring you greetings from Eberhard, Duke of Franconia and Gilbert, Duke of Lotharingia. They have declared your reign over the Land of the Germans to be at an end. In this they have the full blessing of the most holy Archbishop of Mainz. You are urged to accept this peacefully and without dispute. Lord Henry of Saxony has been proclaimed king. All hail King Henry!"

Chapter five

The man barely got the words out before Otto strode over, seizing him by the throat. "I was anointed by the grace of God," he cried, shaking the messenger. "Henry will never be king."

Struggling for breath, the man clawed uselessly at Otto's fingers but Otto only tightened his grip. The man's face went scarlet and his eyes bulged. Eadgyth ran over to them, tugging futilely on Otto's arm.

"Stop it, Otto. This man is just the messenger," she cried.

Otto gave the man a last shake and flung him to the ground. He sprawled on the floor, gaping up at them, red fingerprints marking his throat. Never had she seen Otto so angry. She clung onto his arm, terrified of what he would do next.

"Get up," he snapped at the frightened man. "And get out before I kill you."

As the man stumbled for the door still gasping for breath, Otto thrust Eadgyth away. She lurched backwards and would have fallen if Hermann had not quickly put a steadying arm around her. Otto kicked a chair across the hall before seizing one of the costly platters on the table and hurling it against the wall. It crashed and splintered, splattering its contents over one of the finer tapestries. A jug of ale followed it, the dark liquid dripping down the walls. Eadgyth shrank further back in alarm, glancing imploringly up at Hermann. He was staring in shock at Otto, but Eadgyth's terrified expression restored him to action. He gave her an understanding smile before edging forward to put a hand on Otto's shoulder.

"My lord, you are distressing your wife."

Otto shook him brusquely off, but he turned to Eadgyth, his rage subsiding as he saw how frightened she looked. He ran his fingers through his hair, his chest heaving. "Forgive me, Eadgyth." He glanced at Hermann. "Please leave us a moment."

Hermann hesitated, which only made Otto angry again. "Damn it, I'd never hurt Eadgyth. Now, leave us."

Eadgyth nodded her head at Hermann, knowing there had only ever been a risk of accidental injury while Otto was in such a rage. She went to him slowly and put her arms around him.

"I am sorry, my sweet," he whispered. "I didn't mean to frighten you. Did I hurt you?"

"No and I am not frightened, but you must calm yourself."

"I know." Otto took a deep breath. "Why has this happened?"

"It is not completely unexpected," Eadgyth said gently. "It was obvious Father Frederick and Eberhard were still angry. And Henry has always coveted the throne."

"Thanks to my mother," Otto muttered.

"Gilbert is more of a surprise. I could see he was not the most loyal of men, but I did not expect him to join a rebellion. I suppose Father Frederick has encouraged him."

"I sense my mother's influence there too. She and Gerberga were always close. I do not doubt she filled her head with this nonsense of Henry being born to rule. Gilbert has thrown in his lot with the King of West Francia. I think it is hard to say if Frederick is influencing him or he, Frederick."

"Never mind the reasons. I am sure your mother did not intend for this. You need to focus on what you are going to do now."

Otto gave a short laugh. "I know what I have to do. Yet again I shall have to go to war with one of my brothers. And it may be before the year is out, the blood of another of my brothers will be on my hands. Will you still love me if that happens?"

Eadgyth smoothed the hair back from his face. "This war is

not of your making, my love. I will not blame you or love you any less."

Otto kissed her. "Thank you. I know my mother will not be as forgiving."

∞∞∞

The message Otto sent back to the rebels was short and to the point. "You are all traitors and will be dealt with accordingly."

The next couple of days were spent in frantic planning. Hermann summoned his men north and Otto gave the call to his own army. They were cheered by the unexpected support of Conrad, the young Count of Rhennish Franconia, who sent a message pledging himself and his men.

"That is good news," Hermann said. "I was worried about the thought of the two duchies of Lotharingia and Franconia against us, but it seems they do not have as much support as they think."

"Conrad must be Lady Regelind's grandson. Have you met him?" Otto asked. "I think I have not, although I remember his father, Werner, very well."

Eadgyth smiled at the note of wry humour in Otto's voice as she remembered how Otto had once described him as the most pompous man he had ever encountered.

"I have met him. He is young yet, no more than seventeen I believe. But he is known to be a fine fighter."

"Excellent. I have the support of the Burgundians as well, since I assisted their king."

"My brother, Udo, Count of Wettergau will also be willing to aid you," Hermann said. "I know Eberhard is his cousin, as he is mine, but his son was slain last year by the forces of Eberhard, so his loyalties are to you."

Otto gave his friend a warm smile. "I am not fortunate in my brothers, but I am fortunate indeed in my friends. I think we will soon be ready to march." Otto looked thoughtfully at Eadgyth. "I hope the fighting will not come anywhere near you, but this palace is not well enough defended. You need to go somewhere safer. Unfortunately it would be too risky to return to Saxony."

"I would suggest Lorsch Abbey," Hermann said. "It is in the hills, away from the river. It is as safe as anywhere can be and less than half a day's ride from here."

"Very well. Send a message to them to expect the Queen and the royal children."

"Of course. My lady, may I also commend Ida to your care? I do not want her to risk the journey back to Regelind at present."

Eadgyth smiled warmly. "Naturally you can. Is she not also now one of my children?"

∞ ∞ ∞

Nestled in the hills, Lorsch Abbey was as peaceful as Eadgyth could want and she soon found herself thoroughly bored. The days reminded her uncomfortably of her life at Wilton before her marriage. Although dull as the days were, the nights were terrifying as she dreamt frequently of Hermann arriving at the abbey to inform her of Otto's death, the doors echoing in her ears as they slammed shut behind him.

Resolutely she made herself grateful for the peace and the boredom. The last thing she wanted was fighting near the abbey. She busied herself with the children, finding much of her day was spent trying to keep Liudolf amused, when all he wanted was 'to be fighting alongside my fathers', as he now insisted on referring to both Otto and Hermann.

As always Otto kept her informed of his whereabouts. She was heartened when some weeks after his departure, she received a message stating, "My dearest Eadgyth, be of good cheer. After praying before the Holy Lance, I routed Henry at

Birten and have kicked the puppy out of the German lands. I have every hope this will bring an end to his pretensions and our reunion will not long be delayed."

Their reunion when it came was welcome, but brief. Henry was still in exile, but he had made himself at home at the court of the West Frankish king, Louis, Eadgyth's own nephew.

"He will give Louis control over Lotharingia if Louis helps him become king," Otto commented with a curled lip. "My God, Germany deserves better than that."

"Is the support of Louis and the West Franks not a problem?" Eadgyth asked, surprised Otto was taking this news so calmly.

"Louis is not as powerful as he likes to think. Much power rests in the hands of the Duke of the Franks, my brother-in-law and yours. I have already sent a message, but the last thing he will want is King Louis expanding his power into Lotharingia. The Margrave of Flanders too has pledged his support."

"Arnulf? He is my kinsman."

Otto gave a wry smile. "Is there anyone of note you are not related to?"

∞∞∞

The hope Henry would forget his pretensions was short lived when news reached them of his gains. Regretfully Otto again left Eadgyth at Lorsch, as he moved quickly to prevent Henry from joining Gilbert and Eberhard. For a while Otto besieged Henry and Eadgyth hoped the fight might soon be over, but an attack by King Louis on Verdun forced Otto to release Henry's stronghold while he dealt with the Franks.

If war in the German lands had frightened her, the thought of a war with a powerful foreign power was many times worse. With enemies advancing on them from all fronts, she could not help but fear the worst. It was impossible for Otto to be in so many places at once. But mighty as Louis was, Otto turned out to be the stronger. With Louis gone, Henry,

Gilbert and Eberhard lay low. Otto sent for Eadgyth to come to Mainz, where he intended to negotiate the surrender with the traitorous Archbishop.

∞∞∞

Eadgyth left the children in the security of Lorsch Abbey when she made the day's ride to Mainz.

"Otto!" she cried, as she arrived in the hall of the palace, overjoyed to see her husband standing with Hermann and a man who so resembled him, she immediately guessed was his brother, Udo.

Otto turned and grinned, holding out his arms. Eadgyth flung herself into them. After clinging to him a moment she looked up at him, critically studying his face. Gently she ran her fingers over a long cut which stretched from his cheek, across his neck. She shook her head.

"I see you have not taken care of yourself," she said sternly.

"I am still alive," Otto protested, taking her into his arms again. "Oh Eadgyth, it is good to see you. Are the children well?"

"Yes, although it has been hard to keep Liudolf from running away to join you."

"That lad will be a brave warrior one day," Hermann commented.

Eadgyth hated the thought, but smiled at Hermann. "Ida is well and has been the most charming companion. She and Liutgarde are very much a pair of sisters already. But tell me of the war? Are they surrendering?"

"I do not see what else they can do," Otto said. "It would be better if I had captured them, but their ally King Louis is gone and I have had some decisive victories. Hermann led an army into the heart of Franconia itself, winning support and destroying any who persisted in standing against us."

The meal that night was a merry one as everyone savoured

the thought of Otto delivering the terms of surrender the next day. When Eadgyth rose at the end, Otto got up with her.

"I will bid you good night, my friends. I do not wish to be rude, but I have spent far too much time these last months in your company and not nearly enough with my fair wife."

Eadgyth shook her head, blushing at some of the comments the men returned, but she happily left the hall hand in hand with Otto.

"Do you think the Archbishop will accept the surrender terms tomorrow?" she asked as they reached their chamber.

Otto looked at her, a smile on his face. He removed her mantle and tossed it to the floor, before gently unwrapping her hair, lifting the fair strands so they sparkled in the candle light.

"I do not want to talk about the war this night," Otto said, pressing long and lingering kisses against her lips, cheek and throat.

He pulled her over to the bed, kicking of his shoes before sitting next to her, wrapping one arm tightly around her. Gently he stroked her cheek. "This night is just for you and me. Is that acceptable to you?"

Slipping her arms around him, Eadgyth sank back against the pillows, meeting his lips in joy. "Very," she whispered. "Oh, Otto, I have missed you so much."

Chapter six

Everyone was in a confident mood when the Archbishop of Mainz arrived with his entourage. Otto and Eadgyth walked into the hall to many cheers, as the men settled down to enjoy the spectacle.

"A good day to you, Father," Otto said to the Archbishop. "This will not take long. The terms are very simple. The Duke of Lotharingia, the Duke of Franconia and Lord Henry of Saxony must deliver themselves to my justice. If they do so, I may be disposed to mercy. Their titles and lands will be forfeited and whether they ever regain them will depend on how they display their loyalty to me in the future."

"That will not be acceptable, my lord," Frederick said.

Otto raised an eyebrow and flung himself into his chair with an irritated shake of the head. "Very well. Tell me what will be acceptable to them. I am sure this will be most entertaining."

"We demand that the Duchy of Lotharingia be returned to the overlordship of West Francia. The Duke will negotiate his own terms with the noble King Louis. The Duchy of Franconia is to gain such rights and freedoms as were formally enjoyed by the Duchy of Bavaria."

"Never," Otto spat.

"And that Lord Henry of Saxony is given increased lands and named as your heir. Such a declaration is entirely reasonable given the tender years of your son, Lord Liudolf of Saxony."

"Are you anticipating my death in the next few years?" Otto asked. "Even if my son is too young, I have other options. Lord

Bruno, for example."

"Those are our terms," the Archbishop said.

"You are not in a position to make such terms," Otto replied. "I set the terms for surrender."

"I fear you were misinformed, my lord," Frederick said. "We are making terms for a truce, not a surrender."

"You fool," Otto spat. "I have no interest in a truce. They will surrender or die. That is the only choice they face. Take those terms back to your friends."

Otto stormed from the hall and after a shocked moment Eadgyth followed him. He was already shouting orders.

"Send out scouts. I want to know where the former Dukes of Lotharingia and Franconia are. From this moment their titles are forfeit. Also locate Lord Henry of Saxony. He is no longer a brother of mine. If any are killed in the attempt to capture them, so be it. I shall not mourn their deaths."

"Otto," Eadgyth ran to him.

He did not even look at her. "You will need to return to Lorsch Abbey. Go as soon as you can."

"Already?"

"Your place is with the children somewhere safe," Otto said impatiently.

Eadgyth bit her lip, knowing the last thing she must do was make more work for Otto. "Of course. I'm sorry."

Otto paused, giving her a swift kiss. "No, I'm sorry. At least we managed one night together."

Eadgyth forced a smile. "Yes, we did. I will make arrangements to return to Lorsch immediately."

Hermann had overheard this last comment as he came towards them. "Otto, the Queen will need a good escort. The rebels mostly fled to West Francia. If they return they will come over the Rhine. She could encounter them on her journey."

"You can't spare the men," Eadgyth protested.

"Of course I can spare men to keep you safe," Otto said. "Part of the army will need to go south in any case. If I lead that force you can make most of your way with us."

"With your permission, Otto, I shall head north," Hermann said. "I will send a message to young Conrad in Rhennish Franconia to continue with his efforts."

As Otto nodded his agreement, he and Hermann embraced before the two men parted to organise their forces.

∞∞∞

Eadgyth had never before ridden with an army. She found it hard going, but knew better than to complain. For her it would be just one day's ride. Otto and the men would likely be on the move for some time. Besides, she was dreading the moment they would yet again be parted.

As they were riding along the river frantic messengers rushed to meet them. "My lord, the rebels are attacking settlements along the river. They know your children are at Lorsch and there are rumours they will head there."

Eadgyth cried out, terrified as she imagined the three children helpless in the hands of the rebels. The two children of the King and the daughter of the Duke of Swabia would be hostages of exceptional value.

"Otto, do something," she cried. "Don't let them near our children."

Otto cursed, but kept himself calm. He gestured at some men. "You, ride with the Queen to Lorsch. Eadgyth, get there at all speed and keep the children safe. I will do everything I can to keep them away, but if you need to escape, so be it. I do not mind where you go, as long as you are all safe."

Eadgyth took a deep breath and composed herself. "I understand. I will not fail you." She looked steadily at Otto, trying to smile. Mounted on her horse, there was no possibility of even a farewell kiss. "May God send you victorious, Otto," she said, somehow keeping her voice even.

"May God keep you and our children safe, my love," Otto

replied soberly, as he rode away from her.

The rumours of the threatened attack had already reached the abbey and Eadgyth's arrival was greeted with relief. She clutched Liutgarde and Ida to her as she explained the plan to the Abbot but he would not hear of Eadgyth and the children leaving the security of the abbey unnecessarily.

"Our presence is putting you and your brothers into danger, Father," Eadgyth said.

"My Lady Queen, Lorsch is honoured to provide you with refuge. You are safe here for now and every man here will defend you with their lives. We shall keep a careful watch and will plan as necessary."

"I will defend you too, Mother," Liudolf announced.

Eadgyth had to smile despite her terror. "Thank you, my son, but I pray it will not come to that."

She put aside her anxieties to allow Liudolf to ride out with the scouts who had been sent to check the surrounding area. She knew it was good for him to be involved, despite his tender years, although she could not relax until the boy returned safely. After several anxious days they returned one morning so quickly Eadgyth had no time to become concerned, accompanied by a smiling messenger.

The messenger bowed. "The rebels have been kept away, my lady. The immediate danger to you is past."

"God be praised!" Eadgyth murmured.

Liudolf was bursting with pride. "Can I tell Mother what Father said to the rebel leader once he was defeated?"

"Absolutely, my young lord."

Liudolf grinned. "He told the man he would not allow a swine such as him to advance upon the place where he kept his most treasured pearls."

"Oh, Otto," Eadgyth said, shaking her head in both tears and laughter.

"My lady, this information is confidential," the messenger continued. "Count Udo of the Wettergau is leading a large force to aid the King and he knows where the rebel dukes are. The

King too is marching on them."

"The battle will be huge." Eadgyth twisted her hands together, torn between her terror at the thought and the hope the rebellion would soon be over.

"Yes, it will."

Eadgyth nodded, allowing no sign of the horror flooding through her. "Prayers must be said in the church for the King to be victorious."

∞∞∞

It was only later that Eadgyth found out what a brutal fight the Battle of Andernach had been. At the time all she heard was a brief message from Otto.

"My dear Eadgyth, praise God we have proved victorious. The rebels are either dead or in flight. I am pursuing them into Lotharingia, but I am hopeful this matter will soon be at an end."

Eadgyth had prayers of thanks said in the church and waited nervously while Otto invaded Lotharingia and pressed further into West Francia. At last she was summoned to join him once again in Mainz. Joyfully she hurried there and as before found Otto in the hall. To her surprise Mathilda was also there in a conversation so intense neither noticed her immediately. She took the chance to watch them for a moment, thinking neither of them looked happy.

"Eadgyth!" Otto's mood suddenly cheered as he saw her and he pulled her tightly to him, pressing his lips passionately against hers.

"It is good to see you, Eadgyth," Mathilda said, also kissing her. "Although I know it will be useless to think you will disagree with any of Otto's actions."

"I do not yet know what Otto's actions are," Eadgyth said with a smile.

Otto ran his hand wearily over his hair. "Sorry, my sweet. I have not kept you well informed.

"It doesn't matter. I knew you were alive and that was all I needed to know. Tell me now what has happened."

"Eberhard of Franconia is dead," Otto said. "Count Udo killed him at Andernach."

"A fine supporter of your father," Mathilda commented.

"But a traitor to me," Otto countered. "Gilbert survived the battle. He should have surrendered. He might have found me merciful, but instead he tried to escape over the River Rhine." He laughed out loud. "The fool chose a leaky boat, which sank mid river. The current was too strong for him and he drowned."

Eadgyth's eyes widened at the humour Otto was showing over his brother-in-law's death, although after all fighting he had endured, she could not find it in her heart to blame him.

"You show no sorrow, Otto," Mathilda said. "He should have been a brother to you. He was a son to me."

"If he had behaved as a brother to me he would not have died." Otto narrowed his eyes. "My God, Mother, why do you always choose to side with my enemies?"

"If you had accepted God's will, none of this would have happened. Henry was the first son born of King Henry. You know that. I assume your rule is so strict because you know how weak your claim is. You have offended everyone and are a disgrace to the wise rule of your father." Mathilda glared furiously at her son. "Your morals disgust me."

Otto shook his head. "My morals? You still hold against me some indiscretions from when I was a boy. Nearly ten years I have been married to Eadgyth and I have been completely faithful. Even when she was with child and unable to receive me, even when we have been parted for weeks or months, I have not once strayed." Otto looked at her, a tender smile coming to his lips. "And not only that, I have not even been tempted to stray. In both thought and deed my morals have been beyond reproach for my entire marriage."

Eadgyth, who would never have reproached Otto if there had

been other women on those occasions, felt tears come to her eyes at Otto's speech. There was no doubting the honesty in his tone. She put an arm around him and swallowed the lump in her throat. She wondered if Mathilda would condemn her if she confessed to feeling only relief that Gilbert and Eberhard were dead. "What has happened to Henry?"

"The coward ran to our sister in Lotharingia and when I pursued him, hid behind the King of West Francia. He is finished now. His allies are dead. Good riddance to him."

Chapter seven

Otto had Henry, Gerberga and Archbishop Frederick brought to Mainz for judgement. The gathered people watched in interested silence as Gerberga, dressed in the deepest mourning, collapsed weeping into Mathilda's arms. Eadgyth was torn between her natural sympathy to the widow and her anger that she had abetted the traitors who would happily have widowed her. She glanced at Otto to see his face impassive.

The Archbishop too was completely expressionless, implying he had much better places to be. Eadgyth studied his face, but she saw no sign of any grief for his brother. As always she found his ability to conceal all emotion unnerving. Henry was, as usual, scowling. None of them bowed to Otto and nor did Otto demand it, simply ordering all three to be seated.

"The rebellion is over. None of you now are in any position to make demands of me. You will face my justice. Do you wish to say anything?"

Gerberga wiped her eyes and Henry looked at the floor. "Our Heavenly Father is the only judge who matters to me, my lord," Frederick said.

Otto sent the Archbishop a contemptuous look, but gave no other sign of hearing him. "First the Duchy of Franconia. This will now be under my direct control. There will be no further dukes. Parts will be governed by such counts as are loyal to me. I shall appoint someone to act on my behalf when I am not in the region."

"Might I suggest young Conrad," Hermann said. "As a Frank himself, he will know how to manage the region and his actions show him to be loyal to you."

"Of course," Mathilda muttered. "Your grandson by marriage. How convenient for you, Lord Hermann, to have a kinsman in such a position."

"I suggest him for his loyalty to the King, my lady," Hermann replied. "And because, although he is young, his abilities are impressive."

"He is as skilled as he is loyal," Otto said. "I approve your suggestion."

"What of Lotharingia?" Gerberga asked, raising red rimmed eyes to her brother. "Does my son inherit?"

"Your son is far too young to manage such a region and his father's lands were forfeited. I trust he will grow into a loyal man. If so, one day he shall be rewarded, but I shall appoint some other to rule in Lotharingia."

Gerberga folded her arms and glared at her brother. "Lotharingia is under the protection of the King of West Francia. You have no right to make such pronouncements."

From the dais Otto smiled benevolently. "My men have Lotharingia, so I will make such pronouncements."

"King Louis will never give up. I know it."

"His fight is over, Sister. In any case it will not concern you. You are to marry Duke Berthold of Bavaria."

"I will not," Gerberga snapped.

"She has only just been windowed," Mathilda said. "You cannot marry her off already."

"I can and I will," Otto said. "Gerberga is too much of a trouble maker. I need her wed to a loyal man."

"This is unacceptable." Mathilda looked outraged.

Gerberga had been looking disgruntled by Otto's comments, but at this a hint of satisfaction darted into her expression. "No, Mother. If this is what Otto commands, so be it."

Otto and Gerberga looked at each other, as everyone in the hall muttered. "I thought she would argue more about this,"

Otto whispered to Eadgyth.

Eadgyth too was surprised by Gerberga's demeanour of noble fortitude. "I suppose being Duchess of Bavaria gives her a high rank and I think she will enjoy telling everyone how you forced her into the marriage."

Otto smiled. "True." He held up his hand for silence. "If I might continue. I have wasted quite enough time on this matter already. Henry of Saxony and Archbishop Frederick of Mainz, rise and stand before me."

Otto stared at Henry, who shuffled his feet beneath his brother's withering gaze. "Do you have anything to say?" he asked.

"No."

"No? Men have died, including your own brother-in-law for this and now you have nothing to say?"

"I am the king, Otto," Henry shouted. "It is my right."

"No, I am the king and you are my prisoner. You shall both enjoy a spell in captivity. I may show you mercy when you are ready to acknowledge my rule. Transport them immediately." Otto waved his hand airily at some armed warriors.

"May God forgive you for this, my son," the Archbishop said to Otto, as he was escorted from the hall with an air of injured dignity.

His calm demeanour made a stark contrast to Henry. He was dragged from the hall, still proclaiming his kingship, but Otto ignored him, putting his arm around Eadgyth. "I hope we can get back to normal now."

"So do I, but I would not hope for too much too soon." She gestured to Mathilda, who was coming towards them, her face white. Otto sighed as he waited for his mother's tirade.

"How can you do this? He is your brother?"

"He is no brother of mine," Otto replied. "He is a traitor."

"No, he is not. This is your fault, Otto. Your rule is too arrogant. You have ignored the rights of the noble men of the realm. Why could you not follow the example of your father? He never implied he was better than everyone else, as you do.

Your rule is wrong and I am ashamed of you. Henry would be by far the finer king."

"That is enough!" Otto got to his feet, his voice echoing throughout the hall. "For years now I have heard this nonsense from you, trying to avoid being roused to anger since I consider it wrong for a son to be angered at his mother. But this is enough. You too bear responsibility for the men who have died. If you had not continually poured such nonsense into Henry's ears and Gerberga's, none of this would have happened. I could have won Henry to loyalty. Be grateful I have not punished you."

Otto stormed from the hall, as Mathilda collapsed into tears. Gerberga put her arm around her and Eadgyth too ran to her, concerned by the way she slumped against her daughter.

"How can he speak to me in that way?" she sobbed.

Eadgyth poured her a cup of wine. "Drink this, Mathilda and calm yourself," she said, putting her arms around her. "Come, sit down."

"How can Otto be so cruel? I never thought to be so abused by my own son."

"Otto will calm down and you will be friends again," Eadgyth soothed. "I will see to it."

"I trust you will persuade Otto to beg her pardon," Gerberga put in.

Eadgyth looked up, her gaze narrowing. "I will try to bring peace between them, but I do not see why Otto should apologise. I trust you will encourage your mother to display more loyalty towards Otto and to stop this endless censure of his rule. Henry is in captivity and you will soon be in Bavaria. It will be very much the better for Mathilda if she learns to live amicably with Otto."

Gerberga shook her head. "Oh yes, you never see any wrong in Otto. You support him without question."

"She always does," Mathilda put in.

"At least somebody does," Eadgyth said, her sympathy for the two women vanishing.

She went in search of Otto and found him outside, staring at the river. The boat bearing away Henry and Frederick was still visible.

"Are you going to tell me I am too harsh?" he asked.

"No, my love," Eadgyth said putting her arms around him. The triumph in his manner had gone. "Perhaps you were harsh, but she has provoked you often enough over the years. I do not know how she can think as she does. If Liudolf becomes as fine a man as you, I will be the proudest mother alive."

Otto pressed his lips against the top of her head. "I do not know what I would do without your support. Shall we return to Magdeburg once we have escorted Gerberga to Bavaria? I should be in that area. I have heard there has been some trouble with the Slavs while I have been away."

"I will be glad to return there. You know I love it more than anywhere else. But we will go wherever you need to be. As long as we are together, I am content."

Chapter eight

"Eadgyth." Mathilda approached her hesitantly the next day. "Gerberga is gone."

Eadgyth set down her cup. "What do you mean gone?"

"She is not in her chamber. Her jewels and clothes have vanished. Where can she be?" Mathilda's voice rose in a panic. "I think she's left Mainz."

Eadgyth looked frantically at the doorway, although she knew it was too late. Otto had already left for Rhennish Franconia to consult with Conrad. A number of people gathered around them in a mixture of outrage and excitement at hearing Mathilda's news. She gestured at one of the men. "Ride after the King, as swiftly as you can. Beg him to return." She turned to another group. "Send men in all directions. Locate the Duchess of Lotharingia at all speed."

Mathilda twisted her hands. "Where can she be? Oh, this is all Otto's fault. If he hadn't talked of forcing her straight into another marriage…"

"Stop criticising Otto," Eadgyth snapped, although she suspected there was some truth to her words. "If Gerberga had not caused such trouble for him, none of this would have been necessary. Indeed Gilbert might still be alive. Now, sit down. I am sure no harm has come to her."

Otto returned swiftly, striding into the hall, his face like thunder. "Has that damned woman been found yet?" he snapped at Mathilda. "I do not have time to waste on this matter."

"I have sent men out to look for her," Eadgyth said. "But none have reported finding her." She had hoped Gerberga would have been found before Otto returned. Judging by his clenched fists and narrowed eyes, any delay would be very much the worse for her.

"Are you not concerned for your sister?" Mathilda demanded.

"Oh, she will be fine. No doubt she has taken refuge in some abbey. I am sure it is too much to hope that she has followed her husband to the bottom of the river."

Otto strode away before Mathilda could start her indignant reply and Eadgyth quickly followed him.

"Otto," she called.

Otto turned back. "Yes, I know. Now you are going to tell me I was too harsh. Probably I should not have said that to my mother."

"No, you should not." Eadgyth took his hands. "But I know how vexing this is."

"Yes, it is. I've had to send Hermann to talk to Conrad. I know he will carry out my wishes, but I would prefer to have dealt with such matters myself. And there is trouble in Saxony. The Slavs could be invading, while I waste time dealing with Gerberga's tantrums."

"I am sure she will be quickly found."

"She had better be." Otto scowled, but his eyes softened as he looked at Eadgyth's anxious face. "You did well acting so quickly, my sweet. If she is easily found, it will be thanks to you."

∞∞∞

Some weeks went by with no sign of her. The men they had sent out believed she had fled back to Lotharingia, but where in the duchy they did not know. Otto became increasingly agitated, his mood worsening with each comment Mathilda made. Even the news Hermann was escorting their children to Mainz did not cheer him and he barely glanced up when they arrived. Liudolf and Liutgarde sent Eadgyth bewildered looks and wisely left their father alone. As they were preparing to dine that night, a messenger arrived from West Francia.

"My Lord King," the man started. "I bring demands from King Louis of West Francia for you to withdraw your men from Lotharingia. He is taking control there."

Eadgyth caught her breath, suddenly terrified of another conflict, but Otto merely shook his head in an irritated fashion. "King Louis is in no position to make demands of me. He has no rights to Lotharingia."

"He has every right, my lord," the man continued. "He has the right by marriage to the Duchess of Lotharingia."

A gasp went around the hall and Otto got to his feet. "What did you say?"

The messenger stood his ground. "The noble King Louis of West Francia is wed to the fair Duchess of Lotharingia."

There was a tense silence, as all eyes went to Otto. Eadgyth wanted to warn the messenger away, convinced Otto was about to hurl something at him.

Otto sat back down. "Wed?" His tone was dumb struck and taking advantage of this, Eadgyth laid her hand on his arm, hoping to stall any fury. But Otto shook his head and leaning back in his chair, he began to laugh. "That woman," he said, with admiration flickering in his voice. "The hour grows late, but in the morn return to your king, my friend. Tell him he is welcome to keep my sister, but Lotharingia remains mine. It is a fair exchange."

∞∞∞

"Are you not angry, Otto?" Eadgyth asked, as Otto came to bed that night.

"No." Otto looked more relaxed than he had done for a long time. "Gerberga would have been wasted on old Berthold. This role will suit her much better and keep her too busy for any further trouble, I hope. Besides, a family connection with the royal family of West Francia can only be an advantage."

"I already have a connection," Eadgyth said. "King Louis is my nephew."

Otto grinned, leaning over her to press a long kiss against her lips. "I know. I am well aware how much better connected you are than I."

∞∞∞

Keen to have everything settled, Otto swiftly arranged a meeting with King Louis and Gerberga swept in on her new husband's arm. The gathered nobles watched the spectacle in fascination, anticipating a huge row erupting.

"I will not kneel to you, Otto," she announced. "I am your equal now."

"Oh, I think you always were," Otto replied.

Gerberga raised her eyebrows. "Is that all you have to say?"

"Not at all." Otto took his sister's hands and kissed her on each cheek. "I wish you every happiness."

Gerberga did not look completely pleased and Eadgyth restrained a smile at how she had so clearly hoped to infuriate her brother. She turned to the King of West Francia, delighted to meet her nephew, who she had last seen as a boy in exile at Athelstan's court. The nineteen year old king looked very young stood next to Gerberga.

"I am glad to see you again, my dear aunt," Louis said, bowing over her hand.

Eadgyth studied him. "Why, you have a look of Athelstan, as I remember him from when I was a child."

Louis looked pleased. "I hope I am like him in manner as well as looks, for he is a great king."

THE SAXON MARRIAGE

"He is indeed," Eadgyth murmured.

Otto nodded coolly at his new brother-in-law. "Let me restate the position on Lotharingia. I have taken it and that is how it will remain."

"But…" Louis started.

"No, let me finish. You could fight me for it, but I think you have enough problems dealing with our brother-in-law, the Duke of the Franks." Otto's eyes lit up in a mischievous gleam. "You will also have your hands full with your new wife."

Gerberga shot him a black look, but Louis shook his head. "My wife is a woman beyond compare and the finest queen in Christendom."

"No, my wife is the finest queen in Christendom." The look of mischief on Otto's face deepened. To the fury of his sister and embarrassment of his wife he continued, "my dear Gerberga, do try to emulate Eadgyth's example and I feel sure you will become much admired."

∞ ∞ ∞

The wedding of Gerberga with King Louis was celebrated with great pomp attended by many from both Germany and the Frankish regions. It was obvious to all that in spite of her genuine grief for her first husband, Gerberga was enjoying becoming a queen.

With the celebrations over, Eadgyth, Mathilda and the children made their way east, determined to be back at Magdeburg in time for the Christmas festivities. Otto was delayed while he stationed his men in Lotharingia and consulted with Conrad, his new deputy in Franconia, but he promised to join them as quickly as he could.

Eadgyth was delighted to welcome him upon his arrival, but he came bearing bad news. This time he did not repeat the mistake he had made when Eadhild died, but after greeting her in the hall, he asked her to come to their chambers.

"Why? What is wrong?" Eadgyth asked, recognising the sadness in his eyes.

"Just come."

In their chamber Otto gently put his arms around her. "My dearest, there is news from England. I am so sorry, but Athelstan has died."

Struck by the pain, Eadgyth sank down onto the bed burying her head in her hands. Otto put his arm around her shoulders, knowing there was nothing comforting he could say. She looked up at him, tears in her eyes. "I knew I would be unlikely to ever see him again, but…"

"I know. This is still hard. I wish I had met him. I have heard from so many that he was the finest of men."

"He was. He was the most affectionate of older brothers when I was a child. I know he would have liked you. As a king he was he was so pleased with the advantages our marriage brought him, but as a brother I think he was even more pleased I had found such contentment."

Otto smiled gently at Eadgyth. "Although I never met him, I will always remember him with the greatest of gratitude for sending you to me."

Chapter nine

Eadgyth put aside her grief to ensure it was an enjoyable Christmas at Magdeburg that year. With his enemies either dead or imprisoned, Otto was in high spirits as he relaxed with the court over the festivities. To start with he spoke with Mathilda only when necessary, but gradually the tension between them eased. Mathilda confessed to Eadgyth how much she was missing Henry, but she had the sense not to mention this to Otto. She spent much time in the company of the grandchildren she adored and her mood too became merry. However in the spring she surprised Otto by going down on her knees and begging him to pardon Henry.

"I know he will be loyal to you now," she said. "Please Otto, it is not right for your brother to face such indignity."

Bruno who had also spent Christmas with them added his pleas. "Mercy is a fine quality in a king, Brother."

Otto who had appeared somewhat disgruntled at his mother's request, looked amused at what a churchman mischievous little Bruno had become. "Perhaps the fool deserves a chance. Very well. We will summon him and that wretched Archbishop here. If they swear loyalty, they will be free."

"You need to give Henry some responsibility, Otto," Mathilda said. "Show him he is valued and I know he will be of the greatest value."

"What responsibility do you suggest?"

"Lotharingia is without a duke. Install Henry there," she

urged. "It will be a great honour and he will prove himself worthy."

Eadgyth sucked in her breath, nervous at such power in Henry's hands. She was confident Otto would swiftly dismiss the idea, but to her surprise he was considering it.

"You may be right, Mother. Perhaps if he has something to occupy himself he will be more amenable."

"But Lotharingia, Otto?" Eadgyth said. "It is a powerful duchy. Should he not earn your trust first?"

Mathilda frowned at her but Otto shook his head. "It is not as powerful as it was. As I expected, King Louis has enough problems to keep him occupied in West Francia. With Hermann in Swabia and Conrad managing Franconia, there would be no nearby allies for him to plot with."

"Apart from Father Frederick," Eadgyth pointed out. "Presumably he would return to Mainz."

Otto frowned. "True. I shall have Conrad keep an eye on him."

"Henry will be the finest of dukes," Mathilda said with an icy smile. "You need have no concerns."

Otto smiled at Eadgyth. "I must settle this trouble with the Slavs," he said. "I do need someone to oversee matters in the West, so I can concentrate on the Eastern Marches. Henry gets a chance to prove himself and I, I hope, will gain a useful deputy. It will be advantageous to us both."

Eadgyth considered it even more worrisome that Otto would be distracted with the Slavs while Henry set up a powerbase in Lotharingia, but she kept quiet and smiled brightly at Otto and Mathilda. "Well, we must prepare a welcome for him."

∞∞∞

The tension in the hall was high as Henry and Frederick arrived in the grand hall of Magdeburg. All eyes were on them as they both knelt penitently before Otto. Eadgyth studied them, trying to work out what was making her uneasy, but Otto seemed delighted by their attitude. He rose up from the throne to embrace Henry. "I hope we can truly be brothers now," he said.

Henry gave Otto a wide smile. "We shall be. I am truly penitent."

"Excellent," Otto said, turning to greet the Archbishop.

Eadgyth kept her eyes on Henry. The moment Otto's attention was elsewhere, it seemed to her that Henry's smile slipped. Their eyes met and his expression instantly became winning again. "My dear sister, forgive me for not greeting you. The journey tired me."

She accepted the brotherly kiss on the cheek. "Welcome back, Henry. Your mother too is waiting to greet you."

Mathilda embraced Henry warmly. "It is good to see you, my dearest son," she said. "But you must accept Otto's rule now."

"I know that, Mother," Henry said impatiently.

"Yes, Mother," Otto put in. "Henry has done some foolish deeds, as we all do as boys." He looked pointedly at Mathilda. "It would be unjust indeed to continually hold them against him. I have pardoned him and that, I hope, is the end of the matter."

Henry smiled again, clapping his brother on the back. "Of course it is, Otto. No brother will be more loyal."

Otto grinned. "Speaking of brothers, Bruno is here. He will be pleased to see you. It is good we are all together again."

"Except for Thankmar," Henry said pleasantly.

Otto's face darkened. "Except for him."

∞ ∞ ∞

Eadgyth kept a close eye on Henry over the next weeks, although his manner towards Otto seemed friendly. They frequently hunted together with Henry full of praise for Otto's skill, but there was something Eadgyth could not put her finger on. Some comments, although innocuous enough, seemed to carry double meanings that she was unsure if Henry had intended.

"I have prepared the charters granting Henry the Duchy of Lotharingia," Otto said as he came to their chambers one evening.

"Are you sure about this?" Eadgyth asked. "It confers huge power on him. Is he truly ready?"

"I believe so. I take it you are not sure. Why not?"

"I am not certain. Something in his manner makes me uneasy. I know he seems willing, but I feel his manner is contrived."

"It is natural his manner is a little forced given the enmity which has been between us," Otto replied. "Displaying my trust is the best way to ease that. Besides, he will not have an easy time in Lotharingia. He will be kept far too occupied to have any time for further rebellion."

Eadgyth slipped willingly into Otto's arms as he got into bed. "I pray you are right."

∞∞∞

Otto summoned Henry to him the next day. Eadgyth was sitting next to him in the hall, ever observant for any signs Henry was not the loyal brother he was appearing to be.

He gave a slight bow as he entered, but Otto was in an informal mood. He got up and embraced him. Henry smiled broadly. "Greetings to you, Otto, and you too Eadgyth."

"Greetings, Brother," Otto replied. "I am enjoying your company here at court, but I shall soon be sending you away. There is work for you to do."

"Of course, Otto. You know I will serve you in whatever way I can."

"The Slavs are mounting a force against the border," Otto said. "I am needed over there, but you are to go the other way. Lotharingia needs a duke. I am appointing you."

Henry's eyes widened. "You are making me Duke of Lotharingia? I do not know what to say. I had hoped you might confer an honour on me one day, but I did not expect it to be so great or so soon."

Eadgyth felt better. Henry's surprise was very natural. Otto grinned at his brother. "You have given me your word I can trust you."

"Did Mother ask you to do this?" Henry asked.

"She did," Otto replied. "But, Henry, you know I do not make my decisions on requests. You would not be gaining this honour if I did not consider you worthy."

"I shall not let you down, Otto. I swear it."

"It is not the easiest of duchies," Otto warned. "If you need assistance, you must ask. Hermann in Swabia and Udo in Wettergau will both be glad to help. They are Lotharingians themselves, so will understand the region."

"I can manage," Henry said buoyantly.

"Of course Henry will manage," Mathilda said, entering the hall at that moment. "You should not underestimate him, Otto. Henry will be a fine duke."

"I am sure he will," Otto replied. "It may not be easy, but no doubt he will learn quickly."

"I do not know how soon you wish me to go, Otto, but I have a request," Henry said. "Could I go first to Bavaria?"

Otto raised his eyebrows. "Bavaria? Are you considering matrimony?"

Henry nodded. "I would like to take my bride to Lotharingia."

Eadgyth felt dismayed. She was a long way from trusting Henry and if he did have any further plots in mind, the last thing she wanted was pretty, young Judith embroiled in them. "Is she not still a little young?" she asked.

Both Otto and Henry stared at her. "She is plenty old enough by now, I think," Otto said.

"She was marriageable at our betrothal," Henry put in. "But I agreed to wait a while. It has been three years now. She must be ready."

"What if her uncle does not agree?" Eadgyth said desperately.

Henry frowned. "If he does not agree, I shall break off the betrothal. It is not reasonable to expect me to wait any longer."

"Her uncle will agree," Otto replied. "Why wouldn't he? Eadgyth, you are being foolish. Of course Henry must claim his bride. I wish you every happiness, Brother."

Eadgyth flushed. "Of course, forgive me, Brother. I had forgotten how old she was. I am sure she will make an admirable duchess."

Henry smirked at Otto's rebuke of Eadgyth. "Thank you, Sister." He turned to Mathilda. "Do I have your blessing, Mother?"

Mathilda embraced her son. "Naturally you do, Henry. She was a sweet girl when I last saw her and I am sure she has grown into a charming young woman now."

∞∞∞

Eadgyth found it hard to shake off her foreboding at the thought of Judith in Henry's clutches, far away in Lotharingia from any who might help her. She would be completely at the mercy of any decisions Henry made, however bad. But this was the fate of women and there was nothing she could do. At the feast to celebrate Henry's accession as Duke of Lotharingia she did her best to smile graciously, wishing she could cast off the feeling of impending danger.

On the day of Henry's departure, she watched him as he was giving brisk instructions to his entourage in the courtyard. Handsome and confident, he appeared a man any woman would be delighted to gain as a husband, but Eadgyth wished matters were otherwise. Hesitantly she approached him, smiling as brightly as she could.

"Henry, can you spare me a moment of private conversation?"

THE SAXON MARRIAGE

Henry's smile was equally bright and, Eadgyth felt, equally false. "Of course, my dear Eadgyth. Shall we step in here a moment?"

They went into a small gallery and Eadgyth took out a package, unwrapping the fine fabric. "Will you give this nuptial gift to Lady Judith for me, as a token of my esteem and a wish for her happiness?"

Henry looked startled at the sight of the intricate bangles, inlaid with precious stones and the necklace, studded with emeralds. Eadgyth had chosen it, as the gems reminded her of Judith's beautiful green eyes. "Thank you, Sister. I had no idea you thought so highly of her."

"Oh, I liked her very much. Of course it is some years since I have seen her, but I am sure she has only grown finer."

"I do not doubt she will be honoured to receive such a gift from you."

"You will be kind to her, won't you, Henry?" Eadgyth pleaded, taking advantage of Henry's genuine delight at the gift. "Of course she is old enough for marriage, but she is still so young and she does not yet know you very well. Please be patient and understanding."

Henry's face darkened. "I do not need advice from you on how to treat my wife, thank you, Eadgyth. I shall expect her to be dutiful and obedient. If she can manage that, I am sure she will not have any cause for complaint." He thrust the gift into his pouch. "Now if that is all, I would like to be on my way. I am eager to claim my bride." He gave a lascivious smile. "I do not think it will be hard to mould her into the sort of wife I require."

Henry did not wait for a reply, as he returned to the courtyard. Eadgyth's eyes filled with tears, as she wondered what Judith would have to endure. She murmured a quick prayer for the girl she had become so fond of and followed Henry to where he was bidding farewell to Otto and Mathilda. It was an effort to allow him to kiss her on the cheek. "I thank you for your gift, my dear Eadgyth," Henry said with no sign of any anger.

"Please pass my greetings to Lady Judith and I wish you every happiness, Henry," Eadgyth said properly, even more unnerved by how quickly Henry had concealed his anger. She wondered what other emotions he had been concealing since he had arrived at court.

She remained in the courtyard, staring after the entourage, unable to shake off her feelings. Otto stood behind her, resting his hands on her shoulders. "Is all well, Eadgyth?"

Eadgyth turned, clinging to Otto. "I hope so. Do you truly trust Henry?"

Otto looked amused. "There is only one person I trust unreservedly and that is you, my sweet. But Henry seems sincere in his intentions. If he can make a success of Lotharingia, it will be the making of him."

"I suppose so," Eadgyth replied, clinging even tighter, reminded more than ever how fortunate she had been to gain such a loving husband. She only wished Judith could be as fortunate, but with Henry, so arrogant and impatient, it seemed a forlorn hope.

As she returned with Otto to the palace, she was unable to help one last glimpse in the direction Henry had set off. The anger towards her which he had so quickly concealed reminded her of the hatred he had born Otto. She realised she had never truly believed Henry had overcome that.

"Do not worry," Otto said. "Henry is a fool. To succeed in Lotharingia, he will have to grow up a lot. And if he fails, he will learn he was not cut out for rule after all."

"Are you sure I should not worry? A failed Henry could be more dangerous than ever."

Otto tightened his arm around her shoulders. "I hope it will not come to that."

Part Five: The Year of our Lord 940-41

Chapter one

Otto spent the spring campaigning on the eastern marches, while Eadgyth remained at Magdeburg. She missed Otto, but in spite of that it was an enjoyable spring. With Otto and Henry reconciled, tensions had eased with Mathilda and the days slipped pleasantly by as she, Mathilda and Liutgarde spent much time together in talk and laughter.

Now Liudolf and Liutgarde were growing up, she encouraged them to take more of an interest in Magdeburg and its people, particularly the charities which so interested her. Both children embraced their new roles, leaving Eadgyth increasingly proud as they were cheered everywhere they went. She had come to realise she would likely have no more children. In the previous two years, although she and Otto were as eager for each other as ever, she had not had even the briefest of pregnancies. Through much prayer, she had become reconciled to this knowledge, vowing that as long as Liudolf and Liutgarde remained healthy, she would have no regrets.

She had heard nothing from Henry since his message to Otto that he and Judith had married and were on their way to Lotharingia. Always Eadgyth remembered Judith in her prayers, fervently hoping she was contented.

As summer came she was delighted to welcome Otto back. A few more scars marked his arms, but he was in high spirits reporting that the border was now as strong as it had ever been. Eadgyth wondered if he had seen his illegitimate son while he was in the region. She knew it was likely and indeed she could not wish it otherwise, but the question went unasked. It was better for her not to know. He greeted Liudolf exuberantly, promising him a day's hunting and she delighted in the strong bond they shared.

Otto had not heard anything from Henry, but he did not seem concerned. Now he was back at the heart of government, one of his first acts would be to discover what was happening over in the west. However before he could send out any inquiries, Hermann arrived at Magdeburg. Eadgyth took one look at the strain on his face and knew the harmony was about to be shattered.

"Greetings to you, my lady," Hermann said. "And greetings to you, Liudolf. You have grown much since I last saw you."

"Welcome to Magdeburg," Eadgyth replied, kissing Hermann on the cheek.

"Greetings, Father," Liudolf said with a grin. "Is Ida well?"

Hermann laughed, ruffling Liudolf's hair. "Yes, Ida is very well. She speaks often of you and your sister."

"Hermann!" Otto cried, entering the hall. "It is good to see you."

It was a long time since there had been any formality between Otto and Hermann and he did not bow, but embraced Otto warmly. The more than ten year gap in their age which had been so apparent when Otto first took the throne, had diminished as Otto grew in experience until now it was barely noticable.

"Thank you, Otto. It is always good to see you and the Queen, not to mention having the chance to check on the progress of my young son." Hermann winked at Liudolf.

"Why do I sense you are not entirely happy?" Otto said wryly.

Hermann gave Otto a half smile. "I need to speak with you on a matter which will not make you happy. And I need to speak frankly."

Otto glanced around him. "You can always speak freely in front of Eadgyth, you know that. I want Liudolf to learn more about the duties of kingship, so I am happy for you to speak in front of him, if you do not object."

"It concerns his uncle," Hermann said grimly.

"I thought it might," Otto replied. "I am still happy for Liudolf to listen. Shall we sit? Eadgyth, do you want to remain?"

"I think I should," Eadgyth replied.

"Very well," Hermann said. He took a long drink of ale and looked firmly at Otto. "I support you completely, but you made a big mistake in putting your fool of a brother in charge of Lotharingia."

Otto frowned. It was unusual for anyone to question his judgement so brutally. "Did I or are you afraid to have someone so closely related to me in Lotharingia? Maybe you hoped I would appoint one of your kin to the position."

Hermann met his eyes without flinching. "Are you questioning my loyalty?"

Eadgyth laid her hand on Otto's arm, alarmed at the thought of Otto quarrelling with Hermann over Henry of all people. "Hermann has been your most faithful supporter since you took the throne. At least listen to what he has to say. He would not question your judgement lightly."

"No, I would not," Hermann said. "Shall I continue, my lord or would you prefer I remained silent?"

Reluctantly Otto grinned. "I sometimes suspect you and Eadgyth of being in alliance against me. You both only show me formal respect when you are angry with me."

Eadgyth and Hermann exchanged shamefaced glances and Hermann laughed. "We are most certainly not in alliance against you, although I am flattered to be placed in such company. Seriously, Otto, do you doubt my loyalty?"

Otto shook his head. "No, I am merely angered as I had thought I had solved the problem of my brother and now it seems I have not. I am not angry with you. Tell me everything, as frankly as you wish."

"Your brother cannot cope. Lotharingia is in disarray. The

nobles there are all squabbling among themselves. None will accept the Duke's judgement. I offered my support and I believe my brother did the same, but we were both banned from entering Lotharingia."

"He banned you?" Otto exclaimed.

"His message was under no circumstances was I to set as much as a single foot in Lotharingia. Not that he could do anything to stop me if one of the Lothringian nobles decided to invite me. He is powerless."

"Have you any news on the Duchess?" Eadgyth asked anxiously.

"Not really. She is said to be very beautiful, but I know nothing more than that."

"What are you going to do, Father?" Liudolf asked.

Otto rested his hand on his son's shoulder. "What do you suggest?" He smiled at the look of astonishment on Liudolf's face. "Come, my son, give me your ideas. Most make foolish suggestions at times, but it is still good to make them. It is only your mother and father-in-law to hear them."

"I think I would ride to Uncle Henry and demand he accept help," Liudolf said after a long pause. He looked at his father in trepidation for some reaction.

"What if he does not?" Otto enquired.

"I don't know. Can you force him?" Liudolf asked.

Otto smiled. "Not so foolish after all. However I will not ride all the way to Henry. This mess is of his making. I will demand he meet me at Grona. I do not know if I can force him to accept help, but if he will not accept it, I will strip him of the duchy. I must have a strong man to rule there."

"He will be furious," Eadgyth said. "Is this really wise? He has rebelled against you before."

"I think it is the only course, my lady," Hermann replied.

"I know he will be angry," Otto said. "What difference does that make? It seems he has no power in Lotharingia. Franconia and Saxony are under my control. And, Hermann, I know I do not even need to ask if Swabia will be loyal."

Hermann grinned. "No, you do not, but what of Bavaria? His wife's uncle is the duke."

"Berthold is not the rebellious type. Oh, I am sure he would quickly swear loyalty to Henry if he became king, but I do not think he will stir himself on Henry's behalf at present. Then we are decided. Eadgyth, make the preparations to move the court to Grona."

∞∞∞

Henry did not appease Otto by taking his time before arriving in Grona, one of the smaller royal residences. By this time Otto had summoned many Lotharingians and had found that the situation was just as Hermann had described.

"Not that I doubted you, my friend," Otto said. "But I do not want Henry to accuse me of listening to false words from my favourites."

Eadgyth had hoped Judith would accompany Henry, but he arrived accompanied merely by a small entourage. She received him the hall.

"Sit down, Henry and take some refreshment," she said, unable to help feeling sorry for him. This would likely be a humiliating encounter with his older brother. She gestured to a chair close to the central hearth and poured him a cup of wine. "Is Judith well and happy?"

"She is well enough," Henry said curtly. "She has proved to be an obedient and amenable wife, so I have no complaints."

Eadgyth's sympathy faded, deciding this arrogant young man deserved everything Otto chose to throw at him.

Chapter two

Otto left Henry kicking his heels in the hall for a long time. Eadgyth had long since given up trying to make conversation and so he had been left alone, becoming increasingly agitated. Eventually Mathilda came in, but although delighted to see her favourite son, even she was greeted curtly.

A burst of laughter heralded Otto's arrival and he strode in with Hermann on one side and Liudolf on the other. Eadgyth's heart sank. Henry would undoubtedly be even more outraged when he received his rebuke in front of his nine-year-old nephew. She would have called him away, but Otto kept his arm around his son's shoulder, leaving little doubt he wanted Liudolf to stay.

"Greetings, Brother," Otto said, his smile fading.

Henry looked up from the fire. He got slowly to his feet but did not bow. "I do not know why you summoned me here, when you seem in no haste to see me. I have been waiting an age."

"So have I," Otto replied, folding his arms. "You should have been here before today."

"I have much to occupy myself with. I cannot simply leave Lotharingia on a whim."

"What occupied you, Henry? Trying to subdue your rebellious nobles?"

"The situation in Lotharingia is completely under control," Henry said, flushing. "I do not care what you have heard to the contrary."

"The trouble is, I have heard much to the contrary," Otto replied. "And not just from Hermann, so you can stop glaring at him."

"They are wrong," Henry said.

"Are they? So you will not mind if I come with you to Lotharingia, will you?" Otto gave an unamused smile at the panic in Henry's eyes. "Do not think you can refuse me entry, as you refused Hermann and Udo."

Henry's face turned scarlet with rage and with a roar he launched himself at Hermann, drawing his sword. Hermann dodged the blade swooping towards his ear, as Otto seized Henry's sword arm. Hermann grabbed the other, Henry straining against them both. With a sudden effort he wrenched his sword arm free, but stumbled backwards. Eadgyth screamed as in his attempt to steady himself he lurched towards Liudolf, the point of his sword pressing into his shoulder. She dashed forward, without any thought for her own safety, pulling Liudolf away. The boy had gone white in shock, his hand clutched to the wound.

Henry stared in horror and Otto easily wrenched the sword again from his hand, shoving him to the ground. "Stay there," he snapped. "Guard him. I do not want him moving."

A little away from them, Eadgyth had eased Liudolf into a chair and pushed aside his tunic, despite his protests.

"Mother, I am fine. It is just a scratch."

Eadgyth blinked furiously to prevent the tears rushing to her eyes from spilling over. Never had she felt such fear as when the sword had struck him. "I will be the judge of that," she said firmly, although even in her own terrified eyes it was obviously just a scratch.

With her hands shaking, Mathilda brought over a jug, the wine splashing over the table as she poured it out. Eadgyth attempted to hold the cup for him, but Liudolf shook his head at her and took it with a desperate attempt at a smile.

Otto crouched down next to Liudolf, his hand resting on his

good shoulder. "Your first sword injury already, my son. You are a brave lad."

"Truly it is nothing, Father," Liudolf replied, the colour returning to his cheeks in pleasure at his father's praise.

Otto half smiled and kissed his forehead. He pushed back his own sleeve to show Liudolf a long white scar. "This was mine," he said.

"I think that is more impressive."

"But I was nearly five years older than you," Otto replied. He looked again at the scratch on Liudolf's shoulder. "That may look more impressive once the bruise comes up. Stay here with your mother now." He grinned at Liudolf's look of horror. "I am afraid, my son, the toughest part of a warrior's life is being fussed over by your mother. It is most irksome, but indulge her. She too has had a shock."

Otto stood up and took Eadgyth in his arms. She pressed her face against his chest, trying to keep the tears back. "He will be fine," Otto soothed.

"He could have been killed. If he hadn't jumped back so quickly or if there had been more force behind the blow…"

"Do not think of it, my sweet."

"Henry did not mean to hurt Liudolf," Mathilda said, her voice still shaking.

Outraged, Eadgyth pulled away from Otto's arms. "Do not make excuses for him. If the sword had gone deeper do you think I would care if he meant it or not?"

Mathilda looked down. "No and nor would I. But Otto should not have had Liudolf aside him in such matters."

Otto shook his head. "I had a feeling you would make this my fault, Mother." He looked again at Eadgyth and Liudolf. "I need to deal with that fool. Will you two be well enough for a moment while I do that?"

Eadgyth nodded, putting her arms around Liudolf, who submitted with resignation to his mother's embrace. Otto smiled at them both, as he returned to Henry, who was still sprawled on the floor with Hermann glowering menacingly over him.

"Get up, Henry," Otto said in a voice seething with fury.

"Is all well with the lad?" He stared earnestly up at Otto. "I did not mean it, Otto. I swear."

"He will be fine, no thanks to you."

"Let me apologise," Henry begged.

"No, I do not want him coming near," Eadgyth cried, clutching Liudolf even closer.

"Stay away from my son." Otto glared at his brother. "Now we will discuss Lotharingia. You have failed there and you know it."

"It was not my fault."

"You were under strict instructions to ask for assistance from Hermann or Udo if the situation proved too tough."

"I neither needed nor wanted them meddling."

"You did need it and if you had sought it, you would have remained Duke of Lotharingia. As it is, you can now consider yourself stripped of your dukedom. I shall appoint someone more capable. I have already sent a message to Count Otto of Verdun. I have no doubt he will be glad to take over the duchy and act as a guardian to Gerberga's brats."

Henry's eyes narrowed. "You cannot do this."

"Yes, I can. Who do you think will stand up for you? The Lotharingians will be delighted. They deserve better."

Mathilda darted to Otto. "No, my son. I agree with Henry. This is wrong. Henry is a king's son. He should have a high position."

Otto's lip curled. "Of course. I should not have asked who will stand up for the fool. I do not care that Henry is a king's son. Men do not gain high office in my realm just because of their birth. Men gain it from loyalty to me and serving me well. Henry has done neither of these things."

"This is not the way to rule," Mathilda cried.

"It is the way I rule."

"Am I free to go?" Henry asked, clinging on to his last shred of dignity.

"Of course. Being an incompetent fool is not a crime. But where will you go? The hour gets late."

"I care not. I am returning to Lotharingia to get my wife and then we will go to my lands. I suppose I still possess them or have you taken those from me too?"

"Don't be foolish, Henry. Of course I have not taken the lands our father left you. But why not come to court? You could learn much."

"No, thank you. I do not need to see you strutting around every day. Indeed, I hope I never have to see you again."

Henry was the last person Eadgyth wanted at court, but she would have been pleased to see Judith. She shivered at the fury on his face, suddenly terrified of what Judith would have to endure once Henry returned to her. "Henry, if you are truly sorry for your actions towards Liudolf, do not take your anger out on your wife," she called.

Henry turned. "I will not have you meddling in my marriage. Judith will do as she is bidden and I will take no complaint from her." He spat at Eadgyth. The glob fell considerably short of her, but even so she shrank back.

Otto shoved him. "Get out. I shall be glad if we never meet again."

"No," Mathilda cried. "Otto, you cannot let Henry ride away at night."

Henry had already stormed from the hall. Otto shrugged. "The worst the fool will have to suffer is a cold and uncomfortable night." He turned to Eadgyth and put his arms around her. "Don't cry, my sweet."

"I cannot help it." She wiped her eyes. "I cannot bear what he will do to Judith. Can you do nothing to protect her?"

Otto looked downcast. "I regret that marriage. The girl deserves better, but there is nothing I can do. Every man in the realm would be up in arms if I interfered in a man's marriage. Henry's wife will have to do as Henry commands."

Chapter three

Everyone was subdued that night with none of the usual lively conversation around the great table. Eadgyth personally supervised seeing Liudolf to bed, ignoring the boy's indignant arguments. He inspected his shoulder, taking great pride in the bruise now starting to form. But as she hugged him goodnight, he clung longer to her than she had expected and she knew he too was shaken.

Knowing she would find sleep impossible, Eadgyth wrapped a cloak around herself and sat in the torch lit courtyard, staring for a long time up at the stars.

"Let us talk out here," Otto said, as he came out of the door with Hermann. He looked surprised to see Eadgyth. "What are you doing out here? I had thought you would be asleep by now."

"I couldn't," Eadgyth replied.

"Is all well with young Liudolf?" Hermann asked.

"He is shaken, but determined not to show it."

"Poor boy," Otto replied. "He is brave. I wish today's events had not happened, but I cannot help feeling proud in how he handled himself."

Eadgyth nodded. "So am I. Do you two need to talk alone? I can retire."

Otto took hold of her hand, as he sat beside her. "I do not suppose Hermann will mind if you hear what he has to say."

"No, although yet again I will be telling you something you do not want to hear."

"That does not surprise me, but even so I shall listen."

"The Dowager Queen," Hermann said hesitantly. "She criticises you too freely. Her opposition is so obvious, but you show her such deference. Showing respect to such a woman is making you look weak."

Otto looked taken aback. "I have never despised the counsel of women and have come to respect their wisdom very much. It may be different from the wisdom of men, but I do not consider it any less."

"I would not consider that respect wrong," Hermann said slowly. "Certainly everyone notes the respect you show to your queen, but that further endears you to your people and indeed they share it. As of course do I." Hermann sent a smile in Eadgyth's direction. "But the Queen has long proved herself the finest of women and does not abuse your respect, but returns it tenfold. No one has ever heard a word of censure of you on her lips."

"I have on occasion," Otto said with a smile. "But I agree she is the finest of women."

Eadgyth shook her head. "Hermann, I shall have to disappoint you if you two continue in this vein and call you both fools."

Hermann laughed. "I do not think it improper for you to voice your opinions to Otto in private, but in public you are always Otto's greatest supporter. That support, coming from a lady as well respected as yourself, enhances Otto's standing." He looked apologetically at Otto. "But the Dowager Queen… her intelligence too is respected. Her criticisms of you are outspoken, yet you continue to show her such respect even though she returns none of it. It makes you look weak."

"What can I do? She is not the type of woman to be silenced."

"She does not have to stay at court. You could send her away."

There was a tense silence. "Exile my own mother?"

"She has her own estates and very fine ones," Hermann said. "She would not be destitute."

The torches flickered wildly in the breeze as Otto stared at

Hermann until the silence grew uncomfortable. Hermann put his hand on Otto's shoulder. "Otto, I am your man, always. I do not want you ever to doubt that. I do not consider you weak. How can I? You have impressed me as both a warrior and a leader since your first fights on the Slavic marches all those years ago. If I have presumed too much on our friendship and spoken out of turn, I apologise. I would be grieved to lose such a friendship."

Otto clasped his hand. "I am not that much of a fool. Indeed I appreciate my good fortune in having so wise a friend who is not afraid to speak his mind. You may freely voice your thoughts to me on any, with perhaps one exception."

Hermann glanced at Eadgyth. "That is understood, although if I did freely voice my thoughts on that exception I can assure you they would be nothing but praise."

Otto smiled, but Eadgyth looked sharply at him. "Have any voiced criticism of me?"

"Rarely and it is unimportant," Otto replied.

Eadgyth thought of that sword point against Liudolf's body and shuddered at how easily they could have lost their only son. "Because I have born you just the one son?"

"We do not need to discuss this," Otto said. "Yes, some have made comments. They are ignored. You know I would never do anything to cast Liudolf's legitimacy into doubt, quite apart from how much I need you at my side. Please do not worry."

Hermann nodded at Otto. "I shall bid you good night, my friend, my lady. I know I have given you much to think on."

As Hermann returned to the castle, Otto turned to Eadgyth. "Let me hear your opinions on my mother? Am I too weak? Should I send her away?"

"I do not know, Otto. The manner in which she speaks to you grieves me greatly, but she has always been so kind to me. I would miss her very much if you exiled her."

"I have never stopped hoping to gain her support," Otto replied, a wistful note creeping into his voice. "But perhaps it is time to accept I will never have it."

Eadgyth put her arms round Otto, understanding this was about so much more than power. "Shall I talk to her? Make her understand how she is forcing you to this position? Such a talk may be better received from a woman."

Otto nodded. "Thank you. That might be best." He ran his hand gently over Eadgyth's head. "Come, let us go to our rest and try to forget the events of this day."

Eadgyth nodded, keeping her arm around Otto's waist as they made their way to their chamber.

∞∞∞

The conversation with Mathilda went as so many conversations had gone before, with protestations of her affection, but continued criticism of Otto's rule and Henry's rights.

Eadgyth held up her hand. "We are not talking about that now. I am here to tell you to stop your criticisms or face exile. Otto is being strongly urged to consider such an act and I cannot say I blame him. Why should he put up with so poor a supporter at court?"

"You would support him in exiling me? Yes, of course you would. You support everything Otto does. Why, when I think of how I and my dear husband welcomed you to this land, it is a poor repayment you are giving me."

"Is it?" Eadgyth raised her eyebrows. "When Otto was confirmed as his father's heir, Henry begged me to always support him. I am eternally grateful for the welcome you and Henry gave me and I will honour my promise to Henry until my dying day. I shall never forget Henry's concern for his son or the peace it gave him when I assured him Otto would always have my love and support."

Mathilda wet her lips nervously. "I did not know Henry said such things."

It went against Eadgyth's nature to say anything hurtful to

one she loved, but nonetheless she ploughed resolutely on. "I shall tell you something else Henry said. He knew you could not support Otto. That is why he placed his trust in me. But he also said he thought you loved Otto and would do nothing to harm him. I am grieved beyond all measure that Henry was misled in this belief."

"He was not misled," Mathilda cried. "Of course I love Otto. He is my son. It is because I love him that I seek to guide him in a better direction."

"But your public and unrelenting criticism is harming him," Eadgyth pointed out. "Henry believed you would do nothing to harm him, but Otto is finding it hard to share that belief."

Mathilda suddenly looked very old. "I see."

Eadgyth put an arm around her mother-in-law. "Please do not think me ungrateful for the kindness and love you have shown me over the years. Indeed it is because I am grateful that I am saying such things to you this day. I would be saddened indeed to lose your company, but you are leaving Otto no choice."

A few tears trickled down Mathilda's cheeks, but she nodded. Eadgyth pulled her closer and hoped for the best.

Chapter four

The year ended with the usual merriments at Magdeburg, before the court moved in the spring at Mathilda's request to Quedlinburg. It had become her habit to spend Easter there and to have a mass said for her late husband.

"Otto, can I also invite Henry to join us," she asked tentatively the evening before they set off.

Otto shrugged. "Quedlinburg is your residence. You can request whoever you want."

"I know I can, but I will not invite Henry if it displeases you."

Eadgyth felt touched. Over the Christmas festivities Mathilda had tried hard to remain on good terms with Otto. His face softened and he looked questioningly at Eadgyth. "Henry is tiresome, but I truly believe he did not mean to hurt Liudolf that day."

"I know he did not," Eadgyth replied. "I have no objections to his presence at Quedlinburg. Bruno is coming, so it would be good to have the whole family together."

Otto squeezed her hand gratefully. "It would. And, Mother, I will make every effort to have an amicable relationship with him for your sake."

Mathilda embraced Otto. "Thank you."

"Of course, he may not come," Otto warned. "He did say he hoped never to see me again."

Mathilda looked somewhat shamefaced. "He will come. He sent me a message to ask if he might attend the mass for his father."

Otto smiled. "Perhaps he is growing up at last. Of course. It is only right he should be there."

∞∞∞

When Henry arrived at Quedlinburg ten days before Easter he greeted Mathilda and Bruno warmly, but gave only a sketchy bow to Otto and Eadgyth.

"I am here for the mass and nothing else," Henry said. "I shall speak to you if you command it, but I would prefer not."

Otto shrugged. "As you wish, Brother, but our mother would be pleased for us to be on amicable terms."

Henry shrugged. "There are some actions I cannot do, even for Mother's sake."

"Is Judith well?" Eadgyth asked quickly to try to fill the awkwardness between the brothers.

"My wife is none of your concern, my lady," Henry said, turning away.

"Henry, do not speak to Eadgyth in that fashion," Otto called after him. But Henry did not look back. Otto put his arm around her shoulders. "If that fool stays here after the Easter service, we shall move swiftly on."

∞∞∞

Although Henry remained on stilted terms with Otto, the mood at Quedlinburg was pleasant. The meals were full of the Lenten fare, but were merry enough as everyone anticipated the approaching return to the normal diet. On Palm Sunday Archbishop Frederick of Mainz arrived ready to say the Easter mass. He had been quiet since Otto had pardoned him and his manner was respectful, although as usual Eadgyth was certain there was something false about it. He moved on to greeting the others at court and she watched him thoughtfully. His greeting towards Henry was proper, which surprised her. She had expected it to be friendlier. Otto too was watching them.

"Looks like those two have fallen out," he said with satisfaction. "That is good news."

The meal that night was enjoyable. Archbishop Frederick spent much time talking to Bruno and complimented Otto on his intelligent young brother.

"He will be a fine addition to the church, my lord," he said.

"I agree," Otto replied. "Bruno has excelled even more than we expected and we are all most proud."

"You are studying in Utrecht, I believe," Frederick said to Bruno. "A fine establishment indeed."

"I have been," Bruno replied. "But I wish to continue my studies with a wise man who has recently arrived in the realm, with your permission, of course, Otto."

"I urge you strongly to grant it, my lord," Bishop Balderic said. "Your brother has excelled beyond my wildest ambitions and has learned everything I can teach him."

"Who can provide my brother with superior guidance to you, Father?" Otto asked. "When my father placed Bruno in your care, he said there was no man in Germany more able to teach him."

"There is a fine scholar recently arrived in Trier named Israel. You may know of him, my Lady Queen. I believe he is from Wessex."

"Israel? Yes, I met him once at Athelstan's court," Eadgyth said. "He is Irish and very wise. Athelstan said he was the wisest man he had ever encountered."

"If he had King Athelstan's admiration, he will most certainly gain mine," Otto said. "You have my blessing to study with this man, Bruno. Invite him to court and you can continue your studies there. With envoys visiting from all over Christendom and beyond, it will be a fine place for you to learn."

"Thank you, Brother. I would like that."

Otto nodded. "So would I. Both your company and your abilities will be valuable indeed. I have need of a learned man to act as my chancellor, preparing the documents of the realm and such matters. Will you take on this task once you join my court?"

Bruno sucked in his breath, looking in astonishment at Bishop Balderic. The Bishop nodded. "I think you should accept it, Bruno. There is no one better the King can choose."

"I am honoured, Otto. I must consult first with Israel, but if he agrees I will be glad to serve you in any way I can."

Otto looked pleased and Eadgyth smiled at Bruno, thinking how good it would be for Otto to have such a loyal brother at court.

∞∞∞

Eadgyth and Mathilda left the hall together, arm in arm. Affectionately she bade her mother-in-law goodnight, before making her way to her own chamber. She unbound her hair and removed her jewellery in the antechamber before pushing open the heavy door to the main bedchamber. Always she felt a smile come to her face as she entered. It was where she and Otto had spent their wedding night and many another joyful night since. But on this occasion the smile swiftly faded from her face and she froze in sudden terror.

An armed man in dark clothing was standing before her in the centre of the room. Eadgyth opened her mouth to scream, but the man flung himself on his knees.

"Please do not cry out, my lady. Forgive the intrusion, but this concerns the king."

"Get out," Eadgyth hissed.

"Please, my lady. Grant me a few moments and then if you command it, I shall leave."

Eadgyth's heart thudded with terror, although the man made no attempt to harm her. He remained kneeling on the floor, his head bowed and the knife still sheathed in his belt. She reached behind her for the door handle, her hand trembling so much it took a few attempts to grip it. The cold iron ring reassured her she could easily escape. "Speak."

"I am in the entourage of the Archbishop of Mainz," the man said. "But I was placed there secretly by Count Conrad of Rhennish Franconia. Count Conrad instructed me to watch the Archbishop carefully and report anything suspicious to him or the King."

All of Eadgyth's hatred for the Archbishop rushed back. "Have you noticed anything suspicious?"

"Yes, my lady," the man said. "I would not be here if matters were not desperate. I do not make a habit of disturbing ladies in their bedchambers."

Behind her came a sound of voices and Eadgyth realised her serving women would enter the chamber at any moment. She made a hasty decision. A man sent by Conrad would be trustworthy. Praying he had truly been sent by Conrad, Eadgyth whispered, "Hide. My women are here."

The man swiftly concealed himself behind one of the heavy coffers. As the door to her chamber opened, Eadgyth felt a bubble of hysterical laughter rising in her. Never had she suspected she would be concealing a man in her chamber.

"Just comb my hair this night," Eadgyth said to the women who had curtseyed to her. "I shall not disrobe just yet."

"Yes, my lady," the women murmured.

It seemed to Eadgyth that it took an age for the women to comb the long blonde tresses. It was an effort for her to remain calm and she was surprised neither woman could hear the rapid thump of her heart. It was hard to fight the urge to order the women away from her before they had finished their tasks.

"Shall we wait with you until the King retires, my lady?" one of the women asked.

Eadgyth shook her head. "The King is enjoying a night with his brothers and may be some time. I shall not keep you from your rest."

"Yes, my lady." The other woman took a jug of weak ale to the coffer where the man was hiding. Eadgyth clenched her fists, praying the woman would not hear him breathing. She tried to think of some words to distract the woman, but her mind went blank. To her relief she simply set the jug down and turned away.

"That will be all," Eadgyth said. "I will bid you both good night."

Her shoulders slumped in relief as the door closed behind the women and she waited a few moments until she could no longer hear their voices.

"Come out now and tell me all."

"There is a plot to kill the King. He is to be struck down at Easter as he pays his respects at the grave of King Henry."

Eadgyth sucked in a shocked breath. "Is the Archbishop the instigator of this plot?"

"One of them, my lady. The other is the man who will be proclaimed king in his place."

"Henry."

"Yes, my lady."

A white anger coursed through Eadgyth. Henry had wormed his way to Quedlinburg, claiming to want to pay his respects to his father. Her first instinct was to tear to the hall, to stick a knife straight into Henry's treacherous heart. It was hard to remain calm. Her hands shook as she poured out two cups of ale, handing one absentmindedly to the man. She stared into her cup, horrific pictures of Otto sprawled mortally injured on the bloodstained grave of his father flashing before her eyes. She jerked the cup impatiently, spilling ale over her garments in the effort to drive such visions away. She took a mouthful of the drink and it calmed her enough to look back at the man. "Who knows of this plot?"

"Very few, my lady. I know not who Lord Henry has told, but the Archbishop has told only a select few. Those he trusts to carry out the task."

"Of which you are one?"

"Yes, my lady. He has no idea I am in the service of Count Conrad and am loyal to the King."

Eadgyth suddenly remembered how she had left Otto talking in the hall with the Archbishop. She leapt to her feet. "Is the King in danger now?"

"No, my lady. He is well attended in the hall. I would know if any orders had been issued for this night. But in the church, when men cast aside their arms…"

Eadgyth shivered, remembering Thankmar slain before an altar, his blood spilling over the sacred ground. That had been an act of war. Henry's actions were far worse. She had no great opinion of Henry, but never had she imagined he would come in the guise of peace to defile his own father's grave.

At that moment the door opened and Otto came in. His eyes widened at the sight of them, a mixture of shock and rage spreading across his face.

Chapter five

Again Eadgyth had to repress hysterical laugher, as she imagined the scene through Otto's eyes. There she was, her hair unbound, alone in a bedchamber with a strange man who was drinking from Otto's own cup. She ran to him, clutching his arm. "Otto, please listen. I know how this appears."

He looked dazed. "Eadgyth, I must be the most trusting husband alive, but what am I supposed to make of this?"

"He is one of Conrad's men."

The man had fallen to his knees. "My Lord King. Please forgive the intrusion. I will swear by any oath you wish me to swear that I have not harmed the Queen in any manner, beyond a fright when she entered. I beg only for you to listen to me and then I will accept whatever punishment you wish to dispense."

"Get up," Otto said, folding his arms sternly. "If you have come from Conrad, why have you not requested an audience in the proper fashion?"

"I was placed by Count Conrad secretly in the household of the Archbishop of Mainz. I must not be known to be seeking an audience with you, my lord. Approaching you in public is a risk I dare not take."

"Otto, there is a plot to kill you," Eadgyth burst out.

"By the Archbishop?" Otto asked.

"And Henry."

Otto turned back to the man. "I think you must tell me

everything you know."

Still clutching onto him, Eadgyth could feel the rage boiling in Otto as the man talked. "On my father's grave? My God, I will destroy the brat for this."

Eadgyth was certain Otto was going to ignore the man's pleas for secrecy. From the look on his face, she expected him to storm from the room in search of the conspirators, killing both Henry and the Archbishop in one blow, but he took a deep breath and calmed himself. "I thank you, my friend, for bringing this information." He gave the man a hint of a smile. "I will overlook on this occasion that you cornered my wife in her bedchamber."

"Thank you, my lord. What are your orders now?"

"Continue as you are expected to act. If the situation changes, tell me. Otherwise be ready at the Easter mass. My men will be well prepared."

"Yes, my lord." He bowed deeply to Eadgyth. "My lady, please forgive the intrusion. If I could have spoken to the King in any other way, I would have done so. By not having me dragged immediately from your presence, you have saved the King's life."

Eadgyth swallowed, unnerved by how nearly she had done exactly that as she extended her hand for the man to kiss.

"You must not be seen leaving the chamber," Otto said. "Let me check all is clear."

After the man departed, Eadgyth and Otto clung to each other as they sat down on the bed. Eadgyth dug her fingers into the thick fur of the covers as she tried to make sense of everything she had just learnt.

"What will you do?" she asked.

"I shall have my most trusted men guard me at all times until the danger passes. And not just me. You and the children must also be guarded. If they cannot kill me, they may try to strike at me in another way."

"Can you not arrest Henry and Father Frederick this night?"

"I have no real proof. Only the word of a man I caught alone with my wife in a bedchamber."

In spite of the danger, Eadgyth had to laugh. "I never expected to do such a thing."

"Arresting them now would achieve nothing and give them the opportunity to discredit you. They will be arrested when they act at Easter."

"Not until then?"

"Do you think you can restrain yourself from killing Henry before then?" Otto asked.

"Can you?"

Otto shrugged. "I shall have to try. My God, to think he would defile our father's grave in such a way. I knew he cared nothing for me, but I did not think him capable of such an act."

"Otto, what if something goes wrong?"

"I shall send immediately for Hermann. I do not know if he can arrive in time, but he should at least be here soon after Easter. If anything goes wrong, put the children under his protection and remove yourself from Quedlinburg as quickly as you can."

Eadgyth put her head in her hands, the tears flowing as she imagined fleeing Quedlinburg after being brutally widowed. Without Otto she was not sure she would want to live, but she would have to for the sake of her children.

Otto put his arms around her. "Do not weep. Nothing will go wrong. Henry thinks he can surprise us, but the surprise will be on him when he finds we are ready for him. That gives us the advantage."

∞∞∞

Eadgyth found it almost impossible to get through the following days without anyone realising something was amiss. The men Otto confided in were well trained and discrete, managing to surround their king and his family without making it obvious.

It was as well that Henry had maintained a distant manner with them since arriving at Quedlinburg, as Eadgyth did not know how she could have born to make friendly conversation with him. Father Frederick continued to talk to them in a confident and urbane manner and Eadgyth was certain she had never hated anyone so much. When he spoke of God's wisdom, she had to conceal her clenched fists in her wide sleeves, full of disgust at this man of God who could plan such a despicable act on hallowed ground.

Surreptitiously she watched Henry and Frederick. They had remained formal with each other and a casual onlooker would assume them to be mere acquaintances, but now she knew the truth, Eadgyth was able to detect the occasional glance between them.

On the night before Easter Otto set down his platter with the remains of the stewed eels he loathed pushed to one side and smiled at everyone. "Well, that is the last Lenten meal over. Tomorrow we shall dine well again." He looked casually around the table. Henry twitched but betrayed no other sign that the following day would have anything beyond the usual pious significance.

Otto laid his hand affectionately on his brother's shoulder. "What are your plans for after Easter, Henry? Are you remaining with the court awhile or returning to your lands?"

For a second Henry froze at the question, his eyes wide, but he shrugged Otto's hand away, his face settling back into his usual sneer. "I do not care to remain long at your court, Otto." He got to his feet. "I shall retire early, I think."

Otto stood as well. "A good night to you, Brother. I hope you will change your mind one day about attending my court. You have much to learn, but you are no fool. There could be high honour for you one day."

Henry turned and smirked. "Perhaps there will. Sleep well, Otto."

Otto and Eadgyth exchanged glances and it was not long before Otto brought the meal to an end, rising to his feet and bidding everyone a good night.

Mathilda left the hall with them. She hugged Otto as she reached her chamber. "Thank you for offering Henry the hand of peace," she said. "I shall talk to him after the mass and urge him to accept it."

Eadgyth could see the pity in Otto's eyes as he kissed his mother's cheek. "A good night to you, Mother."

Eadgyth and Otto said nothing more to each other until they reached the privacy of their chamber. "This is going to destroy my mother. Tomorrow she must learn that one of her sons tried to kill the other. She may even lose a son, if Henry is successful or if he is slain in the struggle. She will discover how Henry, her favourite, has used the mass for our father to further his aims and cares nothing for the sanctity of his grave. Tomorrow she must learn what a monster Henry has become." Otto shrugged. "Or if she cannot accept that, she will find a way to blame me, ruining the warmth there has been between us."

Eadgyth squeezed Otto's hand. "Did you mean your words to Henry?"

"Of course. He has plotted, but he has taken no action yet against me. I wanted to offer him an escape from his plans. I can never forget the pain of Thankmar's death. Do you think Henry would feel any regret for killing me? He is my brother, yet he must truly hate me."

Eadgyth put her arms around him, not knowing how to comfort him. It was likely Otto would stop the assassination, but there could be no real joy in that.

Chapter six

It was an effort to get any sleep that night, although Eadgyth did her best. She knew she would need her energy to support Otto and Mathilda through the following days or, if the worst happened, to protect her children. But in spite of that, she had spent most of the night staring into the darkness, trying not to disturb Otto as she knew he needed to be as alert as possible that day. She was envious of his military training which allowed him to sleep so deeply ahead of a dangerous day.

They dressed silently the next morning, Eadgyth barely taking her eyes off Otto as she wondered if this would be the last time she would see him do this. She blinked back the tears obscuring her vision as she tried to memorise every detail of his body. From the dark hair brushing his shoulders to the scar marking his ankle, every part suddenly seemed doubly precious.

Otto caught her eye and smiled. "Oh, Eadgyth." He pulled her against his chest and tenderly stroked her hair. "I will get through this day." He picked up a mail shirt. "I shall be thoroughly uncomfortable, but nothing worse."

It was a relief to see the mail under his elaborate tunic and she felt better still as he concealed a dagger in the folds of his cloak. Outwardly there was no sign of his defences. Otto watched her as she fastened the mantle around her head, securing it under her chin. He rested his hands on her shoulders and looked at her critically.

"Are you ready for this?" he asked.

"Yes, my dearest, I am. I am ready for anything they throw at us."

Otto gave her a swift kiss. "That is better, my sweet. Whatever happens, remember how much I love you. You are the greatest light in my life."

"And you are mine," Eadgyth said. "And that light will not be put out this day."

"No, it won't."

Otto's men were prepared, surrounding them as they joined the rest of the family. Watching the group, it seemed hard to imagine anything was amiss. Henry was talking casually with Mathilda and Bruno, while Liutgarde and Liudolf were laughing together. Normally Eadgyth would have chided them for their levity on such a solemn day, but that Easter she was just glad to see them laughing while they still could. The greetings everyone called as Otto and Eadgyth approached seemed genuine and she straightened her back. Knowing Otto needed her to play her part, she somehow managed to smile in a sisterly fashion at Henry. He gave a brisk bow in return, but she noted how his eyes were darting nervously around and the hatred came rushing back. For a moment the scene had seemed so normal, she had almost wondered whether the intruder in her bedchamber had created an elaborate hoax. Her thoughts were interrupted by the toll of the church bell and she glanced at Otto.

Otto smiled lightly back. "Shall we go to the church?" He gave a nod to his men which seemed a courteous gesture, but Eadgyth knew it was a signal ordering them to take up their positions. Her pulse raced as she rested her hand on Otto's arm and they made their way to the abbey.

Mathilda's abbey at Quedlinburg was taking shape around the church where Henry had been laid to rest. The church was far more elaborate than it had been on that day, but Eadgyth had no heart to admire the gilded icons and frescos lining the walls or the exquisite gold cross adorning the altar. They drew closer to Henry's grave, her heart aching as she wondered what that wise and kindly king would have made of all this. He had worked so hard to secure the succession for his son. She knew how much he would have hated the quarrels in the family.

Archbishop Frederick was already standing before the altar, surrounded by a small group of men, including the one who had warned them of the threat. In furtive glances Eadgyth studied the men, guessing they were the group of assassins. None appeared to be armed, but no doubt they too had concealed weapons just as Otto and his men did. Father Frederick came towards them, a welcoming smile on his face. He took the hands of each of the family in turn, laying his hand on their heads in blessing. With Otto's eyes upon her, Eadgyth made herself accept the blessing, but as he moved on to speak to Mathilda, she had to look down to hide the fury in her eyes. She was repelled beyond all measure at the friendly manner he maintained with Mathilda, while he was planning in just a few moments to murder her son.

Through her lashes she watched the Archbishop, noting how close his men still were. Otto looked sideways at her, giving a reassuring smile as they knelt before Henry's grave. Still very much the dignified churchman, Frederick took up a place before the altar. In a sudden panic Eadgyth looked swiftly around the church. Otto's men were dotted around, seemingly without motive, but they formed a protective ring surrounding the family. Her breathing steadied as she recognised how they would be ready to move at the first hint of trouble. Otto slid his hand under his cloak and she guessed it was resting on his dagger. Eadgyth bowed her head, muttering a quick prayer for her father-in-law, vowing to come back as soon as she could to pray more thoroughly. **On that day she could not concentrate on the prayers he deserved.**

The first movement came soon after the Archbishop started the mass. Out of the corner of an eye which should have been closed, she saw one of the Archbishop's men edge forward. She held her breath, knowing by the way Otto had tensed that he too had noticed it. Several men were now on the move, taking advantage of the bowed heads to sidle closer to the family. Otto's men stood still, their heads bent in prayer. She wanted to cry out a warning, but as Otto remained on his knees, she assumed this was part of his plan.

It was the candlelight glinting on metal as the men drew concealed weapon which made Eadgyth unable to restrain a cry. At the same time those men who had appeared so intent on their devotions, sprang into life. As Otto had hoped the assassins were taken by surprise when men seized them from behind.

Otto leapt up, standing protectively in front of his children with one arm firmly around Eadgyth and his dagger outstretched. The scuffle was brief. The assassins recovered from their shock, struggling hard against the hands which grabbed them, but Otto's men had the advantage. Not being certain how many assassins there would be, Otto had twice as many men as the Archbishop. One by one knives clattered to the floor, as the family and other courtiers scrambled to their feet. A few screams echoed in the lofty space, while others could do nothing but look around in shocked bewilderment. A few tried to flee the abbey, but found their way blocked by guards. Otto urgently surveyed the scene, betraying no relief at finding the situation secure.

"Bruno, take Mother, Liutgarde and..." He glanced down at Eadgyth. Firmly she shook her head. She was not moving from Otto's side until she knew Henry and the Archbishop had been arrested. Otto sighed. "Take Mother and Liutgarde back to the hall. Guard them well."

Liudolf came out from behind Otto to stand on Eadgyth's other side. She smiled tremulously at him, her heart swelling with pride at his bravery. A nearby footstep sounded deafening in the silent building, making Eadgyth shrink closer to Otto, pulling Liudolf with her. Henry had taken a step in their direction.

"No one else move," Otto snapped.

"But..." Henry looked frantically from him to the Archbishop. Frederick's eyes were narrowed, but other than that his face remained in its habitual calm expression. In this, Eadgyth could see his guilt more clearly than ever. Normally a priest would show some feeling at the most sacred of masses being so violently disrupted.

"I said do not move." Otto turned to the rest of the court. "Only able men remain. Everyone else, leave immediately." As soon as the women and children had left, Otto gestured first at the Archbishop and then at Henry. "Arrest them."

"What are you doing?" Henry cried, as two men grabbed his arms. "I have done nothing wrong."

"Lock them up. I shall deal with them shortly."

"Otto!" Henry cried as he was dragged away.

Otto ignored him, pulling Eadgyth against him. "There, I told you there was no need to worry."

"God be praised," she whispered shakily.

"What happened, Father?" Liudolf asked, his eyes wide more with excitement than fear. "Did Uncle Henry try to kill you?"

"Yes, my son and he might easily have succeeded. A King must always be above the others in his realm, but he must never forget that he needs strong friends and allies. My life was saved by one such – Count Conrad. He had the wisdom to keep a close eye on such former traitors and because of that, the plot was foiled." Otto looked around. The man who had warned them of the plot was being held by one of his men. "Release that man." Otto went forward and embraced him. "You have my eternal gratitude, my friend. Your actions have been appreciated beyond anything I can say."

"I am honoured to have been of service, my lord."

A faint smile hovered on Otto's lips. "I fear your role has now been exposed and you will need to return to Count Conrad's household. You shall return with my commendations for your prudence and courage, as well as a handsome reward."

The man bowed. "The greatest reward is that the plot has been foiled, my lord."

"Take the rest somewhere I can talk to them. I may be willing to show mercy to those who are helpful." Otto gave a slight bow to a confused looking Bishop Balderic. "Celebrate Easter as best you can, Father and remember my father's soul in your prayers."

Otto kept his arms around Eadgyth and Liudolf as he went outside. "Take your mother to the hall, Liudolf. No arguing please, Eadgyth."

Eadgyth gave a shaky laugh and kissed Otto. "Now all have been apprehended, I can leave you. Besides, I think your mother may need support. What shall I tell her?"

"The truth. She will not like it, but she needs to know."

∞∞∞

Telling Mathilda proved to be just as hard as she had feared. She and Bruno got to their feet as soon as Eadgyth and Liudolf entered.

"Eadgyth, what is happening?" Bruno asked. He had hold of his mother's hand and Eadgyth was dismayed to see how white Mathilda looked.

"Sit down," Eadgyth said. "Liutgarde, serve everyone a drink. I know we should still be fasting until we have heard mass, but I think God will forgive us on this occasion."

"Eadgyth, please just tell me," Mathilda whispered.

Eadgyth knew there was no easy way to do this, so got straight to the point. "Henry and Archbishop Frederick have conspired to kill Otto. They made an attempt this day in the abbey."

"No." Mathilda shook her head vigorously. "Henry would not do such a thing."

"Mathilda, you were there in the church. You saw what happened." Eadgyth took a long mouthful of the drink Liutgarde had put in front of her. She put her arm around her daughter, suddenly feeling exhausted.

"I saw men attack," Mathilda said. "Henry did nothing."

"Is there truly any proof Henry was involved?" Bruno asked. "I am not doubting you, Sister, but this is a terrible crime Henry is accused of."

"I know," Eadgyth replied. "It was one of Conrad's men who uncovered the plot and told all to Otto. He named Henry."

"He is lying," Mathilda said. "Otto should stop listening to men such as Count Conrad and Hermann of Swabia and show more regard for his own family."

Eadgyth's composure broke. "Stop, Mathilda. Stop believing your precious Henry is so perfect. If Henry had his way, at this moment your oldest son would be lying dead in your abbey, slumped over his father's grave with a knife in his back. A knife placed there on Henry's orders."

Liutgarde shrank closer to her mother and Liudolf too put his arm protectively around her. Eadgyth struggled to calm herself, determined to remain strong for everyone present.

"I have a son, Mathilda. Do you think I do not understand that unquestioning love? Of course I do. But you must stop believing Henry is perfect. He is far from that. He is a monster who will let nothing stand in the way of his ambition. He used his own father's memorial service to get closer to Otto. He thought nothing of defiling his father's grave. Perhaps that will move you, even if the thought of Otto dead does not."

Mathilda had gone whiter than ever. "I do care about Otto," she whispered. "I could not bear his death. What will happen to Henry? Whatever has happened, he is still my son. I can't stop caring for him, whatever he has done, any more than you could ever stop caring for Liudolf. What will Otto do to him?"

Eadgyth suddenly felt very sick. "I do not know."

Chapter seven

They were all sat in silence at the table, occasionally taking a sip from their cups when they heard Otto's voice. The bright banners and fresh cloths lining the chairs created a festive appearance, but the mood was glum.

"Mother, Henry must fight this one alone. Do not implore Otto for mercy. It will only make him angrier," Bruno whispered.

Mathilda nodded and when Otto came in she surprised him by folding him in her arms. "God be praised, you are safe, my son."

Otto shot a startled look at Eadgyth but kept his arm around his mother as he joined the others at the table. Liutgarde poured her father a cup of wine. "Thank you, sweetheart," Otto said, running his hand over her smooth hair. "I need this."

"Otto, please do not keep us ignorant any longer," Bruno said. "We need to know your intentions."

"Several of the men I have questioned have named both Henry and the Archbishop as the instigators of this plot. They shall both face my judgement."

"Of course," Bruno said. "You are God's anointed. Their crime is a serious one. The fact that the Archbishop chose an abbey and one so dear to our hearts as the scene of his crime disgusts me all the more."

"Thank you, Bruno." Otto looked anxiously at his mother. "I shall have them brought before me shortly. You do not need to listen to this, Mother. Why not go to your chamber or the abbey?"

Mathilda shook her head. "I need to know what is happening. But Otto, you look exhausted. Take some refreshment first."

Otto gripped his mother's hand. "You are right, Mother. We shall all need some sustenance. Tell me, Bruno, is it acceptable for us to break our fast now or must I order more Lenten fare?"

Bruno smiled at the lighter tone. "The Easter feast is already prepared. I know we are in no mood for festivities, but we need to eat."

The meal was a downcast one and very far from the usual merriments which accompanied the end of the fasting period. As it neared its end, the thudding sound of running footsteps coming towards the entrance sent cried of terror around the hall. Eadgyth pushed back her chair in alarm and Otto was not the only man leaping to his feet, a sword in his hand. Guards rushed to the doorway, seizing the man entering with his sword drawn. His hood fell back.

"Hermann!" Otto cried. "My dear friend, you must have ridden like the wind."

Hermann's face lit up. "Otto! God be praised. I was so alarmed to get your message. Is all well?"

Otto nodded. "The danger has passed. But on behalf of Liudolf, I thank you for your swift action. It is of great comfort to know my son has so caring a father ready to take my place if the need should arise."

"What has happened to the conspirators?"

"I have them in custody. Take some food and wine, my friend. They shall be brought in shortly."

∞∞∞

Eadgyth was sitting beside Otto as the prisoners were brought in. She had instructed Liutgarde to stay with Mathilda, hoping the presence of her granddaughter would comfort her. Otto had kept Liudolf next to him, putting him firmly in place as his heir, while Bruno was sat on Eadgyth's other side. The gravity he assumed as a man intended for the church made him appear much older than his fifteen years, but she noticed how he glanced often at Bishop Balderic for support.

Otto's face showed no emotion as guards escorted Henry and Frederick in. They had been stripped of all weaponry and their hands were bound, but no one was taking any chances and a ring of guards surrounded them. A stifled sob from behind made Eadgyth glance back to see Liutgarde putting her arm around Mathilda. Eadgyth's heart was heavy as she looked back at the prisoners, feeling more furious with them than ever. Neither were showing any sign of remorse. The Archbishop emanated his usual air of saintly martyrdom, while Henry swaggered as arrogantly as he could with his arms tightly held on both sides.

"Father Frederick, Archbishop of Mainz and Lord Henry of Saxony, son of our late King Henry of Germany, you have been charged with an attempt to assassinate the King of Germany. Do you have anything to say?" Otto looked sternly at them.

"I do not recognise your authority," the Archbishop said. "I regard Lord Henry as the rightful king."

A ripple of shock went round the assembled nobles at this blatant defiance, but Otto ignored the comment. He looked at Henry. "Do you wish to say anything, Lord Henry?"

Henry glared at Otto. "I have no wish to talk to you, Otto."

"I note that neither of you have made any protestation of innocence. Four of the men seized in the abbey this day have named you both as the instigators of the plot, as has the man you involved in the plot who unknown to you was serving Count Conrad of Rhennish Franconia." Otto gave a brief, but satisfied smirk at Henry's twitch of anger, as he realised how Otto had been so well prepared. "Do either of you wish to beg for mercy?"

"I wish only for God's mercy," Frederick said.

"I would rather die than beg you for anything, Otto," Henry

snapped.

Otto stood up. "Then you will die. It is regretful that I cannot carry out this sentence on you, Father Frederick. You will be locked up and await the judgement of His Holiness, the Pope. Lord Henry of Saxony, in the morn you will be hung alongside the men who have not cooperated with me. And I will be rid at last of the one who has so troubled my reign. Lock them both up overnight."

Henry's face went white as he stared in stupefied horror at his brother. Everyone in the hall was also shocked into silence. For Eadgyth there was a churning mixture of relief that the threat to Otto would soon be gone with the horror that a man who, in spite of everything, was a member of her family, would be killed in so brutal a fashion. A sudden picture of the high spirited young boy she had met when she first arrived in Germany flashed into her mind. Tears filled her eyes at the memory of him and Otto teasing each other as they returned from a day's hunting, never dreaming they could ever be the bitterest of enemies. She did not need to hear the sound of Mathilda's sobs for the enormity of what Henry's execution would do them all to dawn on her.

"Hurry up," Otto said impatiently and Eadgyth suspected he did not want to look at his brother for any longer than necessary. "I said to remove them."

"God will never forgive you for this, my lord," Frederick said quietly, as he went without struggle.

Henry was another matter. He was dragged from the hall, but still he made no attempt to beg for his life.

No!" Mathilda screamed, flinging herself to her knees before Otto. "No, Otto. You cannot do this. A punishment, of course, but not this. Do not kill my son."

Otto's face tore in pain. "I am sorry, Mother. I have no choice. He must die or one day he will succeed in killing me. What else can I do?"

"A true king would show mercy," Mathilda cried. "The Archbishop is right. You have no right to be king. It should have been Henry. Why did your father not name Henry?"

"Mother, Otto is God's anointed," Bruno said, trying to pull his mother away. "Stop this attack on him. He has the right to pass judgement on his enemies."

"No, he should never have been Gods anointed. Someone stop this. Otto cannot do this to Henry." Mathilda clung tightly to Otto's knees.

Otto got up, unable to bear the touch of his mother. "My decision has been made."

Mathilda also stood, her grief suddenly replaced by a frightening stillness. "If you do this, I will never again show any loyalty to you, Otto. You are no longer a son of mine. Henry is my son. Henry should have been king. He would have reigned fairly in the manner of his father. You are a disgrace to the office."

Otto turned his back on her and walked away. "I have nothing further to say. The sentence will be carried out."

"I shall never forgive you for this, Otto," Mathilda shrieked after him, tears streaming down her face. "I shall hate you forever. I wish Henry had succeeded this day and that you were dead."

Again a shocked silence took hold of all who had gathered as Otto slowly turned to look at his mother. Eadgyth's heart broke at the hurt on his face, but frozen to the spot she could do nothing. Otto gave his mother a bitter smile. "I would have thought by now that you would be used to me disappointing you."

Chapter eight

Mathilda collapsed weeping to the floor and overwrought by everything she had witnessed, Liutgarde too burst into tears. For a moment Eadgyth thought she would be unable to help joining them as she took her daughter tightly into her arms. She stroked the child's soft hair, relieved to see Hermann had a hand on Liudolf's shoulder and the two were talking intently.

"I am sorry, Mother," Liutgarde sniffed.

"Hush, child. You do not need to apologise. What you have witnessed has been hard."

Mathilda still lay curled up in a sobbing ball on the floor. Bruno was staring at her, but he made no attempt to comfort her.

Liutgarde took a deep breath. "I am fine, Mother. See to Grandmother."

Eadgyth smoothed back her hair. "You are not fine. No one is. This has been a terrible day."

She stared in horror as Mathilda crawled over, prostrating herself before them. Her face was blotched and her hair straggled loose from her mantle in wild disarray. Never had Eadgyth seen her in such a state. "Eadgyth, please beg Otto for mercy. You are the only one who can persuade him."

Eadgyth's face hardened. "No, I will not. Henry would have killed Otto in front of me, in front of my children. You have seen me weep every time Otto goes to battle. We have shared our fears for his life. Always in those days I am braced to hear of his death, but here, at the heart of our family, he should be safe. I do not want Otto to show mercy."

"Please, Eadgyth." Mathilda looked piteously up at her. "I beg you as one mother to another. We have always been friends. Do this for me."

Eadgyth was swamped by pity at the desolate expression on her face, the memories of so many kindnesses flooding through her. But the memory of the pain on Otto's face was far stronger. "You just told Otto, my husband and my king, the father of my children and the man I love more than life itself, that you wished he had died. I will not do this for you."

Mathilda put her head in her hands, weeping afresh. Resolutely Eadgyth turned away from her and found herself face to face with Bruno. She smiled shakily at him. Suddenly it was easy to see that under the dignified churchman was a frightened fifteen year old boy.

"Eadgyth, I truly do not want to quarrel with you, but I think I must go to Otto and beg him for mercy. I hope you will not judge me harshly for it. Henry is my brother."

Eadgyth took hold of his hands. "Of course I will not judge you, Bruno. I would not stand in your way. Do you mind if I accompany you? I need to see how Otto is, but I swear I will not influence him against your pleas."

Bruno nodded and she looked down at her daughter. "Liutgarde, stay here with Liudolf and Hermann. I need to see your father. I shall be back presently."

Knowing Liutgarde's kind heart, Eadgyth was unsurprised to see her ignore her instruction. With a guilty look at her mother, she instead put her arms around Mathilda. Eadgyth shook her head slightly, but deep down she overflowed with pride at her daughter's sweet nature.

With no further words she followed Bruno in search of Otto. They found him in the council chamber, staring moodily at the wall. She went directly to him, putting her arms around his shoulders. He said nothing as Bruno fell to his knees.

"My Lord King and brother," Bruno began. "I condemn

without reservation the actions of our brother and consider your sentence to be a just one. But mercy is the finest of qualities and I would beg you to show it this day."

Otto shook his head sadly. "I am sorry, Bruno. I know this day is hard for you, but Henry will have to depend on God's mercy now for his soul. He will receive none from me."

Bruno looked up at his brother. "Is there nothing I can say to persuade you? The consequences of such an act will be far reaching."

"I know," Otto replied. "Our mother will likely never speak to me again. Perhaps you too will now turn against me."

Bruno shook his head. "No, Brother. I am with you, as ever. I wish I could change your mind, but I do understand why you cannot. All will be well between us."

Otto embraced Bruno. "You are truly the best of brothers. Why are you not a little older and already ordained? I could put you in place of that fool Frederick in Mainz. One day you shall be a bishop."

"If it is God's will," Bruno said solemnly. "I hope you do not mind if I pray for Henry."

Otto gave Bruno a crooked smile and the tears welled in his eyes. "Of course. Do you think I will not?"

"Bruno, please leave us now," Eadgyth said. "I want to talk to Otto alone."

As the door shut behind Bruno, Otto looked at Eadgyth. "Are you also here to beg for mercy?"

"No," Eadgyth replied. "I will be glad to see the threat gone. I would be happy to carry out your sentence myself."

Otto almost laughed at that. "Would you, my sweet? I had no idea you harboured such bloodthirsty ambitions."

Eadgyth smiled too and knelt beside Otto's chair putting her arms around him. "I care nothing for Henry. Do with him what you will. I care about you."

Otto cupped her head with his hand. "I know you do. You do not need to kneel."

Eadgyth pulled a chair over and took hold of Otto's hands,

cradling them between hers as she tried to find the right words. "Because you know how I care for you, I want you to listen to what I say. Henry deserves to die, but are you truly able to carry out the sentence? My love, I saw how you were affected after Thankmar died. I held you in my arms as you woke from nightmares, weeping afresh for your brother. That was a death carried out in the heat of a siege and still it tortured you. Can you live with carrying out the cold blooded sentence on Henry? Oh, Otto, I know you better than anyone. I think it will destroy you."

Otto clutched Eadgyth's hand, his fingers almost crushing hers. "I do not know. What can I do? I have passed sentence. I thought Henry would beg for mercy, but it seems he is more stubborn and perhaps braver than I thought."

"What if someone else begged for mercy?"

"I have already refused my mother and been soundly abused for it. I would look weaker still if I backed down for her."

"What if Bruno did it? You have not publically refused him and all know his loyalty to you. Everyone heard him describe you as God's anointed."

The tension eased out of Otto's face. "Yes, perhaps if he begs me publically. Oh, Eadgyth am I weak?"

"No, my love, you are not. Indeed I would say it is only an exceptionally strong king who can remember he is still a man. Besides, no one is suggesting there should be no punishment."

"That is true. There will be a lengthy imprisonment. Perhaps he will never know liberty again. Tell Bruno discreetly that if he implores me again for mercy, I shall listen."

The door opened at that moment and Hermann entered. "Has the Queen urged you to mercy? I am surprised at that," he commented. "Of course her opinions should be respected and she is wise indeed, but a woman's heart can take mercy to a place where it becomes a fault."

A faint smile flickered over Otto's face at this speech, as Hermann tried to voice his disapproval without criticising the one Otto had long declared was above criticism. "No, she has not. Indeed she offered to be the executioner herself! But she has also urged me to look into my heart to decide if such a sentence is truly one I can carry out. I have decided to commute the sentence to imprisonment as a favour to my brother, Bruno. That is my final decision. I do not want to quarrel with you over it."

Hermann raised his eyebrows and shrugged. "Very well. But I wish to speak to you on another matter."

"Let me guess. My mother?"

Hermann nodded. "Her attack on you in the hall was unacceptable. She has to go. I will find an excuse."

"She was distraught," Eadgyth said quickly.

"It makes no difference, my lady. Such a public outburst against the King would not be permitted in anyone else."

"I agree," Otto replied. "But nothing will be said this day. Tomorrow I deal with Henry and then I will inform my mother she is to be exiled from court. What a day that will be."

Eadgyth could scarcely believe what she was hearing. "Otto, please do not do this. I will speak to her and she will beg your pardon, I know it."

"Until the next time she disagrees and then she will publically air her opinions yet again," Hermann commented.

"She is a mother," Eadgyth cried. "A mother who had just heard her son was to die. Otto, do not hold those words against her."

"She is a mother who has continually sided with her other son." Hermann's eyes narrowed. "You need to do this, Otto."

Sinking to her knees, Eadgyth took Otto's hands in hers. "I am begging you, my dearest. Please do not send her away."

Otto's face softened and he looked uncertainly from her to Hermann. Wearily he pulled a hand away to rub his eyes. "Eadgyth…"

Hermann folded his arms. "I had thought you so devoted to the King, my lady. I always admired that, but it seems I was wrong." He glared at her, raising his voice. "If you truly loved the King you would not beg him to keep traitors at court."

Eadgyth's mouth dropped open and Otto stood sharply. "How dare you speak to Eadgyth in that fashion!"

Hermann too got up. "How dare I? I have been at your side since the beginning of your reign. Do you think I have never been asked to join rebellions against you? Of course I have. How did you think I knew about Lord Thankmar's rebellion? But always I have refused. Always I have maintained my loyalty to you. I have even agreed to give my only child to your son, linking myself still further with you."

"You have been well rewarded for your loyalty," Otto snapped.

Hermann stared steadily back. "Yes, I have. But my reward will last only as long as you. If you were to fall, I and my family would be in danger. Yet even knowing that, I have ridden to support your son this day." He shook his head. "Do what you want, my lord. You always do. Surround yourself with traitors if you must, but do not ask me to support it."

Hermann kicked back his chair and walked slowly towards the door, leaving Otto stunned into silence. Eadgyth stared at him, a cold sweat making her shiver at the thought of Otto losing his closest ally. Scrambling to her feet, she darted towards the door, determined to get there before it shut behind Hermann.

She reached it first, pressing her back against the solid wood. "Sit back down, Hermann," she said. "That is an order."

Hermann frowned. "Please stand aside, my lady."

"No," Eadgyth replied. "You will have to force me."

Hermann's eyes widened and he stared dumbfounded at her, but a corner of his mouth twitched. "That is unfair, my lady. You know Otto would kill me if I laid a finger on you."

"Both of you sit back down." A shaky grin had spread across Otto's face. "And that is an order, although I am starting to doubt if I have any authority over either of you."

Eadgyth looked challengingly at Hermann until, with a sigh, he returned to his chair. Only then did she leave the door to join them.

Otto's shake of the head did not conceal his continued amusement. "Eadgyth, we need to have a talk about your tendency to violence. Since arriving in this room you have expressed a wish to kill one man and attempted to start a brawl with another. It is not at all fitting."

Eadgyth gave a shamefaced smile, but as Otto's look turned to sadness she realised with a heavy heart what he was about to say.

"My love, I have to send my mother away. I know it is not what you want. It is not what I want either, but I must. I hope it will not be for long. Please Eadgyth, support me in this."

There was a painful lump in Eadgyth's throat, but she nodded. Otto turned. "Hermann…"

"I know what you want to say to me, Otto and you are right." Hermann slid to his knees. "My lady, I am truly sorry I said such words to you. I sincerely admire your wisdom and devotion to the king. I only pray one day you will find it in your heart to forgive me."

Eadgyth shook her head and took Hermann's hand in hers, keen to reassure this steadfast man all was well. "No forgiveness is necessary. I am eternally grateful for the loyal support you have given Otto over the years. You came to aid me and my children this day with no regard to your own safety. A few cross words have no significance compared to that."

Otto put his arm around her, laying his other hand on Hermann's shoulder. "Hermann, if you have any regrets about Ida's betrothal…"

"None," Hermann interrupted. "I love Liudolf as my own son. It will be the proudest day of my life when he and my little Ida are wed."

"I am glad. There is no one I consider more worthy for my son, than your daughter. I pray all is well between us. Your friendship has sustained me on many an occasion."

Hermann nodded, gripping Otto's hand. "As your wise wife just stated, we have been through far too much together to allow a few words spoken in anger to come between us."

Chapter nine

Tears came to Bruno's eyes when he received Eadgyth's instructions and he nodded when she added, "Tell Mathilda not to intervene. After her outburst, Otto cannot agree to her request. If she begs for mercy, Henry will die."

He played his part well when Henry was dragged into the hall to stand again before Otto. Beyond the palace walls, the bodies of four men were already dangling. "You are here to pay for your crimes. Do you wish to beg for mercy?"

Eadgyth could not help feeling a grudging admiration for Henry. His face was white and his hands shook, but he stood up straight, meeting his brother's gaze without flinching. He did not reply.

Bruno stepped forward and knelt at Otto's feet. "My Lord King, I humbly beg you for clemency in this matter."

"On what grounds? This man is a traitor who has shown no repentance," Otto replied.

"Because mercy is a fine quality in a king, my lord. Lord Henry of Saxony is the son and namesake of our late King, the illustrious Henry. It would be a fitting tribute to the memory of your father and mine to commute the sentence on his son."

"Please stand, Lord Bruno. Your wisdom and compassion are truly a fine tribute to our father, the noble King Henry. You have proved yourself a loyal and loving brother and I am always willing to listen to the words of such trusty men as yourself. Lord Henry of Saxony, kneel."

Henry was pushed roughly to his knees.

"The death sentence I passed upon you is commuted to that of imprisonment. You will remain in custody until I or my heir says otherwise. Your lands are forfeited and will pass now into my possession. You will be transported to your place of captivity immediately."

∞∞∞

Otto wanted Henry imprisoned a long distance away, so he and Father Frederick were sent to Ingelheim, one of the royal residences on the Rhine. His instructions were that the prisoners were to be housed adequately, but without any luxuries. As the two were dragged away, Otto turned to Eadgyth with a look of relief.

"One act completed. Now I must deal with my mother."

Mathilda was not far away, making it obvious she wished to speak to Otto. Pain flickered across Otto's face and he ordered one of his men to have everyone leave the hall.

"This will be difficult enough without everyone hearing it," he muttered.

As the hall emptied, Otto beckoned Mathilda forward. Other than Liudolf and Liutgarde, only Bruno and Hermann had remained.

"Thank you, Otto, for commuting the sentence." Mathilda's beaming face felt like a dagger in Eadgyth's heart, as she knew what awaited her. "I should have known you would not execute him. He will have learnt his lesson, I know it."

Otto did not smile. "I hope so."

"You will not need to keep him in captivity for long, will you?"

"Mother, this matter is not over," Otto said firmly. "I do not know when, if ever, Henry will be released. Now I must deal with you."

"Me?"

"Since I ascended the throne you have continually undermined me and criticised my rule. I can tolerate it no longer. Your threats to me yesterday have forced me to this decision. You are hereby banished from my court."

Mathilda stared at Otto. "You cannot do this, Otto. You have no right."

"He has every right, my lady," Hermann put in. "We have noticed how much of the royal purse you are spending on your charities."

"Are you accusing me of theft?" Mathilda demanded, drawing herself up to her full height. "Are you going to accuse Eadgyth for the gifts she gives to the church?"

Eadgyth frowned at Mathilda's attempt to drag her into the accusation, pressing her lips together to stop the retort from escaping. Hermann, however, was not to be silenced. "The Queen's pious donations are beyond reproach."

"Do not argue, Mother. My decision has been made," Otto said. "You know why you have to go. The money is the pretext. You are a danger to me and you know it."

Mathilda looked outraged. "Nonsense. I never involved myself in any of the rebellions. You brought those on yourself."

Eadgyth sighed. She had hoped Mathilda would beg for Otto to relent, but she continued to glare at her son.

"Still you undermine your son and king," Hermann muttered.

"I do not know what has happened to you, Otto. You turn against your family to listen to men such as Lord Hermann. Your father would be disgusted." Mathilda's voice trembled. "I suppose you are supporting Otto even in this, Eadgyth."

Eadgyth swallowed the lump in her throat, wishing Mathilda had not put her on the spot. In spite of her promise to Otto, she would have preferred not to publically condemn her mother-in-law. "I prayed it would not come to this, Mathilda. I warned you that you were leaving Otto no choice. I wish more than anything you had listened to me."

"I hope it will not be forever, Mother," Otto said desperately.

"You do not need to move. Quedlinburg is yours. Eadgyth and I will return to Magdeburg in the next few days."

Mathilda straightened herself. "I would prefer to go to my estates at Enger, unless you object to that."

"No, Mother. Of course not."

"May God forgive you for this act, Otto."

"May God forgive you for wishing for the death of your son," Hermann put in.

Mathilda took the time to kiss Liudolf and Liutgarde, leaving Liutgarde close to tears. With an air of resignation she kissed Eadgyth's cheek, before looking again at Otto. He looked bitterly unhappy as she kissed him also. "I do love you, Otto and I always will." She moved slowly away, her head held high, but at the door she turned back again. "Thank you for showing Henry mercy. I am truly grateful for that."

Otto shook his head, his shoulders slumping as she left the room.

"Was that really necessary, Otto?" Bruno's brow creased in pain. "I know her judgements on you have been strict, but to exile her…"

Otto laid his hand on his youngest brother's shoulder. "For now it is. She has undermined me for too long. I blame her in part for Henry's rebellions as I feel she could have done much to persuade him to loyalty. Bruno, will you accompany her to Enger before heading to Trier? I do not like to think of her making the journey with no family present."

"Of course," Bruno replied. "I shall leave with her as soon as she is ready. Will you bid her farewell?"

Otto hesitated. "I think it would be for the best if I did not."

∞∞∞

It was a relief for both Eadgyth and Otto to return to Magdeburg. The news of the attempt on Otto's life had spread and they were warmed by the many cheers which greeted him.

Otto and Eadgyth were for the most part popular throughout Germany, but nowhere as much as in Eadgyth's city of Magdeburg.

"Much has happened since we left here," Eadgyth commented, as they dismounted their horses.

"Indeed," Otto replied, putting his arms around her, a look of outrage which would fool no one on his face. "You took to hiding men in your bedchamber to start with."

Eadgyth laughed and shook her head, heartened by Otto's turn to humour. It was on such occasions as this that she realised how Mathilda's criticisms had worn him down. With her no longer present, he seemed more carefree.

However, he had not completely forgotten his troubles. As they sat down to dine that night, he summoned one of his men.

"In the morn ride to my brother's forfeited estates and locate his wife. I want her brought here where I can keep an eye on her. If my experiences with Gilbert of Lotharingia and my dear sister, Gerberga taught me anything, it is that the wife of a traitor can be almost as troublesome as the traitor themselves."

Chapter ten

Otto was not present when Judith arrived soon after noon a few days later. Eadgyth glanced up as one of Otto's men carried her limp body into the hall, crying out in shock at the sight. She ran to them, alarmed by the pallor of Judith's face and the way her arms dangled listlessly.

"What happened?"

"She fainted as she dismounted her horse, my lady," the leader of the men replied.

"Bring some pillows and blankets. Hurry!" Eadgyth called. She knelt down beside Judith as she was laid gently down onto the pillows. She started to wrap a blanket around her, but stopped abruptly, drawing in a sharp breath at the swelling in Judith's stomach. "She's with child. You fools. She should not have been forced to such a ride."

"It was the King's orders she be brought here, my lady."

Eadgyth bit back the comment that Otto too was a fool, feeling also cross with herself for not considering this possibility.

Judith's eyes flickered open. They widened nervously at the sight of Eadgyth bending over her. She gave a reassuring smile and held a cup of wine to her lips. Judith sipped at it, some colour returning to her cheeks.

"Judith, are you in any pain?"

"No, my lady," Judith murmured.

"Thank God," Eadgyth whispered. "May I feel?"

Judith nodded and Eadgyth pressed her hand gently against

Judith's stomach, letting out a sigh of relief at the faint flutters beneath her hand.

"I think all is well. You are safe now," she said.

Judith burst into tears and Eadgyth put her arms around her. "Don't cry. I know you have been frightened, but that is over now."

"Forgive me, my lady." Judith wiped her eyes.

"Judith, we are sisters. Please do not be formal with me." Eadgyth kept an arm around her. "Can you stand?"

Judith nodded and Eadgyth helped her to her feet, supporting her as she walked gingerly to the table. She slumped into a chair, staring at the platters of bread and salted fish. "I do not know if I can eat."

"Try to eat a little then I will take you somewhere you can rest." Eadgyth studied her, thinking how much she had changed. In appearance she had grown as beautiful as everyone had guessed she would be, but the sweet, friendly mannerisms were gone. Judith sat in silence, nibbling on some bread, casting occasional furtive glances in Eadgyth's direction.

"You are being so kind to me," Judith said later when Eadgyth took her to Henry's chamber.

"Why should I not be?"

"My husband tried to kill yours," she whispered, her eyes cast downwards.

"I do not blame you for anything Henry has done." Eadgyth hated Henry afresh for the misery she saw in Judith's tear filled eyes. She remembered how attentive Otto had been during her pregnancies and how comforting it had been. It was obvious Judith had known nothing of such tenderness. "I will look after you. Now rest. Have a sleep if you can. You do not need to come to the hall this night."

"I will come to the hall," Judith said, holding her head high. "I know everyone will stare at me, as the wife of a traitor. I wish to get that first occasion over with. I will know no peace until that is done."

Eadgyth hugged her, overwhelmed by her courage. "I will come here later and we shall enter the hall together. If anyone treats you as anything other than my honoured sister, they will have me to deal with."

The first hint of a smile Eadgyth had seen crept over Judith's face. "Thank you, Eadgyth. What of the King?"

"Leave Otto to me."

∞ ∞ ∞

When Eadgyth returned to Judith that evening, she found her finely dressed in a pale green tunic, embroidered in creamy threads with the emerald necklace she had sent as a nuptial gift clasped around her neck. Eadgyth was further impressed by Judith. There was nothing in her manner to suggest she was anything other than a noble young lady, attending an ordinary evening meal.

"You look beautiful," Eadgyth said. "If any stare at you, it will be because of that."

Judith flushed. "Thank you. I know it is not true, but at least I can pretend it is."

As they arrived in the hall Judith betrayed no sign she had noticed the murmur of curiosity which greeted her. Liutgarde, who many were saying was starting to rival her mother for charm, came forward, instinctively understanding the normal protocols for welcoming a guest would not apply that night.

"Liutgarde, this is your Aunt Judith. You do not remember her perhaps. We stayed with her long ago, soon after your father's crowning. She was very welcoming to us then and now we will repay that."

Liutgarde dropped into a slight curtsey and gave Judith a warm smile. "Welcome to Magdeburg, Aunt Judith. I fear I remember only a little of our visit to Regensburg."

Judith smiled back. "I remember your visit very well, Liutgarde. But I would not have recognised you. You have grown so much since then."

Eadgyth led Judith to a seat near the top of the table, between her and Liutgarde. It was the correct place for her rank, although she did not know if Otto would approve. Having declared Henry to be a traitor and no brother of his, it was likely the official place of his wife would be much further away from him.

"Is your father here yet?" she asked Liutgarde.

Liutgarde shook her head, but at that moment male voices drifted in from the courtyard. "Liutgarde, look after your aunt for me. I must talk to your father."

Otto was both surprised and delighted at Eadgyth coming to the doorway to greet him, sweeping her into an exuberant embrace which whirled her off her feet. Eadgyth laughed and kissed him. But as he set her down, she looked searchingly at him. "Judith has arrived."

"Good," Otto replied.

"Otto, you will be kind to her, won't you?"

Otto frowned. "I have no intention of being unkind to the girl."

Eadgyth folded her arms. "I did not say don't be unkind. I said be kind. I think you will find there is a difference."

"My lady, she is the wife of a traitor," Hermann put in. "She cannot expect any special treatment."

"She expects nothing. Otto, I do not often ask you for anything, but I am asking for this. She is with child and very frightened. Please be kind."

"With child? When will it come?"

"I think in the early autumn, assuming the ride you forced on her does not cause the loss."

Otto looked away, avoiding the anger in Eadgyth's eyes. "Why did that fool Henry not announce this at Easter?"

"No doubt he was saving the announcement for after he was proclaimed king," Hermann suggested.

"Never mind that," Eadgyth interrupted. "Promise me you will be kind to her."

"Yes, very well," Otto said impatiently. "As long as she gives me no trouble, she will be treated with every respect."

Eadgyth kissed Otto's cheek. "Thank you, my love."

They entered the hall together, with everyone bowing as they passed. Judith struggled to her feet and went to kneel, but Otto quickly strode forward, taking her by the hand. He studied her for a moment, his face softening at the fear in her eyes.

"My dear Judith, you must not kneel to me." Otto kissed her on both cheeks. "I bid you welcome to Magdeburg and apologise heartily for the uncomfortable ride you endured. I had no idea of your condition."

"Thank you, my lord," Judith whispered.

The hall had silenced as everyone waited with baited breath to see how Otto greeted the wife of his traitor brother. Otto looked at them, keeping Judith's hands in his. "This lady is my beloved sister. I expect her to be treated with the utmost respect."

A relieved smile drove out Judith's bewilderment. "Thank you for your welcome, my lord."

Otto's smile became even warmer. "I hope you will be comfortable here. I know Eadgyth will look after you."

"Yes, my lord. She has been most kind."

"Do not fear for anything and do not consider yourself a prisoner here, my dear sister. You are under my protection, as will your child be."

Chapter eleven

Eadgyth, who had been intensely missing Mathilda, loved having Judith at Magdeburg, finding her a delightful companion. As Judith settled in, her manner towards Eadgyth became so affectionate, she truly felt she had gained a sister. The two spent happy days working on tapestries and garments and Judith often accompanied her on charitable missions, bearing the thick blankets and warm clothing they had made to the poor. Soon she became almost as highly regarded as Eadgyth herself. Even Hermann, ever suspicious of anyone with close links to Henry, seemed charmed and before he returned to Swabia in the summer, said he was sure Otto would have no trouble with her.

Although ever respectful towards Otto, Judith soon lost her awe of him and Otto found himself on excellent terms with his sister-in-law, commenting on one occasion to Eadgyth that he wished "that fool Henry had appreciated his great good fortune in having such a wife."

Eadgyth noticed Judith barely mentioned Henry and often caught an unhappy expression on her face. She would not pry but her heart ached as she wondered how Judith had fared at Henry's hands. As the summer wore on and she grew great with child, Eadgyth often prayed that this young woman who seemed to have known so little of happiness would at least know the joy of cradling her child in her arms.

THE SAXON MARRIAGE

∞∞∞

As expected, Judith's confinement started in the autumn. She and Eadgyth had been working together, when Judith suddenly gave a gasp.

Eadgyth flung aside her stitching and knelt at Judith's side. "Have the pains started?"

Judith nodded. "I have felt uncomfortable since I awoke in the night, but I was not sure."

"You will soon have your baby in your arms." Eadgyth hugged her, noticing how her breath had quickened. Her wide eyes too betrayed the fear Eadgyth knew must be consuming her. "Come, let us get to your chamber and summon your women."

In the chamber the women helped Judith into a loose robe and urged some refreshment on her.

"Do not feel you have to stay with me," Judith said, as Eadgyth took a seat beside her.

"Of course I will stay with you, unless you do not want me to."

Judith's eyes filled with tears. "I fear Henry will be so angry that you and the King will see the child before he does."

Eadgyth bit back the angry comment she wanted to make about Henry. "That cannot be helped and whether I attend the birth or not, I will see the child before Henry." Gently she stroked Judith's hair. "Forget what Henry would want. Do you want me here? Having someone who truly cares for you can help so much. I do not know how I would have got through my births without Mathilda to support me."

Judith cried out as another pain tore through her. She clung onto Eadgyth's hand, her nails digging into her flesh as she tensed. "Please do not leave me."

From the beginning the pains were severe and frequent. Initially Eadgyth hoped this would mean a quick birth, but

Judith laboured throughout the night and when dawn came the next day there was no end in sight. Another day passed, with Judith's cries becoming almost constant. Eadgyth had never felt so helpless as in the brief lulls between the pains, she urged Judith to sip drinks the midwife swore would help, already knowing they would bring no respite. In the evening she left the chamber for refreshment, feeling a guilty sense of relief when she could no longer hear Judith's screams. Otto was in the hall and got to his feet as he saw her.

"Is there any news?" he asked.

Eadgyth shook her head sadly. "Judith is exhausted. I do not know how this will end. I fear we will lose them both."

Otto looked grim. "I have no love for Henry, but I would hate to have to tell him his wife and child are both dead."

"We are doing everything we can, but I fear it is not enough." Eadgyth's eyes filled with tears. "Oh, Otto, I do not think I can bear it. Judith does not deserve this."

Otto held her tightly for a moment. "No, she does not. Prayers are being said for her and the child. I wish there was more we could do."

"So do I," Eadgyth whispered, wiping her eyes. "I must return. I just came for some food and ale."

"Sit down a while, my love. You are exhausted."

Eadgyth shook her head. "There is no rest for Judith, yet my exhaustion is nothing compared to hers."

"Very well. Go back to her." Otto kissed her forehead. "I know you will do what you can. You must not blame yourself if the worst happens."

Eadgyth took a quick mouthful of ale and a bite from a chunk of bread, before returning to Judith's chamber carrying a platter. There had been no change in Judith since she had left and she forgot her tiredness as she again took her sister-in-law into her arms.

It was past midnight before Judith at last reported the urge to push.

"That is good," Eadgyth replied, trying to sound confident.

"Your baby is almost here." In her heart she was more fearful than ever. She did not know how Judith would find the strength to bring forth her child.

Sharing Eadgyth's fears, the midwife ordered every knot in the room to be untied in the hope of easing the baby's passage. She stirred up some ale laced with raspberry leaves, whispering some words over it, but Eadgyth could only persuade Judith to take a few sips.

Her worst fears were realised as dawn broke with still only the faintest glimpses of the baby. For all of Judith's agonised efforts the child remained stuck. "Is there any hope?" she whispered to the midwife. They were rubbing Judith with rose oil, chanting prayers to the blessed Virgin.

"Perhaps, my lady. I have known births longer than this which still have a happy ending." But the woman's face was drawn and the mood in the chamber was not hopeful. **Eadgyth turned back to Judith with a heavy heart, wishing she could bear some of the burden for her.**

Judith lost the strength to cry out and Eadgyth found the quiet, broken only by slight gasps, unnerving. For what felt like an age she kept her arms around her sister-in-law, mouthing prayers.

"My lady, the child is almost here," one of the women cried suddenly.

Eadgyth stroked Judith's hair. "Just a few more pushes. Keep going."

It was a relief when it was all over. Judith slumped against Eadgyth's shoulder, her strength completely gone. Eadgyth held her tightly, not daring to ask about the child. The baby had been stuck for so long, she did not think there was a hope, but a soft, squawky cry took her by surprise. Judith turned, her eyes wide as she stared at the bundle in the woman's arms.

"A girl, my lady," the woman reported.

Judith held out her arms, her face suddenly radiant as she cradled her baby close to her at last. Wiping away a few tears, Eadgyth looked at the child, who had quickly latched onto

Judith's breast.

"She is a strong little maid," Eadgyth said, smiling as the baby sucked vigorously.

"I can hardly believe she is here," Judith said. "It seemed it would never end."

Suddenly feeling like an intruder on the moment, Eadgyth kissed Judith's head and got to her feet. "You need some food as well. I shall see to it and tell everyone the news."

Otto was still in the hall, where he had just finished welcoming a delegation of Greek envoys. "I can see there is good news at last," Otto said with a smile, as Eadgyth ran to him.

"Yes, a healthy baby girl."

"And Judith? How is she?"

"She is exhausted. I do not know, but I pray she will recover. She is so happy at this moment. I hope that will give her strength, but she will need a lot of looking after."

"Can I see her soon?" Otto asked. "As Henry is not here, I feel a responsibility towards them both."

"I will ask her."

When she returned to Judith, she found that she had been helped into bed. Eadgyth smiled, while trying to work out her chances of recovery. Although not quite as long, the birth had been even more intense than Liutgarde's and she had nearly died following that one. The extreme pallor of Judith's face frightened her, but the joy in her eyes gave her hope.

"Let me hold her a moment," Eadgyth said. She indicated the serving woman behind her with a steaming bowl. "You need to eat something." Eadgyth felt a slight pang as she took her niece in her arms, knowing how unlikely she was to bear any more. Reminding herself to be grateful for the two healthy children she had born, she sat down on the bed, giving Judith an anxious glance. Her hands were shaking as she held the bowl, but at least she was eating. "Otto would like to see the child as soon as you are ready."

Judith's lip trembled. "Henry will hate that Otto sees her

first." She swallowed. "But we need Otto's protection. I am ready for him to see her."

"It need not be today." Eadgyth gently smoothed back Judith's hair, wishing she had not raised this issue so soon.

"It makes no difference. Let him come as soon as he wishes."

Otto came as soon as he was summoned and knelt next to the bed. "Forgive me for disturbing you, Judith. I shall not stay long. I know you need to rest." He pushed aside the shawl which was half covering the baby's face and smiled. "You have done well. That is a fine child."

"Thank you," Judith whispered.

"Eadgyth tells me that thankfully all seems to be well with her, but she should be baptised soon. Did Henry discuss any names with you?"

"If we had a boy he wanted it named for his father," Judith said. "For a girl he suggested his sister."

"Gerberga?" Otto asked.

Judith shook her head. "Hedwig."

Otto gave Judith a sharp glance. "Are you sure?"

Eadgyth too was surprised. She had expected the baby to be named Mathilda. But she met Otto's eyes, shaking her head slightly to warn him not to argue with her.

"I and my child are in your hands, my lord. The choice of name is yours." Her voice wavered and Eadgyth put her arms around her shoulders, aware of how close she was to tears.

"No, my dear sister. If Henry wanted Hedwig and you are happy with that choice, then of course that shall be her name. It is a fine one."

"Thank you. It is what I want."

"Then it is settled." Otto kissed her cheek. "I will leave you now and hope you can get some sleep."

∞∞∞

Eadgyth remained anxious about Judith, but with each sleep

she grew a little stronger and the bleeding did not seem excessive. After a few days Eadgyth became hopeful that she would recover. Judith had become popular at court, with many admiring her beauty, while pitying her for her uncertain state with Henry in disgrace. The news she seemed to be recovering as well as could be expected was greeted with joy.

Five days after Hedwig's birth, Eadgyth was sitting at the table, talking happily with Otto. It was a merry meal, with much laughter among all assembled when a scuffle at the door drew all eyes. She looked up sharply, shocked to see a guard struggling with someone in the doorway. The hooded figure shoved the guard to one side to enter the hall.

"Father! Look!" Liudolf cried, staring in shock at the doorway.

Eadgyth too cried out. Pursued by armed men, Henry was running towards them.

Chapter twelve

Guards raced to stand in front of Otto and Eadgyth, while others seized Henry. He struggled against them, his face twisted and desperate. Otto got to his feet, staring at his brother in surprise, as well he might. There had been no message that Henry had escaped custody. Henry pulled hard to release his arms, but the men held him tighter than ever and dragged him towards the door.

As Otto pushed aside the warriors in front of them, Henry stopped kicking at the guards. He looked helplessly back at his older brother and for a brief moment pity overwhelmed Eadgyth's consternation.

"Is he armed?" Otto asked.

One of the men pulled away his cloak, tossing it to one side and patted his belt. "No, my lord."

"Allow him to approach," Otto said calmly.

"Otto, really?" Eadgyth clutched onto his arm, her wide eyes fixed on Henry.

Otto nodded, as the men holding Henry's arms released him. He straightened his tunic, before walking slowly towards them. The guards remained close-by, as Henry came closer. Otto pushed Eadgyth back and curled his hand around the knife at his belt. All eyes were on him as the court waited Henry's actions with a nervous fascination.

Henry paused a short distance from Otto to step out of his shoes. He made the last few steps barefoot and fell to his knees.

"My Lord King, I beg most humbly for your pardon for all crimes I committed against you and those I intended to commit. I swear by the soul of our father, the illustrious King

Henry that I truly repent. I pledge undying loyalty to you, Otto, as my brother and my king."

Never had the court been so silent as Henry bowed his head. Eadgyth glanced at Otto, trying to read his expression, wondering if she was being naïve to believe there was an honest ring to Henry's words. She looked back at Henry, his fair head still bowed, wishing she could see the expression on his face.

Otto pulled Henry to his feet. "I thought I had you securely imprisoned."

"I escaped," Henry replied, with a hint of pride. "But if you command it, my lord, I shall willingly return there."

Otto looked searchingly at Henry for a long time in a manner which left most men squirming. But Henry looked directly back, with no sign of insolence. Breaking into a smile, Otto embraced him. "Brothers should not fight. I freely pardon you."

Henry swallowed. "Thank you, Otto. It is more than I deserve."

Otto patted a chair. "Sit down, Henry. Refresh yourself."

Henry hesitantly took the chair next to Otto. Without a word Eadgyth poured him a cup of wine, still unsure what to make of Henry's penitent attitude. He took the drink and stared into it, before looking again at Otto. "I know I have no right to ask for any favours, but I have one request. Could a message be sent to my wife? She was with child last time I saw her and if all has gone well, she must be near her time." He gripped the edge of the table so hard his knuckles turned white. "I need to know how she is."

"That is unnecessary," Otto replied. "She is here."

Henry looked round in bewilderment. "Here?"

"I brought her under my protection. I give you my word she has not been ill-treated in any way." Otto grinned. "If my word is not good enough for you, perhaps Eadgyth's will be. She made it plain I would be forever sorry if I treated your wife as anything other than my honoured sister."

Henry looked anxiously at Eadgyth. "Is Judith well?"

Eadgyth was taken aback at the fear in Henry's eyes. "She was brought to bed just a few days ago. She is still very weak."

"Was it hard? Will she recover?" Henry sat on the edge of his seat, looking terrified of Eadgyth's answer.

"It was very hard and I truly thought we would lose her. But since the birth she has grown a little stronger every day. She will need care for some time yet, but I am hopeful she will recover." Feeling touched by Henry's attitude, Eadgyth noted he had not yet asked about the child. His concern was all for Judith.

"She must have been so frightened," Henry murmured. "Were you with her?"

Eadgyth nodded and Otto put in, "Eadgyth barely left her side for days."

Again Henry flung himself to his knees, but this time before Eadgyth. Fervently he kissed her hands. "Thank you." He looked at her, tears welling in his eyes. "I have no words to fully express my gratitude."

Eadgyth blinked back a few tears of her own. "Get up, Henry. It was an honour to help deliver her child."

"What of the child?" Henry asked at last.

"A strong, healthy girl," Otto replied. "I know you must have hoped for a son, but I do not think you will find yourself anything other than enchanted by your daughter."

"My daughter," Henry repeated, as if he were hardly able to believe the words. "If they both recover, I am truly the most fortunate of men."

Otto smiled at the awe on Henry's face. "Judith requested she be named Hedwig. You must see her soon."

Eadgyth bit her lip, determined not to allow anything to upset Judith, no matter which of the two brothers she offended. "I am not sure about that, Otto. Judith is still very frail."

"But, Eadgyth…" Otto started.

Henry met Eadgyth's eyes, but there was no sign of the anger she had expected. "You are right. Nothing must distress her while she is so weak. I know I have done little to endear myself to her. Please tell Judith I am here, if it will not upset her too much. But assure her I will not force my presence on her."

Eadgyth nodded. Reluctantly she was impressed by Henry's manner. "She was asleep when I left her to come to the hall. When she awakes, I will tell her you are here."

"Take some refreshment while you wait," Otto said, pulling a platter over to him. "And tell me how you escaped from what I thought was a secure prison. I suppose I shall have to pardon the archbishop as well, now." The flicker of irritation which crossed his face at that thought was swiftly followed by an amused gleam. "Just out of interest, Henry, how many horses did you steal in order to beat my messengers across the realm?"

∞∞∞

When Eadgyth returned to Judith, she found her awake, her baby in her arms. She hesitated, tears filling her eyes at the contented expression on her face. She hated having to destroy this tranquillity.

Judith looked up, her face still pale, but a happy smile on her lips. Eadgyth forced herself to return the smile and sat next to her on the bed, taking hold of her hand.

"Henry is here," she said, wishing she could find a way to soften the news.

The look of dismay Eadgyth had been dreading, spread over Judith's face. "Here? But he is imprisoned." Judith pulled her hand free to cover her mouth. "Oh, no. What has he done? Do not soften this, Eadgyth. What terrible deeds has he done?"

"No, he has done nothing terrible. He has gone down on his knees and begged for Otto's forgiveness."

Judith's eyes were wide. "Has Otto forgiven him?"

"They are sat together in the hall, sharing a jug of wine as if there has never been so much as a cross word between them."

To Eadgyth's shock an expression of pure joy transformed

Judith's face. "Then we can be together again. He can see our child. Does he mind that she is not a son?"

"He seemed very proud to hear of her." Eadgyth stared at the radiance on Judith's face. "He wants very much to see you and the child, but he says he understands if you do not wish to see him and will stay away if you would prefer it."

"Of course he must see her," Judith replied. She picked up a mirror and grimaced. "I look terrible."

"Nonsense." Eadgyth picked up a comb and started running it through Judith's golden brown hair. Judith's reaction was not what she had expected. She had thought there would be some fear, yet instead Judith's attitude of wanting to look her best, was the same one she herself would show when reunited with Otto after a long absence. "Judith, do you care for Henry?"

"Of course."

"No, I mean truly care for him. Not out of duty, but truly from your heart."

Judith glanced at her and nodded. "Yes, very much."

"He cares for you too," Eadgyth said, remembering his anxious questions in the hall. Judith was so pretty and accomplished, she did not know why she felt surprised. Perhaps it was because she had always assumed that Henry cared for no one other than himself. "You have barely spoken of him since you came here."

"I knew you did not like him, so it did not seem right to speak of him."

"Oh, Judith, I am sorry. I never meant to make you feel like that." Eadgyth felt a twinge of guilt. "Did he ever hurt you? I do not mean deliberately, but out of impatience or carelessness."

"Never. He has always been gentle with me. I was afraid on our wedding night, but he quickly showed me I had nothing to fear." Judith gave a shy smile. "And much to enjoy."

"Before your wedding I asked him to be kind to you," Eadgyth said. "He implied he would not."

Judith hesitated. "I think you angered him by your assumption he would not treat me kindly. He said you and

Otto always believed the worst of him."

Eadgyth opened her mouth, but swiftly closed it again as she could find nothing to say to that.

Judith smiled apologetically. "I do not blame you. I know Henry has done nothing to make you believe anything else, but he resented it. He believed Otto was secretly pleased when he failed in Lotharingia."

Eadgyth's first instinct was to leap to Otto's defence, but she forced herself to consider Judith's comments. "He may not have been wrong."

"Forgive me. You and Otto have been so kind. I do not want to seem ungrateful."

"I know you are not. I have often blamed Henry for all the troubles, but it seems it was not as simple as I thought."

"As a boy Henry looked up to Otto, but he always feared he was not as fine. Otto was the heir, the battle hero, the perfect one almost everyone at court loved. Henry wanted Otto to admire him, but he said Otto treated him as a child of no account."

"There is a number of years between them, but when I arrived in this realm there seemed to be a true bond. Perhaps with our marriage Otto became a man and so quickly a father, while Henry remained a boy."

"His mother and Gerberga seemed to love Henry more, but they both had such high expectations of him." Judith shrugged. "He often felt they only regarded him so highly because they believed he should be king. I think Henry had always felt torn between Otto and his mother, but by the time he wed me, he had become obsessed with the crown. He believed if he fulfilled his destiny everyone would revere him as they revere Otto. I know he missed his father very much when he died. He once told me that until we were wed only his father and his sister, Hedwig loved him unconditionally and without pressure."

"So that is why Henry wanted his daughter named for her," Eadgyth exclaimed. "But you too love him unconditionally do you not? Your marriage has been a happy one."

"Between us, yes, it has always been happy, but our lives have not been so happy. I hated our time in Lotharingia. We were treated with such contempt and Henry was always so tired and worried. He did try to make a success of it."

"Why did he not ask for help?"

"From who? Hermann, Udo and Conrad had all fought against Henry the previous year. He should have asked for help, I know, but it would have been humiliating to ask for help from them and he did not want to admit to Otto that he could not cope."

Eadgyth bit her lip, again unsure of what to say. Grudgingly she understood Henry's attitude.

"I was happy when we moved to Henry's estates in Saxony. I still missed Bavaria, but everyone in Saxony respected us. I did not need a great position. It was enough for me to preside over Henry's estates there. For a while Henry too seemed contented, although I was always aware of how much of a failure he felt. I think it was the day I told him I was with child that he became obsessed again with being a man of importance. When the Archbishop of Mainz stayed with us just after last Christmas, I felt something was wrong, but I did not know what they were planning when they went to Quedlinburg, I swear it."

"I know," Eadgyth replied, thinking it was at least to Henry's credit that he had not involved Judith in his plans.

"I just want him and Otto to be friends." She looked down at her baby, her face crumpled as the tears welled in her eyes. In the weary droop of her shoulders, Eadgyth could clearly see the toll the family strife had caused.

With a flicker of hope she thought of how she had left Otto and Henry together in the hall. "I think we have a chance of that now. The friendship is fragile, of course. With everything that has gone before, how can it not be? But it can be improved, particularly if Mathilda and Father Frederick are kept away. Judith, if you have any influence on Henry, urge him to loyalty."

"I will," Judith replied.

"And I will urge Otto to be fairer in his expectations and more understanding of Henry's position. I see now that although Henry has committed some grave acts, Otto is not blameless. Between us we shall keep those two in order."

Judith laughed and squeezed Eadgyth's hand. "Thank you."

Gently Eadgyth tugged out the last knots in Judith's hair and smiled. "You look beautiful. Are you ready for a visitor? There is a most anxious young husband and father who is longing to come to you."

Chapter thirteen

When the door opened Henry and Otto came in together. Henry's face lit up as he ran forward and knelt next to the bed.

"Oh, Judith. I am so sorry. I am so sorry for everything."

Judith gently touched Henry's cheek. "It doesn't matter now, Henry. I am glad you are here."

Henry looked at her fearfully. "How are you feeling?"

"I'm fine."

Henry shook his head and kissed her lightly. "No, you're not, but I think you will be."

Eadgyth noticed how surprised Otto looked at the affection between them. She wondered if she and Otto had become so arrogant to have thought only they could find such happiness in marriage. It had never occurred to either of them that Henry and Judith would come to care so deeply for each other.

With a joyous smile Judith turned the baby so Henry could see her. He swallowed as he took in the tiny infant sleeping so peacefully in her mother's arms.

Otto put his hand on Henry's shoulder. "You are a father now. There needs to be an end to all foolish behaviour. Your wife and daughter need you."

"I think he knows that, Otto," Eadgyth said softly. With her new sensitivity to Henry's position she realised he would be right to feel irritated at Otto using such a moment to start a lecture.

However Henry was so mesmerised by the baby, he had taken no notice of his brother's words. Otto smiled. "Yes, I think he does."

"You have done so well, Judith." Henry blinked back tears as he stroked the baby's wispy hair. "She is very beautiful. Just like you."

"She will be much prettier than I," Judith said, smiling at the baby.

"Impossible," Henry retorted. "Can I hold her?"

Judith nodded as Henry tucked his hands under the baby's body and took her into his arms. After watching him for a moment, Eadgyth got to her feet and touched Otto's arm. "Shall we give them some time alone?"

"Wait." Henry put the baby back into Judith's arms. "I know I have already done this before the court, but I want Judith to see it, so she truly knows that all is well." Henry went down on one knee before Otto. "I, Henry of Saxony, son of the noble King Henry, pledge my loyalty to you, Otto, King of Germany for as long as there is breath in my body."

Otto raised Henry up, holding him by the shoulders. "I told you long ago that brothers should not kneel to one another as long as their hearts be true."

"My heart is now true," Henry said. "But I know it will take you a long time to fully trust that."

"Perhaps, but we have made a start. In the days to come we will talk more. However today is not the day for that." Otto pointed back at the bed. "Spend some time with them and enjoy it. It is not every day that a man meets his daughter for the first time!"

Eadgyth smiled at them both, before giving a look of mock sternness. "Remember Judith is supposed to be resting, won't you."

Henry grinned. "Absolutely."

"I wish I had listened to you before their marriage," Otto said as the door shut behind them. "She is far too good for him."

"Nonsense. She is very good for him," Eadgyth replied.

Otto paused and looked at her in surprise. "I did not expect you to say that. In fact I assumed you would not be impressed at my forgiveness."

"I have changed my mind. Judith has explained much to

me. Henry has not always been in the easiest of positions and perhaps your treatment could have been fairer."

"What do you mean? I have been ever patient."

Eadgyth raised her eyebrows. "Can you swear to me by the bones of Saint Maurice that you felt no satisfaction when Henry failed in Lotharingia?" Otto squirmed. "Well?"

"Very well, perhaps you have a point."

"I am not minimising Henry's crimes. He has done terrible deeds and you are generous indeed to forgive it. But I think this time he will not let you down. You can tell a lot about a man by how he treats his wife and in this Henry has proved what a fine man he can be. My father treated his wives as if they were unimportant and that proved what sort of man he was."

"Your father was reckoned to be a good king," Otto commented, but said no more at the flash of anger in Eadgyth's eyes.

"You are a good king and a good man," Eadgyth said, putting her arms around him.

"I try to be. Very well, I accept that Judith will be the making of him. Eadgyth, I know you do not want to consider this, but what if she dies?"

Eadgyth crossed herself. "I pray not. I think then Henry could be very dangerous. Put yourself in his position. Suppose during my pregnancies you had been locked up, unable to get any news of me.

Otto glanced back at the door. "Henry must have been out of his mind with worry."

"Yes, I think he was. As the summer wore on, his fears must have mounted. I do not think it is coincidence that he escaped just as Judith was preparing to give birth."

"Probably not. I know no prison would have kept me from you at such a time."

"Suppose after our brief reunion I had died. What would you do then?"

"I would stop at nothing to kill the man who had kept me from you and I would not care what justification he had. My

God, Eadgyth, take every care of Judith. She has to recover."

∞∞∞

Some time later Eadgyth returned to Judith. After a soft tap on the door brought no answer, she pushed it open and peeped into the room. A smile spread slowly across her face.

Judith was asleep, her baby tucked into her arms. And curled up next to her was Henry, his arm protectively round them both. Presumably worn out from his dash across the realm, Henry too was sleeping.

Eadgyth stared at the family a moment longer, overwhelmed suddenly with the certainty that all would be well. Then she turned away and quietly shut the door.

Part Six: The Year of our Lord 941-42

Chapter one

Buoyed up by Henry's return, Judith recovered quickly, while Henry divided his time between his wife and his brother. Eadgyth watched him closely, but felt his awkward, yet respectful manner with Otto was very natural. It was certainly different to the exaggerated penitence he had shown on the previous occasion he had been pardoned. Gradually the awkwardness eased into a tentative affection.

Otto cautiously welcomed his brother's newfound friendship, although he remarked to Eadgyth that he was glad Judith would be unable to travel for a while since it meant Henry would remain at court under his eye.

He took Henry with him to Frankfurt to officially pardon both him and Father Frederick. Eadgyth waited anxiously at Magdeburg to hear how the matter had passed.

"Henry seemed almost afraid of the Archbishop," Otto told her. "If he was present Henry insisted on staying by my side. I think in the time after our father's death, Henry felt lost. No doubt Father Frederick found him easy to mould, but he now understands what a poor influence that was."

"What of Father Frederick? Will he be loyal now?"

"I will never trust him," Otto replied. "But as long as he has no one of significance to plot with, all will be well."

Accompanied by his family, Hermann arrived at court shortly before Christmas with the words, "I heard you were here. Otto, what are you thinking?"

Otto embraced his friend. "I am thinking you are too quick

to judgement. I am certain that by the time the Christmas festivities have passed, you too will be on excellent terms with Henry."

"I hope we will be," Henry said. "But I do not blame you for your suspicions."

"I think the chances of us being friends are very remote," Hermann said, taking a cup from Eadgyth.

Otto grinned. "More remote than Eadgyth accepting him? I certainly never thought I would see that after she offered to execute him for me!"

Henry darted a look of mock outrage at Eadgyth, who was greeting Regelind. She laughed as she pulled Ida into her arms. "Come Hermann, I know Liudolf is eager to see you."

Away from Otto and Henry, Hermann lowered his voice. "My lady, I have long admired your judgement and I know you are not blinded by brotherly affection. Do you truly consider Lord Henry changed?"

"Yes, I do. Everything in his manner is very different. He has a wife and a child now so I think he has grown up at last."

"Well, I hope so," Hermann replied doubtfully.

∞∞∞

The Christmas festivities were happy ones. Judith was fully recovered and re-joined the court, her baby never far from her arms. Eadgyth thought occasionally of Mathilda and wondered how she was faring. It felt wrong to be enjoying such celebrations without her. She had sent no message of Christmas greeting to the court and nor had Otto sent one to her, although as Bruno sent his from Enger, she knew that at least Mathilda was not alone during the festive period.

Otto was in great spirits over Christmas, abandoning his usual regal manner to jest with Hermann and Henry. By the time the celebrations were over it was obvious Otto had been right. Hermann and Henry, while unlikely to ever be close friends, were at least on good terms. Eadgyth delighted to see Otto so carefree and could only pray that the harmony in the family would last.

∞∞∞

There were thick snow falls around Magdeburg that winter, but as soon as they melted Otto made plans to oversee some matters in the Slavic marches. Although Henry was to ride with him, the young age of the baby prevented Judith from doing the same. Eadgyth had intended to accompany Otto, but after catching a heavy cold, she decided to remain with Judith. With some ceremony Otto declared Liudolf in charge at Magdeburg, saying he was now old enough to take some responsibilities under the guidance of his mother, leaving Liudolf puffed up with pride.

While Eadgyth missed Otto during his absence, she found much to occupy herself. She was delighted that although Regelind departed for her grandson's court in Burgundy, Ida remained with her at Magdeburg. The shy child who had been betrothed to Liudolf, was blossoming into a pretty girl whose friendship with both Liudolf and Liutgarde grew stronger by the day. Often she watched the three children together, feeling overwhelmed with pride at what a charming little family they made. With Judith for company, she found she did not pine for Otto as much as she had once done. However Otto's message in the spring announcing his return filled both her and Judith with joy. They spared no effort in arranging a magnificent welcome feast to greet their husbands.

It was late in the day before the watchmen reported that Otto's banner had been sighted. The feast was on the table and everyone was gathered around it, when Otto finally strode in. With a grin he swept Liudolf into a hug before moving up the hall to greet Eadgyth. There was quite a group accompanying him, but as always Eadgyth only had eyes for Otto. She flung her arms around him, her lips eagerly meeting his.

"You are quite recovered?" Otto asked, the look of anxiety in his eyes surprising her.

"Of course," Eadgyth replied. "It was a trivial complaint and is long gone."

"That is good," Otto replied.

He stood to one side as Henry and Hermann both came forward and Eadgyth began to feel uneasy. There was something forced about the men's smiles and neither quite met her eye.

"Greetings, Sister," Henry said, kissing her hand.

"Welcome back, Henry. You will find little Hedwig has grown much since you left."

"I am eager to see her. Perhaps you will excuse me…" He gave an awkward shrug. Eadgyth's heart sank as Henry hurried to greet Judith.

She glanced at Otto, trying to work out what had happened only to see a meaningful look pass between him and Hermann. It was obvious something had gone wrong. She prayed it was a minor matter as the thought of a return to the days of strife in the family was unbearable.

Hermann's mumbled greeting was even more awkward than Henry's as he turned swiftly to Liudolf and Ida. After a glance at Otto, he quickly moved away, his arms around the two children. Briefly Eadgyth's eyes met his and her mouth went dry at the grave expression she glimpsed before his eyes slid away from her. She looked again at Henry. He had his arm around Judith and both were staring in her direction, but before she could ask Otto what the trouble was, he had pulled forward a young man of around twenty years. He was a striking looking man with dark red hair.

"My love, I have been most remiss," Otto said, his buoyant tone failing to sound cheerful. "It seems strange given the years he has served me so well that I have never presented Conrad to you."

The young man bowed deeply before Eadgyth. "It is an

honour to meet you at last, my lady Queen."

Eadgyth stretched out her hand. "I am very glad to meet you. I know the great debt of gratitude I owe you."

"I am glad to have been of service, my lady."

"And may I present my daughter, Lady Liutgarde," Otto said.

Again Conrad bowed, studying Liutgarde with rather more interest than Eadgyth would have expected the young man to show.

"Serve Conrad a cup of wine, sweetheart," Otto commanded his daughter.

"Of course, Father. Please come this way, my lord."

Otto stared after them. "I am very fond of Conrad. He is as fine a man as I have ever encountered." He looked steadily at Eadgyth. "I would very much like to bring him closer into the family."

"Do you mean a match between him and Liutgarde?" Eadgyth exclaimed. "But she is so young."

"Oh, I know she is far too young at present. I would not even countenance a betrothal for another few years and a marriage a few years after that. But he would make her a fine husband. One day I shall put him in charge of Lotharingia and our daughter will be the duchess."

Eadgyth, who had assumed Henry would in time be reinstated as Duke of Lothringia, was surprised and it made her suspect still further that matters were not good between the brothers. She darted another look at Henry. To her surprise, Hermann was standing with him and they were talking together, casting uneasy glances at her and Otto.

Most of the group behind Otto had dissipated in search of sustenance and now only one remained. There was a lull in the chatter of the hall as Otto pulled that one forward. It was a boy who appeared to be a year or two older than Liudolf.

He looked nervous and Eadgyth smiled at him, trying to work out who he was. It was obvious he was a member of the family. His resemblance to Otto and Henry was startling. She wondered if he was Gerberga's son. It had been some years since she had last seen him, but from her memory he had appeared more like Gilbert than any of Gerberga's family. She looked enquiringly at Otto and she was not the only one. It seemed everyone in the hall was watching them.

"Eadgyth, this is William," Otto said.

Eadgyth stretched out her hand. "Welcome to Magdeburg, William."

He took her hand and bowed, as Eadgyth wished Otto would explain who the boy was.

Otto took a deep breath. "William is my son."

Chapter two

Eadgyth froze and stared at the boy, the awkward manner of Hermann and Henry suddenly making sense. She withdrew her hand from the boy's sharply, flushing slightly as she realised everyone was still watching her. In the time Otto had taken to present Conrad to her, it was obvious his men had spread the news. A wave of betrayal hit her and she swallowed hard to keep back the stammering words trying to leap from her lips. The boy looked so like Otto and a cold fury swept over her that she had to see him there in her city. Grabbing the last remnants of her dignity, she quashed her instinct to order the boy from the hall. Instead she smiled a remote, but gracious smile. "Welcome to Magdeburg," she repeated.

"Thank you, my lady," the boy whispered, glancing uncertainly at Otto.

Otto laid his hand on William's shoulder, briefly meeting Eadgyth's eyes. She could see the disappointment in them and this angered her more than ever. The silence in the hall seemed never ending, as Eadgyth looked steadily ahead, saying nothing more. Otto let out a sigh. "William, go join Henry. We shall dine shortly."

The boy flushed, giving Eadgyth another bow as he moved away. Slowly the noise started up in the hall with subdued whispers, which Eadgyth guessed were about William. She stared down at her clenched fists, wishing she could make some excuse to escape. Desperately she needed the time to gather her thoughts and make sense of Otto's actions, not certain how she was supposed to keep the tears back. She had been so looking forward to his return, but now it was ruined.

"Eadgyth," Otto said in a low, but urgent tone.

She looked up, resenting him more than ever. Determinedly she gave him a bright smile. "I am sure you must be hungry, my lord. Shall we dine?"

Otto flinched, his face darkening, but as Eadgyth had already moved away he had no choice but to follow her. She took her place on the dais at the head of the table, praying she could get through the evening as quickly as possible. The horror of the occasion deepened as she realised William had been seated between Henry and Hermann in a position which clearly demonstrated his high status, a status she had no wish to grant him.

"I gave no permission for anyone else to be seated here." She looked pointedly at Hermann and Henry.

William shrank closer to Henry who patted him awkwardly on the shoulder. Hermann rose to his feet and wet his lips nervously. "My lady, the King…"

"He sits there at my request," Otto said.

They stared at each other. For an instant Eadgyth was torn between arguing the matter with Otto and storming from the hall, but such public displays of fury were not in her nature. Feeling completely humiliated she sat down, praying she would get through the meal without breaking down.

It was a strange meal. Usually the first meal after any reunion was one of merriment, with Otto's arm constantly around her. They would exchange news, almost ignoring the others at the table, as they focused only on each other. There was always good humoured laughter when Otto would bring the meal to an abrupt end, declaring that the moment he and his wife were to be alone was not to be put off any longer.

But that evening was different. Eadgyth huddled in the far side of her chair, ensuring she was as far away from Otto as possible and did not so much as look at him throughout the meal. Liudolf sat next to his father, looking bewildered at the arrival of a half-brother he had no knowledge of. He answered his father's questions hesitantly in a polite tone, so different from their usual easy manner. Eadgyth did her best not to look at William, but on the few occasions she could not avoid it, she saw him crumbling some food between his fingers and eating very little.

Wanting to avoid the pity in the eyes of Henry, Judith and Hermann, Eadgyth spoke little to them, but instead directed most of her comments to Conrad, who being a stranger seemed easier to converse with.

Besides, she reflected grimly, it would be as well to gain something useful from that night and get to know the man who might become Liutgarde's husband. With a flicker of dark humour she wondered if it would be appropriate to ask Conrad if he had any bastard children who Liutgarde would be expected to welcome one day.

Liutgarde found the meal almost as much of a strain as her mother. She looked overwhelmed with relief when she could rise from the table, bobbing into a slight curtsey before her parents and bidding everyone a good night. As Liutgarde left the hall hand in hand with Ida, Eadgyth realised that, although far earlier than her custom, it would not be improper for her too to leave the table.

"It has been delightful to meet you, Conrad," she said, casting the most casual glance she could manage around the table. "It has been a most pleasant meal. I will bid you all a good night." For the first time since the meal started, she looked directly at Otto, her eyes slightly narrowed. "Good night, my lord."

The hurt and anger flashed in his eyes, but he said nothing merely giving a bow as he sat back down.

"Shall I escort you to your chamber, Mother," Liudolf asked, his longing to escape the hall obvious in every word. It was hard to deny him the chance.

"No, stay here and talk with your father," Eadgyth said, kissing his cheek. A shiver coursed through her as she realised how Liudolf might now need to fight for his place with Otto. Certainly she would not allow the bastard son to be left as Otto's only child present. Almost she sat back down, despising herself for her weakness at needing to leave Liudolf alone to deal with it.

Out of the corner of her eye she saw Henry whisper to Judith as she too got to her feet. Judith walked purposefully towards her so they would leave the hall together. Determined to avoid any questions, Eadgyth kept up a bright stream of meaningless conversation until they reached her chamber.

"Good night, Judith," Eadgyth said with forced cheerfulness. She was ashamed of the jealousy she felt towards her. Judith could look forward to a joyful reunion with her husband once he retired for the night. Eadgyth did not even want to look at Otto.

The embrace Judith gave her was nearly Eadgyth's undoing. "Eadgyth, I do not want to intrude, but if you need me-"

"Good night," Eadgyth repeated more forcefully and did her best to open the door to her chamber with dignity.

She summoned no women to help her disrobe, tugging a comb distractedly through her own hair and tossing her jewels carelessly on top of a coffer. Feeling numb she climbed into bed and hoped Otto would have the sense to stay away. Once she snuffed out the candles, the chamber was plunged into darkness, but the turmoil in her mind rendered sleep impossible. She tossed and turned, hurt and anger alternating in her heart.

Eadgyth stiffened as she heard the door open and the light from Otto's candle spilled into the room. She lay very still, hoping he would think she was sleeping, but he sat down on the bed and put a hand on her shoulder.

"I know you're not asleep," he said.

"Go away, Otto. I don't want to talk to you."

"We need to talk."

Eadgyth sat up at that. "How dare you bring your bastard here and expect me to welcome him."

"You did not welcome him. That was obvious."

Eadgyth was furious at the anger lacing Otto's voice. "He got the appropriate welcome I give any to this court. He is no one important to me."

"Nonsense. You welcome everyone, no matter how lowly, with your beautiful smile. I have seen you give traitors a warmer welcome than you gave William."

"You should not have brought him here."

Otto looked steadily at her. "His mother is dead. He has no one else. Strangely I did not think you of all people would want me to desert him."

"You did not need to desert him," Eadgyth snapped. "You could have made some arrangement for him and continued to see him as you have done his entire life. You had no right to force his presence onto me in front of the entire court."

"I am disappointed you see it that way. I hoped you would welcome him for my sake."

"Is that an order, my lord?"

"Damn it, Eadgyth, do not be like that. I have had enough." He glared at her and then shook his head. "Look, we are both tired. I am coming to bed and we shall talk more in the morning."

"I see. You are going to force me to fulfil my duties now."

Otto recoiled as if he had been struck. He stood up, picking up the candle. "I resent that, Eadgyth. I have never forced you."

"If you ever want me again you will have to." Eadgyth was horrified by the spiteful words leaving her lips, but she could not bring herself to relent. "I shall never welcome you into my bed again."

Otto walked to the door, but he turned to look at her, the candle lighting up the serious expression on his face. "I am grieved to hear that. Of everything in my life, your love is the most precious to me. But I will not desert my son. If the price I have to pay is losing the chance ever again to lie in your arms, then so be it. It is a bitter one, but I shall have to accept it. I will certainly not debase the love you once had for me by forcing you. Good night, Eadgyth."

The door thudded behind Otto with an eerie finality, plunging the chamber into darkness once again. For Eadgyth the tears came at last, as she flung herself backward against the pillows, wishing sleep would grant her a brief respite from her misery.

Chapter three

After a night when she got nothing more than the occasional doze, Eadgyth gave up on sleep as the first hint of light touched the sky. She pulled on a simple tunic and did not bother to bind up her hair, but covered it with a mantle. She slipped quietly from her chamber, guessing that Otto was in the adjoining one. The door to that chamber was closed and she stared at it, tears trickling down her cheeks. She didn't think there had ever been an occasion he had slept there when both were well and certainly they had never slept apart because of a quarrel. Knowing him as well as she did, she doubted very much that he was asleep or if he was, it would only be lightly, so she went silently out into the passageway, finding her way almost by touch to the hall.

The guards on duty at the door were dozing and barely stirred as Eadgyth slipped out into the grey dawn. She shivered slightly, wishing she had the sense to have brought a cloak with her. The late spring weather had been warm, but at that hour of day the chill seeped through her clothes.

Swiftly she made her way to the abbey. Candles and oil lamps burnt brightly although the building was deserted. The last of the night services was over and the monks would no doubt all be sleeping until the matins bell rang. She looked around. The abbey was a beautiful building, although she knew it was not yet as magnificent as Otto hoped it would one day be. She caught her breath and walked towards the altar at a more sedate pace.

As she got closer, she realised the abbey was not after all completely deserted. A boy dressed in grey was kneeling before the altar, murmuring prayers, punctuated by occasional sobs. She gasped slightly as she realised it was William.

He started and looked round. Upon seeing her, he got quickly to his feet and bowed. Eadgyth could see the traces of tears on his cheeks and she wasn't sure if it was his resemblance to Liudolf or Otto which brought a sudden urge to put a comforting arm around him. But she had taken only one step towards him before her resentment at seeing him in the abbey she and Otto had founded together brought her to an abrupt halt.

"Forgive me, my lady, if I should not be here," William said. "I wanted to say some prayers for my mother."

"The abbey is here for everyone," Eadgyth replied, cringing at how ungracious she sounded.

"Thank you, my lady." William looked back for a moment at the altar. "But you must have come here at this time hoping to be alone. I shall leave now." He gave another bow and moved away.

Eadgyth stared at the jewelled cross on the altar, the sense of reproach emanating from the figure affixed to it, striking her hard in the heart. She had come there to pray for guidance, but it was unnecessary. She already knew what she needed to do. She turned, but William had vanished from view behind the columns. Swiftly she ran after him, her soft footsteps echoing in the abbey and caught up with him as he was heading out of the door.

"Wait, William. I want to talk to you."

The sky was lighter now and the first sounds of birds were drifting through the still air. William swallowed. "I have long been trained to enter the church. My fa… The King wishes for me to continue my education at court, but it is not necessary. I think, my lady, it would be for the best if I returned to Mollenbeck where I was raised or perhaps some other institution of the King's choosing."

In the grey light Eadgyth could see how pale he looked and this time she did not allow resentment to swamp her natural sympathy. She shook her head. "No, if the King wants you educated here, that is what you must do. I will support him."

"Thank you, my lady, but I do not want you to be made uncomfortable by my presence."

"I shall grow accustomed. You must do as the King wants." Eadgyth flushed, knowing this was not coming out how she wanted. "But this palace is not just a court. It is also the place where those closest to the King gather. The King controls who comes to court and we must all obey that. But none would be admitted into the inner circle of his family without my approval."

"Of course, my lady. I understand and have no intention of intruding."

Eadgyth cursed herself for her failure to state exactly what she meant. The anxious eyes looking at her at that moment were so like Otto's. It should not be so hard to speak the words she wanted to say. Knowing none of the events of the last day were his fault, she stretched out her hand to him. "You misunderstand me, William. I did not say that to imply you are not welcome. I said it so that as you are welcomed, you know you need feel no awkwardness with me." William stared at her, slowly taking her hand. "I know you must miss your mother most grievously and I would not presume to take her place. But if you ever do need a mother's guidance, I hope you will come to me."

William dropped to his knees, tears again falling down his cheek. "Thank you, my lady. I have no right to expect such kindness."

Almost in tears herself, Eadgyth tugged on his hand. "Get up, William. You must not kneel to me on informal occasions. Indeed on such occasions I would like you to use my name. No formality is necessary." The next step was harder, but Eadgyth knew it was the right one to take. "And on such occasions I have no objection to you calling the King, Father."

William's eyes widened in surprise. "Thank you," he breathed.

"Yes, thank you, Eadgyth," Otto said. Eadgyth and William both looked round, startled. They had not heard him approach.

Otto and Eadgyth's eyes met. She did not smile, but neither did she show any anger.

"I hope I can repay you for your kindness one day," William said, oblivious to any tensions between them.

Eadgyth was consumed with guilt that he was thanking her, when so far she had shown him very little kindness. A sudden memory of the contempt her mother had shown to Athelstan horrified her as she recognised how easily she could have treated this motherless boy the same way. Resolving to do better from that moment, she smiled at him, realising it would not be hard to become very fond of William. "Be a friend to Liudolf. That is all I ask. He may find it hard to accept you at first, but do not give up. As he gets older and takes on more responsibilities, he will need a supportive friend and brother."

"Of course. I will ever be his most loyal supporter," William said eagerly.

Otto smiled too and put his hand on William's shoulder. "Go to the hall now, my son. There will be food and ale served shortly and I shall join you there soon."

William nodded, giving them both a slight bow before running away.

Eadgyth looked warily at Otto. He ran his fingers through his hair and sighed. "Both Henry and Hermann urged me not to bring the boy here. They said it was too much to expect of you and I should make provision for him to be cared for either at the monastery or in some similar foundation." He looked pleadingly at Eadgyth, but she did not reply. "When I got the message his mother had died, I had to see him. He was distraught and my first instinct was to bring him to you, to this happy home you have made for me."

In spite of her anger, Eadgyth's heart swelled with pride. Creating a happy home for Otto was what her father-in-law had long ago asked her to do. It felt good to know she had succeeded.

"I am so grateful for what you said to him just now," Otto continued. "Do you still feel I did wrong in bringing him here?"

Slowly Eadgyth shook her head. "It is not that it was wrong for you to bring him here, but to expect me to welcome him without warning…"

"Well, you did not welcome him last night, so you can feel some satisfaction in that."

Eadgyth narrowed her eyes. "I feel no satisfaction in that. The fact that he was sprung on me without warning was not his fault."

"I didn't know I was going to need to bring him to court," Otto protested. "I wasn't even planning on seeing him on this occasion. But when I heard his mother had died, I wanted to take him into my direct protection. He is my son. I want him here."

"And what you want, you always get. Your word is law and no one else matters. Except you have always said that I am your equal."

"You are, Eadgyth."

"It did not feel that way when you presented him in such a fashion. I had no choice, no chance to prepare myself. Can you not understand that, Otto? If you had come to me when I was alone or if you had sent a message, I would still have found it hard, but I could have dealt with the shock before facing the court. Instead I have to cope with you arriving with him in front of everybody. He looks so like you. He is more like you than Liudolf is."

"I would not revere him more just because he looks like me. I love to see your beautiful eyes every time I look at my son. Liudolf is so precious to me as my son, but he is even more precious to me as he is yours."

"Otto, stop this and face facts. When you presented William to me without warning, you made it plain to me and to the court how little you care about my opinions or feelings on this matter. No doubt many are already whispering that you have brought him here because I failed to provide you with more than one son."

"William can never be part of the succession. Nothing threatens Liudolf's place as my heir."

"Everyone at court now knows how little regard you have for me, Otto. And I know it too." Eadgyth's eyes filled with tears. "You could have made it easier. You could have placed him in the care of the abbot overnight, while you spoke to me. But you didn't. You did not think of me once."

Otto looked stricken. "Oh, Eadgyth, I did not mean to make you feel that way. You are right, I did not think of you. But that is not because I consider myself above you or because I do not care for you. Never think that, my love. I was thinking only of William, as I would think only of any of my children if they were as distressed as he." Otto bit his lip. "I am sorry. I do not know what else to say."

"It is done now," Eadgyth said crossly. "There is nothing else you can say."

"You are the last person in the world I ever want to hurt. Please, Eadgyth, will you be able to forgive me?"

Eadgyth sighed. "Of course I will forgive you. You have forgiven men for much worse crimes than this."

"Thank you." He looked pleadingly at her. "Will you welcome me into your bed this night?"

Eadgyth had never been able to resist Otto when he looked at her like that and a smile slipped out from behind her stern expression. "I will consider it."

Otto smiled too and pulled her into his arms. He kissed her, tentatively at first, but as Eadgyth responded the kisses became more passionate. She suspected it would take time for the hurt to completely fade and she was not sure if even now Otto truly understood why she had been so upset. But there was no point dwelling on the pain and she guessed Otto would put the incident swiftly from his mind.

However in this she had underestimated him. He broke off the kiss abruptly. "No, you should not forgive me so easily. It is unacceptable that I hurt you and I have to make amends. I want to show you and the court how greatly I value you. My love, is there anything I can do? Surely there is something you want, something you do not ask for because you believe it is not what I want. If there is, ask it now and I swear, if it is in my power, I shall grant your wish."

Eadgyth hesitated. "Yes, there is something. I have not asked it because you seemed so contented now she was no longer present. But I miss your mother. I know your relationship was not the easiest, but she was always so kind to me. Could she be brought back to court?"

Otto looked resigned. "I should have guessed that was what you would ask for."

"Will it make you unhappy? Because I do not want it if it will."

Otto smiled and shook his head. "Oh, Eadgyth, never mind what I want. I will do this for you."

Her hurt quite forgotten, Eadgyth kissed Otto again. "Thank you. It is the right thing to do. I know she plagued you often enough in the past, but the words she spoke that Easter were not from her heart. She was overwrought. In truth I did not think she should ever have been sent away."

Chapter four

Eadgyth was heartened by the relief she saw in Hermann's face as she and Otto arrived hand in hand at the hall. At least he and the men closest to Otto recognised her importance to him. Otto took a seat next to Liudolf, beckoning William also to sit with them.

Liudolf got to his feet, looking uncertainly at Eadgyth. She smiled at him, understanding the question in his eyes. "Liudolf, perhaps you will show William the town after you have both broken your fast."

Liudolf looked from her to William and for a moment she thought he would refuse. Then he smiled at his half-brother. "I would be glad to."

William smiled back and in that instant Eadgyth was certain a friendship had been born. Otto ruffled Liudolf's hair, but quickly turned his attention to Conrad. With his brow creased Liudolf kept his eyes on his father as the two started an animated conversation.

"If Liudolf is to show William around, perhaps he will show you too, Conrad," Otto said at length, turning back to Liudolf.

To Eadgyth's surprise, Liudolf stiffened. "Indeed, I should be glad to, my lord."

Otto frowned and Eadgyth stared at her son. Liudolf had inherited her ability to deliver a stinging formality. She was shocked as this was the attitude she had expected him to show towards William.

Conrad smiled. "Thank you, Lord Liudolf, but I will not

trouble you this day as I am sure you and William have much to discuss."

As Liudolf looked sullenly down, Eadgyth caught Otto's eye and shook her head, thinking he had enough to become accustomed to for one day. Otto shrugged and got up to talk to Hermann. Eadgyth watched him, suddenly understanding Liudolf's animosity. The affection Otto showed Conrad was very obvious and different to the old friendship he shared with Hermann. She recognised how hard it was for Liudolf to see this handsome, confident young man on such close terms with his father. Befriending the nervous and grieving William was easy by comparison.

"I hear there is fine hunting around Magdeburg," Conrad said, breaking the awkward silence.

"It is fair enough," Liudolf replied, with barely a glance.

Eadgyth was about to chide him for this, impressed that Conrad was betraying no anger at Liudolf's surly attitude. But Conrad pointed at some boar's tusks hanging on the wall. "The King tells me you were the one who slew that boar. That is very impressive."

Liudolf's face lit up. "That was a very fine day's hunting indeed. I never expected bring it down by myself."

"You must be exceptionally skilled to make such a kill at your age. I hope I will have the privilege to hunt with you while I am at Magdeburg."

Liudolf nodded, pushing back his chair. "I am sure you will, although it is not the best time of year at present. Shall we go, William?" He looked at Conrad, his smile widening. "And truly I will be glad to show you the town if you care to join us."

Conrad smiled back. "Thank you, I would like that very much."

Eadgyth watched him in approval, thinking how skilfully Conrad had handled the conversation. Yet there had been nothing false about it. In spite of the years between them, she wondered whether another friendship had been born. She had not yet had a chance to talk to Otto about Liutgarde's proposed marriage alliance, but she found herself agreeing with Otto's assessment that this was indeed a fine young man.

Liudolf darted to Otto, recovering his usual exuberance. "Father, will you join us too?"

Otto looked at Liudolf and smiled. "Yes, my son, I will join you presently." As Liudolf and William raced for the door with Conrad following more sedately behind them, Otto took Eadgyth into his arms. "Is all truly well between us, my sweet?"

"Yes, Otto, it truly is." She looked at the three by the door and swallowed the lump in her throat. "I could only give you one son, but somehow you were able to acquire three. Could Conrad ever be your heir?"

"Liudolf is my heir."

"I know, but…" Eadgyth stopped, unable to voice her deepest fear.

Otto held her tightly. "Married to Liutgarde, I suppose he could be named. He is a kinsman of the old Frankish kings after all, but in truth I would favour Liutgarde's son over her husband. Of course Liudolf and Ida will wed at a similar time to Liutgarde and I hope have sons of their own. My love, you must not worry. You did enough to secure the succession." He pressed a long kiss against her lips. "And you have done more for me than you realise."

Feeling as if a weight had been lifted from her, Eadgyth smiled as she watched him head from the hall to enjoy a happy day with all three of his 'sons'. She could feel the eyes of the court on her and was unsurprised as she turned to see Hermann, Henry and Judith looking at her.

"I do not like to criticise Otto to you, my lady," Hermann said. "But I do feel he has been a very great fool."

"I could have told you that years ago," muttered Henry.

Judith slipped a hand into hers. "Is all well, Eadgyth?"

Eadgyth smiled back. "Yes, Judith. All is well."

∞∞∞

Otto did not forget his promise to Eadgyth and after some days of festivities he summoned Hermann, Henry and Conrad to him.

"I have been asked to invite my mother to return to court," he announced. "I intend to grant this request."

To Eadgyth's dismay there was a long silence, the air growing tangibly heavy with tension, as Hermann shot a narrow eyed look at Henry. "I suppose I do not need to ask who made this request. I think you are making a mistake."

"I did not request it," Henry said hotly. "Although I will be glad to see my mother again."

Hermann folded his arms and looked sardonically at Henry. "Of that I have no doubt. How long until you start plotting with her again?"

"I never plotted with my mother."

"I was not at court when the Dowager Queen was present," Conrad put in. "But I have heard how she undermined you. I agree with Hermann. This is a mistake."

"Who made this request?" Hermann demanded. "I would be very suspicious of their loyalty to you."

Eadgyth held her breath, afraid she had triggered an argument with Otto's closest allies, but Otto laughed out loud. "This request was made by one whose loyalty is without doubt. One who has supported me in everything and very rarely asks for anything in return."

Hermann and Conrad were instantly silenced. Hermann glanced at Eadgyth. "In that case, Otto, I withdraw all objections."

Otto squeezed Eadgyth's hand. "Excellent. I shall invite my mother to return."

"I am glad to hear that." A voice came from the doorway. "But you may have trouble persuading her."

"Bruno!" Otto cried, getting up to embrace his brother. "I am glad you are here."

"I did not know you were coming this day, Bruno." Eadgyth kissed her brother-in-law. "But welcome!"

"I came because Otto tells me I have a nephew who is likely to be following me into the church."

"That is correct," Otto replied. "I shall present William to you in due course."

Bruno's smile faded as Henry came forward to greet him. "Good day to you, Henry. I heard Otto had pardoned you. I do not know why, after your plot to kill him and defile our father's grave."

"Oh, Henry," Otto muttered mischievously. "If only you had the good sense to kill me elsewhere, all would be forgiven."

Henry's face flushed crimson and he did not smile at Otto's remark. "I was in a state of madness then and it brings me great shame to recollect that time. I hope one day we will be friends again, Bruno. I am truly grateful that you persuaded Otto to mercy when I was too foolish to beg him myself."

"It wasn't me who persuaded Otto to mercy. I think it was Eadgyth."

"Eadgyth?" Henry exclaimed. "Do not be foolish, Bruno. Eadgyth was ready to rip my head off with her bare hands. Not that I blame you, Sister," he added hastily.

Otto laughed again. "Come, Bruno. Forgiveness is a fine quality in a bishop."

"I am not yet a bishop," Bruno retorted, but he embraced Henry.

"Well, I am glad you are inviting your mother to return, Otto," Hermann said. "I would be most afraid for you to refuse the request of so terrifying a wife."

Eadgyth shook her head, enjoying the friendly atmosphere. "That is enough nonsense from all of you."

Otto put his arm around her. "Indeed, everyone behave. So, Bruno, what will I have to do to persuade Mother back to court? I have promised Eadgyth I will do it if it is within my power, but I have a feeling Mother's stubborn will may be beyond my powers."

Bruno thought for a moment. "I think it is beyond your power and Henry is not in favour either, so he will be unable to persuade her. I could try, but in truth I doubt I have any chance of success. I think the only person who may influence her is Eadgyth. She speaks often of her with great fondness. Tell her how much Eadgyth wants her to return to court and I think she will listen."

"I had a feeling you would usurp my power one day," Otto said, with a playful glance.

"Do not be foolish." Eadgyth rested her head against him. "Otto, do not invite your mother if she will cause problems for you."

Otto kissed the top of her head. "No. I swore I would do this for you and I will."

Chapter five

The spring was fast merging into summer when Mathilda returned to Magdeburg. Eadgyth was with Liutgarde, Ida and Judith in a sheltered spot against the walls, with baby Hedwig sat contentedly at Judith's feet. They were supposed to be stitching, but all four gave little attention to their work as they exchanged light hearted comments.

"The Dowager Queen has arrived, my lady," a serving man announced.

Eadgyth looked up to see Mathilda standing behind the man. She looked weary from her ride, but other than that, unchanged. Casting aside her stitching, Eadgyth ran to her, pulling her into a tight embrace.

"Welcome back, Mathilda. It is so good to see you," she cried.

Mathilda kissed her warmly. "Thank you, Eadgyth. I have only returned because you wished me to."

"Bruno told us that would be the case."

Mathilda's eyes lit up. "Is Bruno here? I shall be glad to see him."

Eadgyth shook her head, not knowing whether to be amused or infuriated. "I see. Bruno is now your favoured son."

"For the last year he has been my only son," Mathilda retorted. "Liutgarde, how tall you have grown and prettier than ever, I see."

"Welcome back, Grandmother," Liutgarde said, flushing at the compliment as she accepted Mathilda's kiss.

"Do you remember Ida?" Eadgyth asked. "Hermann's

daughter and Liudolf's betrothed."

Ida curtsied, as Mathilda looked at her, her long resentment of Hermann eventually giving way to a smile. "At least you do not resemble your father. So, you are going to marry my grandson are you?"

"I have that honour, my lady," Ida murmured.

Judith had also got to her feet and she came forward shyly. "I do not think you have seen Judith for many years," Eadgyth said, gesturing at her sister-in-law.

"No and you too have grown quite as pretty as I expected." Mathilda gazed at the baby in Judith's arms. "I heard you and Henry had a daughter. May I see?"

"Of course." Judith handed a beaming Hedwig to her grandmother.

Eadgyth smiled at Judith. Whatever Mathilda's opinions on her sons, she had always adored her grandchildren and from her delighted expression, it seemed Hedwig was proving to be no exception.

Eadgyth sent for some refreshment and they sat down to exchange news until a clatter of horses in the courtyard made them look up. From their spot by the walls they had a good view of the men's return. Mathilda's eyes widened as she saw Otto and Henry walk from the stables, laughing together with Otto's arm flung casually around his brother's shoulders.

"Are Otto and Henry truly such good friends?" Mathilda asked.

Judith nodded. "They truly are."

"I never thought I would see the day either." Eadgyth squeezed Mathilda's hand as she noted the tears in her eyes.

"It is wonderful to see," Mathilda murmured. "Who is that boy with Liudolf? He looks so like him they could be brothers."

Eadgyth and Judith both laughed. "They are brothers," Eadgyth said. "The older boy is Otto's son, William."

Mathilda stared at Eadgyth. "And you have accepted the boy at court? My dear, is there anything you would not do for Otto?"

"I do not think so," Eadgyth admitted. "Do you condemn me for that?"

Mathilda shook her head. "No, my child. I admire you. You have a capacity for compassion and forgiveness that is an inspiration to us all."

"Grandmother!" Liudolf cried, running towards them.

Eadgyth got up and put her hand on William's shoulder. Having heard much of Mathilda's disapproval of his birth, it was no surprise he was looking decidedly nervous. Mathilda released Liudolf and looked from William to Eadgyth. Eadgyth looked warningly back and Mathilda smiled. "You do look like Otto as a boy, but I expect you are better behaved. I am very glad to meet you, William."

"Thank you, my lady," William stammered.

"I think, young man, you should call me Grandmother, as the others do."

William gave a shy smile. "Thank you. I would like that."

Eadgyth smiled too. She knew William was still grieving for his mother, but she was glad he was settling in with his new family. For herself she had no regrets at accepting him.

Mathilda suddenly stiffened and her smile faded. Following her gaze Eadgyth saw Otto and Henry had come upon them, with Bruno, Hermann and Conrad just behind them. She sighed. She should have realised the reunion was going too well.

"Well, what do you two have to say for yourselves?" Mathilda snapped.

Otto and Henry exchanged glances. With a sigh Otto went down on one knee. "Mother, if I have judged you harshly, I am truly sorry. Please forgive me."

Henry followed suit. "I am truly sorry for all the animosity I caused between you and Otto, as well as the terrible actions I plotted. I humbly ask for your forgiveness."

Mathilda folded her arms. "You two are a couple of silly boys."

"Yes, Mother," Otto said meekly, exchanging another look

with Henry very much in the manner of a small boy caught stealing cakes.

Mathilda's face softened. "No, you are not boys. You are men now. I shall try hard to remember it and not interfere. Otto, you rule differently from your father, but I think he would be very proud of you. And, my son, I too am most proud."

Otto smiled warmly and Eadgyth could only guess his feelings at hearing those words he had so long wanted to hear. He folded his mother into his arms. "Thank you, Mother."

"Henry, it takes courage to admit the mistakes of the past and to make amends. You are becoming the man your father envisaged you would be. He would be very proud of you too."

"I hope so," Henry murmured.

There was a silence in which everyone felt close to tears. Otto gave Eadgyth a shaky smile. "Shall we have some drinks? We are all thirsty after our ride."

Eadgyth began to pour cups of wine and ale, as Mathilda greeted Bruno. Hermann and Conrad waited their turn, but it truly seemed all the angry words of the past had been forgotten. Suddenly Mathilda turned back to Otto, her face animated. "Otto, you seem truly reconciled with Henry, is that correct?"

"Yes, completely."

"Then will you put him back in charge of Lotharingia?"

"Oh, Mother." Henry shook his head. "You said you would not interfere."

"I am not interfering, Henry. Your father hoped Otto would grant you a noble position, so I think it would be right. Will you Otto?"

"No," Otto replied firmly. "I know the current duke is not in the best health, but when the time comes, Lotharingia is for Conrad. After the years he has acted so loyally for me in Franconia, it is time he has a duchy of his own."

Eadgyth looked nervously at Henry, wondering how he would react to that, but if anything he appeared relieved. She glanced at Judith to see the same expression and remembered how Judith had told her how much she and Henry hated their time in Lotharingia.

"I am honoured, Otto," Conrad said. "I will serve you there to the best of my abilities."

"And your abilities are very fine indeed," Otto smiled.

Mathilda sniffed. "I would have thought your own brother might come first, Otto. You know it is what your father wanted."

"What Father wanted," Henry put in, "was for me to serve Otto well. And that is what I shall do. If, once I have proved myself, Otto chooses to reward me, I shall gladly accept."

"But, Henry," Mathilda started.

"No, Mother. If Otto offers me lands I want to know I have truly earned them. If I suspect you have browbeaten him into it, I shall refuse."

Hermann clapped Henry on the shoulder. "Well said. I never thought I would say this, but on the day Otto does reward you, there will be no objections from me."

Otto smiled at Henry. "I do have a position in mind for you, Henry. It is likely to be a few years off yet, so there will be time to prove your worth. Bavaria."

Henry gasped. "Bavaria? Really, Otto?"

"Why not? The current Duke is not a young man and who better to succeed him than Arnulf's son-in-law?"

Henry looked stunned. "I do not know what to say, except I hope I can fulfil your expectations."

Otto laid a hand on his brother's shoulder. "Do not take your failure in Lotharingia to heart. It was an impossible situation. You had no ties to the land and no experience of rule. I was foolish to send you there. Bavaria will be different. You will be well prepared when the time comes to take over. I shall send you often to Bavaria to act for me, so the nobles will be accustomed to accepting your judgement." Otto gave his sister-in-law a friendly smile. "You will have at your side one who is surely the wisest and most beautiful of Bavarian ladies. In my experience, having so fair and gracious a consort is the greatest of assets."

Judith blushed. "Oh, I would love to return to Bavaria."

Henry put his arm around his wife. "That is true. I saw at our wedding how popular Judith is there. Thank you, Otto. I will not let you down."

"I know you will not, but do not hesitate to ask for help if you need it. After all, I will certainly be asking for Bavarian assistance if I need it."

Eadgyth smiled, feeling misty eyed again. The delight of Henry and Judith was touching to see. She looked around at the group, suddenly struck by what Otto had achieved. Saxony and Franconia were under his direct control. Lotharingia would soon be in the hands of what was likely to be his son-in-law, Swabia was controlled by his closest friend and would one day be ruled by Liudolf and Bavaria would be ruled by his brother.

"Are those drinks prepared?" Otto asked.

Eadgyth was staring speculatively at Bruno and William, the two churchmen talking together. A few days before, Bruno had announced his intentions to remain at court, taking on the role of Otto's chancellor. It was another powerful position now in the hands of one close to him. "Do you have archbishoprics in mind for those two?"

Otto smiled, taking a cup of wine. "You have noticed my plan, have you?"

He took a drink over to his mother and Eadgyth watched as she accepted it, talking animatedly with both Otto and Henry. The affection between all three was suddenly obvious and Eadgyth wondered where it had been all those years. They did genuinely love each other, but the crown had caused so many problems.

For the first time in years Eadgyth thought of her own father without anger. She realised the affection he had shown her as a child and which, according to Athelstan, he had expressed on his deathbed could have been genuine. He had been driven to desert her by his need to increase his power, but perhaps he had, after all, loved her.

She smiled at Liutgarde, Ida and Judith playing a game with the baby and at Liudolf engaged in a lively discussion with Conrad and Hermann, as she took her own drink to stand with Otto.

Otto raised his cup. "Welcome back, Mother. I am pleased you are here."

Eadgyth slipped her arm around his waist and smiled at Mathilda. It had been the right decision to ask her back. "So am I," she said. "I have truly missed you, Mathilda."

"And my friends, I would like you also to drink to someone else." Otto kissed the top of Eadgyth's head. "Someone who I owe so much to and who gets very little recognition for it."

Eadgyth blushed, shaking her head. "Oh, Otto. This is not necessary."

Otto looked teasingly at her. "Do not shake your head, my sweet. I am going to say this. My father always stated he would not have been the man he was without the love of my mother and that is something I can truly understand. You have been at my side through everything since I was little more than a boy, helping me become the man I am today. To Eadgyth, my beautiful wife and queen, the fair lady of Magdeburg."

Eadgyth and Otto

Eadgyth died unexpectedly in 946, as reported sorrowfully in the chronicles of the time. Although her life was not a long one she did at least enjoy sixteen years of what appears to be have been a genuinely loving and happy marriage – a fate denied to many of her contemporaries. She was buried in the Abbey of Saint Maurice (later Magdeburg Cathedral) she and Otto had founded.

There are signs of how deeply Otto mourned for his wife, not least the fact that although he was still a fairly young man with only one legitimate son, he was in no immediate hurry to marry again. His life was long and remarkable, but I have not seen the last of Otto! He will feature again in a future book. When he did die many years later he was buried, at his own request, in Magdeburg next to his beloved Eadgyth.

It is not uncommon for royal graves to be moved and often remains are lost, so it was assumed that the grave in Magdeburg Cathedral was empty. However when the tomb was opened it was found the lead coffin contained bones. These were sent to Bristol for testing and the results showed this was a woman in her mid-thirties, with a high protein diet who was a frequent horse rider, implying someone of noble birth. However most convincing of all was that tests on the teeth confirmed this woman had spent her childhood on the chalky hills of Wessex. Eadgyth had come home.

But Eadgyth came home only briefly. With the tests completed, her bones were buried back in Magdeburg Cathedral close to the man who fell in love with her when he was just seventeen, in the land she had made her own and whose people had taken her to their hearts. I feel sure this is what she would have wished.

Women of the Dark Ages

More than a thousand years before today was a fabulous period where history and legend collided to form what is often known as the Dark Ages. Peering through the mists of time figures emerge, often insubstantially becoming as much legendary as historical. And if the men are hard to see, the women are even harder. But they lived, they were loved, they mattered and they should be remembered. Each of the books in the Women on the Dark Ages series tells the stories of the forgotten or uncelebrated, but very remarkable women who lived through these tumultuous times.

God's Maidservant

The story of Adelaide of Italy, the widowed queen who calls for Otto's aid.

Dawn Of The Franks

Bitter betrayal, forbidden love and the visions sent by the Gods as Queen Basina of Thuringia seeks her destiny.

Kenneth's Queen

The tale of the forgotten wife of Scottish king, Cinaed mac Alpin.

The Girl From Brittia

The curious tale of a sixth century warrior princess, known

only as The Island Girl.

Three Times The Lady

A Frankish princess, a Wessex queen, stepmother of Alfred the Great, a scandalous widow – the exciting true story of Judith of Flanders.

Quest for New England

It is the 1070s, England is reeling from the Conquest and an epic voyage is about to begin…

1066 is probably the most famous date in English history and we all know what happened. Duke William of Normandy invaded England, winning a decisive victory at the Battle of Hastings, bringing as end to the Anglo-Saxon era.

But not all Anglo-Saxons were quietly absorbed into the regime. There were rebellions and when these failed, some preferred exile over submission. The Quest for New England trilogy is based on a true story, following a large group of Anglo-Saxons in their search for a place to call home.

Rising From The Ruins

After the defeat at Hastings, the failure of rebellions and the devastation of the North, England desperately needs a new hero. Will Siward of Gloucester be that man?

Peril & Plunder

Siward and his Anglo-Saxon exiles have escaped England, but can they escape the ghosts of the past. Can they even escape the Normans?

Courage Of The Conquered

Sinister secrets lurk beneath the splendour of a fabulous city. Will Siward's Quest for New England end in heart-breaking tragedy?

Tales of the Wasteland

The year 536 has been called the worst year to be alive, spanning a decade of cold, famine and disease. The world was a wasteland.
But like all good wastelands it is also a spiritual wasteland inhabited by disreputable and damaged kings.
These are their stories…

Tyrant Whelp

Custennin was King of Dumnonia.
Legend names him a kinsman of King Arthur.
So why did a monk write the words to damn him for all time?

Fisher King

Told around firesides, retold into legend, his anguish echoes down the centuries… The tale of the Fisher King – the man behind the myth.

About The Author

Anna Chant

Anna Chant was born and spent her childhood in Essex. She studied history at the University of Sheffield, before qualifying as a primary teacher. In her spare time she enjoys walking the coast and countryside of Devon where she lives with her husband, three sons and a rather cheeky bearded dragon. 'The Saxon Marriage' is her fourth novel. Her first novel was 'Kenneth's Queen', telling the tale of the unknown wife of Kenneth Mac Alpin. Anna has fallen in love with the Dark Ages and in particular the part played by the often unrecorded and uncelebrated women of the time. She plans to tell the stories of as many as possible!

I hope you enjoyed reading The Saxon Marriage. With its cast of some of the most remarkable women of the Dark Ages, it has been a joy to write! Good reviews are critical to a book's success, so please take a moment to leave your review on the platform where you bought the book. I look forward to hearing from you!

For more news, offers, upcoming releases and all things Dark Age please get in touch via
My Facebook Page
https://www.facebook.com/darkagevoices/
Check out my blog: https://darkagevoices.wordpress.com/
Or follow me on Twitter: https://twitter.com/anna_chant
For more information on the characters, places and events of this book take a look at my Pinterest board, where I have pinned many of the sites and articles I used in my research.
https://uk.pinterest.com/annachant/eadgyth-and-otto/

Printed in Great Britain
by Amazon